VITÆ

Heirs of the Five: Book One

Ametra S. Rayford

Cover typography and layout by Arrayed Formats™

This book is a work of fiction. Names, characters, places, and incidents either are products of the author's imagination or are used fictitiously. Any resemblance to actual persons, living or dead, events, or locales is entirely coincidental.

Printed in the United States of America
ISBN: 978-1-737-01482-9

Published by Arrayed Formats™

DEDICATION

For my amazing baby sister

vi·tae

[vahy-**tee**, vee-**tahy**; *Latin* wee-**tahy**]

noun, plural
1. The course of one's life.
2. A brief biographical sketch.

Prologue

"You must be joking. That can't be right!"

The quintet of girls sat in a wide circle on the floor of an immense dormitory bedroom. Three queen-sized wrought-iron canopy beds lined each side of the candlelit room. All three of the beds on one side were neatly made, draped in silks and brocade, and topped with pillows in coordinating splashes of color. Only two on the opposite side were similarly appointed. The third held a plush pillow-top mattress on a low-profile box spring, bare of linens or pillows.

Thirteen-year-old Rhia pushed her wire-rimmed spectacles up the bridge of her nose and nibbled her bottom lip. She sat with a heavy book in her lap, her long legs tucked beneath her, wearing a short-sleeved, blue velvet nightgown embroidered with silver ivy along the neckline and hem. Her berry-kissed dark brown hair hung in a thick braid down her back. The end of the braid swayed as she shook her head.

"It has to be right," she said. "It came, didn't it?"

"Yes, but look at it!" the first girl said, leaning forward. Candlelight highlighted wide, heavy-lidded, dark green eyes and olive-hued skin. "Is that really what we've been waiting for this entire time?"

"It's right, Ani," Rhia said again, "I assure you."

Aniela snorted, taking in the situation with one sweep of languorous lashes before shrugging, smoothing the bodice of her gold-flecked, dark green nightgown. "I say we should let it go and try again."

"Let it go?" another girl said. Her finely arched brows furrowed beneath a shock of red curls. "After all the time it took to get it here?" She shook her head and folded her arms, exquisitely pretty in a gold nightgown upon which was sewn a scattering of tiny red rosebuds. "No, that will not do!"

"There's still steam coming off it, Elyse," Rhia said to the redhead, leaning in for a closer look at the creature.

Rhia's oval, chestnut-colored eyes were bright with wonder, and a smile lit her smooth, dark brown skin. The two girls, best friends from the first day of the school term, giggled in unison.

"That is certainly no surprise," Aniela declared. "You remember where it came from, don't you?"

"Did you do it right?" Elyse asked, to which Rhia responded by rolling her eyes. Elyse was immediately repentant. "Yes, yes of course—I know you did. You always do since you're smarter than the rest of us..."

"Stop this!" another of the girls hissed, flinging back a mass of dark curls as her eyes flashed. "Matron is due to come through on patrols in a quarter of an hour. We need to get this done, clear up, and be back in bed by then! It's already taken much too long!"

"We know how long it has taken, Lee-ahna," Elyse said in a singsong tone, a mirthful twinkle in her light green eyes.

Rhia responded with another giggle, and Elyse continued to smirk even after Liana shot her a look that would have intimidated anyone else.

"Who wants to be the one to do it, then?" Liana asked carefully, studying the monogram of LRD stitched in black thread on the cuffs of her silver robe.

The group once again studied the damp, leathery, reddish-black creature. It reclined at the center of an intricate drawing, glaring up at them through eyes of a strange matte black.

Triangular ears, much like those of a cat, adorned a small round head. Its forehead was deceptively smooth for its kind, and its nose was long, pointed, and almost humanoid. The mouth was curled into an angry sneer, and the tips of jagged yellow teeth peeked from the underside of its top lip.

Though it was only two feet long, sharp black talons protruded from the ends of the three digits on each hand, and equally lethal-looking claws adorned the toes on both feet.

It lay prone, spread-eagled and unmoving, studying them through endless black eyes that caressed each girl. At last, its gaze rested upon Liana as it waited to learn its fate.

"It's not going to move, is it?" Elyse asked softly.

"It can't," Aniela offered in clipped tones before picking up a silver goblet and sipping from it. "Immobility is part of the spell Rhia cast. A better question is whether we're even sure it can do anything. It looks like a baby."

"Because it *is* a baby," the fifth girl offered with a shake of thick, golden-blonde hair as she held the tip of a silver, hook-handled dagger to her lips. She then pointed to a sketch on a page in the open tome sitting in Rhia's lap with the stiletto tip of the dagger. "But it's really not so much different from the drawing in the text."

"Only by maybe eight feet and six hundred pounds, Van," Rhia said with a smirk. "Besides, we've been trying to summon one for months," she reminded them, "and this is the first one to answer us. Do we really want to risk letting it go and having the next one take even longer, if one shows up again at all?"

"No!" Liana said, reaching over to take the dagger from Vanja with one hand as she snatched the goblet from Aniela with the other, dumping the contents onto the floor. "We're already running out of time, and I refuse to wait any longer than I already have!"

There was a collective gasp from the other girls as she used the dagger's edge to slice into the thigh of the creature, ignoring its shrieks of pain as she positioned the goblet to collect the blood seeping from the wound. Dropping the dagger with a clatter, she twisted the flesh around the cut, milking enough of the viscous greenish-black fluid to fill roughly a quarter of a cup.

"There!" she said with a satisfied smile. "That should be enough for all of us. Who's first?" Her friends stared at her in various combinations of shock, admiration, and disgust.

"Since you're so eager for the blood, why don't you go first?" Aniela challenged, tucking a silken lock of long, black hair behind one ear. "This was your idea."

"It was not just my idea!" Liana countered. "It's Rhia's book!"

"It was your wish," Aniela shrugged.

"That's because you don't know what it's like!" Liana complained. "All of you have the gift and I, despite being from a powerful family, have somehow been born without." Her gray eyes appealed to Aniela. "Ani, whatever ailment we've had, from a paper cut to a broken limb, you can heal it almost completely just by touch." She looked at each girl. "Rhia can read ancient spell books as though they're written in modern language. Even my dad was impressed by it when he heard.

"Elyse finally stopped being teased by that harpy Natalia Betencourt after encouraging that pregnant wolf spider to give birth behind Natalia's bed. She also talked those squirrels into going to the kitchens through the courtyard window to pinch treats for us." She nodded toward Vanja. "Your overall marks have made you first in our class. You'll probably be promoted two levels at the end of the term and get to graduate early.

"Meanwhile, I'm only here as a favor to my father. My parents thought this was a good idea… and that it would somehow coax some untapped ability out of me. I am no closer to that now than I was when I came here six months ago, and I'm tired of people looking at me with such… pity in their eyes. So, yes, this was my wish, Ani. What else could I do?"

"No one pities you, Liana," Aniela said. "No one looks at you any differently just because your abilities haven't manifested yet. They still could, you know. There are others here who've experienced that very thing."

"Those people may not have had power before," Liana insisted. "But they do now. I still don't."

"Power is not everything," Elyse offered.

"Easy enough to say when you have it," Liana said stubbornly.

"Dare I point out that, while we have this spirited discussion, the blood is losing its potency?" Vanja asked with an arch of a sandy eyebrow. "Plus, this thing is screaming its head off, and I don't know how much longer my insulation spell will keep anyone from hearing what's going on. Drink it, Liana, and let us be done with this."

"Don't any of you want anything?" Liana asked as she clutched at the goblet. "You should get something, too."

"We did this for you," Aniela answered. "After all the time it took, I don't think any of us thought it would ever work, so who had the foresight to think of what to ask for?"

They exchanged guilty looks during the silence that ensued. After a time, Liana chuckled dryly and then nodded.

"The foolish hope of the non-magic," she mused, staring into the goblet. "All the same, girls, I'm glad for the help. Shall I begin, then?" She cleared her throat and paused briefly, lifting the goblet with both hands above her head. Her voice, when she spoke, was clear and commanding. "Father of Night, heed the call of a devoted daughter. Behold your servant. We have lured him from your realm into ours, and now I hold his life in my hands.

"I bind myself through him and to you, forever loyal and faithful. As his life's blood passes through my lips, grant me my wish for the safe return of your acolyte to your plane.

"You know the dreams of my heart. I seek favor and redemption. Let me see power, O great Guardian. Allow me to be enlightened. Let me no longer be forsaken, but embraced and uplifted with the equality I deserve." Liana's voice faltered and she took a shuddering breath as a tear rolled down her cheek. "From the depths of my soul, I beg you. I offer to you my oath and the oaths of my sisters."

She took a deep breath before bringing the goblet to her lips and taking a healthy swallow of the contents. She winced, slapped a hand over her mouth, and gagged as she struggled to keep it down. They passed the goblet until each girl had drunk, and then they glanced at one another in silence. The thing lying on the drawing had long since ceased its shrieking and now held Liana in its dark stare.

"Well?" Rhia asked through green-tinged lips. "Now what? Did it work?"

"Try something!" Elyse requested. "Put out the candles, or lift the bed!"

Liana did her best, trying everything the girls suggested, from attempting to levitate a feather to conjuring a wall of fire. Nothing worked, not even a simple illumination spell. All Liana created was a massive headache and, after a short while, a nosebleed.

In tears, she buried her face in her hands, smearing a mixture of red and dark green blood onto her cheeks. Nothing had changed for her at all, and her best friends had witnessed her defeat. How would she face them in the light of day, knowing that they were still so superior to her?

She struggled to understand why her parents and older brother were so accomplished, and yet she was... plain. Liana felt so inferior to them. She could never compete with her mother's inventiveness, her father's intelligence, or her brother's charm, and she wanted desperately to stand on equal footing with them in some other way.

Then she heard the throaty little chuckle. With a gasp, she raised a face wet with blood and tears to look upon her friends, wondering which of them found such joy in her misery. Her eyes locked with each of theirs until Vanja finally lowered her azure gaze toward where the thing still lay. Liana followed the look, shocked by the twisted leer upon the being's face. Its dingy, decaying teeth were on full display. It was laughing at her.

"Kill it," she said softly, fresh tears springing to her eyes. Stony silence greeted her. The creature was not laughing anymore.

"Liana, we can't do that," Rhia said. "It's against the rules. We have to send it back."

"The rules state that it's supposed to give me what I've asked for in exchange for safe passage back to its realm!" she shouted. "It hasn't done that, so kill it!"

"You don't know that!" Elyse said.

"Don't I!?" Liana countered. "Was I able to do anything I tried!?"

"But you could wake up tomorrow and your wish is granted! And you would have killed it and violated the pact, damning us all in the process!"

"What's the alternative?" Liana shrieked. "Do I wait to wake up tomorrow and find out that I'm still nobody? By then it'll be too late because it'll be gone!"

"You took an oath," Vanja reminded her, "and, you made us a part of it. If you hurt it, we'll all have to pay."

"KILL IT!"

"We won't," Aniela said, her green eyes wide. "We brought it here for you, Liana, but not for that. Never for that. It's over."

"Then one of you didn't drink the blood!" Liana's eyes were wild as she stared at each of the girls. "The exchange only works if everyone drinks the blood of the conjured!"

"You saw us drink it," Vanja said calmly. "I understand that you're upset, but we've done all we can."

"Then you didn't do the right spell after all!" Liana accused Rhia.

"Now just hold on a moment," Rhia said, closing the book in her lap and tossing it aside. "It took a while, yes, but it showed up, didn't it? I know it upset you, Liana, and I am terribly sorry because I know—we all know—how much you want this. But, you are taking this too far! We've done all we can—all anyone can—to help you."

"Yes," Aniela agreed. "And, as Elyse said, you could still wake up tomorrow and find that you got what you wanted. There is nothing more to it now, though. Look at what you have done to it already. There's blood on your face and hands. We have to send it back."

"I'll send it back!" Liana screamed, taking up the dagger once more and raising it high above her head, poised to strike as the girls protested in various screams and shrieks.

When the dagger struck home, the little body was no longer there. All that remained were the oily smears of its blood on the diagram upon which it previously reclined. Liana's glare shifted from one girl to another, anger etched into her pretty heart-shaped face.

"This isn't over, I promise you," she began breathlessly before her voice faded and she collapsed into a sobbing heap. "Which one... Which one of you denied me?"

The rest of the girls exchanged looks, then stared at Liana, who had curled her body into a fetal position and was moaning in misery. Rhia went to her first, followed quickly by Elyse. Aniela joined them shortly thereafter, while Vanja simply stared at the group through icy blue eyes.

The imp's chuckle echoed around them.

PART ONE

Chapter One

Kynedal was a coastal city nestled within clusters of low green hills and lush trees. The landscape offered privacy to its inhabitants while still conveying warmth and openness to visitors.

Light winters and moderate summers kept the land rich and the soil fertile. While the temperate climate drew visitors, it was the reputation and quality of Kynedal's wares that kept them returning, boosting the economy and keeping the city's coffers overflowing.

The city was wholly self-sufficient, trading primarily within its own unguarded walls. However, their offerings were of such high quality that visitors came from distant regions to purchase premium cheeses, fabrics, spices, and even breeds of animals local to the area, and otherwise unavailable.

"I'm off to Kynedal during the next fortnight," a buyer often said. "The missus has a hankerin' for their marble jack to nosh before bed. Might as well get some sacks of grain, too. None of my heifers will eat anything that doesn't come from Kynedal!"

To their credit, those setting up shop in the area did not use the uniqueness of their offerings as an excuse to gouge those seeking to do business. While haggling was commonplace, the resulting deals were always more than fair. Kynedal's reputation for unrivaled goods and unmatched prices was both a boon and a blessing to merchant and patron alike.

In the furthest corner of town, nestled within what at first glance appeared to be an enormous green bowl, were tracts of land belonging to the Chatelains. Encompassing nine hundred acres, the Chatelain estate included three houses and a large farm. The farm housed a dairy, butchery, stables, groves of fruit trees, neatly built accommodations for the staff in Servants' Row, and a large, clear lake teeming with fish ready to leap into an open net at a moment's notice.

Each of the two smaller houses sat upon fifteen acres of land with its own gardens. The dwellings were furnished in décor independent of that which filled the principal residence and provided the perfect retreat within a retreat.

'Liana's Den' was the primary residence of nearly 40,000 square feet, a sprawling, multi-level residence built in her honor. They had spared no expense, from the hand-carved columns that adorned the outside of the house to the marble floors contained within. Each brick, tile, slab of granite, and piece of hand-cut, stained glass was commissioned for the enjoyment of the lady of the house.

Liana Chatelain, née Dhamon, was an ethereal beauty of only twenty-four. Her dark hair, usually hanging in thick curls, was styled in soft waves. A band of silver sweetheart roses pulled the crown of her glorious mane away from her heart-shaped face, the rest spilling over her bare shoulders.

When she moved, the hem of her silver silk taffeta dress whispered around her ankles as the heels of her strappy silver sandals tapped against the mother-of-pearl inlaid stone floor.

Sunlight streamed through the domed, stained-glass ceiling that topped the solarium. The colors danced over the richness of

Liana's honey-beige skin as she sat consulting a list. She wrinkled her lightly freckled nose, checking off an item with her quill pen before adding another in her delicate script.

Just as she began reading over her notes, she heard first a sigh and then a gurgle coming from the lilac silk-draped bassinet behind her. Smiling, she put her list and pen to the side and walked over to the bassinet, drawing back the silk organza veil. Liana smiled sweetly at the baby girl who looked up at her beautiful mother and, with a kick and squeal of glee, displayed a toothless grin.

"Did you have a good nap, my little sweetheart?" Liana crooned, rubbing the baby's belly, causing the baby to shriek and thrust her chubby fists into the air as if to say that yes, she had indeed slept well. Liana scooped her up, planting several kisses onto the baby's smiling face as she returned to her seat and cradled the child in her lap.

Reaching up, the baby captured a lock of her mother's hair in a tiny fist as she cooed. Liana laughed and kissed the infant's forehead, nestling her nose within the sweet-smelling black curls.

"You are such a delightful baby, Mahari," Liana said as she gave more kisses. "It will amaze your grandmother how much you've grown! She'll think I'm feeding you one of her special concoctions!" Mahari shouted in agreement before trying to shove the lock of her mother's hair into her mouth.

"Liana, are you in here?" a man's voice asked from somewhere outside of the room.

Liana briefly froze. "Yes," she called back. "I'm here."

"Good, good!" Evium Chatelain said as he entered the solarium. "Liana, a word, please. A messenger's just come from Tilehn."

Liana smoothed the tumble of curls away from the baby's forehead with another sweet smile and reclaimed her lock of hair before turning a concerned, soft gray gaze toward her husband. She

15

could usually hear him approaching before seeing him. Since converting to the steam-powered wheelchair earlier in the year, the large house seemed to almost continually echo with the 'Puff-puff-wheeze' sound made by Evium's latest innovation.

"Tilehn?" she repeated in a gentle tone. "Is it my mother?"

Evium puttered to a stop as he nodded, and Liana's eyes flicked toward the folded sheets of black linen paper in his lap. She found it easy to visualize her mother's ornate handwriting in the silver ink she often used, but her brow furrowed. Liana knew that the timing of the letter could mean only one thing.

"She's not coming," Evium stated plainly, confirming her thoughts. "She sends her regrets and promises to visit as soon as she's able, but there's been an incident regarding your brother."

"Rael?" Liana breathed, wide-eyed. Evium took one of her hands, giving it a reassuring squeeze.

"He's fine now," he soothed. "There was an issue at the sanitarium, though. There is to be an inquiry and your mother doesn't think this is the right time to leave. Right now, she seems to be the only one he's responding to without aggression."

Liana nodded. "Did she say what's happened?"

"He had another of his episodes," Evium answered. "This time, however, there were injuries to some of the other patients and substantial damage done to the property itself."

"Episodes!" Liana scoffed, taking her hand from his and rubbing the baby's back. "You know I hate it when you call them that! It's not like Rael can help having uncontrolled bursts of magic! He never means to hurt himself or anyone else, and for you to so easily dismiss what he's been through as an episode..."

"I'm sorry!" Evium said, raising both hands in supplication. "I'm not trying to be disrespectful of your brother, and I know what he's been through. I realize it hasn't been easy for you or your mother since he's been ill."

16

As Liana focused on the child in her lap, Evium took a moment to scrutinize his wife. His blue eyes softened as he visually feasted upon the striking woman who had consented to be his bride nearly seven years before. He did not think it possible to love anyone as much as he loved her.

Evium was at the marketplace in Tilehn, looking for a last-minute birthday gift for his then-fiancée when he walked into a well-known florist at the center of town. He had already met the proprietress, Kaileih Dhamon, and was a repeat customer. Kaileih was a charming and peculiar dark-haired and dark-eyed beauty with a gift for cultivating the most exquisite flora available for thousands of miles—many of which were hybrids exclusive to her shop.

Kaileih's daughter, Liana, was working behind the counter that evening while her mother labored in one of the extensive greenhouses on the property. When Evium entered the store, their eyes locked. With thoughts of his fiancée and the intended gift melting away at the sight of Liana's warm smile, he approached her and began a conversation. The conversation ended with an invitation to dinner, and a whirlwind courtship ensued. She made an exquisite bride a mere four months later.

There were two noteworthy occurrences during their lengthy honeymoon. Evium, frantic with love for his new wife, began the initial sketches for the home that would eventually become Liana's Den. Another occurrence of a more collaborative nature took thirty-nine weeks to complete before being brought into the world amidst cries of exultation, delight, and relief. Evium, having insisted upon assisting Kaileih during the birth of his first child and her first grandchild, held the crying, bloodstained bundle in his powerful arms, kissing an exhausted Liana upon the lips in gratitude.

Unable to help himself, and despite the happiness of the memory, Evium's focus drifted to the baby in his wife's lap. His wistful look gradually faded, and his brow slowly creased. The child, relishing in the attention and incapable of understanding its origin, cried out in glee as she kicked. Liana looked from the baby to him, noticed his expression, and hugged the child protectively to her body. Evium lifted his gaze to meet that of his wife, still frowning.

"Huison will still attend, though," he commented softly as he looked at her. "I'm sure he's practically beside himself with excitement now that he's fully recovered from his illness." The couple continued to stare at one another before Evium slowly steered the wheelchair backward several inches, turned, and took himself from the room.

Liana blinked back tears as she bounced the baby in her lap with a sniffle. At the sound of approaching footsteps, she sat up straighter and quickly composed herself as a young man entered the solarium. His uniform included a black poplin tunic with rosette chains stitched in silver thread at the neck and hem, matching pants, and thick-soled black leather shoes with identical silver detailing.

"Lunch will be ready in thirty minutes, Lady Chatelain," the young man offered in his thick brogue. "We've set a table in the east garden as you requested, and it's a lovely day for it."

"Thank you," Liana said in a steady tone.

"My pleasure, ma'am. Shall I take Miss Mahari up to the nursery?"

"Please do, Shaz," Liana replied. "She's just awoken from her late-morning nap, so be sure that the wet nurse is ready for her, and that the nanny has her bathed and properly dressed. Where is my son?"

"Mr. Jahd is upstairs in his suite," Shaz replied as a still-gurgling Mahari changed hands. "After he came in from playing, I drew a bath for him and set out his clothes."

Liana could not resist a laugh. "Terribly dirty, was he?" she asked.

18

"Sweat-stained," Shaz responded with a smile.

"I'd better check on him then," she said as she got to her feet. "Shaz, after you've seen to the baby, please find out if my husband intends to join us for lunch or if he'll need something brought to the workshop."

"Yes, ma'am," he replied with a careful bow as Liana swept past him.

As she approached the stairs, she examined an enormous arrangement of flowers cut from her own gardens just that morning. Ivory hydrangeas, blush sweetheart roses, and peonies nestled within a crystal bowl that sat atop a hexagon-shaped accent table with chrome accents and a frosted glass top. Liana dearly loved the piece, as it was her own design that was crafted in Evium's workshop, along with several other items within the Den.

With a gentle smile, Liana closed her eyes and indulged in the sweet smell of the flowers. The alluring combination of scents always drew Liana into a torrent of memories—not all of them pleasant. She didn't have her mother's talent—that was impossible—but, Liana's gardens and the blossoms she cultivated brought a following that was undisputed. She only wished she could take full responsibility for their creation...

"Why can't I do that, Mama?" Liana asked, her gray eyes wide.

She knelt in the grass beside her mother, her dark curls pulled back from her face into two tight bunches and secured with ribbons of the same shade as the mint green pinafore dress she wore.

"We don't know yet that you can't," Kaileih answered with a smile. "You're only three years old, Li. There's plenty of time to find out who you are."

Kaileih's almond-shaped dark brown eyes were trained on the recently turned plot of soil beneath them. She had already treated a series of sections throughout the sizeable garden before planting and covering her chosen seedlings and visiting each area to provide the final, special touch. Liana, fascinated, had accompanied her to watch her care for the last.

Mimicking her mother's movements, Liana placed her chubby hands atop the damp soil and took a deep breath. Kaileih exhaled and Liana felt a gentle, humming vibration beneath her palms as warmth coursed through the earth. Though she had seen her mother's power manifested dozens of times, she still could not resist the shriek of glee when the first sprout poked through the topsoil, followed by others.

"You're doing it, Mama!" Liana laughed, clapping her hands.

Kaileih smiled as she sat back on her haunches, and they both watched the sprouts continue to grow. Liana stood and bounced on the balls of her feet as she scampered over to one of the raised garden beds. A row of strawberry plants had unfurled, and she gasped in wonder as one plant gently sunk to the side as it became weighed down by clusters of sweetly fragrant berries the size of Liana's hand.

"Oh, Mama," she breathed. "Next time, can I? Please?"

Kaileih held her arms out to her youngest child, and Liana quickly went back to her. "We don't know what you can do yet, sweetheart," she said, gently tugging at one of Liana's ponytails as the other tracts flourished around them. "It's a little different for everyone, so you may not do exactly what I can."

"Or Daddy or Rael?" Liana prompted.

"Or your father or brother," Kaileih agreed. "As you know, your father is excellent at changing the way spells work. Rael just started showing his abilities this summer so they're still developing."

"He can move things without touching them!" Liana offered. "He made my stuffed bear dance when I was sick in bed last week. I tried to do it, too, but I couldn't!"

"It can be different for everyone, just as I've said. You might even find that you're unable to do anything at all, and that's fine, too."

Liana's smile melted. "No, Mama... that's not fine. You can do things. Daddy and Rael can do things. So, I'll be able to do things."

"Baby," Kaileih said, "it doesn't always work that way. My father could create localized storms when it suited him, but my mother's gifts lay in how she raised me and took care of her home and family. They brought me up to be prepared for either possibility and to have respect for both."

"So, you could have been born plain like Grandmama?" Liana frowned.

"Not plain, Liana," Kaileih corrected, her smile fading. "There was a time many, many years ago, when being without special abilities was normal and expected. But, even now, every person is born with the possibility of never becoming a spellweaver."

"Not me!" Liana replied, stubborn as she disentangled herself and hopped up from her mother's lap. "I'm gonna be just like you, Daddy, and Rael! I may even be better! You'll see—everyone will!"

"Mama?"

Liana felt chilled as she emerged from the depths of her thoughts. She turned to find a miniature, male version of herself staring up at her with eyes the exact shade of her own. Dark hair framed his heart-shaped face in a damp halo of curls that dripped water onto the collar of his light blue shirt.

"Jahd," Liana said as she finally smiled at her son. He rushed over and hugged her, holding her tightly around the waist as he peered up at her. "Hello, my darling. I hear you've been out playing."

"Yes, ma'am, Mama," he said. "But, I came in like Shaz told me to and took my bath." He looked around. "Where's Mahari? Are we having lunch soon?"

"Your baby sister is with her nurse," Liana explained, smoothing back Jahd's curls much as she had done for his sister. "Lunch will be ready shortly, but you can go play with her after, if you'd like."

Jahd nodded. "I would. I wanna show her a trick I learned this morning."

Liana stiffened. "A trick?" she quickly asked. "What sort of trick, Jahd?"

Her son was nearly seven years old and had so far not shown signs of being able to perform magic. Liana felt a quiet, unsettling sense of gratitude about this, as it meant the likelihood that her children would never rise above her the way other loved ones had.

"Shaz taught me!" Jahd announced with pride as he released her and stepped back. "I'll show you, but don't tell Mahari how I did it... promise? I'm gonna do it for her after lunch." Not trusting herself to respond, Liana simply nodded. "Lean closer, Mama."

"What?" she asked in surprise.

"Do it!" Jahd said excitedly, prompting Liana to bend until she was nearly eye level with her son.

With a giggle, he reached forward to caress a lock of his mother's hair. Tucking it behind her left ear, he gave the lobe a gentle tug and then drew back a fist. With a shy smile, he slowly opened the fist to reveal a silver coin. Liana first stared at it and then looked at his beaming face.

"Shaz taught you this?" she asked.

"Yes, this morning!" Jahd said. "He knows other tricks, too, and I wanna learn them all!"

Liana straightened, taking a deep breath.

"No," she said. "You shouldn't be learning these things and I'll be sure to speak with Shaz about it."

"What?" Jahd shrieked before wailing. "Mama, no! It's so much fun, and I wanna learn..."

"It's not suitable for you to learn such things and Shaz should know better."

"But, why not?" Jahd demanded, his breaths coming faster as his face reddened. "It's no different from what I've seen from Nana, or from what Grandpapa would show me before he died."

"Jahd, sweetheart," Liana began, once again lowering herself to eye level, "it's vastly different. Your grandparents were born possessing magic—real magic. They did not do parlor tricks or hand magic and that's what this is! I did not know that Shaz practiced common street lore, but that's not something I want you to have anything more to do with from this point. Such a farce is not allowed in this house and it is insulting to who we are. Do you understand?"

"No, Mama, I don't," Jahd answered honestly, looking at his mother through rounded eyes filling with tears as he shoved the silver coin into the pocket of his blue plaid shorts. "I wanna learn. That's all, I promise. I'm not trying to be a street person."

"Jahd Dhamon Chatelain," she sighed as she stood upright, lightly rubbing her temples as they throbbed. The approaching sounds that accompanied Evium's wheelchair then silenced her.

"Hello, you two!" Evium greeted as he stopped, his dark blue eyes dancing from wife to son and back, taking in the condition of both. "I thought we were heading out for lunch."

"We are," Liana answered, "but, I'm glad you're here."

"What's happened?" Evium asked softly.

"You'll need to have a word with Shaz. I want him dismissed before day's end. Immediately, if you can manage it."

"Shaz has done nothing less than stellar work for us," Evium said calmly, once again looking at his son. "What's happened that he should warrant such treatment?" Jahd hitched a breath and stared at the floor as tears spilled onto his cheeks. Evium looked past the trembling body of his son and studied his wife. "Li?"

"Shaz is a magician," Liana sniffed in a dismissive tone. "He's been sneaking around teaching our son tricks."

Evium exhaled as he settled back in the wheelchair. "And for this you want him to be sacked?" he asked, his tone still even.

"As he should be!" Liana flared, gray eyes flashing. "He's not being paid to teach our son to be common! Jahd is not destined to be better than most, but he will not be low-class!"

"Jahd," Evium interrupted carefully, eyeing the child. Jahd sniffled in response, but was still having trouble looking his father in the eye. "Come to me, son." Evium reached over, carefully wiping the tears from Jahd's cheeks after he approached. Evium then placed a finger beneath his son's chin, tilting it upward until their eyes met. "Go wash your face," Evium told Jahd gently. "Your mother and I will meet you outside to have our lunch in just a moment."

"But, Daddy!" Jahd burst, weeping afresh, "I promise I don't wanna be on the streets! Shaz was only trying to..."

"Shhh," Evium interrupted. "Do as I say, Jahd Dhamon. Allow me a moment to talk privately with your mother." His eyes settled upon his wife. "We won't be long at all."

"Shaz is upstairs, settling the baby in with her nurse," Liana said when they were alone. "Perhaps when he comes down, you could..."

"There's no need," Evium interrupted quietly.

Liana paused, dark brows raised. "Excuse me?" she queried.

"Shaz isn't going anywhere. I won't be dismissing him."

"But, I've already told you that..."

"It doesn't matter," Evium said. "I won't let this continue."

"You won't what?"

"Liana, in five years we have lost eighteen members of staff. Eighteen. Each one performed his or her duties well and took excellent care with whatever task was given."

"That's not true, they..."

"And yet," he went on, interrupting again, "their worth to you and to this estate was diminished at once after you claimed to have discovered that they possessed magic."

"You saw yourself what that Jakea did at our son's fifth birthday party, she..."

"Liana," Evium said again, his tone unwavering, "you need to stop. Sorcery, magic, spellweaving—whatever you want to name it—is prevalent in this world. It is nothing to be hidden or ashamed of. I don't come from a magical lineage, but neither do I persecute those who do.

"I keep hoping that you'll come around on this. Look at your own family, Li! Before he died, your father was among the best spellbreakers in the world. His ability to dismantle and then rebuild spells was unlike anything seen for centuries. Your mother is practically Kore come back to us with the way she makes the earth do her bidding. Rael..."

"Don't talk to me about Rael!" Liana snapped as she wrung her hands together. "What happened to my brother hasn't a thing to do with the topic at hand! I don't want those kinds of people teaching Jahd anything that might cause him to hope to do something he'll never accomplish!"

"We don't know what he will be yet, Liana! With us as his parents, he could be anything, and we must be ready for that. Whatever Shaz has shown him, whatever the others may have shown him, does not mean the end of the world and will not shape his destiny!"

"A hand wizard?" Liana snorted, toying with the platinum bands on the fingers of her right hand. "Do you care so little about his prospects?"

"Liana," Evium sighed, "Jahd is just a child. Allow him to be one. His shoulders are much too narrow to bear the weight of whatever vocation it is that you have in mind for him."

"What will you do when Mahari is his age?" Liana laughed, an edge to her voice. "Will you be so accommodating then?"

"I will speak with Shaz and explain that his actions discomfited you," Evium said, "but, I will not dismiss him. He is a bright young man who has helped with many projects on this estate, even after ensuring that his work for you was done for the day. I'll switch his primary duties so that he can attend me solely in the workshop, and you may hire a new retainer to replace him."

"That's practically a promotion!" Liana said.

"It's rewarding someone for his excellence," Evium countered, "something that I should have done for the others. Shaz has been the best at what he does for us since the day we hired him. If you refuse to understand and capitalize on that, I cannot help you. But, I will not dismiss him, and I'm done entertaining these panicked notions of yours." He paused and took a breath. "As for Mahari, I don't deign to assume any plans for your daughter. I commend her to your excellent care, and I'm sure you'll continue to serve her best interests well."

Evium studied his wife, exhaling as she stared back at him, and he could see realization dawning in her gray eyes as she flushed.

"We should go to lunch," he said quietly, extending a hand as an offering of peace. Liana's gaze went first to the proffered hand before once again meeting his eyes.

"I'll be having my lunch upstairs," she said icily, "with my daughter."

Evium watched, lowering his hand, as Liana turned away from him. She was graceful on dazzling silver heels as she ascended the elaborate winding staircase without looking back before disappearing into one of the suites.

Chapter Two

Evium emerged from his custom-designed bathroom in the sturdy black-and-silver wheelchair he used when showering. He was still nude, a plush, cream-colored towel draped across his lap as he made his way over to the antique mahogany bureau and opened it.

Liana, raised in wealth and privilege, was used to the benefits of having her wardrobe maintained and her outfits perfectly coordinated by a small team that consisted primarily of a stylist, valet, and seamstress. Evium, who had inherited his father's moderate fortune and turned it into a massive one, refused many of the amenities his wife suggested even when Liana insisted he hire extra help after the accident that left him partially paralyzed.

Even his recent ascension to Lord Mayor, largely a vanity title granted by the grateful citizens of Kynedal because of the economic boon provided by wares from his estate, had done nothing to entice Evium to make many changes. His only compromise had been to increase the staff in the workshop for the tasks he could no longer perform personally. Modifications were underway to allow him to one day handle anything he chose again.

Evium sighed, pulling on a soft gray nightshirt from the bureau. Using his upper body strength, he lifted himself first with one arm and then the other as he pulled the hem of the nightshirt past his hips and then used the towel to dry his hair.

It did not surprise him to hear a knock at his bedroom door. Though his attendants were respectful in keeping their distance so that he could see to his own needs in the evening, Shaz still often checked on him before retiring for the night.

"Come," Evium answered with a sigh, thinking of his earlier conversation with the young man.

Evium was certain Shaz understood why he had been summoned that afternoon, but Evium steered clear of Liana's accusations. He was careful to say only that, effective immediately, Shaz's duties would change and that he would report to the workshop instead. Shaz, seemingly grateful to not be wholly dismissed, readily accepted before being sent to the steward for a briefing, and to be fitted for everything needed for the transition.

Evium's breath caught as the bedroom opened and, rather than Shaz or another attendant, he found Liana standing there instead. No matter how often he contemplated his wife, her beauty still startled him. She was lean and finely muscled, with a figure that gave no hint to the reality that she was a mother of two.

Her eyes, a disarming shade of gray, were her most interesting feature. Evium, having been well-acquainted with Liana's mother, Kaileih, initially wondered about the origin of Liana's eyes. Kaileih's eyes were a beautiful, warm shade of dark brown. It was not until he finally met Amriel Dhamon, Liana's famous father, and regarded the icy gray eyes of the pale, wraith-like figure that Evium understood.

"Liana," Evium said softly, taking her in as the towel dropped from his hand and into his lap, "hello."

She looked freshly scrubbed, a rosy tint beneath her honey-hued skin. The smell of coconut wafted into the room. He recognized the scent of oil worked into her skin and hair, which was pulled back into two thick braids and still looked slightly damp from a recent washing.

"Jahd hoped he could say good night to you," she said shyly, as if she had not once shared that same bedroom with him before taking up residence in another suite.

"Oh!" Evium answered, inwardly embarrassed.

Not that he did not care to see his son. He had hoped she might be there for another reason. Before he could give it any additional thought, Jahd came bouncing into the room and climbed into his father's lap, wrapping his skinny arms around Evium's neck.

Evium hugged his son warmly while still scrutinizing the stationary figure of his wife. She had not left her place in the doorway, yet seemed to make no effort to venture further into the room.

Evium kissed Jahd on the forehead and lightly rumpled his still-damp curls. "Sleep well, son," he said with affection.

"Yes, sir, Daddy! You, too!"

Jahd disentangled himself from his father with a smile, climbing down and running past his mother and out of the door. Liana was lightly toying with the sash on her periwinkle-colored silk robe, and Evium hoped, almost desperately, that she might stay.

"Would you like to sit with me a bit?" he asked, hoping that his anguish did not show. "I could call for some wine, or anything you'd like."

"I didn't mean to intrude," Liana answered softly, stirring a bit yet still not advancing. "I only meant to bring our son..."

"You don't," Evium interrupted. "You never intrude, Liana." He shrugged and chuckled dryly. "How could you intrude in your own rooms?"

He watched as her gray eyes roamed over the space, and he hoped she was thinking of occasions much more endearing than those last intimate moments they shared in the room. When he saw her body become rigid, he felt certain that the battle had once again been lost.

"Liana, about earlier..." he began.

"How long have you known?" she asked at the same time.

Evium settled back in his seat, picking at the elaborate stitching on the towel. "Six months," he admitted.

"She's seven months old!" Liana exclaimed.

"I am well aware," Evium told her.

Liana stepped further into the room, closing the door behind her and leaning against it. "And you said nothing this entire time?" she whispered fiercely. "Was it your intention to just lord it over me, or to blurt it out in conversation as you did this afternoon to shame me?"

"That was not to shame you, Liana. I didn't know what to say or how to say it. It's been harder to keep inside, and it just slipped out."

"I knew something was wrong," Liana said softly. "You never hold her. You barely even look at her."

"You knew that something was wrong?" Evium mocked. "Meanwhile, you said nothing! What were you hoping would happen?"

"As you so aptly put it, I didn't know what to say or how to say it. I still don't."

"I suggest you put some thought into it," he intoned.

The couple stared at one another for several moments. Evium could hear his heartbeat thudding between his ears and wondered if Liana could hear it, too.

"I should see to the baby," she muttered at last.

Evium sighed, feeling defeated. "No! Now that this is finally in the open, stay!"

"She looks for me before bed," Liana said, examining her fingertips. Having recently bathed, she was not wearing rings, and she fiddled with the sash on her robe again. "It's as if she wants me to be the last thing she sees... And, I have no answers for you right now, Evium."

"After," he pleaded, unable to help himself, "come back after?"

At last, Liana moved from her place against the door and crossed through the room. Evium's breath caught again as she leaned forward, putting her hands upon his shoulders, and he felt the chaste kiss she placed upon his forehead. It was so much like the one he had given Jahd. He reached for her, inhaling the sweet, tropical scent that surrounded her as his hands landed upon the curves of her silk-draped hips.

"Evium," she sighed.

"Just for a little while," he said, rubbing his face against the cool fabric, no longer caring how he sounded. "Liana..."

"I... wouldn't want to disturb you," she stammered, her hands still fidgeting as they often did when she was distressed. He heard the knuckles crack.

"You don't," he said firmly as he looked up at her. "You never have. This needs to stop! I dislike what's happening. I want it to stop!"

"Evium..."

"It's been too long!" he blurted out, the knot in his emotions having loosened. "We can't keep going like this."

"Evium, please..."

"Do you still love me?" he demanded. "Do you love me at all anymore? Is that why you can't think of what to say to me, because it's Huison that you love now?"

"Stop this!" she hissed, wriggling from his grasp and going back to the door, sighing before speaking in her normal tone. "I need to go to her."

He did not follow. Instead, Evium turned the wheelchair so that his back was to her, and he did not have to watch her leave. He could still hear her uneven breaths, though, and hoped that it meant she changed her mind and would be staying.

"I'll see that Shaz comes to attend you," she said, a slight quiver to her voice. "I know you find his presence to be comforting."

"I don't want Shaz!" Evium said, turning around again. "I want you!"

But, she was gone, closing the door behind her. Exhaling in frustration, Evium yanked the towel from his lap and tossed it across the room before burying his reddening face in his hands as he tried to steady his breathing.

Evium did not know how to salvage the most important relationship of his life. Much had transpired in the last two years, and though Liana had moved out of their bedroom, she had not left him entirely. He, too, could have gone anywhere else that he wanted, yet they were still there together. That had to mean something. He prayed it meant something.

Evium missed his wife; not only the whispered, giggling conversations they once shared late into the night, but also the passion and openness in which they expressed themselves to one another. They had often touched and held hands. No one could make him laugh as Liana did, and he loved the mischievous twinkle that illuminated her eyes.

Among their last attempts at lovemaking, one of the few intimate interactions since using a wheelchair became a necessity for Evium, was an embarrassing blunder ending in frustration. He had been nowhere near understanding the changes in his body and had not learned how best to please Liana in a way that satisfied them both.

His level of annoyance, combined with Liana's lack of understanding what she could do to contribute to the situation, caused Evium to pull away from his wife as he ignored her pleas to tell her how she could help. So heated was their parting that Liana had her things moved to a separate suite the very next day.

Evium sniffled, wheeling himself over to the vast four-poster bed. The bed was immense; finished primarily in chestnut, but with accents of burl, pecan, and elm. The carvings along the sides of the canopy and upon the massive headboard, footboard, and the thick legs of the bed were elaborate, and the four structures holding the canopy aloft were made of platinum marble.

The insert decorating the underside of the canopy was of a sheer, billowy, silver-colored fabric that undulated gently, looking so soft and cloud-like that Liana was mesmerized by it from the start.

The bed itself was neatly made and topped with several pillows of different sizes and shapes, each covered in fabrics that complemented the colors in the black, silver, and white coverlet draped over the bed. Evium had steadfastly refused to have the bed replaced after his mishap. Part of the reason for his stellar upper-body conditioning was so that he could still get in and out of his marital bed with ease. He wanted nothing to impede that, not counting on the fact that the eventual absence of his wife would grind to a halt any plans to ensure that they still enjoyed the bed for anything other than sleeping.

Lowering the armrests on either side of the wheelchair, Evium drew back the coverlet and sheets on one side of the bed and knocked some pillows over before pulling his frame into the massive structure. He shifted himself, using his hands to straighten his legs before tugging the bedclothes up and over his body and settling back onto the pillows that remained.

He wondered if Liana was still in the nursery or if she had also gotten into bed, and if she ever thought of him while lying there. She looked so beautiful. The color of the robe suited her, and her skin was glowing. Evium could never again associate the alluring scent of coconut with anything other than his exquisite wife, and he could not help thinking of the early years of their marriage when he would frequently be the one to apply the oil to her lithe body.

Evium's brow furrowed as he drew in a breath. Though he could not feel the sensation, he was certain that the thought of Liana's smooth skin brushing against his as they tangled and teased had physically affected him. There was no need to slide a hand beneath the sheets for verification, as there was nothing to be done about it anyway, and he had no one with whom to share his ardor. In a twist of cruel irony, his thoughts gradually shifted to Huison Loromin, Evium's friend of over twenty years.

Pandoufuli Academy was a military-style boarding school just outside of Scio. Evium, as the son and grandson of successful graduates and future sponsors, earned a scholarship to attend. The fees at Pandoufuli were so exorbitant that payment would have been otherwise impossible for a family of modest means.

Huison, distantly related to the founder of the school, Yannic Pandoufuli (and the distance of the relationship changed nearly every time the story was told), had both the wealth and clout to attend, though he was lacking in the courage to explain to an overbearing mother the reasons he would rather not.

It was expected that Evium, already tall and stocky for his eight years, would have clashed with the thin and reedy Huison. What was unexpected, however, was which turned out to be the perpetrator and which was the prey.

Things came to a head almost immediately at the completion of orientation. The boys were filing out of the auditorium after initial roll call, standing in various queues in the hallway to await dormitory assignments. As Evium passed the swarthy kid with the long, curly dark hair, weirdly colored eyes, and wearing expensive robes, he first heard a whisper and then tripped over his own limbs as his papers were strewn across the hallway and he landed on his face. Some boys snickered, others looked confused, but the only one to look at Huison was Evium.

As Evium got to his feet, a stream of blood trailed from his nose, sending droplets to splatter upon the bright white marble floor. Professors immediately spirited him away to the infirmary with much ceremony, where he was fussed over by the school physician.

Already fiercely independent, even for one so young, Evium endured the ruckus made over him with minor complaint, though he could not wait to leave so that he could get his dorm assignment with the other boys. Instead, his assignment—as well as his recovered possessions—were brought to him at the infirmary. Only after three hours of unnecessary monitoring was he allowed to leave.

He rushed in excitement to his dorm, pleased to find his trunk of belongings already at the foot of his bed, before changing out of his bloodied shirt and making it to the dining hall in time for lunch. He noticed that the curly-haired kid was glaring at him when he entered, but he thought nothing more of it when he sat with the others assigned to his dormitory and tucked into a hearty meal.

What are you on about?

Evium, on his way out of the dining hall to the library, stopped and turned in confusion. Other boys were rushing on either side of him, many of them chittering like excited monkeys. In fact, the noise in the hallway was deafening, and there were only two students standing still in the corridor. The other was Huison, who leaned against the far wall with a scowl on his face. Considering the noise level, Evium knew he could not have heard the other boy that clearly by normal means.

Carefully crossing through the swarm of students, Evium approached Huison, brows raised. Huison seemed to be coolly surveying Evium with amber-colored eyes framed by dark lashes.

"You're a bold one to do that here," Evium told him, causing Huison to redden beneath his olive complexion. There was little need to whisper, considering the noise level. "You know that sorcery isn't allowed at Pandoufuli—this is a school strictly for those lacking the ability."

"What could you possibly think you know about me?" Huison challenged.

"I think I know that I just heard you ask me a question in my head from clear across the way," Evium answered. "I also heard a whisper earlier, just before I fell. It had to have been you. Why'd you do it?"

"Why did you not tell anyone I did it?" Huison hissed between clenched teeth. "You were certainly gone long enough to have made a full report!"

"Why would I tell? I don't even know you!"

"You do not have to know me to know, as you were so quick to say, that sorcery is not allowed here."

Evium studied him. "You'd be expelled if they knew," he said. "It was just a nosebleed. Were you trying to hurt me more than that?"

Huison groaned. "No, you idiot! I actually..." he shook his head. "What difference does it make? You were supposed to tell! I have heard everything about you. You come from a non-magical lineage. Your kind is not supposed to like me—it is why I picked you!"

"Who's making you come here?" Evium asked, narrowing his eyes. "Is it that you don't have a choice? Is that why you want to be kicked out?"

"What difference does it make!?" Huison said again. As the student population had finally started dwindling, his voice carried farther than intended and caught the attention of two of the faculty that had been shepherding the boys nearby. "Damn," Huison muttered.

Evium turned to look at the adults that eyed them with curiosity. "There's your shot," he said, looking back at Huison. "If you want out so badly, you'd do better to tell them."

"I made you trip in the hallway without touching you," Huison nearly pleaded, his voice lowered. "I just talked to you from across the hallway, using my mind. Surely, that means something that needs to be broached with the proper authorities!"

"It means you're remarkably gifted," Evium said, matching Huison's tone. "And, you apparently haven't heard everything about me because you're wrong. I have no issues with people who can do magic. Truth be told, I envy you for it and I'm not doing your dirty work."

"I will do something else," Huison threatened. "I need you and your family name behind this, and I will make it so that you have to tell."

"Try to keep from breaking my nose, then, will you?" Evium said with an affable grin. "I'll never get a pretty wife if my face gets messed up." He turned and walked away. "I'll be in the library getting a head start on some studying when you're ready," he called over his shoulder.

Huison stared after him, his delicate hands curled into soft fists as he swore and then stomped after Evium.

Evium wiped at the wetness in his eyes, blinking up at the creamy canopy as it billowed above, while his thoughts continued to overwhelm him.

Huison was on an extended sabbatical when Evium and Liana married. When Huison was first introduced to Liana at the event celebrating the completion of Liana's Den, nothing at all seemed amiss.

Evium, aware early on of his wife's selective disinclination toward those with magical talent, informed her that Huison, despite being from a family known for not possessing any special abilities and even for having founded a school for those without, was more than talented in his own right. Though Huison's gifts—as he displayed them to others—had not manifested themselves as much more than telepathy and mild telekinesis, his level of intelligence was such that it was easy for him to understand some of the most complex spells... even if he could not always duplicate them.

Liana seemed willing to accept this, but only after Evium pleaded with her to do so. Huison was his oldest friend, and though he would have sacrificed the friendship if Liana asked, he hoped he would not have to.

Evium reflected upon recent events and wished he had not convinced Liana to be so accommodating. It was at his insistence that Huison first became Jahd's godfather and then, once the child turned three years old, his tutor—with the stipulation that the focus of study was to be solely on academics and not on sorcery.

When had the affair begun?

It was surely after the collision, of that Evium had no doubts. He had endured months of rehabilitation, though it was purely out of respect for his wife that he adhered to the more traditional methods of treatment. Even his mother-in-law, the formidable Kaileih Vance Dhamon, tried to extol the benefits of a hybrid therapy that would combine convention with charms. However, Liana, having recently lost her father to death and her brother to magical psychosis, would not hear of it.

It was likely then, during the lonely months and failed couplings between man and wife, that Huison's role in Liana's life shifted. Did she cry to him about the goings-on, or lack thereof, in her marriage bed? Tears led to comfort, and comfort to caresses?

What could they have been thinking? Did they care for nothing else at all but their base and foolish pleasure? The worst of it was that Evium did not know at first. They were so good, the two of them, at keeping their secret between them and never betraying it when the three of them were together. It might have continued undisclosed for however much longer, if not for...

The distant sound of a baby crying startled him from his thoughts. His fingertips dug into the tufted coverlet as he exhaled slowly and thought of that night nearly eighteen months ago.

He had already been in bed; the candles snuffed by the attendants an hour before, but he was having trouble sleeping. Liana had looked so tired and drawn the last few days and moved about the grounds of the estate with no purpose. When asked what was wrong, she would only shake her head without answering. Jahd was in perfectly good health, an adventurous and intelligent boy of only five years old, so Evium was left to wonder.

Just as he thought he might get into his chair and travel to the lower levels and his workshop, Liana appeared in the doorway. She had come to Evium breathtaking in a delicate white satin robe, with flowing sleeves of scalloped lace and wearing nothing underneath. Liana's long, dark hair hung in loose curls and Evium stared at her in speechless adoration and open longing as she slid wordlessly between the sheets after removing the robe. She was warm, soft, and sweet-smelling. He held her to him as he kissed her mouth, neck, and shoulders.

Evium wished—oh, how he wished!—that he could flip her over onto her back and feel the warmth of her long legs around him. But, he could not. He could only wait as she tugged his nightshirt upward and sat astride him. He touched the soft skin and kneaded the supple flesh, watching her motions but unable to feel them, until she arrived at her completion and assured him he had, too.

After taking great care to clean him with a warm, wet cloth, she climbed back into bed beside him after having a shower. It did not take long for him to fall asleep, as he was so content to have her with him again. Yet when he awoke in the morning, she was already gone.

Days passed as he waited for her to move back into their rooms, but she did not. Their night together seemed to have changed nothing—until a couple of months later.

"I'm going to have a baby."

Evium looked up from his breakfast plate and stared into the weary gray eyes of his wife as a smile slowly spread across his lips.

"Li!" he said happily, and he tossed his napkin to one side. "Are you sure?"

"Yes," she said with a gentle smile. "I am. I'm more than sure."

The next several months flew by in a whirlwind of preparation, as they built a new nursery. Jahd was moved into a larger suite of rooms connected to the nursery by a bedroom with its own adjoining bath. A wet nurse would inhabit that bedroom for the first few months after the baby's arrival.

Evium ensured Liana wanted for nothing, though she had none of the same cravings with this new pregnancy as she did with Jahd. She was also not as lively or excited. Instead, she was often fatigued and napped frequently.

Liana's figure, which had ripened into curvaceousness when she was carrying their son, was deceptive this time around. Unless one was looking right at her or saw her in profile, it was nearly impossible to know she was with child.

"I should send for her mother," Evium confided in Huison after Liana had gotten up from the dinner table, leaving behind a barely touched serving of food. "Surely she'll know of something or can make a posset that will encourage Liana to eat a bit more."

"I do not think it wise to cross Liana in this," Huison cautioned, examining the shine of his buffed fingernails. "Did she not say just this afternoon that her plan is to wait before summoning her mother?"

"I know she says that she isn't due for another couple of months," Evium said, lowering his voice just to be safe, "but, even though she's smaller overall than she was when she carried Jahd at this stage, her belly seems more prominent." He grinned. "Do you think she might have twins?"

Huison waved a hand. "Could be. Could be not. We will know when it is time."

Evium was right to be concerned. Only a week after the conversation with Huison, Liana's cries awakened him during the night. He heard a torrent of commotion further down the hallway near Liana's suite and rushed into his wheelchair, still in his nightshirt. The door to Jahd's room was closed, likely to shield him from what was happening with his mother, as a handful of servants bustled in and out of Liana's rooms.

"What's happening?" Evium demanded, not wanting to roll over anyone's feet, but anxious about his wife's condition. "What's going on with my wife!?"

He finally made it far enough into the bedroom to find Liana panting and groaning as she tugged with all her might against a thick rope looped behind the headboard. The ends of the rope were fitted with sturdy, triangular handles to make it easier for Liana to pull during contractions.

One maid was dabbing at Liana's forehead with a moist cloth. A second maid stood to the right of the bed, holding what appeared to be a small stack of clean towels. The third perched between Liana's spread, blood-smeared thighs, shouting encouragement.

As happy tears sprang to Evium's eyes at the thought of the arrival of his child at any moment, a slight shift in the darkened corner of the room caught his eye. Evium squinted and focused, not wanting to move from where he had been watching Liana. It was Huison, doing his best to remain still and concealed as the glow of the candlelit room reflected from his amber eyes.

There was no time to ponder the reasons for Huison's presence while Liana gave birth, for Liana emitted a piercing wail that immediately diverted Evium's attention. Evium's cry of encouragement lodged in his throat as he realized. It could not be! It was too soon! Liana was not due for another couple of months.

"No—wait!" he demanded. "Can't something be done to soothe her?"

A fourth maid came into the room carrying a silver tray upon which sat a flagon, goblet, and a small bowl of assorted berries. She smiled warmly at Evium, placing the tray upon a nearby side table, her green eyes twinkling merrily.

"It's all right, sir," she said as she walked back over to him. "Her pains came on rather suddenly, but she's going to be fine! She's doing wonderfully!"

"But, she can't!" he exclaimed. "It's too early! She isn't ready!"

They were interrupted by a cheer from all three ladies at Liana's bedside. Evium looked over to find his wife slumped backward onto the pillows as the maid positioned between Liana's legs whooped in exultation.

"There's a good lass, ye've done it!" she said. A few smacking sounds later, and Evium heard the outraged cry of an infant. "Well done, well done! Y'have a beautiful, healthy baby daughter!"

In the weeks following Mahari's birth, life on the Chatelain estate returned to a semblance of normalcy. Jahd, excited by the birth of his sister, lingered in her nursery during every spare moment—talking to the baby about many things, reading to her from one of his books, or simply sitting beside her crib humming a variety of songs that he made up on the spot.

When not in the company of her brother, or any of the staff hired to care for her, Liana often took the baby on long walks through the grounds. It was usually after those walks that the baby was given over to her nurse and Liana would retire for a nap.

It was during an early afternoon that Evium returned to the principal part of the Den from his workshop, maneuvering his wheelchair through the foyer and to the custom lift he designed and had installed to help him easily travel from one level of the home to another.

As Evium moved through the stillness of the house, he wondered if Mahari's birth meant that he could hope to share a bed with Liana again soon. Not that he expected more children, he simply missed his wife. Surely, she missed him, too? In the months following the announcement of her pregnancy, they coexisted in an environment that, while not fiery with passion, was mostly peaceful. Evium felt it was a brilliant start to what he hoped to rebuild with his intended.

An hour later, Evium had finished showering and changed clothes so that he did not reek so much of sweat, oil, and any other residue resulting from time spent in his workshop all morning. He first went to Jahd's bedroom, hoping that he could entice the child to accompany him on a kitchen raid of some of the leftover elderberry and custard tart initially served at dinner the previous evening. Finding his son's suite of rooms empty, he went through the open door connecting Jahd's room with that of the nurse and approached the closed door on the opposite side that would lead him to Mahari's nursery. He froze, his arm held aloft in reaching for the latch on the door. His eyes narrowed as he focused, and he leaned forward a bit, straining to listen.

"Mahari Siera, I have for so long dreamed of a daughter just like you," a voice said. "You are the spit of your remarkable mother, but you are also of my formidable line. With the combined power of our respective lineages, no door will remain closed to you. Your mother and I love you dearly and will work together to ensure that you take your rightful place in the world."

With chilling realization, Evium realized that the voice belonged to Huison. Trembling, his arm fell to his side as his stomach cramped, and then turned over. Evium felt nauseous as a line of sweat appeared on his brow. What was Huison saying? How could this be? Dreaming of a daughter?

Evium's thoughts traveled to the night Liana gave birth and Huison was in the room. Evium did not know why, but now it made sense. He was lurking in the shadows as he had always done, seeming inconspicuous so that Evium would never have cause to suspect. After Mahari's birth, the incident was quickly forgotten and now Evium cursed himself for being so easily deceived.

The child had been born early—or so Evium thought. The dawning truth was that his wife had already been pregnant on the night she appeared in his bedroom, and he was so enthralled by her presence that he willingly allowed her the use of his body as part of her eventual ruse.

Evium slowly turned away from the door, going back through both rooms to reach the main hallway. Somewhere in the back of his mind he caught the acrid smell that came from having soiled himself. That he had done so failed to register, as he wheeled himself into the lift, going back to the lower floors and the entrance of his workshop.

Shutting himself away in his office, Evium approached his worktable and reached for a large sheet of paper and a charcoal pencil. Tears ran unchecked down his cheeks as he sketched, refined, and sketched further the design for a new wheelchair that steam would power. He would no longer be silent in Liana's Den. He wanted his presence heralded in advance of wherever he went, so that he would not risk bumbling unheard into another secret.

He moved through his own home like a stupefied ghost for days, barely acknowledging his wife and distancing himself from their daughter. Her daughter. Huison's child. He did not know what else to do, so he did nothing.

He completed the new wheelchair in a brief span; the original prototype somewhat cumbersome, though the design would improve. If the change surprised Liana, she said nothing. Then again, she did not know the reason for its creation.

Evium did not give Huison a second glance, knowing that to focus on him for too long would send him into a rage that his body could not convert to action. Jahd was his sole source of comfort, a lovable and affectionate boy with an engaging smirk, and they often spent an hour together for lunch while Liana was napping and Huison was in the library working on updates to the lesson plan for Jahd's studies. It sometimes pained Evium to see Jahd so carefully carrying his baby sister about the house, talking to her and explaining the different things they would encounter along the way.

"Our daddy had a hand in making this—isn't he brilliant?" he would say about many items within the Den.

But, that wasn't true, was it?

"The only thing Huison has had a hand in is Liana," Evium thought bitterly, leaving the child and his sister as he went to the workshop one early morning, where much of his time was spent.

Evium had been working steadily since breakfast, having given no thought to lunch, so fixated on the design for an intricate indoor pool he was keen to build. There was already a substantial lake on the property that was more than suitable for swimming when weather permitted, but Evium wanted something climate-controlled and heated for the off-seasons.

He was busy studying a blueprint of the layout of the grounds so he could best determine the placement of the facility that would house the pool, when his nostrils twitched at the enticing and robust aroma of something delicious. He suddenly looked up, puzzled. The kitchens were much too far away from the workshop for the smell of anything to reach him, not that it would have been able to cut through the stink of a forge and machinery at any rate. Yet, he was tantalized, and his stomach growled loudly in response.

"Well, at last I have your attention," came a voice from behind him.

Turning his wheelchair in a half-circle, Evium came face-to-face with his guest. She was dressed in a jumpsuit with a corseted waist, the top half designed in a white, scalloped lace blouse with long sleeves, while the pants were of black velvet.

The front of her hair, dark but for a silver forelock, was pulled away from her face in a dozen thick, twisted braids, some decorated with silver cording and gathered at the nape. The rest of the dark, deeply waved tresses hung past her shoulders, ending at the middle of her back. Burgundy-colored lips were curled into the same smirk he saw so often on his son, and her dark brown eyes were twinkling. In her neatly manicured hands, bereft of any finery except for a bejeweled band on the ring finger of her left hand, she held a covered silver tray.

"Kaileih!" he said in shock.

"Yes, I know, I'm a surprise," his mother-in-law said, walking over to his worktable and pushing his papers aside with a pinky before setting down the tray. She looked him over, wrinkling her nose. "You've gotten scruffy—don't you shave anymore?"

Evium's hand quickly went to his face, feeling the whiskers along the jawline. He could not readily remember when last a razor touched his face.

"I'd imagine it's a bit more difficult nowadays," she said lightly, the heels of her black velvet boots clicking against the smooth stone floor as she walked about, glancing at a few of the books on the shelves lining the walls. "The first months after a birth can be chaos."

"I didn't know you were coming," Evium said feebly.

Kaileih turned to him again, the light of her smile suffusing the smooth brown skin that belied a woman of her years. It was difficult to believe that she was fifty years old, as anyone looking at her would be hard-pressed to believe that she was a day over thirty. Evium always felt sure that there was much more to Kaileih than simply being the product of good genes.

"I am late," she admitted with a delicate shrug, "but, surely you expected me eventually. I'm sorry to have missed the birth of my granddaughter; however, she came a bit earlier than expected and I couldn't get away then."

"How is Rael?" Evium asked gently.

"Weakening," she answered simply. "Each occurrence seems worse than the last. He's going farther away from me and there doesn't seem to be a thing I can do about it."

"Kaileih... I..." Evium stammered. "I don't know what to..."

"Never mind that," she said, sweeping over him with one glance. "What's gone on with you and my daughter?"

Evium blinked. "Gone on?"

"I've been in this house for four hours—not that you would know because you're holed up in here," Kaileih said. "When little Jahd was born, you and Liana could not keep your hands off each

48

other: holding hands, lingering glances over his crib, clandestine caresses... I thought she would end up pregnant again before her body had fully healed from childbirth, you were so relentless.

"Now, she is thin and as pale as her complexion will allow, sleeping the day away and doubtless others before now. Her son—my grandson—is responsibly raising himself, with the aid of that smarmy tutor of his, who seems more at home here than ever."

At the mention of Huison, Evium frowned and turned back to his desk, removing the cloche covering the tray to find a meal of beef and vegetable stew atop a serving of herbed rice, his all-time favorite dish of Kaileih's, along with a half loaf of crusty bread and a drink served in a silver goblet.

"And there it is," Kaileih said behind him, and he knew she wasn't talking about the food.

His eyes burned as he spooned up some of the stew, cramming the bite into his mouth. As always, it was delicious, and he knew the bitterness he tasted was no reflection upon the talents of the chef.

"My daughter has always been impulsive," Kaileih said in a gentle tone. "She has faith in neither time nor patience and will act rashly in the name of self-gratification—particularly with things she doesn't understand."

Evium continued to eat with his back to her, tears streaming down his face. "Despite our best intentions, preparations, and reassurances, she couldn't comprehend the reasons she was born with an inability to do magic on any scale," Kaileih went on. "Her refusal to accept it nearly got her and four of her friends expelled from Breaton Academy when she was thirteen. Some nonsense about being caught trying to cast unsanctioned magic. I could go on."

He picked up the goblet and drank deeply of what turned out to be some of the honeyed mead his multi-talented mother-in-law had expertly brewed. Kaileih moved to lean against the right side of the table, facing him as he replaced the drinkware and took up the bread, breaking off the end to swirl about in what remained of the stew.

"A loving marriage to a young and virile husband," she continued, taking care to not comment on the tears. "Her first and, I'm sure, only love—the ideal love for a girl whose dream is to be swept off her feet and made to forget the troubles that exist only in her mind... until an accident alters the course of that dream and clouds the world in uncertainty.

"Maybe there is someone else... incomparable to the one she loves in every way, except for whatever physical comforts he can provide. Impulse yet again." Kaileih sighed. "How long has it been going on?"

"I don't know that it still is," Evium answered with a loud sniffle, cramming the bread into his mouth before chewing. "I just know that it once did."

"The baby?"

The bread felt like lead when he swallowed it. Unable to trust his response, Evium simply shook his head.

"You've only just recently discovered this, or Huison would likely be on his way back to Scio nursing a singed arse," Kaileih surmised. "What of my darling daughter? Is this why she's haunting her own home like a ghost?"

"I haven't told her I know," Evium managed, clearing his throat.

"You're afraid that she'd choose Huison Loromin over you, if put to the test."

Evium glanced sharply at his mother-in-law but did not answer. Though Evium had thought about that very thing countless times since discovering his wife's affair, it was even more heartbreaking to have it voiced by someone else with such certainty.

"I don't know the extent of what's transpired between my daughter and Huison," Kaileih went on, "but, I know this: he would have to move both heaven and hell for her to turn away from you completely."

"I'm fairly certain that you've spent the better part of the last four hours cuddling with the extent of what has transpired between Liana and Huison," Evium countered, draining the cup of the remaining mead before spooning up the last of the stew. "Does it matter whether she can turn away from me?"

"That's a question to ask yourself," Kaileih said. "She'll hear from me about this, though. I can promise you that. But, not before you've had time to compose your thoughts. I will not force your hand. When she comes to me afterward, and I know she will, I'll have my say then."

Evium chuckled, though it sounded harsh and forced. "No lectures, then, about a young woman's inability to choose, to supplement the reminder that Liana is impulsive?"

"You know, or at least you should, the depth of what you have with Liana," Kaileih said. "You, and only you, can decide whether it's worth fighting for. I have seen you two at your best, and I do not believe that the best is behind you.

"I am sorry, though, so deeply sorry for what she's done. I hope for her sake that this can be made right. But, Evium... Mahari is blameless. Be mindful of that."

Kaileih ran a hand through Evium's blond hair before leaning over to place a kiss upon his right temple. She then replaced the cloche atop the tray before picking everything up with a chuckle.

"You know, Huison has always cared for my mead," she said. "I'll make sure he has a cup. I'll even take it to him personally." She laughed again. "I'll let you get back to work. I can have your dinner brought up to you later if you'd like. I've picked some marvelous vegetables from the gardens, and I've set the butcher to trim up a roast for us."

Balancing the tray with one hand, she gave Evium's right shoulder a reassuring squeeze before leaving.

There were streaks of dried tears on Evium's face, and those that collected upon the pillow behind his head had cooled while he continued to stare up at the undulating canopy. Six months—that was how long it had been since the truth about the state of his marriage became apparent.

Kaileih stayed with them for a week before needing to return to Rael, and she was true to her word. She mentioned nothing to Liana about what she knew, and her care of baby Mahari was infinite. Kaileih was also true in making sure that Huison had some of her honeyed mead, though Evium suspected she added something special to the drink beforehand. Huison became violently ill that very evening and was carried from the Den on a litter during the night with barely a word of farewell.

Jahd, freed early from tutoring sessions that rarely ended until the start of summer, divided his time between Mahari's nursery and Evium's workshop. Evium was thrilled to have his son by his side, and he shared with him the plans for the indoor pool. It touched him when Jahd added to the layout with an idea of his own for a wheelchair-accessible transitional reservoir comprising water even warmer than that of the rest of the pool.

"For you to soak in, Daddy," Jahd told him as they both bent over the plans, pointing to one section of the drawing. "You're using something to make the water warm, right? Can you have more of that stuff here, so this part is a little warmer than the other?" Jahd peered at his dad through narrowed eyes. "What about something on the sides to make bubbles around you?"

Jahd's birthday was in a matter of days. With it would come Huison's return: Huison, who would be none the wiser about the change in climate on the Chatelain estate. Evium's only correspondence from his old friend was the reminder that he would attend Jahd's celebration, and an outline of his plans to start the next tutoring session a bit earlier in the season, because of having lost time after leaving so abruptly.

"You'll see," Evium said into the empty room. "By the time you get here, there'll be no doubt that things are different. First, I'll talk with my wife. Then, Huison my friend, I'll deal with you."

Chapter Three

Evium sat at his worktable early the following morning, working on a sketch. The entire multi-level workshop—fitted with a steam-powered lift to help Evium and his staff move between floors with ease—was at his disposal. Evium's personal office was at the very back of the first floor of the space with insulated walls and a vast steel door to aid in keeping the office quiet.

He had not slept well the night before, choosing to begin his day before dawn rather than pretend he might get any rest. After two hours, Shaz appeared to begin his new duties and found Evium in the office. After bringing in a breakfast tray for his employer, he busied himself with the obviously overdue task of cleaning and then organizing every inch of the space. After another two hours, the tray was still untouched, but Shaz knew better than to press the issue as he continued with his own work.

So immersed in his work, Evium did not realize he was no longer alone until a shadow fell across the page he was working on. It startled him to find Liana there, resplendent in a cream-colored wrap dress with long, frilled sleeves and small black dots. The tied sash showcased her slender waistline, and the hem ended mid-thigh, giving a wonderful glimpse of Liana's long, shapely legs and finely muscled calves.

Evium's first fleeting thought was of how Liana always made it look so easy to flit about in the strappy, high-heeled sandals that were making a comeback after decades of obscurity. The second was that her talent for entering his office unheard rivaled her mother's.

"Good morning, Liana," Evium said, turning back to focus upon what he was doing.

"Good afternoon, Evium," she corrected.

He looked up again in surprise. "Afternoon, is it?" he said.

"It is," she said, "almost a quarter after one."

"My, how time flies," he said, looking back to his sketch.

"I thought I might find you still in your bedroom," Liana ventured. "I thought... maybe after last night..."

"I was still sulking because my wife doesn't love me anymore and prefers to sleep on the opposite side of our home?" Evium offered flatly, smoothly sketching. "You couldn't even force yourself to sit and have a glass of wine with me. Not even out of pity."

"I don't pity you!" Liana said.

"That much is obvious," he said with a snort.

"What is it you expect of me, Evium?" she asked. "One minute, you look upon me with so much love... but then sometimes your eyes are so cold..."

He tossed his pencil down and looked at her. "Are you prepared to tell me you don't know why that is?" he snapped. "Will you really bat those long lashes at me and pretend to not understand why I'm so hurt by you?"

Liana shook her head, her mass of long, jet curls becomingly tousled and framing her face.

"I know why," she whispered. "What I don't... what I don't know is what I can do about it."

"Do you want to?"

"What?"

"Do something about it—do you want to?" Evium asked louder.

"Yes, of course," Liana answered. "But you can't always be angry with me or look at me with such... disappointment in your eyes!"

"Liana," Evium sighed, "you can't do certain things and behave in such a way that affects me so deeply, and then expect to dictate how I respond." He sat back in his chair. "I live each day with a gurgling, cooing reminder of what's become of our marriage. I silently endured it for months for love of you, when you still cannot even look at me to say that my love is returned.

"Huison, my best friend of over twenty years, is coming to our son's seventh birthday celebration next week. Jahd loves him. Huison's become much more to him than just a tutor. Jahd calls him 'Uncle,' and he would not understand why I would be content to never allow Huison Loromin anywhere near this home ever again." Evium narrowed his eyes at his wife. "You want to talk about anger and disappointment?" He shook his head and returned his attention to the worktable. "You can accept how I feel—or not. At least you won't have to worry about any retaliatory bastards from me. Who'd have me?"

Evium heard Liana's choked sob behind him, and he cursed himself for going too far. His own eyes stung, and he expected Liana to leave so that, once again, things would remain unresolved. In the minutes that followed, he could hear her struggle to control her tears and steady her breathing.

When at last he turned to look at her again, he was surprised to find that she had not even turned away. Tears she had wiped away stained the cuffs of her dress, but she countered his resigned look with one of sad determination.

"I don't want to keep doing this," he whispered. "I don't want to fight with you, Li. This is tearing me apart. Our home has turned into a powder keg, and I don't know which of our frequent disagreements will provide the spark that blows everything apart." He extended an arm, and Liana placed her hand in his.

"I don't know where to begin, other than to say that I'm sorry," he told her. "What I said was uncalled for. Mahari is innocent in all this." He cleared his throat. "Huison, however, is another matter. He'll have to go after the party, and for good. I don't yet know how to go about it in a way that won't ultimately damage our son, but it's going to happen." He studied his wife. "Do you disagree?"

"No," she said. "It has to happen, I know that."

"This will be more effective if we present a united front, Liana."

She nodded. "Yes, of course," she said, sniffling.

"We have things to discuss," he said solemnly.

"We do," Liana agreed, "and we will."

Evium pulled her into an embrace, sighing into her hair as he held her close.

She stiffened in his arms.

Suddenly, she gasped and pulled away from him, moving closer to the worktable.

"What is this?" she demanded. "What?" Evium asked, alarmed.

Liana snatched up the most recent sketch he had been working on, a miniature construct unlike anything she had ever seen. Evium spared no details, considering it ranked among his best work, and took pride in the way he could highlight the key aspects of the transport from the whitewall tires to the accents made of chrome.

"What *is* this!?" Liana asked again.

"I was hoping it would be Jahd's birthday present," Evium shrugged, confused.

"You're giving our son a drawing?" she asked evenly.

"No, we're going to work on the life-sized model today—this afternoon," he said. "Since this will be scaled for him, it should take only a few days to complete and will be ready in time for the big day."

"Why would you do this!?" Liana screamed, clutching the drawing in one hand and shaking it in Evium's face. "It's not enough that you nearly got yourself killed in one of these contraptions! You mean the same for him!?"

"No, of course not!" Evium said, wresting the paper away from his wife before she destroyed it. He turned to his worktable, doing what he could to smooth the wrinkles from the sheet. "This is to be nothing like my vehicle. Mine had a motor of sorts... one that was too powerful, obviously, or the impact of the crash wouldn't have damaged my spine. This one is completely manual with a pedaling mechanism inside. He'll go no faster than his little feet and legs will take him." He turned back to his wife and seized her hands in his as he stared up at her. "I promise. I would never, ever do anything to endanger our son."

"He won't be hurt?" Liana asked in a small voice, her eyes filling again.

"On my life," Evium swore as he pulled her to him again.

Liana nodded. "I should let you get back to it, then," she said with another sniffle before turning away. Evium watched as she walked toward the large steel door and paused. He waited, wondering what more she might be thinking, but she seemed to think better of it as she left the office, closing the door behind her.

Chapter Four

Evium groaned in his sleep, instinctively reaching out to his left and to what was once Liana's side of the bed. Sighing as he was roused from slumber, he ran a hand through his hair before pushing himself into a seated position on the bed.

As he sat rubbing his eyes, Evium noticed the delicate smell of coconut. He looked around the vast suite, his eyes adjusting enough to the darkness that he could see the slim figure sitting at the dressing table.

"Li?" he whispered.

The figure got up and walked toward the bed. As she crossed a beam of moonlight from the window, Evium could finally see her clearly. She leaned against one bedpost and shrugged. He could see the hint of a bare shoulder peeking from the pale-yellow chiffon and lace robe she wore.

"I couldn't sleep," she said.

"Is something wrong?" he ventured.

"No," Liana answered with a small shake of her head, a curtain of dark curls falling forward. "I think our son's enthusiasm is contagious. It took three bedtime stories to get him to calm down. He's really excited about his birthday tomorrow."

"Ah," Evium said, lightly picking at the coverlet upon the bed. "Is that the only reason you're unable to sleep?"

"What do you mean?" she asked, pushing her hair from her face with one hand.

"What will happen tomorrow?" Evium asked.

"With Jahd's birthday celebration?" Liana asked, and Evium could see in the moonlight that her brow was furrowed.

"Huison will be here," he reminded her. "He arrives first thing in the morning."

"Yes, and?"

"Things are different now," Evium said. "We haven't discussed everything, but..."

"Nothing is going to happen," Liana said.

"Nothing?"

"No!" Liana said before sighing, first rubbing her hands together and then interlacing her fingers. "This isn't about Huison. It's about our son's birthday."

"I'll not have him stay in the main house this time," Evium said quietly, determined to make the point. "I have instructed Clea to prepare one of the guest houses for him." Liana nodded but did not comment. "All those nights he stayed under this roof." He slowly shook his head. "All those nights with me alone in this bed, and you in your suite of rooms..."

"Don't worry yourself over it," Liana suggested.

"How can I not?" Evium asked loudly, his hands curling into fists. "Each time I try to put it out of my mind so that we can move forward, I think about what went on in this house under my nose!"

"It can't matter now—not like that."

"Then tell me what does matter!" Evium said, still angry. "Tell me something that will keep me from pummeling Huison on sight at our son's party! Say something that'll make all of this..."

Liana moved to Evium's side of the bed and took a seat, silencing him. "You asked me before... the last time I was here... if I still love you," Liana began.

Evium went rigid, his body suddenly chilled as his hands went slack.

He didn't speak.

He did not want to think of that night or any other awful night they'd shared in the bedroom. He wanted only to focus on future possibilities that would bring them closer to being happy again.

"I do love you, Evium," she whispered. "I love you. My heart aches... it burns so deeply inside of me... with what I feel for you. The passion we have shared, the things you have awakened within me, the caresses and kisses... and not just that... The way we used to talk to each other, and our adventures together are scorching reminders of what we have, and I know that my behavior and the things I've done betrayed all of that.

"I'm not making any excuses for what happened. I cracked the foundation of what we have built. I was willful. I was greedy. I acted as my mother has always said—without thinking. I thought I needed something... someone... to tell me I was still desirable, as if what happened to you was a personal attack upon my sensuality.

"I was wracked with guilt about what happened each time we attempted to make love after your accident. I should have discussed it with you, but didn't know how to approach it in a way that you could accept as not being your fault... because you were always so apologetic on those nights as you tried to take the blame."

"The fault is in that we didn't talk with one another," Evium agreed. "We were so busy dancing around eggshells that we moved away from what was important."

"I originally went to Huison intending to talk with him about you," Liana admitted, reddening. "You've known each other for so long, and I hoped he might guide me in how best to approach you."

"You confided in Huison about my... inability to..." Evium struggled with the words, looking away from his wife as his hands retracted into claws that dug at the bed linen.

"No, no," Liana said quickly, "I offered no specifics. I said only that we were having problems communicating, and that I was afraid." She shrugged. "I didn't know what it meant, and I desperately wanted to fix it. If my father..." She paused and took a breath. "My father is dead, or I would have gone to him. Rael is ill... and I have no other close male figure in my life, so... I went to Huison." Liana looked down to study her hands and a few curls fell into her face. "He was very easy to talk to at first, but then he became a convenient diversion."

There it was—the admission that Evium needed but was afraid to hear at the same time.

"So there was no spell. No enchantment," he managed, blinking back tears.

"No," Liana scoffed angrily, though Evium did not feel that her anger was directed at him. "I won't demean the gift of magic by naming what happened to me as an enchantment. Huison wanted me to love him for himself and never would have imposed his will upon me—though I think he regrets that now."

"Regrets it?"

"Because he never bound me to him, and my feelings faded."

"It's really over?"

"Yes."

"When did it end?"

"When I realized I was carrying Mahari," Liana answered. "It came as such a surprise to me. You and I hadn't conceived again in the years between Jahd's birth and the accident. I thought perhaps I was no longer capable. Relieving myself of the pregnancy was not an option, though, despite the circumstances of Mahari's conception.

But... I knew things were over, and I told him so, right after revealing that I was expecting."

"I didn't know things had ended," Evium admitted. "He's behaved no differently, which is one thing that makes this so maddening! I saw no difference in him when you were apparently together, and now that you say it's been done for over a year, I can't think of any instance where I can look back and pinpoint when it happened."

"Because he still has hope," Liana revealed. "I believe Huison harbors the idea that as long as you remain unaware and he still has a place in our lives, there's a possibility that I will change my mind.

"I don't know that he ever planned to supplant you fully. We discussed nothing resembling a future together. I think he's content to remain in my life in whatever capacity I'd allow."

"Because he loves you so much," Evium said.

"He does," Liana replied, examining her fingernails.

"Do you love him?" he whispered.

"No," she insisted, looking up at her husband. "Huison has only ever heard that word from me as it related to you or to our son."

"You came to me..." Evium could barely say the words. He placed a hand upon his chest as if he could touch his heart to comfort it, his words punctuated by hitching breaths. "That night... you showed up a-and you... made me think..."

"I told Huison that I was pregnant," Liana revealed in a whisper. "Instead of leaving with him as he asked, I ended things. He then suggested that I go to you, and..."

"Huison!" Evium choked out the name. "He bade you... to go make love to your *invalid of a husband*—and you acted on his command?"

"As I told you... I ended things with Huison when I realized I was carrying the baby. He knew he would lose any chance of seeing me or his child if I went back to my mother in Tilehn. Both his hopes and mine were pinned on you, though for hugely different reasons."

"No, not different. You were both selfish."

"I love you," Liana said again. "I *was* selfish, and I was wrong." She took one of his hands, clutching it between both of hers as her eyes searched his. "I want this to work, and I'm willing to do what it takes. I'm telling you all of this now to show you I know what I've done wrong and I'm willing to correct it." She frowned as her eyes filled with tears. "If you think it would help you see your way clear... I can send Mahari to Tilehn." Evium stared at her, aghast. "I hope you wouldn't want it to become permanent, but if she needs to stay with Mama while you and I work things out..."

"Liana, what do you take me for?" Evium asked, shaking his head.

"I know you didn't ask this of me," she rushed on, "but, it's something I'm willing to do for a while. I know you don't care for Mahari now, but I hope that in time..."

Evium was infused with guilt. "It is not that I don't care for her," he said. "She's a sweet, beautiful baby... and she looks so much like you, but..."

"...another man fathered her," Liana finished. "I know, Evium. I know. And, I am sorry, for what I've done to you and to our marriage. I have hated every moment of us being apart, and I'm willing to do what's necessary to fix things between us. I just... I just hope that... I..." She blinked through the tears that fell. "I hope that I'm not too late."

A light tapping upon the closed bedroom door interrupted Evium's response.

"Oh, what is it?" Liana wailed in irritation, releasing Evium's hand and rushing to fling the door open. She found Alena, the young wet nurse, who was startled into a quick curtsy because of the ire in Liana's moist eyes.

64

"Begging your pardon, Lady Liana!" Her pale blue gaze went beyond Liana and toward the bed where Evium sat, which caused Alena's blush to deepen as she curtsied again. "Forgive me, sir!" She looked at Liana again. "I went to your bedroom and then came to find you here. I was reading the young sir a story before taking to my own bed for the night. It's the wee babe. She woke from her sleep, screaming something fierce. I can't get her to calm down. She's got her brother in a right state as well. Sick with worry, the poor lad."

"I'll be right there," Liana told her, to which Alena responded with yet another curtsy before fleeing.

Liana sighed, closing the door and returning to the bed to once again sit beside her husband. "I'd like to finish this conversation tonight, Vi," she breathed. "I can't go to bed another night with this weight on my heart."

"Of course," he agreed.

"I'll come back, then... after I've seen to the children," Liana said, preparing to get up from the bed. Evium reached over, taking her by the wrist. Liana looked back at him.

"Not alone," he said gently. "Let me go with you." When he saw how Liana's brows rose in shock, the depth of how he had treated Mahari in the short time she'd been alive descended upon him in a tremendous blow, and he blinked back the sting of more tears.

"You go to Jahd," he insisted. "I want to be the one to comfort Mahari. I need to... make this right. I don't want you to send her to your mother. I'm sorry that you ever felt a need to make that offer. I'll go to her, be there for her, and you and I will talk things through."

Evium accepted the hug from his wife, holding her tightly.

After a moment, they parted. He took a deep breath.

He then reached to his right, pulling the wheelchair to him as Liana got up from the bed and pulled the covers back for him.

Moments later, settled in, he pressed a few buttons and the chair sprang to life. Liana went to the door, holding it open for him, and they moved a short distance down the hallway together until Evium stopped.

"What is it?" Liana asked. "If you've changed your mind, and you'd rather check on Jahd..."

"No," Evium said. "I'd rather you go in through Jahd's bedroom and I'll go in through the nursery door. If... if Mahari sees you first, she might never let me..."

Liana nodded. "I understand," she said, doing her best to smile, though her eyes were filling again. "Take all the time you need, Vi. I'll be waiting for you in our bedroom."

The full effect of his wife's words did not strike Evium until she had already gone into Jahd's room, and he was reaching for the latch to Mahari's.

"Our bedroom."

He wiped at his eyes, smoothed back his hair and inhaled deeply before going into the room. Alena, surprised to see him come in rather than his wife, knew better than to say anything as she bobbed yet another curtsy before leaving, closing the door behind her.

The baby, sitting up in her crib with tear-stained cheeks, hiccupped softly as she looked at Evium through big, red-rimmed gray eyes. He knew she was uncertain of him, and he cursed himself for all the times she had smiled at him or reached for him, only to be greeted by a blank stare before he turned away from her.

Her little body trembled, and he made note of how her eyes wandered toward the doorway, likely hoping that her mother would come soon to rescue her from this staring stranger. When her brow furrowed and fresh tears filled her eyes, Evium's voice caught in his throat as he spoke.

"It... it's okay, Mahari," he whispered.

She looked at him again as the tears crept from the corners of her eyes. Evium approached the crib, using the latching mechanism to slide the door from left to right. He slowly held his arms out to her and then smiled, feeling the wetness as it spilled onto his own cheeks. Mahari contemplated the gesture for a moment, timidly scooting toward Evium until she was nearly at the edge of the mattress. Suddenly, she keened and reached for him. He quickly scooped her up and held her to him, rubbing her back as she cried.

The baby smelled lightly of chocolate, and Evium knew it was likely because of a whipped butter that Liana applied to Mahari's skin. It was the same variety of cream she routinely lathered Jahd in from the time he was born, and fond memories of the aroma caused Evium to inhale deeply before kissing Mahari's cheek.

He steadily rocked her in his powerful arms, gently shushing her while she cried. Eventually reduced to mostly sniffles, Mahari pulled back to study Evium. She touched his face, and the tousled shards of his blond hair, before wiping at the wetness on his cheeks. Her eyes were rounded, and Evium sensed she was still unsure of him after having been rejected for months.

"Hello," he said simply. "I think that it's time for us to be properly introduced. I know you are Mahari Siera Chatelain." He continued to hold her in one of his arms as he wiped the tears from her face with a free hand before gently tousling her glossy ringlets. "I'm your father," he said, "and I'm so sorry that it took me this long to come to you.

"I'll make you a deal, though. I won't be taken away from you again, all right? No more nightmares, Mahari, for either of us. The nightmares are over."

As if in response to that, Mahari leaned forward and rested her head upon Evium's chest as she nestled in his lap. He lightly cleared his throat, at first humming and then crooning a melody from his childhood and one he sang to Jahd often as a baby. Evium felt that

Mahari had relaxed, and he continued to rock her even after the song was completed.

Though he could tell from the gradual steadiness of her breathing the moment she fell asleep, he was reluctant to disturb her or return her to the crib. Instead, he continued to hold her gently, focusing on the lively beat of her heart and her gentle snores, wondering why he ever felt that his mistreatment of her was justified.

Chapter Five

Activity on the Chatelain estate was in overdrive on the morning of Jahd's seventh birthday. Messengers began arriving just before dawn; one after another, bearing cards, gifts, and well-wishes to Jahd and his parents. The vast kitchens and pantry were filled with perishable offerings for the household from the townsfolk of Kynedal, and tables were erected outside to hold all personal presents for Jahd to open later.

While the servants bustled downstairs, the upper levels of the home were still quiet. Jahd and Mahari, having stayed awake well past midnight to indulge in hearty early birthday celebrations, were sound asleep in their respective rooms. Evium and Liana were also sleeping in their shared marital bed.

Liana sighed in slumber, rolling over onto her right side and scooting closer to her husband. He instinctively put an arm around her without opening his eyes, pulling her to him as he also sighed.

On the night of Mahari's nightmare, Evium returned to the bedroom after tucking the baby back into her crib to find Liana patiently waiting. Evium was pleased to see that she had made herself comfortable by getting into the bed and, once he settled in beside her, she slid over to rest her head upon his chest. He hoped it meant that they were on the path to setting things right again, a hope further reinforced the next morning when Liana instructed members of the staff to move all her belongings back to the bedroom she intended to—once again—share with her husband.

In the mornings since, it was Evium who went into the nursery every morning to greet an increasingly delighted Mahari. He couldn't play with her the way Liana and Jahd did. There was neither hiding nor seeking, but Mahari took just as much comfort from sitting in Evium's lap as he steered through Liana's Den or on estate grounds. It did not take long for Mahari to adapt to a relationship she wanted all along, and Evium did not find as much difficulty in the change as he previously assumed.

"Uncle Hui!"

Jahd wove his way through the crowd of children, running to greet Huison as he stepped through the back doors of the Den and into the spacious backyard. The grounds were decorated primarily in blue and silver, with balloons, banners, and gaily waving flags throughout.

There was an array of picnic tables nearby, each able to seat six comfortably, and a larger table at the head of the group. As Huison enveloped Jahd in a hug, his amber eyes took in the sight at the head table: Evium and Liana sitting side-by-side, with Mahari, seated in Evium's lap, shrieking and clapping with delight at a petite young woman wearing a harlequin costume, who was turning cartwheels at lightning speed.

"I'm so glad you're here!" Jahd said breathlessly, his face flushed with excitement. "I haven't seen you in so long! Mama said you got sick—are you better?"

Huison looked over at Liana again. As if sensing his stare, she turned—and locked eyes with him. Evium, ever alert, noted his wife's expression and turned to study Huison.

"I am better," Huison said to Jahd, looking down at him and smiling as he touched the top of his head. "Happy birthday to you, young man! I have brought with me some new books for your studies. I believe it is time to add to your already immeasurable catalogue of knowledge."

Jahd giggled. "Sounds great, Uncle Hui! I can't wait!" he said.

"Tell me, my grand sir," Huison said charmingly, pantomiming the straightening of an invisible bow tie at Jahd's throat. "Have I missed anything fun by being away?"

"Not really," the boy answered with a shake of his head. "I've still been studying. I finished the rest of the lesson plan after you left." His face brightened. "But, it has really been great to say good night to both Mama and Daddy at the same time now!"

Huison stiffened, his smile locked into place. "At the same time?" he asked steadily.

"Yes! They both come into my room like they used to!" Jahd said, causing Huison to sigh inwardly in relief. "Or, I'll go into their room and say good night before going back to bed on my own so that they don't have to get up."

Huison's worried gaze flickered over to Liana again before he glanced once more at Jahd and nodded.

"You are certainly growing into such a considerate young man, Jahd," he managed. "Your parents are truly blessed in this. Now... I do not mean to keep you from your festivities. Please—go on and enjoy yourself. We will have plenty of time to catch up, yes?"

"Yes, sir, Uncle Hui!" Jahd agreed happily before scampering off, leaving Huison to collect himself in silence before walking across the yard and toward the head table.

"Ah, forgive my tardiness!" he said in mock jubilation as he approached, arms spread in supplication. "I meant to be here early this morning, but one of my horses cast a shoe in the middle of nowhere. We had to move carefully until reaching the next town to have her shod again." He bowed to Liana. "A pleasure as always." He then turned to Evium, noticing now that he was closer, that Mahari was comfortably seated. "Hello, my old friend."

"Huison," Evium answered with a brief incline of his head as Huison took a seat at the opposite side of the table. Shortly after doing so, a uniformed attendant approached the table and bowed.

"Chamomile tea, no sweetener," Huison requested. The young man nodded and walked away.

"Chamomile?" Evium asked. "Are you still ill after all this time?"

"It is nothing more than the road sickness I am plagued with whenever I travel," Huison answered. "It will pass in time as always, but the tea helps."

"Well, there are more convenient ways to travel," Evium said. "You could have easily traveled by train. There are those who feel that traveling by carriage is antiquated these days, even by today's standards."

"Yet it is still infinitely safer than traveling by the steam-powered train," Huison shrugged before arching a brow, his gaze taking in Evium in his wheelchair, "or via a motorized conveyance."

In the silence that followed, the attendant returned carrying a steaming mug, which he placed in front of Huison.

"Is there anything else I can do?" the attendant asked.

"Take the baby to her nurse," Liana said. "She can stay out for another thirty minutes, but then I want her taken upstairs for a nap."

"Of course, Lady Liana," the young man said, scooping Mahari up and taking her away.

"I still say that you're looking ragged, Hui," Evium commented in an off-hand manner a short time later, "despite your claims of travel sickness." He smiled, though his blue eyes were cold. "You haven't been visiting Heingraf again, have you?"

Huison chuckled as Liana contemplated the arrangement of flowers nearby. "I have not been to Heingraf since the trip at the end of our school days," he said, knowing that Liana wouldn't likely take kindly to knowing that her husband had once frequented the place known as, "Brothel City."

"Nice try, that," Evium commented, reaching for one of Liana's hands. "My wife and I have no secrets from each other." He looked from Liana's paling complexion to Huison's reddening one. "No secrets at all... anymore."

Evium lightly kissed Liana's hand, watching the way she fought to keep her eyes firmly trained on the floral centerpiece atop the table. He saw the way Huison stared at Liana, as if willing her to meet his gaze. When she refused, Huison's brow furrowed, and he frowned. For the first time in months, Evium felt triumphant.

"I have been working on something," Huison answered softly, casually toying with the handle on the mug of tea. "Admittedly, it has consumed quite a bit of my time—though I would not have missed today for the world."

"Another of your experiments?" Liana asked with a wry chuckle as she tried, or so it appeared, to lighten the mood.

"No," Huison responded with a smirk. "This is no experiment. It is already proven—I am merely taking part in a re-enactment of sorts. You will actually find this interesting, Liana." Huison's gaze slid briefly to Evium. "I based my research upon a thesis written by your father."

Liana started, removing her hand from Evium's grasp before straightening her posture, her gray eyes appearing huge as she stared at Huison. "What did you say?" she asked.

"Your father continues to be an authority in the subjects of spellbreaking and spellweaving," Huison said lightly. "In the years since his death, no one has come close to being able to understand his abilities—let alone duplicate them. Those who have tried..." He shrugged slender shoulders.

"How is it you're able to understand Amriel's work?" Evium asked, his blue eyes still frosty. "While I don't deny that you have some talent, Amriel's level of competency is—as you've alluded—unmatched and unsurpassed."

"Hence the reason I look—as you said—ragged," Huison agreed, turning his attention back to Liana. "It is difficult, attempting to copy what your father has written about." He cleared his throat. "I must also guard against meeting the same end as your brother."

"Now, wait a moment!" Evium began as Liana leaned forward, one hand to her bosom as she studied Huison.

"What do you mean?" she asked. "What about Rael?"

"Has your mother never divulged to you how your brother came to be at the sanitarium?" Huison queried.

"Huison..." Evium warned, knowing how volatile Liana became when speaking about her brother.

"Of course," Liana answered, ignoring her husband. "Rael went to my father's laboratory at my mother's command to summon Daddy to dinner. He found our father had collapsed and tried to help him."

Huison nodded. "That is a very simple way of describing the complexity of the truth."

"How would you know?" Evium demanded. "How could anyone know? Only two people were there, and one of them had already died. They have institutionalized the other for almost five years."

"I know from reading his work," Huison said. "Obviously, Amriel Dhamon took some secrets with him to his grave, but there are enough pieces hidden within the body of the research he published to glean the facts. It would take a rare and determined individual to piece it together. I am, and I believe I have."

"Tell me!" Liana demanded.

"Li, no!" Evium said, grabbing her hand again.

When Liana pulled away from him a second time, he huffed and sat back in his chair. His gaze moved to where the children were playing, under the watchful eye of both nanny and nurse. Mahari was shrieking with laughter as her big brother performed a series of cartwheels nearby, doing his best to imitate the young lady performing previously.

"It happened much as you said," Huison told Liana. "I believe your brother found your father collapsed in his workroom and tried to resuscitate him. His manner of doing so is likely to be the reason for his mental degradation." He, too, seemed to look over at the children, and his smile was chilling. "The bond between father and son," he said before looking at Liana again, "was not quite enough in that moment. I believe your brother tried to lift the veil of death from your father and ventured to a plane he was not trained to face."

"What does that mean?" Liana asked.

"Rael tried to bring Amriel back from the dead," Huison stated plainly. "What he saw when he followed your father... drove him mad."

"That makes no sense!" Evium interjected.

"Because you do not understand it," Huison responded.

"No, Huison—Evium's right," Liana said, to Evium's surprise and relief. "How would Rael have even known to do that, or that it could be attempted?"

Huison looked at Liana, and then his eyes softened. "You do not know the full extent of the work your father has done," he surmised.

"Your father is much more than the man who revolutionized the way spells are first broken down into elements of power and then rebuilt in a way that enhances the intent of the user. The skills he possessed are not just of this world, but of others. He visited other realms, Liana—which is why his work is so difficult to recreate. Some of it is born of his ties to alternate planes.

"We will likely never know why your father risked an inter-planar shift, since he has never written of those reasons, but I can only imagine that his motives were profound. It took some time to realize the truth in what likely happened to Rael, but everything points to an attempt by your brother to emulate what your father had done, and his mind was consumed by a being he encountered and was not strong enough to deflect." Huison leaned forward in his chair. "After he awoke from the coma, his power had increased, yes?"

Liana nodded slowly, her face flushed. "Yes," she admitted in a whisper. "We couldn't figure it out." She looked at Evium and shrugged. "He'd always been able to move things with his mind, but this was different. There were other things—things he couldn't do before. He caused a marble bust in the foyer to bubble and then melt onto the floor. He...once got a headache and a cluster of dark clouds hung over our home for a week, causing a downpour and flooding the grounds. Those were just the minor incidents."

"He could not control himself," Huison offered.

"No," Liana said, still whispering as she looked back at him. "After a time, Mama thought it best to have him moved from home to a place that specialized in tending to those who'd suffered accidents related to spellwork."

"Spell sicknesses," sneered Huison. "But they were and still are ill-equipped to deal with the challenges of someone as unique as Rael Dhamon."

"Now that you have forced my wife to relive what is likely the most painful memory she has, perhaps you'll now enlighten us about what any of this has to do with what you're researching," Evium challenged.

Huison grinned, steepling long fingers beneath his nose. "It is simple," he revealed. "I am on the verge of uncovering the way to rid Rael of his malady and return him to the path of full recovery."

Chapter Six

The table fell silent for several moments as both Liana and Evium first looked at each other with incredulity before turning to a smugly satisfied Huison, who was taking a sip of his tea.

"What sort of game are you playing, Hui?" Evium asked, covering Liana's trembling hand with his.

"No games, my friend," Huison answered. "I am on the brink of a grand discovery, and I intend to see Rael relieved of his ailment."

"Rael has been ill for five years," Evium stressed. "His mother, Kaileih, has afforded him excellent care, considering the uniqueness of his condition. The consensus is that there is no successful treatment for him. Everything that's been tried has failed."

"No one has tried this," Huison shrugged. "The thought has not even occurred to anyone to do so. I do not think anyone else is capable."

"*You're* not capable," Evium snapped. "You have a modicum of talent, Huison, I'll grant you that... but, you're talking about duplicating Amriel Dhamon's work. If research alone has you looking so drawn, how do you expect to attempt this? Just what is it you plan to do?"

Liana placed her free hand to her throat and took a shuddering breath. Evium turned to his wife in concern, his expression softening at how distressed she looked. He then sighed and turned back to Huison.

"If you lack the decency to tell us anything more about what you're devising," he began, "would you at least exercise a bit of sense about this? Take your findings to Claerendon."

"Claerendon?" Liana asked suddenly as she stiffened.

Evium's grip on her hand tightened as he turned to her. "I know, sweetheart," he said soothingly. "I know, but this is important. Claerendon University is the nucleus of some of the most brilliant minds in all subjects, especially spellwork. Your father sometimes consulted with the board, remember?" He looked at Huison. "They would be the most qualified to handle this."

"I have been doing well with the research on my own," Huison said crisply. "I do not need them or anyone else to aid in this." He fixed Liana in his yellow gaze, and his tone softened. "If this is of some concern to you, Liana, or if you find you would prefer that I not do this... I would have no choice but to cease in my efforts. My goal has never been to distress you."

"What is your goal, then?" Evium interjected. "What is it you want to accomplish by doing all of this, Huison? Are you aiming to be successful and get what you want when it's all done?"

Huison settled back in his chair, the dual nature of the questions asked not lost on him.

"I only hoped," he said quietly, staring down at his mug. "I hoped with no plot, plan, or design and lived only in the moment. I am, apparently, too frightened to look too far ahead for fear that those hopes will be lost." His eyes met Liana's. "And it would seem that they have been, in part, all the same."

"I can't keep you from researching whatever you choose," Evium said, "even though you have to know the effect this will have on my wife and her mother."

"I am counting on it," Huison said, his expression unchanged.

"I do, however, need to make certain things clear regarding my wife."

Huison smiled gently as he focused on Evium. "I have brought with me several books," he responded mildly, providing a slight shift in subject. "I have told Jahd about them. What I was remiss in explaining is that I will no longer be his tutor." Evium exhaled deeply as he felt Liana's fingers interlacing with his. "I have struggled with this, but it is best for several reasons." He shrugged again. "Clarity is not needed, old friend. It is obvious where things stand... for now."

"I won't keep you from visiting from time to time," Evium said, glancing over to where the children were. Mahari was the central point in a circle of applauding children, lolling on her side in the grass and doing her best to imitate a cartwheel as she shrieked with laughter. Jahd dove onto the lush grass to roll beside her, equally jubilant. "It wouldn't be fair to bar you from the estate entirely, considering."

"Kind of you," Huison commented carefully, his eyes once again on Liana as Evium watched Mahari. "Should I decide to visit, I will send a messenger well beforehand." He paused. "Or perhaps she... can visit my lands in Scio. I have harbored the desire for her presence, and she will one day be mistress there should she desire it." He allowed the duality of those words to linger for a moment. "But if I may... I would like to be the one to speak with Jahd." Evium arched a brow as he turned back to the table. "I will only talk to him about the need for me to focus on my research. I will not tell him the subject of said research or the reasons for the change. My only thought is that it might seem better to come from me. There would be fewer questions for you to have to answer later."

Evium looked at Liana. "What are your thoughts on this?" he asked her.

"The research you're doing for my brother," Liana said after lightly clearing her throat, "it would continue undeterred? You wouldn't end it out of spite?"

"On the contrary," Huison said with a smile. "I am more determined than ever to see this through."

"What Evium suggested, though, about Claerendon?" Liana pressed.

"I will do this alone," Huison said with a shake of his head. "It will take longer, I admit, but I have taken ownership of this and do not trust that anyone else will serve my interests."

"Liana's interests," Evium prompted. "Kaileih's interests."

"Of course," Huison said, smiling once again. "I will also ensure that you are kept abreast of my findings, should the situation call for it."

"Generous of you," Evium said, "considering Liana's familial ties to all of this." He released Liana's hand and leaned forward, locking Huison in his sights. "If, at any point, my wife tells you to stop—you will listen and do as she asks immediately. Is that clear?"

Huison looked at Liana, taking in the way the light breeze toyed with a cluster of her long curls. The coloring of her cheeks nearly matched that of her dress, and he did his best to capture this image of her; soft and resplendent in blush, even though she was reaching for her husband's hand and not his. She blurred in his vision only briefly, until he blinked the situation back into clarity.

"Crystal," Huison said, his smile unwavering.

Chapter Seven

Evium sat up in bed silently, watching Liana run a brush through her damp hair. His sapphire gaze drank in his wife, who had emerged from her private bath swathed in an intricately embroidered dark red silk nightgown that skimmed the tops of her delicate feet.

Even before the main house was completed, Evium tried to convince his bride to allow the installation of modified electric lighting, at the time one of the latest innovations from his busy workshop. His creation nearly duplicated the warmth and spectrum of natural sunlight and would bathe the structure in its glow, no matter the time of day or year. Liana declined to have it established in the Den, stating that she preferred the atmosphere created with candlelight, no matter the cost of upkeep for the number of candles needed to illuminate such a large house.

She did consent, however, to having the lighting modification installed in the greenhouses to benefit the various flora contained therein. Looking at her now, he had to agree with her logic. Electricity, revised or not, could never duplicate the way candlelight enhanced the softness of Liana's skin and the silken sheen of her hair.

Evium picked at the coverlet, his fingertips tapping in staccato against the brocade as his brow furrowed. He opened his mouth to say something and then snapped it shut with a shake of his head.

"What a day," Liana said with a sigh as she placed her brush atop the vanity and coiled her mass of hair, securing it into a thick knot at the nape. "The children enjoyed themselves so much. I didn't think we'd ever get them to bed."

Evium could not help chuckling. "I think they were two of the grimiest children ever born," he commented. "How did Mahari fill her pockets with so much grass and dirt?"

"Likely the same way her brother had his filled with wild mushrooms and at least one slug," Liana said with a laugh as she dipped her fingertips into a jar atop the vanity, extracting some cream that she applied to her face and neck.

Evium was still watching as Liana smoothed the cream into her skin, switching focus to her arms and elbows as she applied more of the decadent substance. He saw the sudden change in her expression, and his stomach tightened, wondering what she might say next.

"We've wasted so much time, Vi," she whispered. "Today was the happiest I've seen Jahd in so long. My heart is so full, and yet it also aches in part because of what we have deprived him of. I was stubborn. You were confused and angry. The effect on the children..."

"No, stop," Evium said with a shake of his head. "We can't go back and change that, though I wish we could. We'll do our best for them both, and for each other."

Liana turned in her seat to look at Evium. "Is it too late? Can we make up for it?"

Evium sighed. "Li," he began, "it's not too late at all. We still have a little over a year."

She frowned. "You still mean to do it, then? You haven't changed your mind?"

"We've been planning for him to go away to school since he turned a year old," Evium reminded her. "He would either have attended the Junior Academy at Breaton until he became old enough to transfer to their senior levels, or Pandoufuli if he reached the proper age showing no signs of being a spellweaver." He ran a hand through his hair. "There's been nothing, Li... nothing at all, so Breaton isn't a consideration anymore. I started at Pandoufuli after I turned eight, and so will he."

Liana went to the bed, curling up against her husband with her head upon his chest. "It's so soon," she said. "We're only just getting our family back."

"A lot could happen in a year," Evium said, wrapping an arm around her and caressing her hip. "We'll change the plan as needed, but he'll still end up attending either school. He'll be better for it."

Liana nodded, sitting up. "What about Mahari?" she asked softly. "Do you, as you said before, have no plans for her care?"

"Oh, Liana," Evium said with a deep sigh. "I was angry. I was hurt. I will assist however you need when planning Mahari's future. I will solidify a place for her and care for her as my own, but surely you don't mean for me to override whatever her father might have in mind for her."

"I don't know that he has anything in mind," Liana admitted.

"Well, he's already planning for her to take over his holdings in Scio one day, to hear him tell it," Evium said.

"That was certainly news to me!" Liana said. "We had discussed nothing like that before, and now..." She shrugged. "Now, I feel he would accept whatever you allowed, if only to keep the peace. He might be afraid to press the issue as long as he's working on the investigation of ways to assist Rael."

"How do you feel about that?" Evium asked with a tilt of his head. "It's an ambitious undertaking. Your father's brilliance is... consummate."

"If he can help my brother, I would be eternally grateful," Liana said, catching Evium's glance. "That gratitude, however, doesn't extend to the possibility of any rekindling of my indiscretion with Huison.

"Should he be doing this, Vi? As you mentioned, he looked exhausted—and he expects to keep this up for months yet."

"We tried to talk him out of it," Evium said. "He seems resolute. I'm just hoping that his efforts are fruitful." He grabbed her hand and squeezed it. "It would be marvelous to have Rael back, for you and your mother primarily, and... he'd be a tremendous influence on the children."

"He would," Liana could not help smiling. "He was so good with Jahd before... so patient and attentive." Evium watched as her eyes briefly clouded with memories before she shook her head and looked at him, her smile sad. "You sent the inquiry to Claerendon for a tutor?"

"Late this afternoon," Evium said, patting her hand as he relented to the change in subject. "I imagine we'll start receiving responses early next week. Jahd can enjoy an extended summer, or he can work on the material that Huison prepared for him."

"Very good," Liana said as she got up from the bed to return to the vanity and study her reflection. "Speaking of, I should go check on Jahd and Mahari."

Evium's breath caught as his hands nervously tapped against the coverlet once again. "I'm sure they're fine," he said in a cheerful tone, as he slid both his hands beneath the bedclothes, wringing them together. "The nanny came to us, remember? She told us they were both stuffed with sweets and sleeping." He frowned as Liana rose and reached for her red robe, slipping into it and tying the sash around her comely body.

"Would you like to come with me?" she offered, looking back at him from over her shoulder. "You can use the manual chair, so as not to risk waking them."

"Do I need to come with you as you see to our children, Liana?" he asked plainly. "Have I anything to be fearful of?"

She turned to him then. "No," she answered simply. "I am going only to see our son and daughter. I have no interest in anything or anyone else. You could come with me, Evium."

"I want to trust you," he said. "I shouldn't need to feel as though I have to watch every move simply because Huison isn't returning home until tomorrow."

"Will you wait up for me, then?" she asked. "I shouldn't be too long." She chuckled. "I might even see if there's any cake left."

"I'll wait up for you," Evium said, unable to share her smile. "I'll be right here."

She swept through the door, closing it behind her. As Evium debated whether to go after her, he realized that doing so would go against the trust he needed so desperately to rebuild. He did not want to think of the many nights he was alone in bed while Liana and Huison roamed freely about the grounds of the estate. He instead preferred to focus on events such as what they experienced that afternoon: as a loving husband and wife sharing laughter with their son while celebrating his seventh birthday.

Under the watchful eye of her former lover, and with the sound of laughter coming from the child she had with him, echoing in the background, Evium thought.

With a quavering sigh, Evium Chatelain lay back against the cool softness of his pillows, sniffling lightly before taking another deep breath.

Liana crept into the darkened bedroom, careful to make minimal noise as the door clicked softly behind her. Barefoot, she padded through the space over the lush carpeting as she approached the figure on the bed.

Jahd was fast asleep, one arm casually thrown overhead while gently snoring. He was also practically tangled in the bedclothes, Liana noticed with a silent giggle. After making sure that none of the tangles posed any danger, she moved through the room toward the open door that connected Jahd's suite to the in-house nurse's quarters.

Alena, having served as Mahari's wet nurse since she was born, ceased to occupy the suite once Mahari began sleeping through the night at four months old. She then returned to her primary dwelling in one of the servants' cottages on the estate, where she lived with her three small children and her husband, Fayal, who maintained the stables on the property. Liana's dearest wish was that Alena might return to the main house one day soon, to serve as wet nurse to a new baby Liana hoped to conceive with Evium.

Mahari's snore was even heavier than that of her brother, and Liana stifled a laugh at the way both the baby's arms were flung overhead as though she was prepared to take flight at any moment. She was still neatly tucked in, nowhere near as careless with her bedding, with curls fanned out around her head in a dark halo.

Exiting the nursery through Mahari's bedroom, Liana felt invigorated by the love she felt for her children. She moved further along the hallway toward the stairs, hoping to snag a bit of leftover birthday cake. She was determined to grab two forks so that Evium could share.

"Li…"

Liana looked up in time to see the slender body of Huison Loromin emerge from among the shadows further down the hall. She froze, glancing behind her toward the bedroom she shared with Evium, before moving closer to where Huison stood.

"What are you doing here?" she hissed, her gray eyes flashing up at him. "How long have you been watching me?"

Huison smiled gently; straight white teeth contrasting against his olive skin.

"I have been watching you for years... did you not know?"

"Don't toy with me, Huison! What are you doing here?"

Huison shrugged. "Despite what seems to be a very unfortunate turn of events, you asked me to stay the night," he said calmly. "As you well know, it is a long journey back to..."

Liana took a deep breath and tried again, slowly. "What are you doing *here* in this hallway? What are you doing in this *house*? You're staying in one of the guest houses, remember?"

"I had trouble sleeping," Huison admitted. "The full impact of recent dealings has left me a bit... unsettled. I went for a walk and habit brought me here."

"Went for a walk?" Liana sneered as her gaze flicked over him. "Dressed like that?"

Huison's shoulder-length curls were loose, and the red silk robe contrasting nicely against his skin was worn open to the waist. Liana's eyes danced over the muscles in his chest and stomach before quickly flickering away. Huison simply smiled at her.

"I hoped to check on Mahari," he said. "I do not know how long it might be before I see her again."

"No one has restricted access to your daughter, Huison," Liana said. "Evium would never do that—he told you as much earlier today."

"Would he not?" Huison countered softly. "She is my link to you, and always will be."

"A link to a time that no longer exists," Liana stressed. "You'd do better to forget about it."

"As you seem to have done," Huison said, "particularly when you refer to it as 'a time' when it was more than that. Over a dozen such instances as I remember it."

"I don't need to listen to this!" she told him, her face flushed. "Go on—spend time with Mahari, but you're not to wake her up and you're to go back to the guest house immediately after! You shouldn't be here like this in the middle of the night."

"Liana," he breathed, "come with me—please. Let me gaze upon our daughter, and you, just this one last time in private."

"No," she said sternly. "You can do it alone. There's no need for me to bother with..."

"I am not trying to bother you, really," Huison interrupted quickly. "I... just want..." Huison's amber gaze took in Liana's attire with unconcealed hunger. "I miss you, Liana, so very much." His voice lowered to a whisper as he took a step forward. "It does not need to be exactly as it was before, but must you shut me out entirely?

"What have I done to be treated in such a way? Evium would not allow us a moment of space at all today, not even just to talk things out. Why else would I wait here for you, willing you to come out? I need... Just one touch, a simple caress... an embrace so that I can go away having felt you one more time..."

"Don't!" Liana hissed, with a quick glance toward the bedroom again. "Just don't! It's done! It's been done for over a year! Why can't you just leave it be?"

"Why can you not understand how I feel?" Huison insisted. "My dearest Liana... for years I have loved you. For years I have watched you. When you close your eyes, I know what you wish for." He stepped even closer. "I can see your dreams and I can feel your desires. This was not merely a dalliance for me. My soul cannot so easily dismiss you, and now you expect me to leave it be, just as simply as that?"

"Yes, just as simply as that! I don't ask that you love me! I've explained this to you."

"I hoped," he whispered. "I have always hoped you might reconsider. I hoped you would one day look upon me with love."

"There can be nothing between us—not anymore!"

"There will always be something between us," he began, "especially because of Mahari. She is, as I said, a link."

Liana straightened and locked eyes with Huison. "Evium still loves me, despite everything. Don't make me use that love to banish you from her life forever."

"That you could hurt me like this..." Huison said, crestfallen. "But I would still do anything for you, and I have already done more for you than you realize, Li. I have always belonged to you, and I know what it is that drives you.

"I know now that the desires of your heart are within reach. No matter what, my greatest wish is to see you attain them." He took a step backward and bowed, his eyes never leaving hers. "I will be gone by the time you awake in the morning. Sweet dreams, Liana... my beauty... my love."

Liana watched as Huison maneuvered through the darkness before vanishing from sight. Smoothing the fabric of her robe, she proceeded with her plan to check the kitchens for any remaining birthday cake to share with her husband.

Chapter Eight

The servants had come through to snuff the candles in the master bedroom, having already done so in the other parts of the house. As tired as Evium was, he was equally determined to wait up for his wife in the darkness. He needed some comfort from her; some kindness, a sign of the love they were rebuilding.

Liana stole into the room, and he held his breath as she slid between the cool sheets of the king-sized four-poster bed. She lay with her back to him. Despite the plushness of their bedding, Evium could feel that she was trembling, and her sigh was audible.

What happened?

Everything in him ached to reach out to her and ask if anything was wrong, but he was afraid of her answer. He wondered if Huison caused her discomfort. Had she seen him? Had she found returning to bed, and to an invalid husband, so repellent that her body shook in defiance? Would he wake in the morning to find her packing her things, intending to leave—not to return to another suite—but to assume residence in Huison's home in Scio?

If Liana and Huison rekindled their relationship, Evium did not know what he would do. He felt the familiar burn in his eyes, and he clenched his teeth in the darkness, wishing he had the power to get up from the bed and escape the feelings of loss and loneliness despite being next to the woman he cherished more than anything in the world.

They were doing so well, or so he thought. It was likely a mistake to allow Huison to return at all. Evium closed his eyes, doing his best to ignore the wetness collecting on the pillow, and settled into a troubled sleep.

The sudden and insistent banging upon the bathroom door startled fifteen-year-old Liana. She jumped, knocking a decorative frosted bottle from her vanity as she whirled around. It shattered upon impact with the floor, spraying her ankles with perfume and bits of glass.

"Liana! Dinner's getting cold!"

"I'm not hungry!" Liana yelled back, pressing a clean wad of tissues against her nose while looking with dismay at the mess on the floor.

"You know that excuse never works with Mother," he said. "What are you doing in there? Is that perfume I smell? You DO know that there are better ways of concealing the scent of your..."

"Get OUT, Rael!" Liana shrieked, kicking at the closed bathroom door.

"I'm not in," her brother countered with a chuckle. "But I will be if you don't come out of there."

"Don't you dare!" Liana said, looking into the mirror above the vanity and quickly dabbing at her nose. She whimpered at the sight of blood, smeared not only across her nose and top lip, but also splattered upon the bodice of the pearl-accented pale blue dress she wore.

The doorknob rattled and Rael laughed. "You know that a lock can't keep me out!"

"I mean it, Rael!" Liana scurried about, sweeping other crumpled, blood-stained tissues from the vanity and into a nearby wastebasket while still attempting to keep the wad against her nose.

"Oh, Liana," Rael sang, and the sound of clicks emanating from the lock horrified Liana. She spun around, dropping the wastebasket.

"No!"

Liana sprang toward the door, dropping the tissues. She snatched them up from the floor, piercing the tips of her fingers on various shards of glass from the broken bottle. She swore, hating the tears that burned her eyes.

"Ha!" Rael crowed as he entered, "I win aga—" He stared, and his dark brown eyes rounded. "Liana!" He rushed over to her, cupping her face in his hands. "What happened!? Why are you bleeding?"

Liana looked at the tissues, the lacerations on her fingers, and the mess upon the floor before looking up into Rael's eyes, crying. Rael pulled her into his arms, smoothing her hair.

"Don't," he pleaded. "Don't cry, little sister."

"I... I asked you not to..."

"I didn't know you were hurt! I thought you were playing with me! We always joke around with one another!"

"I have to clean it up," Liana sniffled. "I have to... and then I'll come down for dinner."

Rael released her, his own eyes shining. His dark gaze shifted toward the still-open bathroom door, which slowly closed. The click of the lock seemed deafening to Liana. He then reached into his back pocket, extracting his own handkerchief, which he then used to wipe the blood from Liana's nose.

"I'll clean it up," he announced. "I can't fix the broken bottle. There are too many pieces, and I haven't learned how to direct my power on something so small yet, but... I can clean it all up the regular way. You'd better get changed. Mother will have a fit if she sees you like this."

Liana shook her head. "You shouldn't waste your gifts on me anyway, Rael. Besides, plain people like me must learn to clean up our own messes. You go on before our parents start to wonder. I won't be long."

"I'm staying here with you," Rael insisted. "I want to help." He grabbed the hand that was uninjured. "I'll always help you. I'll never leave you behind, Liana."

Liana awoke with a start, a thin line of sweat upon her brow as she sat up in bed. It did not take long for her eyes to adjust to the light, as it was nearly dawn and the sun already peeked through the drapes.

"Are you going to tell me what's wrong?" came Evium's gentle voice from her right.

It had been a while since Liana last dreamed of her brother. She knew that the earlier conversation with Huison and Evium about Huison's plans had a lot to do with it. She was also conflicted about how much she should tell her mother, and whether she should do so right away.

"I had a dream," she said at last. "I dreamed of Rael when we were younger. The dream was so vivid. He... he promised to never leave me behind." She looked at Evium. "Is that what I've done, by refusing to go visit him and just hoping he'd miraculously recover and come home? Have I left him behind?"

"Oh, Liana," Evium said sympathetically, and she immediately went to him.

Evium folded her in his arms as she clung to him, smoothing back the stray locks of her hair that had sprung free. He loved the feel of her against his chest, and he indulged in the sweet smell of her skin.

"Do you need to talk?" he asked.

"About?"

"Anything," he said. "Rael, the dream..." he paused. "Maybe about your thoughts on seeing Huison again?"

"He was here," she admitted quietly, "in the house last night. I was on my way back from looking in on the children when..." The sharp intake of Evium's breath briefly silenced her and she raised her head to look at him. "Nothing happened, Evium."

"Not because of any restraint on his part, I'll warrant."

"It wasn't like that," Liana said before pausing again. "Well, it nearly became that. But I told him again that things are done and that, while he isn't barred from seeing Mahari, any further attempts to restore a relationship with me won't be taken lightly."

Evium could not resist a chuckle. "You told him that?"

"I had to. Nothing will come between us again. I love you, Vi."

Evium opened his mouth to repeat the sentiment but found himself unable to do so as he became choked up and relief flooded his entire body. He felt as though he could easily melt away between the soft sheets of his marital bed with the woman he loved more than life cradled in his arms.

Liana leaned over and kissed him. The first kiss was gentle, the second more insistent, and the third left both breathless. Liana caressed the side of Evium's face, her hand trailing down to his chest. The nightshirt Evium wore had no buttons in front and, though Liana could not see his chest and stomach, she could certainly feel the muscles through the thin fabric. She had taken for granted that he had kept himself in excellent physical shape even after the accident. The feel of him, warm and hard, sent fluttering waves of heat throughout her body.

She kissed him once more while lightly scratching at the space just below his sternum. An involuntary groan escaped Evium's lips, and they were both startled by it. Another flick of fingernails garnered a similar vocal reaction and a sharp intake of breath. The response did not go unnoticed, and Liana smirked mischievously. Evium had not been sensitive in that area before, and she wondered if it had anything to do with the way his body and nerve endings had essentially rewired after the accident. Whatever the cause, the result was impossible to ignore.

Liana was soon relieved of the red silk, and it soared overhead into the darkness of the bedroom. More than adept from hours of tinkering in the workshop, sculpting and hewing, Evium's firm hands teased and shaped Liana's lithe form until she arched upward from the bed with a quavering cry.

She could feel his eyes upon her as she struggled to catch her breath, her long hair now free and tumbled loose at her sides as she turned to him once more. Her kiss was passionate upon his lips, muffling his exclamations of surprise and delight as she tugged the hem of his nightshirt upward and shifted so that her body hovered over his.

Chapter Nine

Huison stepped from the ornate, four-wheeled carriage with assistance from Fayal, the young man in charge of the stables on the Chatelain estate. Huison, unsteady on his feet, wiped at his mouth with a lace-edged black silk handkerchief before pressing a clove-studded orange against his nose. He then looked at Fayal, who studied him with a carefully neutral expression.

"Will you be needing anything from the carriage to be brought to the main house, sir?" Fayal asked in the crisp accent that belied his upbringing in the northern region. "Or shall I have the attendants unload and take everything to your lodgings?"

Though there appeared to be no underlying duplicity apparent in the question, Huison could not help but wonder how much Fayal had learned in the year since Huison's last visit. What sort of servant gossip had there been within the Den? Had Huison's absence even registered among the help? Rather than appearing foolish by taking too long to answer, Huison simply shrugged.

"There are several wrapped parcels inside the leather valise," he sniffed. "Those are to be placed among the rest of the birthday gifts. The satchel inside the cabin comes with me." Fayal responded by snapping his fingers. The footman immediately fetched the bag from its resting place inside the carriage and brought it to Huison. "I have not arrived too early, have I? The household is awake?"

"The young sir and his sister, the little lady, enjoyed quite a late evening," Fayal revealed, unable to resist a smile. "They, as well as the lord and lady of the residence, were still abed as of roughly three quarters of an hour ago."

"Ah," Huison said with a resigned nod, "then perhaps I will just go to my accommodations." He hoped he might scurry away unnoticed before running into anyone he would sooner not see, especially in his current physical condition.

"I'm awake, though, Huison. You're always welcome to visit with me."

Huison, his spine stiffening in a combination of fatigue and trepidation, turned at a snail's pace until he met the amused, dark brown gaze of Kaileih Dhamon.

She had obviously just come from one of the greenhouses, standing tall despite being barefoot, balancing a basket filled with assorted vegetables on the curve of one hip. Her brown skin was aglow, likely because of the delight of working at her favorite hobby. Though there was one small smudge of earth upon the crest of her left cheek, she looked otherwise immaculate and comfortable in a soft pink linen jumpsuit.

"Oh, Huison," she chided with an impish grin, "you are a fright. I can only imagine what's got you in such a state."

"My intention is not to foist myself upon you so early," Huison said with a stiff bow. "I merely thought to go to the guest quarters until..."

"Nonsense," Kaileih interjected softly. "As I've said, you can come and visit with me. We can catch up." She chuckled. "Traveling certainly refuses to agree with you, though the roads have little to do with your overall condition, I think. You'd better come in."

She turned away from him to walk toward the main house. Her mass of dark and glistening twisted braids was tied with a gold cord into a bundle that swayed as she moved. Huison followed, finding himself unable to do anything else, as both the swaying bundle and the woman to whom it was attached seemed to beckon him along. A young housemaid, one unfamiliar to Huison, met them at the door.

"Do not touch these even to give them a wash," Kaileih told the maid as she handed the basket of vegetables to her. "You're to take the basket to the pantry nearest to my section of the kitchen as-is and leave it there. I'll tend to it shortly."

"Yes, ma'am," the girl responded, delivering a graceful curtsy despite the weight of the parcel before fleeing further into the house.

"Now then," Kaileih continued, turning to Huison with a sardonic smile, "let's get you away from that citrus concoction you're clutching for dear life. I've picked chamomile flowers and mint for your usual tea."

"I would not want to intrude," Huison began, abruptly pausing when Kaileih arched a brow at him. Unable to gaze at her for too long, and certainly not after all he had learned of her, he glanced away and cleared his throat.

"Yet intrude you have," Kaileih remarked, "upon my daughter many times... and now also upon my son."

Huison started, squeezing the orange in his hand so hard that juice squirted from it and the sharp edges of a cluster of cloves pierced his palm and he yelped, dropping the fruit.

"Huison," Kaileih sighed, "pomanders are infinitely more effective when you allow the fruit to dry first before studding it. Now you've made a mess." She glimpsed his reddening face and bleeding palm. "Come along, then. Leave the orange where it is. Its freshness will brighten the day."

When Huison entered the house, he was awash with the smells of plumeria, lilies, and petunias. He could not help himself, pausing in the foyer to close his eyes and breathe deeply as he savored fragrances he had so dearly missed.

How often had he indulged in similar aromas while a frequent guest at the Chatelain estate? How often had he unpacked his books after returning home from a lengthy stay at the Den, only to find pressed flowers nestled within the pages? How often had Liana come to him in the darkness, her skin petal soft as he, much like a hungry bee, drank in her warmth?

Huison's own shuddering sigh roused him from his cocoon of memories, and his heart ached. He opened his eyes again to find Kaileih watching him, her face an unreadable mask.

"A mess indeed," was all she said as she turned away and continued walking.

"It's superficial," Kaileih announced, having finished cleaning the blood from Huison's palm. She was now dabbing at the puncture wounds with a gel extracted from the freshly cut leaf of an aloe vera plant. "You'll heal quickly. The injury was likely more to your pride than anything else. Have you any, Huison? Pride, that is."

Huison, knowing better than to respond, only watched as Kaileih continued to administer aid. They were sitting across from one another in what had always been known as her section of the kitchen. It was a cozy nook just off the main pantry, neatly supplied with many of the old-fashioned accoutrements that Kaileih loved, and Liana had never quite learned to use.

Among the offerings was a contraption that, when cranked by hand, made the most delectable frozen confection Huison had ever tasted. Even Evium had steadfastly refused to update the machine to more modern standards, so enamored was he of the product it created.

"Did you advise my daughter not to tell me what you've been up to at Vespers Glen?" Kaileih asked lightly, deftly removing what appeared to be a sliver of clove from one of the inflamed dots in Huison's palm.

"I did not," he answered, surprised by how calm he sounded.

He felt anything but calm while this woman, this paragon, tended to him. He hoped that if she could hear the rapid rhythm of his heartbeat, she might attribute it to travel anxiety. Kaileih would not think it could be anything else, would she? She was obviously aware of his visits to Rael, but how much more did she know?

It was easier for Huison to study Kaileih like this, while she was busy applying a light bandage to his hand. She was awe-inspiring. Though he had known Kaileih for years, Huison felt as though he was seeing her through a fresh set of eyes, and he was. Huison was gazing upon Kaileih through the eyes of one who loved and cherished her above anything, and who had altered the planes to be in her presence.

"Rael has been improving," Kaileih said, securing the bandage before moving away to clear up the remnants of her makeshift infirmary. "You would have heard from me otherwise once I realized what's been going on. Though why you didn't come to me at the start is baffling. My newest shop is in the same city as your home, after all. You needn't travel too far."

"I did not wish to provide any misleading expectations," Huison answered.

"Yet you had no problems bringing my daughter into this," Kaileih said, scoffing at him. "It quite surprised me to bring the news to her, only to find out that you revealed your intentions months ago."

"I know how deeply troubling this has been for Liana," he said, once again shifting his amber gaze away to focus on his hand. "I meant only to bring her a glimmer of hope."

"You only meant to try to further endear yourself to a woman who, if she truly meant to, would have left her husband to be with you long ago. You'll soon see how futile a hope that has become."

Huison's stomach gurgled, and the moan of distress escaped him before he could stifle it. He neither needed nor wanted to be reminded of the loss of Liana, which he was still determined to think of as only temporary. The last year had been nearly unbearable. He tried to fill every waking moment with research and regular visits to Vespers Glen. Liana Chatelain still infiltrated every second of Huison's downtime, haunting him with reminders of their time together that left him shaken and empty.

"Do not presume to know my reasons," Huison said through clenched teeth.

"Don't presume to think that you're fooling anyone," Kaileih countered. "Huison, your motivations are selfish, but so are mine." Kaileih leaned with her back against the counter across from where Huison sat. "As I've said, Rael is improving. There has been a significant decrease in the number and intensity of incidents at Vespers. He's even spoken a little."

Huison's stomach turned over again as he did his best to sound distant. "Rael speaks to you?" he asked.

"As I'm told he does to you," Kaileih said, "though no one at Vespers can attest to what the two of you talk about since you hold your sessions with him in such privacy."

"Kaileih..."

"Huison," she interrupted, "nothing about you has ever led me to believe that you have a modicum of philanthropy in you. Despite that, I'm willing to be generous and pretend that I'm unaware that your reason for doing all of this has everything to do with Liana.

"While I am pretty sure that this won't at all turn out the way you wish and won't be the catalyst that lures Liana away from Evium for good, I'm willing to allow it to continue as long as there is some benefit to my son." Her gaze hardened, though her tone stayed sweet, and her smile was a breathtaking vision. "But, I promise you this: your world, your aspirations, and everything you've dreamed of will devolve into your darkest nightmare if this goes wrong." She leaned forward. This time, Huison could not look away. "There will be no escape for you. I will execute your demise with exuberance and delight. I'm not all valerian root and lavender, you know."

"Mama, who on earth are you talking to?"

Huison, chilled to his foundation, could barely tear his gaze away from Kaileih in time to notice that Liana, her glorious mane of curls in a tumble about her head and shoulders, had ventured into the kitchen wearing oversized, silver satin pajamas. Her eyes rounded upon noticing Huison sitting at the table, and she reddened, folding her arms low across her stomach. Neither the action nor the voluminous sleepwear hid the swollen curve of Liana's belly.

Huison's body went rigid, and a wave of cold sweat swept over him as realization dawned. Liana, despite her embarrassed expression, was beautiful. She would always be beautiful to him, even though her current physical state heralded the reality that their separation was not as desolate for her as it had been for Huison.

The vision of Liana crinkled, blurred, and was completely obscured in the silence that followed. Liana looked in bewilderment as Huison suddenly bolted from the table with tears streaming from half-closed lids as he fled to the servant's bathroom on the opposite side of the pantry. Liana contemplated her mother's bemused expression as they both heard him gag and retch through the door he had just slammed shut.

"Travel sickness," Kaileih said with a dismissive shrug. "I'd better get started on that tea..."

Chapter Ten

The estate surged with activity. Servants bustled through the massive space, each with a task. Streamers were hung and balloons were gathered into colorful clusters, placed at various points within the Den and throughout the grounds.

The kitchen was cocooned in a cloud of tantalizing aromas — each dish supervised by Kaileih, who thrived at the center of the commotion after having showered and changed into a gold, one-shouldered, wide-legged jumpsuit. Her bundle of hair had been freed from its cord, the long twists spilling in a becoming dark waterfall over her shoulders.

Huison, having also cleaned himself up before resting briefly in his comfortable lodging, sat alone at one of the back tables far away from the upheaval. When he eventually emerged from the servant's bathroom near the pantry that morning, sickly and sour-smelling, it relieved him to find Liana no longer there. He was greeted by Kaileih, who informed him that a housemaid would bring the chamomile-mint tea to the guest house, after giving him enough time to make himself more presentable. She even managed a look of concern.

As though it mattered whether he still smelled of bile. Liana was pregnant. Everything he had accomplished over the last several months had come to nothing. Liana's reconciliation with Evium had not been in name only, as Huison had so fervently hoped.

Huison replayed the image on loop in his mind: Liana entering the kitchen, dark coils of hair surrounding her exquisite face, her surprise to find Huison sitting at the table, and then the fleeting, guilty look of a child caught doing something she shouldn't as she feebly attempted to cover her expanding waistline.

"It is almost left too late," Huison muttered into his empty mug, having long since drained his third serving of Kaileih's impeccable tea. "My return could not have been better timed. I will free Rael of his affliction, Liana will have everything she has ever wanted, and I will have Liana."

"Uncle Hui!"

The sight of the coltish boy running toward him, shoulder-length dark curls fanned out, startled Huison out of his reverie.

"Jahd," Huison whispered as he got to his feet, taken aback by how much the boy had grown in a year. He would be very tall; there was little doubt of it, as he was already taller than Evium at that age. He was also graceful, flitting through the obstacle course of people and party favors with little effort as he made his way over to Huison.

"Uncle Hui, at last!"

Wrapping his arms about Huison's midsection, Jahd grinned up at him, displaying a wide smile with a missing tooth.

"My dear boy," Huison said thickly, returning the hug and inhaling the clean smell of Jahd's skin and hair.

Huison's eyes stung as he closed them, overwhelmed by varying thoughts. He could not be sure if he wanted to turn time back or thrust it forward. He only knew that the present felt insurmountable, lonely, and bleak.

"I'm so glad to see you!" Jahd said with a sniffle, and the sight of moisture on Jahd's thick eyelashes deeply touched Huison as they separated.

"And I you," Huison replied, touching Jahd's cheek.

"When did you get here?" Jahd asked as they sat across from another at the table Huison had just vacated.

"Earlier this morning."

Jahd frowned. "They didn't wake me..."

"Nor should they have," Huison said. "I was told that you and Mahari had quite the late evening. It is ideal that you be well-rested for today." Jahd's grimace deepened as he looked away. "Something troubles you?"

Huison watched as Jahd appeared to mull something over. After nearly a minute, the child nodded and then leaned forward, fixing Huison in a serious gray gaze.

"Why didn't you tell me, Uncle Hui?"

"What is it I should have told you, Jahd?"

"About Mahari," Jahd said in a lowered voice. "About you. That you're her father."

Huison sat back in his chair, stunned. "Who told you such a thing?"

"No one told me," Jahd said after a pause. "Not exactly. I overheard Mama and Daddy talking a few nights ago. It was late, and I had gotten out of bed hoping to ask if I could have a glass of juice. Mama's voice was raised so I could hear her as I was coming down the hall."

"I see," Huison said with a sigh.

"It wasn't anything bad, Uncle Hui! Mama just wondered..." Jahd's face reddened. "She wondered if Mahari would know who you were when you came here for my birthday. She said... she said that... You haven't tried to visit Mahari, even though you could have." Jahd swallowed hard, and his voice trembled. "She doesn't know you anymore, Uncle Hui. Mahari doesn't miss you like I do. If I would have known sooner, I would have shown her your pictures and made sure she never forgot you!"

"You sweet boy," Huison said with a sad smile. "This is all so far beyond your years. These are matters for adults. I shudder to think of what your mother would say if she knew we had broached the subject between us."

"Well, she won't know!" Jahd said stubbornly. "I won't tell her and risk not seeing you for another year!"

"Jahd..."

"Is that the real reason you left?" Jahd insisted. "They made you go because you gave Mahari to Mama?"

"Jahd..." Huison tried again, but Jahd banged both his fists against the tabletop.

"Are you leaving again after my birthday is over? Will I have to wait another year to see you?"

Huison looked around, hoping that Jahd had failed to attract the attention of anyone milling about. So far, it seemed he had.

"Jahd," Huison began carefully as he leaned forward, "the decision to leave was mine, as I told you when last we saw one another. I would not deign to cause your mother distress, and my presence had done so. Do you understand?"

"How could Mama be upset when you gave her Mahari?" Jahd asked, puzzled.

Huison reached across the table and clasped Jahd's hands, giving them a gentle squeeze.

"Enough of this now," Huison said. "Had I a millennium, it would still not be enough time to explain this to you properly, and it is not my place to do so at any rate."

Jahd's eyes focused on their clasped hands when the next question came in a whisper. "Will it be another year before I see you again? It doesn't have to stay that way!" He looked up again. "I'm going to Pandoufuli at the start of the new year, and you can come and see me there! It's practically your school, isn't it? They'll have to do as you say."

"It will be as your mother and father dictate." Huison then smiled, knowing that the fruition of everything he had worked toward was now in his grasp. "But, that does not mean that I have failed to organize something truly memorable to celebrate the occasion."

Jahd's face lit up, and he grinned. "Oh, Uncle Hui, have you?"

"I have, Jahd. I truly have."

Jahd pulled his hands away and clapped gleefully. Huison's stomach gurgled at the simple purity of the gesture, and he could only smile.

"Is the present at the gift table?" Jahd asked.

"There are presents there, yes," Huison said before clearing his throat. "However, the gift I speak of is one that I hope to give before the festivities commence."

"Before?"

"Yes, dear boy. Fancy a walk with your old uncle?" Huison managed a smile. "It can be like old times, such as those when we escaped from the confines of the library to enjoy our lessons on the grounds."

"Yes!" Jahd's grin widened. "Will we have a lesson, Uncle Huison?"

Huison took a moment to engrave in his memory the excitement and happiness on Jahd's face.

"Oh, yes... one to take with you for the rest of your days."

"Where are we going, Uncle Hui?" Jahd asked, happily skipping beside Huison as they walked a short while later. "Why are you carrying your satchel?" Jahd's face lit up as he stopped. "Are you going to become my tutor again? Is that the real reason Mama and Daddy were talking about Mahari needing to be used to you again? Is that the surprise?"

Huison also stopped and turned to the boy with a slight shake of his head. "No, Jahd," he said. "Though it would please me greatly to tutor you again, that is not what this excursion is about. I need your help, though."

Jahd grinned and bounced on the balls of his feet. "Do you? Oh, Uncle Hui, do you?"

"I most certainly do, dear boy," Huison answered, reaching over to place a hand upon Jahd's dark curls, gently ruffling them before dropping his hand and continuing to walk. "As to where we are going," Huison continued once Jahd caught up, "I thought the mine would be a good place."

"The mine?" Jahd's brow furrowed. "There isn't anyone at the mine, Uncle Hui. Daddy closes it during the summer because it gets so hot inside the tunnels. He doesn't think it's safe."

"Yes, I know. That is precisely what makes it the ideal environment for the particular lesson I have planned for you."

Jahd clapped his hands again. "Of course!" He cast a shy, sidelong glance up at Huison. "Professor Kenworthy is a nice man and all, but it isn't the same as when you were my tutor, Uncle Hui."

Huison stopped walking again and turned to look at Jahd, unable to help a small smile. He nodded, swallowing the lump that had formed in his throat as he slid the strap of his black leather satchel from one shoulder, allowing the bag to fall to the ground with a gentle thud as he lowered himself to one knee.

"I have greatly missed you for this last year, Jahd," Huison explained. "My work took me away from you. But, I have returned to your side this one last time so that you may aid me in the most important task of my life." He caressed Jahd's cheek as he tilted his head. "I do not suppose I ever genuinely appreciated how much you resemble your mother. I want you to think of her. Focus upon those things you love best about her."

"I don't understand, Uncle Hui," Jahd admitted.

Huison nodded. "I know," he said. "Would that I knew how best to explain it to you."

"You seem so sad, Uncle Hui," Jahd observed softly. "Can I help you to not be sad? It's my birthday. My wish is for you to be happy."

Huison seemed to stare at Jahd for the longest time without answering. His amber-colored eyes drank in the form in front of him as he kneeled on the ground. They were alone on the walking trail leading from the lively Chatelain estate to the solitude of the apparently abandoned mine, and Huison knew that the timing could not have been more perfect.

"Thank you for that," Huison said at last. "I have no doubt that your wish will come true. The sooner we begin, the sooner it will happen."

Huison got to his feet, hefting the satchel as both he and Jahd continued the rest of the way. Upon arriving at the entrance to the mine, Huison glanced back once before turning to Jahd.

"Once we are inside, be sure to stay close to me," Huison said, leaning his satchel against the inside wall closest to the entrance.

"Will we need a lantern?" Jahd asked, pointing to the first of a series of shelves upon which were placed dozens of identical lanterns.

Huison shook his head. "I will not venture far enough to be claimed by darkness," he answered. "Shall we?"

"Yes!" Jahd said with another excited little bounce.

"Excellent," Huison said. "Remember—stay close."

"I can't wait for you to see Mahari," Jahd was saying as they ventured through a tunnel several minutes later. "She's gotten so big!"

Huison was only half-listening. From the moment they entered the vast mine with its intricate network of tunnels, he had trained his attention on their surroundings. He made note of the number of access shafts and transport tunnels they passed along the way. Jahd was right. It was extremely hot inside the mine and, though heat rose, Huison imagined it was likely stifling even on the lower levels. But, they wouldn't be venturing too much farther.

"She tries to be a big girl and sit in with me on my lessons sometimes," Jahd continued. "Mr. Kenworthy thinks it a waste of time, though he'd never tell my parents that."

"Oh!" Huison exclaimed suddenly as he stopped walking, causing Jahd to pause and look up.

"What is it, Uncle Hui?"

"In my excitement at the prospect of your surprise, I seem to have forgotten my satchel." Huison sighed and rolled his eyes. "I leaned it against the wall when we initially arrived and neglected to reclaim it before we came all this way."

"That's okay!" Jahd said. "I can go get..."

"No, no! Doing so will take me much less time as my legs are longer." Huison looked at Jahd and placed a hand atop his curly mane. "Stay here. Do not move. I shall only be a moment."

"Of course, Uncle Hui," Jahd said warmly.

"Of course," Huison repeated, patting the curls before turning away.

As he retraced the steps that would take him back to the entrance, Huison's memory locked upon the look of love and trust in the young boy's eyes. It was a look, Huison knew, that would never be seen again.

The remorse he felt was fleeting.

Huison's satchel was exactly where he had intentionally left it. After quickly loosening both buckles and opening the bag, he extracted a thick parcel wrapped in black velvet. Dropping the satchel to the ground, he snatched the velvet away to reveal a book bound in dark green leather, from which protruded a scrap of black fabric.

Using the tip of his thumb, Huison slid the nail along the top of the book, opening it at the exact page marked by the fabric. He then cleared his throat and began reading aloud.

Jahd was thrilled. This had so far been his best birthday yet, and he could not wait for his uncle to return so that they could continue their walk and chat. Gasping in sudden delight, Jahd's eyes fixed upon a small, glittering chunk of raw metal on the ground. Snatching it up and turning it over in his hands, he wondered what kind of material it was.

He would ask his father later.

Chapter Eleven

The torment was beyond anything he had ever known. Every inch of his body flared, and the dank air was thick with the combined smell of blood and excrement. He shivered and attempted to focus but was thwarted by the pain and mingled streams of blood and sweat that had run into his eyes and obscured his vision. He whimpered, hoping that the thing would not find him. He also prayed that it could not smell that he had soiled himself.

"Uncle," he whispered, a tremor in his voice, "Uncle Hui, where are you?"

His voice echoed around him. It was silent—too silent. He could no longer even hear the growl of the beast that had attacked him. Had it gotten to his uncle, too? Was that why there was no answer? Was he now alone? Though he knew the way back home, how could he ever get past that thing and return to his parents?

Jahd wriggled his slight frame from the crevice along the wall into which he had squeezed himself. He wiped at his eyes, struggling to see through unrelenting tears and continually bleeding cuts. He hurt so badly. He was certain that there was not a spot on his body left untouched, but despite the pain, he was determined to find his uncle and escape the hell that had been thrust upon them.

"Uncle?" he queried again, a little louder.

Jahd felt his blood run cold at the chuckling growl that came in response. It had not gone after all, and it sounded as though it was awfully close. With fresh tears springing to his eyes, he turned to shimmy back into his hiding spot, only to find it blocked by the very thing he had been trying to conceal himself from.

The screams were heart-wrenching. Huison stood near the entrance to the mine, his back straight as Jahd's cries echoed behind him. There was a look of exasperation upon his thin, olive-hued face, and he wiped away a bit of dirt that had fallen upon his silk-draped shoulder as the walls shook during the attack. He sighed, smoothing a silver-threaded dark coil of hair, though none of his silken tresses were out of place.

Squinting as the sun reflected from the thick silver bangle upon his right wrist, Huison straightened the embroidered cuff of his left sleeve and then the right before reaching into a pocket to withdraw a delicate, silver lace-edged handkerchief. He dabbed a bit of sweat from the bridge of his long, straight nose and wondered how much longer this would take.

Jahd was calling for him. He had done so almost immediately after the thing set upon him, likely trusting in his dear uncle to come and save him. Jahd did not know yet that what was being done was the necessary result of more than a year of timing, research, and planning. It was almost a shame that Jahd could never know why Huison would not save him, but the sweetness of this eventual victory and the acquisition of the ultimate prize would far outlast the unpleasantness of the methods employed.

"Uncle! Uncle Hui, please! Where are you!?"

Huison examined his fingernails, buffing them with the handkerchief as the shrieks began anew. They sounded closer this time, as if Jahd had made a little progress in getting away. Huison arched a brow. That would not do at all. He glared at the sounds of nearby scuffling.

"Help... p-please... it's... Uncle... Uncle, it's going to... It's biting..." The child suddenly screamed shrilly. "IT'S KILLING MEEEEEEEE! PLEASE! P-PLEEEEASE DON'T LET..."

The cries were silenced by a vicious crunch; so abruptly that Huison became concerned as he heard the throaty cackle punctuating the sounds of gurgling and wheezing. He hoped it had not spoiled the body before completing the act—how would he explain that?

Minutes passed. Finally, Huison heard the slow, lurching shuffle of footsteps approaching. For the first time since the adventures of that early morning, Huison trembled as his heartbeat quickened. Keeping his eyes glued upon the entrance to the mine, he waited.

Huison almost did not recognize him. The curly hair was matted with dirt, blood, and grime, and the clothes were soiled with various bodily fluids and excrement. He was limping; his body twisted and broken to the point of being on all fours. The face was grotesquely distorted; stretched, cavernous, mottled, and the flesh of what remained of the right cheek dangled obscenely by a shred of skin.

A show of weakness or, more accurately, disgust would not do. Though his stomach turned, Huison steeled himself and scowled at the figure. As if in response, the body folded itself forward with an echoing, guttural hiss, shuddering violently as bones crackled and the skin bubbled. Huison tasted the bile as it rose in his throat, but he resisted the urge to retch as the form fell to the dirt floor of the entrance, twitching and writhing as shrieks of intense pain tore from its throat.

Huison took a tentative step backward, his eyes flitting about as he prayed that no one just happening along might hear the noise.

He counted on the mine being closed to aid him in preventing any passers-by.

After several moments, it was done. Huison's breath caught in his throat as the thing got to its feet in a fluid motion and stood perfectly upright. Huison was, once again, looking down at Jahd. Though still quite dirty, the face was repaired, and none of the other prior abnormalities remained.

They studied each other in silence for a time, and then Huison gradually felt comfortable enough to smile. It was not returned. Instead, Jahd stared at him silently, his gray eyes clear and wide despite the rest of his appearance.

"Well?" Huison demanded after moments of silence. The flash of resentment was not lost on him, but he could not suppress a shiver of unconcealed pleasure as Jahd slowly and stiffly bowed.

"It is as we agreed," the entity now known as Jahd said in a hoarse, grating voice. "I am now yours to command. What will you have me do?"

"Fix yourself up and do something about that voice. Be quick about it. We need to get back before someone comes looking. We have almost left it too late. Why did it take you so long? What were you doing in there?"

"Playing," Jahd replied in his normal tone, grinning. "I like to play with fresh things."

"Playing?" Huison snapped. "That is not why I brought you here! You forget yourself!" Huison responded to the second flash of angry gray eyes with a glare of his own. "Do not dare get any ideas. I rescued you from the body of that half-wit you had the misfortune of inhabiting for the last six years. You owe me now. Remember the rules of the binding."

"Oh, I can assure you that I do, Huison Loromin," came the reply.

Huison watched with something resembling fatherly pride as Jahd slowly closed his eyes. The matted curls were restored to their luster, and his skin glowed as every trace of dirt and filth melted away. The soiled and shredded clothing was cleaned and repaired, and Jahd once again looked as fresh as he had when they departed the estate over an hour before. Opening his eyes again, Jahd's grin with the missing tooth was chilling.

"We are ready," Huison said.

Chapter Twelve

Liana walked through the open double doors leading to the backyard, glancing over her surroundings. Everything had gone as planned, and she had her mother to thank for supervising the preparations. Liana intended to do so herself, but she felt a little more fatigued with this pregnancy than she had with the other two. She often slept late and struggled with the feeling of being lazy and useless in her own home.

Not that Evium ever told her so. To him, Liana had never been so beautiful, even during the early days of her pregnancy when she was pale and unable to keep anything down. He had immediately written to Kaileih, seeking the means by which he could properly tend to his wife's needs, not only during her more delicate moments but for the duration.

Armed with weekly deliveries from Tilehn and a set of detailed written instructions, Evium took charge of the Den and Liana blossomed under his care. She lacked for nothing, and Evium remained within earshot as often as he could. Over the course of twelve months, Shaz had become invaluable in the workshop, exhibiting skills that encouraged Evium to elevate the young man to a higher position—which allowed Evium more time to spend with his family.

Liana smiled as she arranged one of the table settings. As inseparable as Jahd and Mahari had been from the start, it still did not stop Evium and Mahari from spending quality time together. Despite having an open invitation to visit Mahari when he wished, Huison had not done so, and Evium became the only father that Mahari knew and dearly loved.

Huison.

The thought had briefly occurred to Liana that she might consider writing to Huison before Jahd's birthday celebration to warn him of her condition. However, she realized that the element of surprise might be more effective, cementing the end of their relationship. Unsure of what his response might be upon seeing her, and not wanting to risk a scene at her son's party, Liana formed a plan.

She was almost sorry that the plan worked so well, but the fact was that Huison was a creature of habit. Unless some unforeseen incident prevented the timeliness of his arrival, one could usually set a timepiece by Huison's schedule. Liana knew when to expect him at the Chatelain estate, and it was fortuitous that her mother had invited Huison into the main house. It made Liana's seemingly unexpected appearance, and the revelation of her pregnancy, seem spontaneous.

As she moved through the yard, she could make out the figures of Huison and her son sitting at one of the back tables, their heads close together as if they were sharing trade secrets. They stopped speaking immediately as she approached, and both of Liana's brows rose as she studied their faces.

"Good morning, Liana," Huison said softly.

There had been little time to look closely at him during the morning charade, but, as she stood before Huison now, Liana could see that he had lost more weight. Threads of silver streaked through his dark curls. Though she wondered how draining the investigation involving Rael had been, she quickly dismissed the notion. Huison had shared no concerns in any of the updates he sent, so she chose not to concern herself with him.

Jahd appeared to be staring at her. Something about the way his eyes, so much like her own, traveled from her head to her feet and back up again before settling upon her stomach was unnerving. Liana stared back, wondering what had gotten into him.

"Good morning, you two," she said with care. "You're awfully isolated back here on your own." She focused on her son. "You'll need to get washed up soon, Jahd. Our guests will arrive in about an hour and the party will begin shortly thereafter."

Jahd slowly got up from the table, his eyes still trained on Liana as he made no moves to obey. Their gray gazes locked, and they said nothing more for several seconds before a gentle nudge from Huison, one that would have gone unnoticed by a less-observant bystander, made Jahd's face suddenly light up.

"Mother!" he exclaimed, rushing over to Liana and wrapping his arms around her waist as he embraced her. Liana, slightly shaken by the way he had looked at her, did not return the embrace as Jahd nuzzled his cheek against her stomach. Liana instead examined the curly top of her son's head before her eyes flickered briefly toward Huison.

"Well, good morning!" Evium greeted, coasting to a stop near the table. Huison's hands tightened into fists, hidden beneath the tablecloth.

Evium's wheelchair was sleeker, quieter—he approached without a sound. Huison's eyes narrowed as he gazed at his old and distant friend. Evium had never looked healthier. Sunlight reflected from the lighter blond streaks in Evium's hair, and his skin was golden, as if he had been baptized in sunshine.

"Guests will arrive soon!" Evium continued. "I came out looking for you earlier and was told that the two of you had gone on a walk together. With as long as you were gone, I thought that we'd have to celebrate without you!"

He smiled at Jahd, who had released Liana and was now studying him.

"It was my fault, Father," Jahd said. "I had not seen Uncle Huison in so long. We had such a good time together and time got away from me. I was... playing."

Evium laughed and reached over to tug gently at one of Jahd's curls. "That's all right, son," he said. "You're allowed. It's not every day that a boy turns eight, is it? I think we can make some exceptions today of all days."

Jahd grinned and looked at both Evium and Liana.

"I am so glad to hear that!" he responded before his gaze rested solely upon Liana.

"Huison," Evium greeted coolly with a brief incline of his head.

"Evium," Huison returned. "You are looking well."

Evium's smile came easily. "It's been a good year," he said. Huison also glanced at Liana.

"No doubt," he responded. "Now here we all are again to celebrate this amazing day." Jahd turned to Huison, and they smiled at one another. "So many years in the making."

"Huison, you are fluent in extravagance and exaggeration," Kaileih said, chuckling as she approached, carrying a basket filled with freshly cut dark blue anemones. "Jahd has turned eight, not eighty. Carrying on like this, I can only imagine the uproar when he turns eighteen."

Huison's amber-colored eyes glinted in the sunlight.

"As can I," he mumbled.

A gleefully shrieking bundle interrupted the quintet as it whizzed by. Huison, confused, sat up in his seat as his eyes widened.

Alena, despite being heavily pregnant, ran by shortly after, her attempts to sound stern contradicted by her giggles.

"Come back!" Alena panted. "Miss Mahari, you come back here this minute!"

A strangled cry escaped Huison. He whirled around in his chair as his eyes frantically sought the fleeing child. He finally saw her — standing on tiptoe and reaching with a chubby hand to grab a handful of candies from a crystal bowl atop one of the dessert tables. Huison pressed a hand upon his chest, as though somehow able to suppress the rapid beat of his heart.

Jahd was right. In a year, Mahari had grown into a miniature version of her mother, with a waterfall of curls spilling over her shoulders and smooth, light brown skin. Alena reached her just as Mahari shoved a candy into her mouth, ducked Alena's grasp, and ran back to where Liana stood with the others. Her large eyes, so similar in shape to her mother and grandmother, fixed on Huison for only a moment before she moved closer to Evium and climbed into his lap.

"'ello, Papa!" she said through sticky lips before planting a kiss upon Evium's cheek while throwing her arms around his neck.

"Hello, sweet girl," Evium said, hugging her back. The look he gave Huison was not triumphant, but it still cut Huison to the core, causing him to catch a breath and look away.

"Beggin' yer pardon!" Alena said, panting. "Miss Mahari! Y'come on, now! Let's go n'get dressed!"

"I am dressed!" the child exclaimed.

"And too smart for your own good," Kaileih laughed. "Be mindful, young lady. Go on now and get changed."

The sound of a whimpering protest drew every eye in Mahari's direction. She looked back at everyone in confusion before sticking another candy into her mouth as the whimper came again.

"Jahd!"

Huison bolted upright in his chair at the echo of distress in Liana's tone. He could see the color draining from her face as she rushed to Jahd, who stood rigid and unmoving as he stared at Kaileih. While Huison slowly looked from Jahd to Kaileih, his stomach cramped.

"Take her quickly!" Evium said to Alena as Mahari, sensing that something was amiss, sniffled as her little face crumpled.

"Baby, what is it—what's wrong?" Liana said as she kneeled in front of Jahd, placing her hands on either side of his face. She recoiled. "He's freezing! Mama!"

"No..." Jahd moaned as his eyes rolled upward and his knees buckled.

Mahari wailed as Huison, with the speed of a striking snake, got to his feet and moved around the table in time to catch Jahd before he fell backward and nearly hit his head against the edge of the table on his way down.

"Take her NOW!" Evium roared to a frozen Alena, helplessly reaching toward Jahd but physically unable to move to his side.

Mahari's cries grew distant as Alena whisked her into the house. Evium watched helplessly as Jahd's lithe frame arched upward from where he was being held by Huison. Jahd's mouth hung open as bulging veins protruded across his forehead and near his temples. His entire body then collapsed, shuddered, and was still for only a moment before he began flailing, startling Huison, who allowed Jahd's convulsing figure to fall completely onto the ground as he skittered to one side.

"Liana, move!" Kaileih hissed, having tossed aside the basket of flowers as she bent easily to pull her daughter up from the ground just as Jahd's left leg extended and he missed kicking his mother.

Evium pulled his pregnant wife onto his lap as Kaileih got on her knees beside her grandson, draping her body over his and pinning his flailing legs down with one knee. Jahd's breaths were erratic, and his attempts to scramble away from Kaileih proved useless as she held him in place, putting a hand on either side of his head.

"Shhh," she crooned, stroking his temples. "Still yourself, sweet boy."

She continued to speak to him in whispered tones, keeping her hands in place and her body positioned so that he could not squirm away. After several moments, Jahd's violent movements ceased, and his body relaxed.

"Nana?" Jahd whispered, tears spilling from his eyes and mingling with the sweat upon his skin. Huison started, staring at Jahd as his brow creased.

"Of course," Kaileih said gently, smoothing his curls back. "How are you feeling?"

"Hurt," Jahd whimpered, groaning. "It hurt me... it... was killing me..."

"We'll take you inside," Kaileih promised. "I'll make you something to help you feel better."

"Yes," Jahd agreed tiredly. "Please... help me..."

He then closed his eyes briefly, turning his head slightly to his right. When he opened them again, he looked at Huison, who was still sitting on the ground nearby. Huison's breath caught as the gray eyes locked on him before rolling upward again as Jahd convulsed once more, grew still, and his eyes slid shut.

Chapter Thirteen

Liana paced outside of the closed double doors leading to Jahd's suite. He no longer shared connected accommodations with Mahari. His younger sister had been given his old rooms while the nursery she once occupied was renovated for the impending birth of the new baby.

"I want to see my son!" she demanded once again.

"Liana, please!" Evium said, grabbing and holding onto Liana's hands. "Your mother is tending to him and she's taking excellent care of him."

"I should be taking care of him!" Liana retorted, snatching her hands away and wringing them together. "I need to see him. I need to know."

"You need to stop!" Evium said firmly, taking her hands again. "You have another child to think of as well. It won't do to get yourself too worked up."

"He is correct," Huison said from where he leaned against the wall opposite the couple. "Have a care, Liana. I am sure that your awe-inspiring mother is doing her best."

"You!" Liana continued, her eyes flinty as she turned to Huison, once more removing her hands from Evium's grip. Huison flinched as she approached. "What's your role in this? Why is my son sick?"

"Liana!" Evium said.

"He'd been fine—just fine—this last year!" she went on. "First day you show up, and this?"

"Li, that's enough!" Evium said as Huison crumpled against the wall.

"Where did you two get off to this morning!?" Liana demanded.

"We went for a walk," Huison said, unable to meet her eyes. "As you pointed out, I had not seen Jahd in a year. I wanted time with him before the start of the festivities."

"Liana, surely you don't think that Huison could have anything to do with whatever's gone on with our son," Evium interrupted.

"Do you?" Liana demanded of Huison.

"Liana, calm down!" Evium said. "Think of the baby."

"I'm thinking of all my babies!"

"Perhaps, then, you should go check on Mahari," Evium offered. "I'll stay here to await word from Kaileih. I'll send for you the moment I hear anything."

Liana continued to glare at Huison, who remained folded against the wall as he focused on anything other than the heated glance directed at him. When at last she turned away, Huison shuddered and slid into a sitting position as beads of sweat decorated his brow.

"The very moment you hear anything," she said to Evium.

"You have my promise," Evium said.

Kaileih sat at Jahd's bedside, gently stroking the side of his face as she gazed down at him. Though his eyes were closed, his brow remained furrowed while his jaw tightened. Occasional shudders shook the bed, signaling that the seizures had not yet ceased.

"Why do you struggle so?" Kaileih asked gently.

She reached over to the bedside table, upon which sat a large glass bowl filled with handfuls of small, bright green leaves mixed with purple buds and covered with water. Condensation fogged the rim of the bowl, and though additional steam rose from the surface of the liquid, Kaileih dipped her fingers into it with no sign of discomfort before rubbing the mixture into Jahd's left temple.

"Jahd Dhamon," she said, "stop this nonsense and come back to us. Open those big, beautiful eyes of yours. Your baby sister had to be given something to calm her nerves, and your mother won't be too far behind at this rate. She's worried about you. We all are."

Kaileih paused at the sounds of distant commotion in the hallway, shaking her head as she dipped into the bowl again.

"Perhaps I should tranquilize the lot of them," she commented, rubbing Jahd's right temple. "I'll have to soon if you keep this up." Jahd groaned, turning to nuzzle his face in Kaileih's palm as his features seemed to relax. "That's better," Kaileih said, as she withdrew her hand and arched a brow. "Now, wake up."

"The way she looked at me just now," Huison said in a trembling voice once Liana departed, "I never imagined..."

"We've certainly had our differences of late," Evium said. "But, I know how much you love Jahd and that you'd do nothing to hurt him. Liana knows it as well, she's just overwrought."

"I only want the best for her," Huison said softly. "Everything I do is to that end."

Evium considered Huison carefully before moving closer and leaning forward in his seat, narrowing his eyes.

"Liana has what's best for her," Evium said. "That's always been the case, and it's not for you to think differently."

Huison glared up at his old friend with moisture building in his eyes.

"You have nerve sitting there in judgment of me!" he said. "Is it so easy to assume my role as the villain?"

"Aren't you?" Evium asked. "Or are you implying innocence, Huison?"

"She came to me," Huison said through clenched teeth. "For years, I only watched from a distance. I never dared to hope that my dearest dreams could bear fruit and she would give me favor, but she came to me."

"She was confused!" Evium shouted. "Liana was upset, and she came to you as my best friend! She trusted you! You twisted her cry for help..."

"...into cries of passion!" Huison said as a slow smile spread across his face and his voice hardened. "Believe as you like, Evium. I will neither sully what Liana and I share, nor lay myself bare for your absolution or amusement.

"Liana does not have what is best for her and you are wholly incapable of providing it because you do not know the secrets of her soul. Enjoy your time now, but I will be who she ultimately turns to in the end!"

"She will do no such thing and you've run mad if you think it!" Evium said, reddening. "Fine. Fine! I don't know why I bothered at all. You've left me with no choice. You need to leave this house and the grounds for good. It was never a good idea to have you back here, despite your ties.

"You are no longer welcome. You'll be permitted visitation with your daughter at a location well outside of this estate—not that you'll bother since you haven't in a year—and since Kaileih now knows what you're up to with Rael, you can communicate your findings to her and she'll relay them to Liana. Stay away from now on, Huison, or I'll..."

"You will what?" Huison said. "Are you threatening me now?"

"I am merely enlightening you," Evium said. "I have spent months cultivating, reclaiming, and rebuilding what's mine. You were only allowed to remain part of our lives because of Mahari and for what you are doing with Rael. But, not even those factors are enough, and I won't be held responsible should you choose to cross me again."

"You *are* threatening me!" Huison said. "You want to take my child away from me only because of how she came to be!"

"Only because?" Evium repeated nastily. "Don't trivialize what you've done! Liana isn't anything more to you than a conquest. You only want her again now because she's happy—happy without you, mind!"

"I love her!" Huison said, getting to his feet. "Simpleton that you are and have always been, lacking the innate ability to comprehend anything other than that which you can see and touch. You have spent months cultivating and reclaiming what is yours? Yours!? You talk of her as if she is a trinket built in that laboratory of yours!

"Did you really think that exclusion would dampen the intensity of my feelings? Do you think full-on banishment will? It will endure far beyond what you think you know of us."

"You *have* run mad," Evium said in astonishment. "I don't understand what's happened, Huison, but something has gone wrong with you. You are not my friend. I don't know that you ever were. That you could do as you have and then say this to me now as if you carry no blame..."

"Because I do not," Huison said, shaking his head. "Believe as you like. You will soon see that you cannot get in the way, Evium. As I said, this is beyond you now. It is beyond all of us. Go on, expel me, but this will not be the end."

"What happened?"

Jahd stared at Kaileih for so long that she was unsure that he had heard her question. He inhaled deeply, the smell of lavender and peppermint wafting from the still-steaming bowl nearby as the tips of his long lashes brushed against the swell of his cheeks during his slow blink.

"I became ill," he said in a whisper.

"That you did," Kaileih confirmed, stroking his forehead. "Tell me about it."

Jahd frowned. "There's nothing to tell, Grandmother," he said. "I just felt... separated from myself for a while."

"Ever feel anything like that before today? Maybe without getting as sick as you did?"

"No," Jahd said after a brief pause.

"How are you feeling now, sweetheart?"

Jahd sat up, first looking around the massive bedroom, before peering at Kaileih again. He then reached out, capturing a cluster of her long twists in one hand and allowing them to roll along his palm. When he looked up at her again, he was smiling, though his eyes were moist.

Kaileih tilted her head at him. "You look at me as though you've never seen me before."

"Your face is well known to me, Grandmother," Jahd said. "I couldn't ever forget you."

"So formal now that you're a big boy of eight," she said, tossing her head back in laughter. She kissed Jahd's forehead before drawing him into a tight embrace. "Please don't scare me like that again?"

"I would never," he said as he snuggled against her.

"We've had to cancel the party," she said as they parted.

"I don't mind," Jahd said.

"Your parents may choose to reschedule, though not right away. You should rest."

"Yes, ma'am," he said obediently as he settled back against the pillows again. "Where is my uncle?"

"Outside waiting for word," Kaileih said with an arched brow, "along with your parents."

"May I see him?"

"As I said, Jahd, you should rest..."

"Just for a moment? Please?"

Kaileih considered him, shaking her head and sighing. "Five minutes," she agreed. "It'll give me time to talk with your parents."

"Thank you, Grandmother," Jahd said solemnly as she exited.

"How is he?" Evium said, wheeling himself over to Kaileih as she entered the hallway.

"Much more in charge of himself than the adults appear to be," Kaileih said after looking from him to Huison and surmising the situation with a glance. "Where is my daughter?"

"With Mahari," Evium said, "but, she wanted to be informed the moment you finished with Jahd."

"I have not finished with him, as you put it. I'll need to watch him closely over the next few days at least to make sure he doesn't have another spasm."

"What caused it, do you know?"

"You're awfully quiet, Master Loromin," Kaileih said as she looked past Evium, ignoring his question to focus upon Huison. "Have I you to thank for the earlier commotion I heard while inside tending to your ailing nephew?" She looked at Evium again. "I suppose I have you to thank as well." Evium flushed and looked away. "Collect yourself, Huison, Jahd would like to see you."

Huison blanched as Evium reddened even more.

"My son wants what!?"

Kaileih placed a hand upon Evium's shoulder, silencing him.

"Go on," she said to Huison. "You have a few minutes while I update my daughter and son-in-law."

The aroma of fresh lavender and mint overwhelmed Huison as he entered the room, closing the door with a soft click behind him. Jahd looked small in the massive bed, and his eyes were stony as he reclined upon a set of pillows.

"What happened?" Huison whispered as he carefully approached the bed. "What came over you?"

"You don't know?" Jahd said in an icy tone.

"Of course not! How could I?" He glanced briefly at the closed door. "We have only minutes. There is no time for riddles."

Jahd nodded, conceding the point. "She happened."

"She?"

"It happened almost immediately after seeing her. She came over me. I... I almost lost myself and he came back for a moment."

"What!?" Huison hissed. "How could that happen? I did not think it possible!"

"You think I did?" Jahd said. "It happened because she recalled him simply by being there. You heard, and he nearly told everyone what happened. I couldn't stop it until we looked over at you and fear allowed me to take over again." Jahd narrowed his eyes. "You've got to let me have more control. I appreciate your graciousness in allowing me to clean up after myself at the mine, but I need more!"

"That is not what we agreed," Huison said with a shake of his head.

"I'm no better off than when I was trapped in the talentless carcass you found me in!"

"We both know why this body is the best one for you!" Huison said. "Your ties to this specific bloodline will allow you to flourish. You must give it more time."

"There won't be more time if another slip like that happens! You don't understand how dangerous this is. It's early days yet. I don't... I don't know if I can control it."

"Did anything happen just now?"

"What?"

"Just now, when you were here alone with Kaileih, were you in control?"

Jahd paused. "Yes," he answered. "I was apprehensive, but I didn't lose myself again."

"Then you are already acclimating," Huison said. "It may be early days, but there will be improvement. It will become easier to conceal yourself from her. You have already done so this long. You underestimate yourself."

"You underestimate me if this goes wrong."

"Nothing will go wrong," Huison said. "It will all be as intended."

"While I'm left here alone to languish? We won't see each other often. You aren't very well liked."

"That is brilliantly understated," Huison chuckled. "Not to worry, though. We have Mahari in common. I would like to be closer to my child and I do not see you being denied the opportunity to visit me when she does."

"Are you genuinely fond of her," Jahd asked, laughing, "or is she only a means of securing ties to her bitch of a mother?"

The infuriated expression on Huison's face cut the laughter short as he studied Jahd. Seconds ticked away as the silence lingered before Huison finally smiled, though the hatred in his eyes was undiminished. When the door opened, Jahd looked more than a little relieved.

"All right, you two?" Kaileih said as she entered, Evium wheeling in behind her.

"Of course," Huison said, giving Jahd another look before turning to Kaileih. "He is already much improved. I take it that Liana is pleased?"

"Not so much that she doesn't intend to come see for herself once she's done tending to Mahari," Kaileih answered as Evium coasted past Huison without a word and approached the bed.

"I thank you for your care, Kaileih," Huison said, lowering his voice. "I could not ask for more capable hands than yours to minister to Mahari... and Liana."

"We've come to this, then?" Kaileih surmised. "Your farewell speech?"

"Surely, it does not surprise you. You may have even hoped for it."

"I hoped for neither a heartbroken daughter nor granddaughter," Kaileih said.

"Mahari is far from heartbroken," Huison said with a sigh. "Kaileih," he said, gently leading her out of the bedroom and into the hallway, "would you consent to advocating on my behalf?"

"In what way?" she asked, arms folded.

"I have been lax in my approach to being a proper father to Mahari. I realize she does not know me, and I would not force my presence upon her, but... I would like to foster a relationship with her and maintain the one I have with her brother, perhaps during scheduled visits to Scio."

"Only Mahari and Jahd?" Kaileih asked.

"It would facilitate the arrangement suggested a year ago. I did not capitalize on it then because..."

"...you hoped for something more."

"A hope that remains, albeit more unrealistic by the day," Huison admitted.

"If this was already suggested, why do you need me to do anything?" Kaileih asked. "Liana and Evium won't go back on their word."

"Liana looks to be having a child within a few months," Huison said. "She and her husband will be caught up in the bliss of that event and I would sooner not tax them further."

"Fair enough," Kaileih said with a nod. "I'll see what I can do." Huison acknowledged her assent with a brief incline of his head. "What will you do now?"

"Pack my things," Huison said with a shrug. "If I can get back on the road within the hour, I can be home long before nightfall."

"You're leaving today?"

"You have canceled the festivities, Jahd is on the mend, and I... have finally exhausted my welcome. Kaileih, I cannot stay. What would be the point?"

She nodded again. "You threw away your pomander," she commented.

"I shall simply have to manage without one," Huison said with a laugh.

"I'll prepare something, and have it brought to you."

"Your generosity is unmatched, Kaileih Dhamon."

Huison turned to glance at Evium, who sat at Jahd's bedside in quiet conversation with his son. Locking eyes with Jahd only briefly, he turned away to walk down the hallway toward the stairs.

Chapter Fourteen

As he had yet to unpack after his arrival earlier that morning, there was little for Huison to do while he waited for Fayal to prepare the coach for travel. He did, however, take care to remove all remaining books belonging to him from among the shelves of the bookcases in the guest house. They were of little consequence, however, as he had already removed the better tomes a year prior, and the action served as nothing more than busy work.

Huison paced the study, recalling the day's events. He wondered how Amriel Dhamon would feel to know that his own work was used to ultimately lure his daughter into a permanent liaison with a man such as Huison—and with his own grandson as the bait.

Poor little Jahd. Huison did care for him, of that there was no doubt, but Liana was a prize for which Huison would sacrifice everything. Now things were in place and Huison needed only to wait. Liana would have her wish, and he would have his.

"You're ready, then?"

Huison whirled around to find the subject of his thoughts standing in the study's doorway. She had changed out of the pumpkin-hued, mini trapeze dress she wore to the party and into a light blue, soft knit, ribbed maxi dress that clung to her blooming figure.

"I did not assume that Kaileih would make you her messenger," Huison said.

"I'm sorry?" Liana asked. Huison then noticed that she was not carrying anything.

"I thought your mother sent you with something to help with my travel sickness," he said, turning back to review the bookshelves once more. "My mistake... yet again. Perhaps, then, the Puppet Master has deigned to inspect her work." He shook his head. "What are you doing here, Li?"

"I let myself in," Liana said, stepping further into the room.

"I did notice that, yes," Huison said. "Why?"

"I wanted to talk with you. My mother told me you'd like to start visits with Mahari."

"I would. And?"

"And I can't help but wonder why. I'm finding it hard to believe that you're agreeing to this so quickly now when you hadn't bothered before..."

Huison turned to face her again. "Is it your intention to bar me from seeing our daughter?" he demanded.

"Of course not!" Liana said, reddening.

"Then why are you bringing it up? No one cares about before. You certainly do not. Why are you even here, Liana? I am mere minutes from being on my way back home and away from you— exactly as you wanted. I only ask that you and your husband honor the initial offer."

"We will, Huison," she said. "Nothing's changed in that regard."

"Not only in that regard," he said acidly.

"You're angry."

"I am hurt," Huison countered before taking a deep breath. "I am tired. I am bereft and bewildered. I am also weary of talking about it."

"I thought things might have been different," Liana said. "It's been a year, after all. You had to know. You should have known. Things ended so long ago, Huison."

"No, you should have known. You are incomparable to me, Liana. Being away from you for all this time has changed nothing."

"Some things have definitely changed," she said, caressing her belly.

"Do you really think that deters me?" Huison asked, taking a step toward her. "It was an initial shock to see you in this condition, yes. Has it wounded me? Yes." He pointed at her stomach. "Even now, I want you. You will always be a treasure."

"Huison..."

"What?" he scoffed. "Were you unaware? Had you hoped to put me off for good? Tell me, Liana, what did you expect might happen when you visited me here? Did you come to wallow in what you presumed would be my misery? Were you hoping for a fight or some reason you might deny me visitation with Mahari?"

"That was not..."

"Did you hope to be rid of me on all counts but for what you expect me to do for your brother?"

"Huison, please..."

"You know why I started helping Rael," he said, his voice growing louder. "It was never a secret, was it? I have done things you cannot fathom for love of you."

"I should go," Liana said, turning toward the door.

"Liana, please!" Huison said, his tone softening. She paused, but didn't turn to face him. "I love you. Nothing has or will alter that fact, and I have tried to make sense of it but find myself lacking."

"It's madness," Liana said softly as she faced him.

"I agree," he said good-naturedly, managing a smile though moisture had collected in his eyes. "I know it sounds odd. I have tried to understand what draws me to you, and it is overwhelming. Nothing you have done, including reconciling with and becoming pregnant by Evium, has affected what I feel for you. Everything I do is for you."

"Why are you saying this? This isn't why I came."

"Then why did you come here?" he shot back, the edge returning to his tone. "I was ready to leave without a word. I had already spoken with Kaileih about mediating the arrangements, which she agreed to do. You came here. You sought me out."

"I shouldn't have," Liana said, once again turning toward the door.

"I love you," Huison said again.

"Stop saying that!" she yelled.

"Liana Rose Dhamon, I love you!"

"Well, I don't love you!" Liana said, equally stubborn as she faced him.

"You did," Huison said, "and you will again." His smile was knowing, and the sight of it caused Liana's breath to catch. "You were good at it—loving me. So attentive... so thorough...

"Your husband believes I seduced you... that you came to me in a desperate state, and I took advantage." He tilted his head. "If he only knew. If he had seen what we were together... You underestimated it when you told him. I know you did.

"Have things truly gotten better? Is he able to..." Huison paused and shook his head. "Liana, this is all so unnecessary. I understand it frightened you when you realized you were pregnant. Evium, in his predictability, represents a haven. I should have fought harder for you."

"It would have made no difference," Liana said. "You're too volatile, Huison... too impulsive."

Huison's laugh resembled a short bark. "The irony!" he said, his smile fading as his tone became serious again. "Liana, tell me what I need to do to show that I am worthy of you."

"It's not about worthiness!" Liana said, "It's never been about that!"

"Then tell me what it is about, and do not give me any nonsense, please. You snatched me up and then just as easily discarded me without ever fully explaining the reasons."

"That's not true!"

"You were toying with me..."

"I was doing no such thing!"

"Even though he cannot begin to give you what I can or ever love you as I do!"

"That's enough!" Liana hissed. "Get out! You get out of this guest house and off this property right this minute..." Huison took a sudden step toward Liana, silencing her. He took another step, his warm amber gaze fixed on hers. "What?" Liana asked. "Why are you..."

Before she could continue, Huison's steps quickened, and he pulled her to him, wrapping her in his long arms. Liana wriggled in his grasp. Despite her physical condition, they were pressed tightly enough that Liana felt every line of him.

"Look at you," Huison said huskily. "You have not forgotten me after all. Does Evium make your heart race like this? You know I can hear it. Does he make you this warm?" He sniffed at her hair, the tip of his long nose grazing her left cheek as he pressed his lips against her ear. "Say it once more," he whispered. "Tell me to leave. Tell me to never touch you again... and mean it."

When he drew back to look at Liana, a rosy tint infused her skin and she was panting. They were also no longer alone.

"I seem to have caught you at a bad time," Kaileih said amiably. Her eyes moved from Huison to Liana and back before she arched a brow.

"Mama," Liana said, still breathless as she wriggled away from Huison, "it isn't what you think."

Kaileih slowly turned to her. "You do not want to know what I think," she said. "Go back to the house. To your husband. Your children. Now."

"Mama..."

"Liana Rose!" Kaileih's voice was sharp, causing Liana to flee from the room without a backward glance, leaving Huison to endure Kaileih's acidic gaze alone.

They stared at one another for a time until Kaileih reached into the pocket of her jumpsuit to extract a small, stoppered vial she held out to Huison. He took it without breaking their gaze.

"This is?" he asked.

"A concentration of the same extract that was used to make your tea," she said. "Drink it." He uncorked the vial, sniffing at its contents. Kaileih laughed. "You don't trust me."

Huison tossed his head back, emptying the contents of the vial in one swallow. She was right. It was thick, but tasted of a stronger, slightly sweeter version of the very tea she had served him that morning. It was delicious.

"Thank you," he said as she reclaimed both vial and cork. "Kaileih, I..."

"Save it," she said. "I know what I saw. I'm no fool. But, you must let this go, Huison."

"Kaileih, I cannot," Huison said. "Do you not see that?"

"What game are you playing? I will not have you using Mahari as the means to get to her mother. I've warned you already."

"And, your warning is noted," Huison said. "You have my word, on my soul, that I would never use Mahari in that way. I want a relationship with my child."

"Mama!" said a panicked-sounding Liana from the doorway.

"Liana, I thought I told you to..."

Kaileih paused when she turned around to find that Liana was not alone. A thin, bespectacled young man with short dark hair and green eyes had joined her. Kaileih's eyes widened in recognition, as she had seen him before, and recalled the uniform of a lightweight tan tunic and matching pants he wore.

"What is it?" Kaileih asked, her words sounding far away and seeming to echo and swirl around her.

"I've come from Vespers Glen, as you know, my lady," the young man said, bowing. "They have sent me to fetch you immediately. Please come. There isn't much time."

PART TWO

Chapter Fifteen

Eight-year-old Rael Dhamon sat at the edge of the pier, absently gazing out at the water. He sighed, idly swinging his legs as his toes grazed the water's surface.

"Look at you, Rael... you're so far away, no wonder you couldn't hear me."

He turned to grin at his mother as she approached before he absently tossed a handful of cracked corn into the water from the bag in his lap. The gathering of ducks, patiently waiting until that moment, helped themselves to the offering.

"I'm sorry, Mother," he said, watching the ducks eat as Kaileih settled beside him.

"Dinner's been ready for twenty minutes," she said, kissing him on the temple before running a hand through his shock of curly hair. She smirked. "You're going to need a haircut before heading off to Breaton in a couple of weeks." Kaileih paused, noticing her son's grimace. "What is it?"

Rael tossed out another handful. "Liana," he said after a moment. "Mother, she's been so upset. She hardly talks to me anymore."

Kaileih frowned. "How long has this been going on? You've both been behaving normally from what I could tell."

"About a month."

"A month!? Well, what has happened? Did you two have a fight?"

"No, Mother. You know we don't fight; it's just..." Rael shook his head, keeping his dark brown eyes trained on the ducks. "She's upset about me going to Breaton."

"Oh, sweetheart," Kaileih sighed, wrapping an arm around Rael's shoulders. "She's only six years old and hasn't ever been separated from you before. She's just having trouble processing..."

"That isn't it, Mother," Rael interrupted, staring down at his lap. "Forgive me for interrupting you, but you've got it wrong." He looked up at Kaileih with rounded eyes. "She's mad because I can do magic and she can't. I get to go to Breaton, and she doesn't."

"I'll have to talk with her again," Kaileih said after a pause, her frown deepening.

"I'm not trying to get her into any trouble!"

"It's not about that, Rael. That you have magical ability isn't your fault any more than it's her fault that she doesn't. I have never understood where this... quest or thirst for power stems from. No one has ever treated her any less and, as I've told her many times, there is still a chance she could manifest abilities..."

"But it's perfectly fine if she doesn't," Rael finished dutifully. "I know, Mother. I've always known, and I was ready to be either way, but... she takes it so hard. I want to spend time with my little sister before I have to leave for the term, but she makes it impossible every time I try!"

"I know you do, baby," Kaileih said, enveloping him in a hug. "It'll be okay."

"No matter what happens, Mother," Rael said shakily, "I promise I'll never leave her behind. When you talk with her, would you tell her that for me, please?"

They were in formation like soldiers at attention. Swathed in black, Kaileih was flanked by Evium and Jahd on one side and Mahari and Liana on the other, watching as the highly glossed, solid mahogany casket was slowly lowered into the ground.

Mahari clung to her mother, not fully understanding what was going on, yet sensing that she should remain still and quiet. She looked around at all the faces of the people nearby. None of them were smiling. None of them sang or clapped their hands. It was so different from what she was used to, and the melancholy caused tears to fill her large, gray eyes.

Jahd was expressionless as he stared at the descending casket for only a moment before casting a sidelong glance across Kaileih to Liana, who was pale, trembling, and unable to sit fully upright. As the casket, upon which lay an arrangement of silver-veined dark blue orchids, lowered out of sight, Liana emitted a wail that startled Evium and frightened Mahari. Kaileih reached for her daughter, catching her before she slipped from the chair, and they both sank to the ground as they clung together.

"Mama, why?" Liana cried brokenly.

"It's all right, Liana," Kaileih assured her.

"It's not! He always promised not to leave me behind... but, I'm the one who left him! Mama... I never went to see him... I just sat back and waited... for him to get better and come to me... I should have gone!"

A soft whimper to her left caused Kaileih's gaze to shift from Liana's anguished face to the faces of Jahd and Mahari. Tears covered Mahari's cheeks as she held onto her brother. But Jahd was only watching... dry-eyed.

"Stop this," Kaileih said, looking at her daughter. "This isn't good for you or for the baby. The past cannot be reclaimed. I know you loved your brother, and he knew it as well."

"But, Mama!"

"Liana, don't! Rael wouldn't want this for you. You know how he hated it when you'd get upset."

Kaileih helped Liana up and back into her chair, making sure that she was sitting comfortably with Evium holding her before focusing on the children. As she approached, Mahari unwound herself from her brother and fled over to Kaileih, whimpering. Kaileih picked her up as she looked over at Jahd.

"I'm all right, Grandmother," Jahd said in answer to the unasked question.

Kaileih opened her mouth to speak, but was interrupted by another cry from Liana.

"Kaileih, help!" Evium said at that moment.

Kaileih quickly turned, with Mahari still in her arms, as the color drained from Evium's face. Following his glance, she noticed the streaks of blood near Liana's feet. There were also smears on one of her shoes and along the inside of her left ankle.

"Fayal!" she shouted, summoning him at a run from where he stood at the back of the gathering. Without being called, Alena also appeared and took Mahari from Kaileih's arms. Neither of them yet knew the reason for the call. The urgency in Kaileih's tone was enough. Kaileih looked at Alena, who was doing her best to comfort Mahari. "Get her and Jahd to the house now!"

Kaileih kneeled before Liana, keeping her tone even as Alena departed with the children. "Sweetheart?" she said softly. "Are you in any pain?"

"Cramping," Liana answered, tears rolling down her cheeks. "In... my lower back. I may just need the restroom..."

"When did it start? Just now?"

"Yesterday morning," Liana whispered. "It comes and goes... I thought nothing of it."

Kaileih's sharp intake of breath seemed to mirror the alarmed expression on Evium's face. Clenching her jaw hard enough that her temples protruded slightly, she turned to Fayal. He had finally noticed the blood and, though his thoughts were of his own wife's advanced pregnancy, he did his best to be present for his employer's family.

"Swiftly, but carefully," Kaileih told him. "Get her to the house for me, Fayal. Never mind trying to reach the master suite. A bedroom on the first floor will suffice until we can stabilize her, do you understand?"

"Yes, of course," Fayal said.

"On your way, then," Kaileih said, standing up and to one side as Fayal scooped Liana up and whisked her away without effort.

Once Liana was out of the chair again, both Kaileih and Evium looked with equal dread at the blood covering the vacated seat. Kaileih looked up at Evium, who was staring at her with tear-filled eyes. She could see the helplessness in them, knowing that he wished he could have been the one to carry his wife into their home or that he, even now, could run along to make sure she was all right.

There was no time for lengthy assurances. Wordlessly, Kaileih reached out to squeeze Evium's shoulder before going after the others.

Kaileih found Evium sitting in the solarium, gazing through a window with Mahari curled up and fast asleep in his lap. As she drew closer, Kaileih could see matching stains of dried tears on their cheeks.

"How is she?" Evium asked in a hoarse whisper. Mahari stirred and sniffled, but didn't awaken.

"Resting," Kaileih said. "We'll wait awhile before moving her upstairs." She peered over his shoulder to glance at her granddaughter. "Alena said there was some trouble?"

Evium gazed down at Mahari. "She was anxious," he answered. "I talked with her, sang to her... she settled down. She only just fell asleep a quarter of an hour ago." He looked up at Kaileih as she moved to face him. "Son or daughter?"

"Daughter," Kaileih said, sitting on the windowsill and reaching over to place her hand atop Evium's, giving it a pat.

"I should see to Liana," Evium said after exhaling shakily.

"You should take a moment for yourself first," Kaileih cautioned.

"No," Evium said. "I... she..." He swallowed hard, briefly closing his eyes. "She needs..."

"Vi," Kaileih said, getting up again and moving closer as beads of perspiration appeared at Evium's brow.

He groaned in response as his blue eyes filled with tears and a hiccup forced him to choke back a moan. Kaileih reached forward to scoop Mahari into her arms, flicking her dark brown gaze toward the arched entrance of the solarium. As she stood cradling her granddaughter and Evium slumped slightly in his chair, Shaz rushed into the room.

"You called for me, ma'am?" he asked before looking over at his employer in alarm.

"Take the baby, please, Shaz," Kaileih said in a level tone.

"But... Lord Chatelain..."

"No buts, Shaz," Kaileih said, her voice firm, though not raised. "I will see to him. Please take Mahari to her room. Make sure she isn't left alone, or it might frighten her when she awakes."

"Shall I call for Alena, ma'am?" Shaz said. "I believe she is already with the young sir."

Kaileih frowned. "Alena should also rest, and you may tell her I said so. She is further along than Liana was. Have Clea or Linet join you in the nursery and then make sure that Fayal tends to his wife. Jahd can also keep his sister company. I'm sure he'd like that."

Mahari emitted a sigh as Kaileih gave her over to Shaz, who lovingly cuddled her sleeping form as he rushed from the room. Kaileih then turned her attention to Evium, pulling him in his wheelchair closer as she assumed her previous position at the windowsill.

She only watched as the tears continued to fall from Evium's bloodshot eyes, silent as the minutes ticked away. It was only until he seemed spent and was reduced to the occasional hitch in his breathing that Kaileih settled back.

"She must be going out of her mind," Evium said at last, running both hands through his hair. "I need to go to her."

"I don't disagree on either count," Kaileih answered. "But, you needed to rid yourself of the rawness of your emotions first. There will be more tears, but you must remember to take time for you, Evium. You're no good to Liana or to those children otherwise."

Evium nodded. "I hear what you're saying, Kaileih, and I thank you for it."

"Did you know that she'd started having pain?"

"No," he groaned. "I swear I didn't! I would have told you!"

"All right, all right," Kaileih said. "I'm just... I should have seen. I should have known."

"She'd been so quiet over the last couple of weeks," Evium remarked. "She's been grieving. We've all been grieving." He looked at his mother-in-law. "Kaileih, I am so sorry. I thought that with all the positive reports we were getting about Rael..."

"What was positive about them is that he was getting no worse," Kaileih said.

"I hoped we could have learned more. Was Huison close to bringing Rael out of it, you think?"

Kaileih's laugh seemed bitter as she reached up to sweep a mass of braids from one shoulder. "I sometimes wonder if Huison really knew what plagued my son," she admitted. "He seems to enjoy a pleasant fantasy. His logic could have been born of something he wove together in the hopes it would benefit him in the end.

"He could reach Rael on some level, though, and I envy that. Those private moments between Huison and Rael are irretrievably lost. Was Rael close to a breakthrough, though? How can we know?"

"Huison thought he'd learned something from the things Amriel studied and wrote about," Evium said. He moved his wheelchair backward a couple of inches so that he could focus fully upon Kaileih. "How much truth is there in what Huison surmised? He seemed convinced that Rael's affliction stemmed from an attempt to help Amriel in death."

"It did," Kaileih said softly.

Evium ran a weary hand over his eyes, sighing. "Kaileih," he said, "how deep did Amriel's research take him?"

"Not deep enough for anyone, particularly Huison Loromin, to traverse."

"You appear to doubt him and yet you let him try to help."

"I had to," she shrugged. "If there was even the slightest chance that Huison could make enough sense of Amriel's work to make a difference, it was worth it because I wanted my son back! There were moments..." Kaileih smiled sadly. "I could see him there, Evium. He was not fully himself, but he wasn't so tormented, either. He was close. He was so close."

"Huison wasn't at the service," Evium said. "I would have allowed it, considering the circumstances."

"That call was mine to make," Kaileih said. "There was no need for him to be here." She folded her arms across her abdomen. "One thing you need to be sure to allow, though, is for Huison to have visitations with Mahari." Evium involuntarily grimaced. "You said that you would."

"I didn't expect him to ask," Evium admitted.

"Yet he has. He would also like to maintain his relationship with Jahd, which benefits the arrangement. Mahari won't feel as alone if her brother is there."

"Must we discuss this now?" Evium asked after a moment. "I'm beyond spent and would like to sit with my wife."

"Fair enough," Kaileih said.

"Thank you."

"Not so fast with the gratitude," Kaileih said. "Before you go, there's something else we need to talk about."

"Hmm?"

"Evium, I hope that once you've returned to yourself and look back on today that you will forgive me," Kaileih said.

"What?" Evium looked at his mother-in-law through bleary blue eyes. "What do you mean?"

"I'm going to tell you something that you need to hear and retain. Liana will never be in the proper mindset for this, but you are the more sensible between you so pay attention to what I'm about to say regarding your son."

"Jahd?" Evium's brow furrowed. "What about him?"

"I buried my son today. Since Jahd's birthday when the attendant from Vespers came to collect me, I've had ample opportunity for reflection. What happened to Jahd before his party began... the convulsions and incoherence... was not my first experience with such events."

Evium stared at Kaileih, his mouth slightly opened before he shook his head. "What do you mean, it wasn't your first experience? Jahd had a seizure before, and you didn't tell us?"

"Not Jahd," Kaileih said with a shake of her head. "Rael. Liana was incredibly young when it happened. I'm sure she doesn't remember, but... Rael had convulsions, off and on for a few months before his abilities manifested themselves. Amriel insisted it was his body's way of trying to adjust for the changes that were taking place inside of him, and that it happens to some occasionally."

Kaileih got up from the windowsill again and padded around the solarium in bare feet. Evium turned to watch her, his mouth still agape.

"After Rael cast his first spell, he never had another seizure... until his father died..." Kaileih continued. "I'm always reluctant to bring these things up with my daughter. You know how she is... and this doesn't appear to be the right time."

"Yet it's the right time for me?" Evium said with a sigh.

"Yes," Kaileih said firmly. "As I said, you're more sensible. You can see these things clearly. Feelings of being cheated will forever cloud Liana."

"Kaileih, even though no one in my family possessed the qualities of a spellweaver, my parents did not bring me up to be prejudiced against those with the ability. However, the more I have seen and learned since becoming part of your family, I am convinced that the only thing Liana has been cheated out of is a life destined to end in heartbreak and pain.

"What has being a spellweaver brought to the Dhamons? Rael is dead after years of being institutionalized because of the related strain stemming from the death of his father. Those who prefer to think of you as the widow of Amriel Dhamon overshadow your prowess as a horticulturist. I didn't understand or support Liana's fear that either of our children might grow up with magical talents. Now... I'd prefer they didn't."

"Did I really just say that you're more sensible than my daughter?" Kaileih mused. "Heartbreak and pain are not exclusive to spellweavers. Your comments are born of both, with maybe a splash of ignorance for added kick." She turned away to walk toward the door. "Regardless of what you feel now, I'd advise you to monitor Jahd. He could be changing. Your plans for him to attend Pandoufuli would have to as well."

"Kaileih," Evium said after clearing his throat. "Since we're being transparent... you realize you don't have to go back to Tilehn, right? I mean... it was easier to travel to Vespers from there, but... you... you won't be going to Vespers anymore." Kaileih turned and raised a dark eyebrow at Evium, though her expression remained unreadable. "I... I just... We have such a large home here, Kaileih. If you do not want to stay in the main house, you can have your pick of either of the guest houses... or we can have something built to your specifications."

"I have something built to my specifications," she said with a gentle smile.

"Don't you want to be with us? The children love when you're here, and I see what it does for you, too."

Kaileih's dark brown gaze danced over the solarium, admiring the care that went into the details and the overall warmth of the room.

"You have built a magnificent home for my daughter," she said. "It borders on palatial, though why any humanoid would require something so large has always escaped me. I've no doubt that you'd go out of your way for me and your generosity is but one reason I love you and that I love you for Liana, but... despite the adventure that has been my life, I have always favored simplicity."

"Then we'll build you a simple house..." Evium protested, stopping when Kaileih held up a hand.

"I mean not only my physical surroundings," she said. "I did my best to instill a sense of practicality in my children. It worked with Rael. Liana... not so much, which likely suits her well in the role as wife of the Lord Mayor, however much of a decorative title it may be. Despite whom he was and what he could do, Amriel was effortless. He never needed to try too hard. I am much the same.

"Even though Liana and I deeply love each other, we will always clash on fundamental levels. I will never understand why she lives to fight for more, and she cannot understand why I'm content to exist with less. You don't want that sort of conflict in your home or any of the homes you hoped to build for me, though I appreciate the thought. Periodic distance is, and has always been, the cure for what ails us."

"When will you leave?" Evium asked softly. Kaileih smiled at him, walking over to tug lightly at a tuft of his blond hair.

"Not just yet," she assured him. "I have something to attend to first thing in the morning but will return before I'm missed." She stepped back, turning again to resume her walk toward the door. "Now... remember what I've said about Jahd," she warned. "Wash your face before seeing Liana. I'm going to see to the children."

"Kaileih?" Evium said. She faced him once more. Evium wheeled closer. "You also need to take a moment for yourself. You buried your son today." His eyes filled again as he shrugged helplessly. "I'm sure you've also seen to the final care of your granddaughter before coming to see me. Don't you... don't you need time?"

Kaileih reached over and gently stroked the side of Evium's face. "Thank you for that," she said, "but, I assure you that one thing I've never lacked is time. The rest will fall into place."

She turned away again and left the solarium.

Chapter Sixteen

Huison looked up from the drawings on his desk, his brow furrowed as he stared at the black-attired attendant. "I have a what?" he asked.

"A visitor, sir."

"At this hour?" Huison sat back in his chair, the task at hand forgotten for the moment. "Has Alford Brandon come early?"

"No, sir," the butler said with a slight bow. "It isn't about your appointment later this morning. This visit is from a young lady who claims to come from Kynedal and the Chatelain estate."

Huison paled. "From Kynedal? Who is she? What does she want?"

"She didn't say, sir. But knowing your frequent dealings there, I thought it might be important and came to alert you straightaway."

Huison rose, coming around the desk as a chill swept over him.

"She did not say?" he asked, brushing past the older man to venture along the hallway toward the foyer. "Idiot!"

Huison had already been advised of Rael's death via a messenger from Vespers, followed by a brief note from Kaileih advising him against attending the services. Huison wanted to be there for Liana, but knew he couldn't do so in the capacity that he wished. Though Rael's demise was unfortunate and unexpected, Huison was glad to have been able to extract the means of ensuring that his plans would succeed. But why would anyone come from Kynedal now?

Huison skidded to a stop as he reached the foyer, and the hooded figure turned around with a smile.

"Kaileih!" Huison said, wide-eyed. "I... This is... rather unexpected! When I was told that someone was here from Kynedal, I thought that there had to be some error. I would have never thought it would be you."

"I was in the neighborhood," she smirked, pushing back the wet hood of her cloak to reveal a neatly braided updo.

"You must have departed before dawn to get here," he commented, his stomach knotting up at the sight of her. "Unless, surely, you did not make the trip in one of those motorized contraptions courtesy of your son-in-law?"

Kaileih chuckled, removing her gloves and tucking them into the pocket of the cloak before allowing the hovering manservant to slip the garment from her shoulders.

"Not at all," she said, smoothing the chiffon cape-style sleeves of her black velvet jumpsuit. "I rode one of the horses. I didn't count on it starting to rain when I was only half an hour outside of town, though. He's being tended to in your stable."

"Wonderful, then..." he cleared his throat. "Please—join me in the living room. It is infinitely more comfortable than the foyer."

"Thank you," Kaileih said, walking with Huison as the attendant followed several paces behind them.

"I planned to have breakfast shortly," Huison said. "It would be no trouble to have the cook make something for you, and I would welcome the company."

"Oh, no, thank you," Kaileih said. "I had something before leaving. I also don't intend to keep you for exceptionally long, so you'll still be able to enjoy your meal with no delays."

"Such a long way for a brief visit," Huison said. "Perhaps something refreshing to drink, then?"

"All right, then," Kaileih conceded with a brief nod. "Have you any mint tea?"

"Of course. With honey?"

"Please," she said, to which Huison responded by snapping his fingers at the waiting attendant, who quickly departed.

"Your home is so open, Huison," Kaileih remarked once they were alone. The heels of her black suede boots clicked against the marble floor as they ventured through the space and into the living room. "My daughter has always found comfort in filling spaces with the most unnecessary things." She smiled, taking Huison in with one glance.

Huison laughed nervously, directing Kaileih to the sofa. She settled comfortably upon the cream-colored leather, leaning against the button-tufted back as she draped one arm over the nail-studded arm roll. Kaileih tilted her head slightly as Huison sat in the matching armchair nearby. He was wearing black slacks beneath a matching silver-embroidered thobe. Upon his feet were soft black leather socks.

"I've practically caught you in a state of undress," she said with a straight face. "My apologies."

"I have a meeting later this morning," he said, almost apologetically before brightening. "In fact, your timing is impeccable. I have completed a series of sketches based on the work I intend to have done to some rooms here at Dalenbeigh. These will be the rooms belonging to Mahari and Jahd during their visitations. I... wonder if you might like to see them?

"I certainly have no gift with a charcoal pencil like my former friend, but... the drafts should show what I intend. I am having them converted into something of a blueprint so that the work can begin within a week."

"I'm sure that what you've planned will be lovely," Kaileih said, crossing long, velvet clad legs.

"It will be nothing like they are used to," Huison said softly. "The Chatelain estate is above reproach. Nevertheless, Mahari will inherit Dalenbeigh someday. Everything I have will go to her. She should be comfortable here."

The reappearance of the butler carrying a tray interrupted them. He placed the tray on the coffee table in front of Kaileih, who visually noted two delicate gold-edged cups filled with steaming amber liquid sitting next to a matching saucer of cookies topped with slivered almonds.

Beside the cup closest to her was an etched glass jar filled with honey, a small honey dipper clipped to the side. Another attendant swept by, placing a charcuterie board on the coffee table beside the tea service along with additional saucers, utensils, and white linen napkins with gold stitching.

When the servants departed, Kaileih looked over the abundant offerings. She spied the cluster of Moon Drops nestled among the varieties of smoked and sliced meats, as well as a dish of burrata with cherry tomatoes. When Kaileih looked up at Huison, he was watching her with a smile on his face, his amber eyes aglow.

"You've been studying," she commented.

"I have had a wonderful teacher over the years," he responded. Kaileih chuckled and uncrossed her legs, leaning forward to take up the cup of tea. She used the honey dipper and, with a fluid flick of the wrist, allowed just enough of the honey to trickle into the hot liquid before using a spoon to stir the result. "For you, I could do nothing less," Huison continued, reaching over to take one slice of prosciutto-wrapped melon, biting into it.

"Careful, you'll spoil your breakfast," Kaileih warned, her dark eyes reflecting the gold from the cup's rim as she brought it to her lips and sipped.

"Is that what you have come all this way to tell me?" he asked with a chuckle.

"No," Kaileih said, taking one of the almond cookies. "I've come to tell you that Liana has lost her baby."

The color drained from Huison's skin, giving him the undertone of a corpse. He coughed as he got up from his seat and, as if realizing for the first time that he was holding something in his hand, he tossed the half-eaten slice of melon toward the coffee table. It landed on the edge of his cup, flipping it over with a clatter and spilling the contents. His hands alternated, clenching into fists and relaxing in rapid succession as he paced first in one direction, then another.

"When?" he asked, panting, when he stopped walking long enough to once again face Kaileih.

"Yesterday," she answered. "She went into distress during the service for Rael and gave birth thereafter. It was too soon."

"I did not attend," Huison said, his hands compressing again. "I wanted to be there for her, but your message forbade me..."

"I don't regret my decision on that," Kaileih said with a sigh, placing both cup and cookie onto the tray. "You wouldn't have been able to do anything, anyway. It happened suddenly. There wasn't even enough time for me to do anything other than make her as comfortable as I could... before and after."

"How... how is Liana now?"

"Numb," Kaileih responded. "Also, angry. This baby was symbolic of what she sought to regain with her husband."

"Is she... is she physically hurt? Did she sustain some injury?"

"No. She was under a tremendous amount of stress, though, and this was the result."

"Why?" Huison demanded when he took his seat again. "Why are you telling me this?"

"You're hoping to have Mahari and Jahd here soon, yes?"

"Yes."

"You're meeting with someone today and plan to begin construction on those rooms you mentioned, yes?"

"Of course," he said with caution. "Why do you ask?"

"Though highly intelligent, Mahari is still a baby. She won't fully understand what's happened with her mother or even that anything has. Jahd will, though, and I cannot have you falling to pieces in front of either of them if Jahd deigns to share the incident with you.

"I knew that if you were genuinely serious about spending time with your daughter that you would want to do so immediately. That you have already taken the time to set aside a room in your home proves that I'm right. Huison, I need you to keep your wits about you on this."

"Of course," he said again, some of the color infusing back into his skin. "Of course. What you say makes perfect sense. I... I just worry for...for..."

"Liana... and Evium... will be fine," Kaileih stressed. "They're still young."

"Is it now your intention to comfort me with assurances of their ability to fill the expanse of their home with more children?" Huison said sharply. "I must ask that you refrain." Kaileih reached once again for her cup, wordlessly taking a drink. She had nearly drained it before Huison spoke again. "Kaileih, forgive me for being so abrupt."

"Not so fast," she said with a smile. "I actually didn't come only to talk about Liana."

"No?"

"What exactly is it you did for my son, Huison?"

Huison blanched again. "I... pardon?"

"You were so certain that you could bring him out of his malady. Now Rael is dead. Was that your goal?"

He crumpled a bit, sitting back in the chair. "No," he said. "The death of Rael would not have served my ultimate purpose. He was coming out of it, Kaileih. Of that I am convinced. He just... left us before I could complete the task."

"Now that he has left us," Kaileih began coldly, "everything stops. I expect a report with a full compilation of your findings. Whatever you can tell me, and I don't care how innocuous you deem it, I want in that report, and I want it within a week's time. I, admittedly, have something of a blind spot when it comes to my children and grandchildren. However, the truth always reveals itself.

"Don't let me find out in any other way that something untoward happened in your dealings with my son. I also stress how serious I am that you do not utilize any more, in any way, Amriel's research from this point on."

"There is no longer a need to," Huison commented.

"Don't assume that I was presenting you with an option," Kaileih said. "Read it for fun. Make it into a bedtime story to help keep your sheets warm at night, if you must... but, your obvious failure at a task you feigned proficiency in is proof of your inability to grasp what my husband devoted part of his life to. I'd rather you not stumble into something you lack the resourcefulness to extract yourself from."

"What did Amriel find during his studies?" he countered in a wheedling tone. "So many enquiries and tomes of knowledge left behind. Yet, he never explained why he was so fascinated by the workings of other planes, and no one has figured it out."

"Do I need to repeat myself?" Kaileih asked in a tone so saccharine that Huison felt sure that the slightest movement from him, even to blink, might leave him in danger of soiling the chair. Her smile widened when he found himself unable to do anything more than slowly shake his head. "You wouldn't be served well in this, Huison. Let it go."

His breaths were shallow as he struggled to regain control of his faculties. He watched as Kaileih reached for the cookie she had discarded earlier and took a bite. He watched her nibble delicately, then cleared his throat.

"What is it like?"

"What do you mean?" Kaileih asked, before taking the last bite of the cookie.

"You are so deeply loved," Huison whispered. "I cannot help but wonder how that feels." Kaileih did not break eye contact as she plucked one of the Moon Drops from the cluster. "You and your husband raised Liana and her brother to be accepting of whatever hand they were dealt. Spellweavers or not, you were primed and ready for the acquiescence of and devotion to who they were as people.

"I come from a long line of non-magical people. I was raised in the belief that there was only one way to be and anything else was undesirable. My family established Pandoufuli on a foundation of intolerance and the refusal to embrace spellweavers, as if they controlled being born as they were." He shrugged. "I was expected to follow suit, and even perpetrated the lie for years and successfully graduated before I was found out and disowned."

"This line of conversation seems vaguely familiar," Kaileih mused. "And? Look at what you've accomplished since then. You've made a name for yourself among scholars, you're quite wealthy..."

"I want to know what real love feels like," Huison interrupted. "I want to give, and have it given back to me. It was my honor to bestow upon Liana everything denied me. She was my chance to pour love into someone that I wished was shown to me."

"You're seeking redemption and validation in the wrong place," Kaileih said, finishing the Moon Drop. "My beautiful daughter will not find satisfaction in that kind of arrangement. You can love Liana to the ends of the earth, and she will gladly take it, but what she wants more than anything is power. That isn't something you can give." Kaileih got to her feet as Huison ran the tips of his fingers along the smooth tops of the brass nails adorning the arm rolls of his chair. "I should head back."

"Would you?" Huison asked softly. "If in your power, would you grant your daughter the abilities she so craves?"

"If?" Kaileih asked with an arched brow. "Huison, I adore my daughter. I also know her well enough to be acutely aware of what would happen if she ever tasted a mite of what spellweaving is. Things happen for a reason."

Huison stood, having finally reclaimed himself, his lips curled into a sly smile. "I cannot say that I agree, Kaileih. To have her lifelong dream come true? She would fall upon the giver of that gift with incalculable gratitude."

"Lucky for you I'm not a betting woman," Kaileih chuckled. "You would have a lot to lose on that wager."

The attendant returned, this time with Kaileih's cloak. Huison waited as she was helped into the voluminous dark fabric.

"No need to see me out," Kaileih said, as she ventured through the living room to return to the foyer. "I can definitely find my way clear from here. Besides, your breakfast will get cold."

Huison could not help chuckling as he strolled along. "Now that you know the way, will I have the pleasure of another visit from you? Perhaps under decidedly less-menacing circumstances?"

"I may venture out with Mahari and Jahd from time to time," she said as she pulled on her thin leather gloves. "I'll surprise you."

"Are you certain that I cannot see you out, at least to the stables?" Huison asked as they reached the massive black matte iron doors with an arched top.

"And risk the ruin of those charming socks?" Kaileih said with another smile as she exited.

Huison and the attendant looked at one another as the latter closed the door.

"Were you listening in on our conversation?" Huison demanded as the bolt slid into place.

"No, sir," the attendant said, shaking his head. "Of course not, sir!"

"Then explain to me how you knew to bring her wrap at that moment? We were discussing something especially important, and you interrupted us!"

"Yes, sir, of course... but... sir... it was because the lady called me," the servant said, his eyes wide.

"I beg your pardon?" Huison said. "What foolishness is this? I ought to send you to muck out the stables with a spoon for telling such a lie!"

"I swear to you, sir! I was seeing to the completion of your meal when I distinctly heard the lady calling to me... asking me to bring her things. I would never have come in otherwise!" At the earnest expression on the older man's face, Huison's uneasiness returned. "Sir, I..."

Huison hissed at him, causing him to abruptly stop speaking. Seconds ticked by with only the sounds of periodic nervous gulping coming from the trembling servant.

"Go clean up that mess in the living room," Huison said at last.

"Right away, sir. Shall I bring your breakfast directly after, Master Loromin?"

"I am no longer hungry!" Huison snapped, glaring at the man as he turned on his heels to walk away. "I am returning to my study. You are not to disturb me until Alford Brandon has arrived."

"Yes, sir," the attendant said, bowing at Huison's departing form. "Of course, sir."

Chapter Seventeen

Kaileih entered the sprawling nursery, pausing near the doorway. She laughed, glimpsing her granddaughter sitting on the floor among half a dozen assorted dolls and stuffed animals. Mahari's little face was compressed into a stern visage as she chattered at her audience, pointing at one page of an open book that she charmingly held upside down. Kaileih found the lilt of a Northern accent in Mahari's speech pattern—likely inherited from Alena—to be endearing, and her smile widened.

Kaileih turned to find Jahd sitting on the floor in the corner nearest the door. He watched Mahari, his hands folded in his lap, a long tangle of curls partly obscuring his eyes. His head shifted slightly, and he glanced up at his grandmother. Pushing the handful of spirals from his face, he finally smiled.

"Good morning, Grandmother," he greeted.

"Good morning to you," Kaileih returned, joining him at the corner and sliding downward into a seated position beside him. She glanced over at him. "You're going to need a haircut soon."

"Yes, ma'am," Jahd answered with a slight smile.

They sat beside one another for several minutes, silently watching as Mahari continued her animated lecture. She suddenly shook her head in mock dissatisfaction, bringing the book closer to the face of one of the dolls, who had obviously missed the point being made. As Mahari traced the page of the book with the tip of a chubby finger, Jahd leaned over and rested his head against Kaileih's upper arm. Kaileih responded by lifting her arm so that he could scoot closer as she held him.

"Have you eaten?" Kaileih asked.

"An omelet," Jahd responded with a nod. "Mahari had pancakes. Have you been out, Grandmother?"

"I have. There was an errand that needed to be taken care of."

"Because of the baby?"

Kaileih looked over at him. "Let's talk about that, Jahd. How do you feel about what's happened?"

"I honestly don't, Grandmother," he said after a pause. "I know others are sad. Alena is also sad, even though that's one less baby for her to take care of."

"But, you don't feel anything?" Kaileih asked.

"We had the same blood, but I didn't know her. It's not the same as Mahari." He shook his head. "Nothing is the same as Mahari."

Kaileih's smile was wistful, as she could not help reflecting upon Rael and Liana's relationship when they were young. "I'm glad that the two of you are so close," she said. They watched while Mahari nodded as if listening to feedback from her audience before turning to another page in the book to begin the next part of the lecture.

"So am I," Jahd said.

"Jahd," Kaileih asked after a moment, "has Huison ever taught you anything about spellweaving?"

"He wasn't allowed to, Grandmother."

"That is a very well-crafted statement, Jahd Dhamon," Kaileih said with a hint of amusement. "Try again."

"He has discussed magic with me," Jahd said. "But he hasn't shown me how to actually do any."

Kaileih nodded. "Fair enough," she said. "Is that something you want, Jahd? Do you want to do magic?"

"Very much," he said firmly.

"What makes you want it so badly?"

Jahd lowered his eyes to his clasped hands. "It's in my blood," he said to his fists.

"You are equally likely to do magic as you are not to," Kaileih told him, "because of your blood." She tilted her head. "How does that make you feel?"

"Trapped," Jahd said in a voice barely above a whisper.

"Jahd, look at me." Jahd slowly raised thickly lashed gray eyes until they met the warm eyes of his grandmother. "We love you," Kaileih said in an unyielding tone. "A proclivity for spellweaving isn't what defines you."

"Yes, Grandmother, but…"

"Who's been telling you otherwise? Is it your mother?"

"No, Grandmother," Jahd said, his hands relaxing until his palms rested atop his knees.

"Explain, please."

Jahd sat fully upright as Kaileih released him from the embrace. "I could never be like you," he said with shining eyes. "I wouldn't dare to try, but… there is something better out there for me than this."

"Jahd, you are only eight years old!" Kaileih said in astonishment. "You don't even have a concept of what 'this' is!" She grabbed his hands, smiling down at him. "Don't sprint before you've even gained your footing. What should be yours will come in time, and that includes whether you ultimately become a spellweaver."

"And you'll love me, regardless?"

Kaileih caressed Jahd's cheek with one hand, smiling. "We all love you, sweetheart."

"Do I still have to go to Pandoufuli?" he asked softly.

"Yes," Kaileih said, pushing the hair out of his face again. "There's no reason for you not to. But, that's still months away."

Jahd looked over at Mahari again. She was still deep in conference with her primarily stuffed staff.

"We'll see what happens in that time," he said.

Somewhere within the depths of her personal darkness, Liana's olfactory senses suddenly came alive. She felt her body shiver as she groaned, shifting slightly. As she struggled to awaken, two thoughts immediately came to mind. The first was that someone was gently stroking the side of her face, even as she felt enveloped by the smell of roses and peppermint. The second thought was a reminder that she had felt no pain at all in days. When she remembered the reason, she felt the sting of tears.

Liana opened her eyes to find her mother smiling gently down at her, a handkerchief in hand to wipe the tears away. Liana scooted until her head was in her mother's lap, and Kaileih gently stroked Liana's hair as she held her.

"You've been tinkering," Liana said of the aroma.

"Perhaps a little," Kaileih admitted.

"Peppermint and roses... together?"

"Yes, one of the hybrids," Kaileih said. "I brought in a small arrangement from the greenhouse this morning."

"I've always loved that," Liana said. "I've always envied it. I used to go out to the gardens with you at home... just knowing that one day I'd be able to do what you did, or maybe something better." Liana sat up with a sniffle, running a hand through her hair. "Where is everyone?"

"The kids are with Linet in the nursery. Evium didn't have any breakfast, so I've lured him away with a frittata."

"He has a weakness for frittatas," Liana said with a chuckle.

"I can teach you to make one while I'm here," Kaileih offered, to which Liana responded by wrinkling her nose. "Ah, whatever was I thinking?" Kaileih smirked, lightly tweaking her daughter's nose.

"Mama... I've been thinking about a lot of things over the last few days."

"Oh?" Kaileih said, getting comfortable by leaning against the headboard of the massive bed.

"Yes," Liana said, "and I need to ask you something..."

"I'm listening."

"I've never questioned you before. I wouldn't now except... so many things are replaying in my head." Liana twisted her fingers together. "I know who Daddy was to me... and who he was to the world. There is so much about his work that I don't understand, probably because I was born plain, but... what really happened to Rael?

"Huison seemed to feel he'd figured it out based upon Daddy's work, but now Rael is dead. Could it mean that Huison was wrong?"

"Huison was not wrong, Liana," Kaileih began carefully. "But, the complexity of the truth has been oversimplified. Huison based his intervention on something that, as it's turned out, he didn't really understand."

"Then explain it to *me*," Liana pleaded, "because I waited six years for my brother to come back and tell me what happened to him. Now, he never will."

Kaileih sighed, rubbing at her temples with her fingertips before sitting fully upright.

"Your brother had already graduated from Breaton and was spending a lot of time in the workroom with your father," she said.

"I think that's where an interest in following your father's work came in."

"Rael could do the same things Daddy could?" Liana said in awe.

"Obviously not, Liana," Kaileih said in a chilled tone.

"But you said..."

"Rael was interested," Kaileih clarified. "He was brilliant at deconstructing magic. Your father and I believed he would excel as a spellbreaker. He would often aid your father by disassembling the craft into pieces, and then your father would finish the work by rearranging it to his will."

"And he could move things with his mind," Liana said softly.

Kaileih nodded. "Yes, he could," she said, "but, that was a reflex for him. He never needed to work at it, and he didn't much like it. What he wanted to do more than anything was study. He was an intellectual."

"He didn't much like it," Liana repeated, shaking her head in annoyance. "What I would do... for a throwaway gift like that... and to travel to other planes, other worlds. The things that Daddy must have seen and the people he must have met." She studied her mother. "What do you think it was like? Do you think there are other worlds like ours?"

"With some differences," Kaileih said. "Some are farther behind than ours... some are remarkably similar, except spellweaving is the stuff of legends for which countless have lost their lives to death by fire. Other worlds have advanced to a point where even Evium's ingenious inventions are commonplace if not entirely obsolete. Some are virtually uninhabitable, but for a certain type of creature. But, no matter where your father's studies may have taken him, this was his home."

"Because you were here," Liana said with a dreamy sigh before her eyes hardened. "Meanwhile, I got to see none of it," she continued, her jaw tight. "Daddy was getting Rael prepped to follow in his footsteps, even if only to a certain point, and I can't do anything at all!"

"You need to listen to me, Liana Rose," Kaileih said. "You insist upon glamorizing something that, when one is improperly prepared or maliciously motivated, can be extremely dangerous. You have two examples right in front of you—what happened to your brother when he tried to save your father, and now what has happened to your brother when Huison tried to save him! That is what you should focus on! That should be what you take from this—those examples!"

"I understand that, Mama!"

Kaileih sat back again, looking at her daughter. "No," she said. "No, I don't think you really do, Liana. No matter how hard I have tried since you were a little girl, you're..." Kaileih grabbed one of Liana's hands, interlacing their fingers. "Let this go, Liana. I'm afraid that your unwillingness to embrace reality and appreciate what a rich life you've been blessed with might lead you into something you cannot escape from. I can't lose you, too."

"I know, Mama, and I'm not trying to do that..."

"You also have two children of your own to think about. Jahd and Mahari look to you as an example. Do you want them feeling like they're not good enough?"

"Of course not!" Liana said.

"Then you need to stop this and stop it now!" Kaileih said. "I mean it, Liana!" Kaileih squeezed Liana's hand, leaning closer until their gazes locked. "I love my son very much. I feel certain, though, that he died along with your father that day. I don't know the extent of the damage done when he attempted to go after Amriel. But he was not himself when he returned, and you need to grasp the reality that there are consequences to overreaching."

"Then why did you let this go on for so long?" Liana demanded. "If Rael—the Rael that we knew and loved—has been dead for six years, why didn't you let him go then?"

"If something were to happen to you... to Jahd or Mahari... is that what you'd expect? Do I count you as a loss and move on with my life? Any hope... any hope at all... of getting Rael back was a hell of a lot better than the thought of throwing him away for good."

"You lost him anyway, Mama," Liana said coldly, snatching her hand back. "What difference does it matter when?"

"Liana," Kaileih began with shining eyes, "I hope that you never have to answer that question when it comes to your own children."

Chapter Eighteen

Huison walked through the gardens of Dalenbeigh, gesturing as he moved about. The landscaping was immaculate; nothing at the level of the Den, but magnificent in its own right. He crossed a narrow, arc-shaped stone bridge as a school of colorful fish swam through the crystal waters of the artificial stream underneath. Continuing along a stone walkway, Huison cleared his throat and resumed his imagined conversation.

"I am so glad that you both could visit me today," he said. "I have looked forward to this moment, and I have commissioned rooms for you..." He faltered, frowning. "No. That sounds... No."

Huison shook his head, walking past the clusters of azaleas, blue irises, and purple rhododendrons.

"I cannot accurately express what this day means to me," he began again. "In the last month I have been working to ensure that you will... No, no! Mahari is a child. She will not understand what I am trying to say..."

"Excuse me, Master Loromin," said a voice behind him. "You wanted to see me?"

Huison turned to find that he was being watched by someone on the opposite side of the stone bridge he had just crossed. The man was deeply tanned from years of working outdoors, with sun-bleached blond hair and bright green eyes that seemed in the habit of squinting. Though somewhat covered in patches of dirt from head to foot, his posture was relaxed as he wiped at a line of sweat upon his brow.

"Ah, Seph," Huison said, turning back as Seph crossed the bridge to meet him. "I am glad of your arrival. I meant to discuss this with you before, but things have been busy as of late."

"Yes, sir, Master Loromin," Seph answered, wiping his palms against the rough fabric of his shirt. "What can I do for you?"

"Everything is ready for the initial visit from my daughter that is to take place later this morning," Huison said. "I want her to feel fully at home here and, since you command my stables, I feel you are in the perfect position to put a last piece into place."

"Of course, sir, whatever I can do."

"I need a duo of well-trained and temperate ponies, one each for her and her brother, and I want them to be the exact breed as the one ridden by her grandmother when she came to see me. I think that familiarity will help the two of them to feel comfortable. I did not see the beast, but since you cared for it in the stable, you should know the breed I mean."

Seph scratched at his head as his squint deepened.

"I'm afraid I can't do that, sir," he said.

"Why ever not?" Huison asked. "Are you saying that you, who boast of being one of the finest horsemen in the region, cannot acquire the breed in question?"

"No, sir, that's not what I'm saying."

"Then what is it?" Huison asked, gritting his teeth.

"I'm just saying, sir, that I don't recall any such lady. You're saying someone came to see you some weeks back, and she was on a horse?"

Huison stared at him. "Of course, she did!" he snapped. "It was an incredibly early morning a little over four weeks ago, on the same day we received unexpected rainfall. Surely, you remember that! A good amount of hay was ruined because you had not yet brought it all in and it was caught in the deluge!"

"And you rained a storm over my head because of it, yes," Seph said, unable to resist a chuckle. "Well, I remember that day for certain. But I promise you sir... there was no lady."

"You hardly remembered at first," Huison said. "How can I trust you to recall anything else?"

"Because I have an eye for the horses... and for the ladies."

Huison paused, his eyes widening. What trickery was this? How could Seph have missed Kaileih or the horse she had brought onto the property?

"Perhaps you passed one another," Huison said, feeling less sure of himself. "If you were out attempting to salvage that hay, she might have escaped notice."

"I suppose that's possible, Master Loromin," Seph conceded, "but, I was consistently in and out of the stables even while the rain was going on. I would have remembered seeing an unfamiliar horse in one of the stalls."

"Yes," Huison said, distracted. "Yes, I suppose you would have."

"I will keep an eye out for the lady from now on, sir... so we can get those ponies for your little girl and her brother."

Huison was so immersed in his own thoughts that he did not notice Seph watching him for a few moments before politely bowing and walking away.

"I believe we should arrive shortly, dear," Clea said.

Jahd, who spent the bulk of the trip alternately reading and gazing out of the carriage window with an occasional sigh, turned away from the view of the sprawling countryside to study the older woman.

"That's good," he said. "I can't imagine how Uncle Huison made this trip so often."

He glanced at Mahari, who was still curled up atop the plush seating after falling asleep when they were only an hour outside of Kynedal.

"Jahd," Clea began, keeping her tone sweet and her pale green eyes focused on her knitting, "do you remember what your parents said about the visit and about making sure that your sister is comfortable?"

"Of course. If Mahari doesn't want to stay, then we're not going to."

"Are you all right with that?"

Jahd shrugged. "Have I any choice?" he asked.

The speed of the carriage decreased before making a left turn and continuing along. Though the ride had not been bumpy at all, Jahd could feel an improvement in the road's smoothness beneath them. When he looked out of the window again, he could not see much beyond the splashes of green, yellow, and orange encompassing the line of maple trees along the road.

As the carriage began slowing down again, Clea dropped her knitting into her lap and raised the flap covering the window on her side of the cabin. Jahd looked past her and out of the window as they passed an open, wrought-iron gate being held open by a uniformed attendant.

"All right," Clea said as she carefully tucked her knitting into a small tote. "Looks like we've arrived."

"Should I wake Mahari?" Jahd asked.

"No, dear. Perhaps this is for the best. I can have her brought inside and sit with her until she wakes. Might be easier on her that way, and it will give you the opportunity to catch up with Master Loromin."

"If that's the type of horse you meant, Master Loromin, it'd be my pleasure to seek such a remarkable specimen," Seph said in a voice filled with awe.

Huison stood in the paved courtyard as he watched the approach of the large silver-accented black carriage. The horses pulling the carriage were unlike any that Huison had seen before: large, muscled specimens with flowing dark manes and a shining coat that made them appear to have been chiseled from blocks of oiled mahogany.

He had never had occasion to study the horses housed within the Chatelain stables. Huison felt certain, though, that this specific breed was unique. The musculature of both animals bespoke endurance that likely made the trek from Kynedal an easy one. While part of Huison felt that this was likely the exact horse that Kaileih journeyed upon, that Seph claimed to not have seen it still troubled Huison greatly.

The carriage came to a stop, the horses standing powerfully straight and seeming to suffer no ill-effects from the journey as the coachman climbed down from where he sat. Removing his hat, he bowed in Huison's direction, keeping his eyes respectfully lowered.

"I bid you a good morning, Master Loromin, sir," the young man greeted.

"I am unfamiliar with you," Huison returned. "Where is Fayal?"

"Pardon me, sir! Fayal is with his wife, who just gave birth to their fourth child some time during the night. I am Millard, sir. I've been apprenticing with Fayal in the stables of the Chatelain estate."

Huison was not at all comfortable with someone he considered a stranger in charge of transporting his child. However, there was not much he could do about it. He realized it was best to stifle his true feelings on the matter rather than bringing them up via courier to Liana and Evium, risking any future visitations.

"Very well," Huison consented, waving a hand dismissively. "How was the trip?"

"Smooth, sir," Millard said. "The young lady fell asleep almost immediately after departing. I believe she's still dozing."

"Mahari is asleep?" Huison said with a frown.

"That she is, Master Loromin," Clea said as she moved through the open door of the carriage, holding onto the hand of the footman as she descended the steps. Once standing securely on the slate-colored driveway, he handed over her tote. Smiling politely at Huison, she bobbed a curtsy. "I was hoping to get her inside, sir, and then she can be well-rested for later."

"Of course," Huison said, turning to his right to signal that another of his staff should go over to the carriage.

He then froze briefly as Jahd alighted from the carriage, ignoring the outstretched hand of the footman as he shook his curls out of his face and moved to stand beside Clea.

"Well," Huison said after taking a deep breath, "I am exhilarated to have you all here. Welcome to Dalenbeigh."

"I trust you find your lodgings comfortable?" Huison asked a short while later, his voice lowered. He turned to Clea, who was hovering nearby, and she smiled with a brief incline of her head.

"Indeed, sir," she said, matching his volume. "It's more than enough, and thank you so kindly for attaching the space to the room here, in case the young lady needs me."

"Of course," Huison said, turning back to the large loft-style bed in which Mahari peacefully slept.

The color scheme for the large bedroom and playroom—primarily rose gold and mauve—was chosen based upon the design of Mahari's nursery when she was born. Reluctant to ask, Huison instead hoped that Liana had maintained those colors so that Mahari would find comfort in an environment like what she was used to.

Huison had spared no expense, from the rose gold-flecked accents on the textured walls to the lush carpeting upon the floor, and even the supple sheets upon which Mahari lay. The second "story" of the immense bed was covered in a variety of colorful stuffed animals and dolls.

"Has Jahd settled in?"

"Yes, sir," Clea answered. "He was on the bed reading a book when I left him just now."

Huison could not help a wry smile. "He has not yet unpacked, correct?" He turned back to Clea. "I imagine you have asked him to refrain until we see how his sister fares?" Clea blushed to the roots of her silver chignon and opened her mouth as if to explain. "There is no need. The logic is sound." Huison got up from the bed and fixed Clea in his amber gaze. "How much do you know, Clea? Be frank."

Clea's blush deepened, and she averted her eyes. "Master Loromin, it isn't my place..."

"I only ask for the truth," Huison said, moving away from the bed and through the extensive suite. "Was there some directive given instructing you to withhold any information from me regarding Mahari?"

"No, sir!" Clea said as she walked alongside him, clearly appalled on her employer's behalf.

"As you will likely be the caretaker each time Mahari visits, there should be some rapport between us." He arched a dark brow as he turned to face her again. "You know she is my daughter, yes?"

"Yes," Clea answered after a moment. "Lord and Lady Chatelain brought me into their confidence in the days before the children were due to visit Dalenbeigh."

"And, that coachman..."

Clea shook her head. "No, sir. Millard knows nothing. They shared the information only with me and it will go no further."

Huison nodded, glancing behind them and toward the bed before looking at Clea again.

"I will leave you to sit with her," he conceded. "Someone will also come up shortly to see if there is anything you need personally. It is such a long trip from Kynedal."

"Thank you, sir," Clea said, waiting until Huison turned away from her before moving back toward the bed.

Departing the bedroom, Huison moved along the hallway, the soft soles of his leather moccasins silent against the bloodwood flooring. He reached the double doors leading to the suite designated for Jahd and, finding them closed, lifted a fist to knock.

"Come in, Huison," came Jahd's voice from inside. Steeling himself, Huison entered and shut the door behind him.

"You need a haircut," Huison said in greeting. "It surprises me that Liana has not seen to that by now."

"She's been a tad busy of late," Jahd commented, turning a page in the book he held. "I'm sure you've heard."

"About that," Huison began, extending a hand in Jahd's direction. The book Jahd held was snatched from his grasp, floating across the room to land in Huison's outstretched grip. "You withheld information," Huison said as he idly flipped through the pages. "You did not see fit to tell me that the extraction could prove deadly."

"You never asked," Jahd said, an amused expression on his face.

"I was there to help him!"

"You were there to help yourself," Jahd countered, folding his hands in his lap. "So, where do we stand now?"

"What do you mean?"

"It was very cute what you did just now," Jahd said, nodding toward the book. "Is that the extent of what magical talents you possess?"

"I am an academic," Huison said tightly. "As such, my abilities are vast."

"Actual abilities, though? You pieced enough together to discern my presence and cast me out, but... what else is there? You couldn't even keep Rael Dhamon alive." Jahd smiled, tilting his head. "You never told me, Huison. When we made our deal, you promised to relieve me of that invalid's body in exchange for something you wanted and that only I could give you... but, you haven't yet told me what that is."

"And, yet you so readily agreed." Huison moved through the room, book still in hand.

"Of course. I wanted out."

"How did you blunder into becoming trapped inside the body of Rael Dhamon?" Huison asked, changing tack. "You latched onto him and remained for six years... why?"

"His mind shattered because of his time between the planes," Jahd muttered. "He had no will left... no soul. I meant only to remain long enough to find someone else to graft onto, but... I was essentially paralyzed inside of him, and it became too late."

The duo locked eyes for several moments, after which Huison simply smiled. "So, you were waiting for someone in particular," he said. "Surely not Kaileih, of whom you have spoken in nothing but reverent tones."

"I could never!" Jahd blurted, reddening before taking a breath and speaking in a calmer tone. "It was she that found us in the laboratory on the night that Amriel was taken. Had it been... Had anyone else discovered us, I could have made my escape sooner. But, I would not use her in that way, not even for a moment."

"You refuse to tell me why that is. Even though you have so willingly touched upon your adoration of her, the origins of that affection have remained concealed."

Jahd's expression gradually blanked, though his eyes became icy, causing Huison to chuckle.

"We are still keeping secrets from each other, my good friend," Huison said. "You choose not to tip your hand, and I shall not show mine."

"How can I help you, Huison, if you don't tell me what you want?" Jahd said acidly. "You thought to win the love of a woman by curing her brother. Now he's dead, which is no direct fault of mine. What can I possibly do for you now?"

"I will divulge my intentions," Huison said amiably, "at the right moment. It will take time."

"Fair enough," Jahd said with a nod before extending a hand. "As will I, at the right time. May I have my book back now, Uncle Hui?"

"Not even able to take it back from me, are you?" Huison said with a chuckle, walking over to hand the text back to Jahd. He continued to laugh as he returned to the door and opened it, leaving Jahd to glare after his departing form.

Chapter Nineteen

Mahari watched with rounded eyes as the okonomiyaki took shape on a griddle set beside the dining room table. She awoke from a nap absolutely famished. Huison was adamant that she have whatever she wanted. Savory pancakes were the safest bet.

After selecting from an array of first-rate ingredients, much to the delight of Huison and the resident chef, she was served the aromatic result of her combined choices, garnished with dried bonito flakes, pickled red ginger, and sliced morsels of karasumi. The look of joy on her face while she tucked into her meal nearly brought tears to Huison's amber-colored eyes.

"I hope you find the accommodations to your liking," Huison said after clearing his throat, toying with the stem of his wineglass. "If you find that something is distasteful, of course, please let me know. I am happy to make modifications until you are satisfied."

Mahari stopped chewing as she cast a sidelong glance at her brother sitting to her left. Jahd, adding sauce to his okonomiyaki creation, returned a reassuring smile.

"Do you like your room, Mahari?" Jahd translated for his sister.

"Yes," she said clearly, a bit of green onion stuck to her bottom lip as she nodded. "It's pretty."

"It really is lovely," Clea offered from her place across from Mahari as the latter returned to her lunch. "I'm sure that both the children appreciate it."

"Yes, Uncle Huison," Jahd said as he stabbed his fork into a serving of green salad. "You've done a great job. Your decorating skills are top-notch."

Huison narrowed his eyes and refrained from commenting as he ate his own salad.

"I don't think you need to worry, Master Loromin. Mahari is enjoying herself immensely."

Huison was jarred from his thoughts, turning to look down at Clea as she smiled beside him. He did not know how long she had been standing there; he had been so immersed in his own reflections as he watched Mahari tumbling around in the large backyard under the watchful eye of Jahd. Huison found her breathless shrieks of laughter musical and could not help dreaming of what it would be like to have Mahari at Dalenbeigh permanently flourishing under the loving gazes of both her parents.

"You're doing the right thing," Clea continued as Huison looked back toward the children. "By allowing her space and the chance to become comfortable, she will come around."

Clea was obviously referring to the way lunch transpired with Huison's repeated and failed attempts to engage Mahari in conversation until the child became so discomfited that she had stopped eating altogether. Huison, unable to finish his own lunch because of the distress he had unwittingly caused, remained mute at his own table until Mahari finally resumed eating. He had not yet tried speaking to her again.

"I'm sure that you feel there's already been enough space as it is, with her being nearly two years old and all," Clea surmised. "All good things in time, sir."

There was a spark in Huison's eyes as he smiled.

"I could not agree more," he said.

Huison sat back with a sigh, setting the quill atop the desk before rubbing his eyes. The rest of the day went as well as expected, though Huison could not help feeling resentful at having to maneuver a wide berth around his own child. It was, however, an arrangement that Mahari easily settled into. Though most of her attention was still paid to Clea and Jahd, it warmed Huison's heart when she at last smiled in his general direction.

Dinner was a modest affair, scaled down from the initial plans discussed with kitchen staff. The quartet dined on fish stew in a rich broth with vegetables, after which Clea surprised them all by baking decadent double chocolate cookies. Huison had indulged in enough of Kaileih's baked offerings to recognize the recipe as hers. Though Clea's were not as indulgent, it didn't stop him from sampling a few.

Only after both children were dispatched to their respective suites for pre-bedtime baths did Huison retreat to his study to reflect upon the day. He wondered how, at this rate, he'd be able to win Mahari over before Jahd would have to attend Pandoufuli two months hence. Huison cursed himself for not starting visits sooner. With things as they were, Mahari would not likely feel comfortable visiting Dalenbeigh with only Clea in tow.

Huison was glad that Jahd would attend Pandoufuli. Huison's parents summarily barred him from contact with anyone within the Loromin family once it became known that he exhibited magical ability. He still, however, maintained various connections within the academy with those who, if discovered to have a forbidden interest in magic, would lose their own livelihoods. Through them he hoped to monitor Jahd and make sure that things remained on track while Huison organized plans for his next move.

He was lucky. To stumble upon the find of a lifetime while at his wits' end had been nothing but providence. Huison wondered why Kaileih, as astute as he knew her to be, had not gleaned that something otherworldly caused her son's distress. Then again, she was likely unaware of the intricacies surrounding her husband's work and did not know what to look for. Her point of view was also likely clouded by the love and pity she felt for Rael. As Huison had no such impediment, his view was unhindered.

Rael's mind was not his own, and the adulation of Kaileih Dhamon had been drilled into the creature within for years, causing the reluctance to even use Kaileih as a temporary means of escape. Huison found her to be more awe-inspiring by the day.

He sighed again, rubbing at drowsy eyes with one hand. Though the extraction and resulting binding into Jahd's body had taken place some time ago, Huison still had not fully recovered, and he wondered how long it would be until he did. It did not thrill Huison to find silver strands infiltrating the darkness of his hair, however distinguished they made him look. He was, after all, not yet thirty. Visible signs of aging were not something he expected to be concerned with for many years. Perhaps once Jahd was at school and Mahari a regular presence at Dalenbeigh, could Huison finally afford the rest he deserved.

Huison's amber gaze flicked toward the closed door at the sound of a series of light knocks. Wholly uninterested in getting up, he instead used the power of his mind to twist the latch and open the door.

"Excuse me, Master Loromin," Clea said, smiling from the doorway. "I wanted to bid you a good night, sir, and thank you so much again for your hospitality."

"You are quite welcome, Clea," Huison said with a weary smile. "Are the children settled in?"

"They are, indeed, sir. The young sir is in his room reading, but his sister has already fallen asleep, bless her. Such a day she's had! She really enjoyed playing in her room after dinner, with so many nice, new things to choose from."

"That pleases me to know," Huison said. "Please do rest well, Clea. I will see you in the morning at breakfast."

"Yes, sir. Of course, sir."

As Clea closed the door softly behind her, Huison stared out into nothingness. Though the day had not gone as he hoped, it was still ending with his child under his roof rather than on the road back to Kynedal.

Huison got up from his desk, hoping as he left the study for the kitchen that there was at least one cookie left for him to enjoy. A short while later, after he had bathed and changed into his pajamas and robe before heading along the hallway toward Mahari's room, he could not help smiling. His daughter was in his home, the home that would one day belong to her. His own grandchildren would someday travel along the same hallway.

He did his best to enter the bedroom, making no noise, even closing the door softly. He could hear Clea's snores through the open door that connected her room with Mahari's, and he wondered how Mahari could sleep at all. As his eyes adjusted to the darkened room, however, he realized that Mahari's bed was empty.

Huison paused, brow furrowing. Had she crept into bed with Clea? It was not unexpected, considering the strangeness of the environment. But he certainly did not intend to sidle into Clea's bedroom to gaze upon his daughter. With another sigh, he turned away from the bed, preparing to leave, when he paused again, tilting his head.

Was that singing?

Huison glanced back over to the bed, this time at the loft above it. Mahari was not there. Where was she, then? Turning on his heels as he surveyed the room, his eyes finally landed upon the double doors leading to the walk-in closet. His breath caught as he listened. Mahari *was* singing, and though he could hear her stumble over some words, her enunciation of the lyrics and overall pitch were remarkable for a child so young.

The song was sweet, and the words that Huison could make out seemed sad and he wondered if the original composition was the same way or if Mahari had somehow made it so. As much as he did not want to disturb her, though, he could not allow her to remain where she was.

"Mahari?" he called gently, rapping with his fingertips against the left closet door.

When the singing abruptly stopped, he gently slid the door open to find her wrapped in a blanket and sitting on the floor with her short legs crossed in front of her. Huison smiled down at Mahari before lowering himself on his haunches until they were closer to eye level.

"Hello," he greeted.

"Hi," Mahari responded after several seconds.

"We thought you had fallen asleep," Huison said, keeping his tone light.

"I was."

"Did something frighten you? Did you have a bad dream?" When Huison realized no answer was forthcoming, he struggled for the best way he could communicate with Mahari without causing her to shut down as she had at lunch. He cleared his throat and decided on a fresh approach. "I heard a beautiful song just now. Was that you?" To Huison's immense relief, Mahari's face lit up, and she nodded. "Do you like to sing?"

Mahari's eyes lowered as she fiddled with the surrounding blanket. "I sing with Papa," she mumbled.

A chill froze Huison's smile into place before traveling through the rest of his body, rendering him immobile.

"Your... he... sings to you?" he stammered.

Mahari nodded again, continuing to twist a corner of cloth around her tiny fingers. Huison found himself unable to look at her and he instead focused upon the blanket which, the longer he looked at it, he realized was not a blanket at all. It was a light blue, long-sleeved tunic, one of many tailored creations he had seen stretched across the broad upper body of Evium Chatelain.

She had brought Evium's shirt along for emotional support. Huison's eyes stung, though he did his best to keep his voice steady.

"I am sorry that I do not sing," he said, a gentle crease in his brow. "Perhaps when you find yourself ready, you might teach me to?"

The briefest of smiles appeared on Mahari's little face as she nodded. "Okay," she consented in a whisper.

"Would you like to return to bed? You can continue to sing there if you like."

Mahari unfolded her legs, getting up from the floor without using her hands to push herself up or steady her balance. Huison got to his feet as well, and the duo walked wordlessly back to Mahari's bed. She settled in, the shirt still wrapped around her, as Huison tucked her in.

"All set?" he asked, to which she responded with yet another nod. "Are you in need of something to drink?"

"No, thank you," she said before yawning.

"I bid you a good night, Mahari," Huison said.

"Good night," Mahari said, closing her eyes and turning with her back to Huison.

Huison remained bedside, watching his daughter as she succumbed to slumber. Only after several minutes did he turn away, finding Jahd standing in the now-open doorway, watching. As Huison approached, Jahd backed away and watched warily as Huison continued down the hallway to return to his suite.

Chapter Twenty

Liana stepped outside, slightly breathless. She turned back to the house, shaking her head as her brow creased, before continuing through the backyard toward the west gardens.

As she grew closer to her destination, it did not surprise her to see a familiar figure ahead. She paused briefly, unsure whether she wanted to disturb anyone, and considered returning to the house.

"You should be resting."

Liana shook her head again, not at all surprised that her mother sensed her presence before seeing her. She slipped her hands into the pockets of her black and red gingham shift dress. The dress was comfortable and slightly oversized. In it, Liana felt safe in the illusion that she could hide her shrinking midsection.

"I was just about to tell you that!" Liana said in return.

Kaileih turned to look at her daughter. She was kneeling near the plot into which Rael had so recently been lowered, and a polished black granite Kerber memorial concealed the freshly covered patch of dirt. The name 'Rael Sage Dhamon' engraved upon the arched headstone blurred in Liana's vision until she blinked and looked away.

"I'm not the one who needs it," Kaileih commented quietly, lightly digging at a small patch of earth nearby.

"I beg to differ," Liana said. "I don't think you've slowed down at all." Liana sighed. "You should come inside, Mama. It looks like it'll rain at any moment."

"Good! I have only a few more flowers to plant before I complete the border. The rain will help once I'm done. Is that why you're here? Afraid I'll melt in a little drizzle?"

"They're dismantling the nursery," Liana said, taking a seat upon the polished top of a nearby basalt bench. "I'm not supposed to know they're doing it."

"And you wouldn't if you'd stay in bed as you were told," Kaileih said.

"Ah, Mama... I'm tired of being in bed." Liana picked at a loose stitch on one of her pockets. "Mama... did you tell them to take the nursery apart?"

"I did not. It wasn't my decision to make."

"Evium said nothing about wanting it done."

"It has nothing to do with want, Liana," Kaileih said, looking up from her work again. "We are all feeling this loss differently. Your husband is only trying to protect you now in a way he doesn't feel he could before."

"Protect me how?"

"He had to sit and watch while another man did something that he could not. You were bleeding and in distress, and Fayal was the one to bring you inside the house so that I could tend to you. Evium's sense of loss is about more than the child."

"I hardly ever think about Evium's disability anymore," Liana insisted. "I thought we were past all of that."

"You might be."

"But what more can I do about it? I thought... this was..." Liana studied her fingernails. "I thought this was what we needed to make

195

things right between us again, but... I lost my daughter. Evium's daughter. The one I owed him."

"Stop that!" Kaileih said in a sharp tone. "Evium loves Mahari. In his heart, she is his, and he never sought to replace her. You don't owe him that and realizing that will help you heal, too." Kaileih shook her head as she busied herself with the flowers.

"You're planting hibiscus for him... just like you did for Daddy," Liana commented softly after watching Kaileih for several moments. "They'll attract every butterfly for miles. Rael would love that." When Kaileih did not respond, Liana's smile faded as she sighed again. "Mama, Evium told me you declined his offer to come live here with us." She twisted the wedding rings on her finger. "I thought that by having Rael here, you'd also want to be here."

"This was not for me, Liana Rose," Kaileih said as she finished her work. "As considerate as it is for you and Evium to allocate a section of property on your land as a last resting place, this was to assuage the guilt you felt over not visiting your brother at Vespers."

"I can't go back and change that, though!" Liana rose from the bench and sat beside her mother on the grass. "Don't you want to be here with us? Why are you staying in Tilehn? Couldn't you have Daddy moved to a plot out here? We should bury him near Rael and..."

Liana's gaze shifted until she was looking several feet away toward the center of the west garden and the small, bronze memorial plaque affixed to a granite base and resting in front of a newly planted cedar sapling.

"What did you put on the inscription?" Liana asked, as tears streamed from her eyes. "We never got to pick a name."

Kaileih leaned over, wrapping her arms around her daughter and pulling her close.

"Beloved," Kaileih said, "because that's what she is."

"Please don't leave," Liana whispered, clinging to her mother.

Kaileih sighed and said nothing.

Chapter Twenty-One

Liana swept along the hallway, the slits on either side of her burgundy silk dress giving brief glimpses of her long legs as she moved. Embroidered floral accents dotted the dress from collar to hem, set with the same seed pearls woven through the braid in Liana's dark hair.

"Ah, good morning, Miss Liana!" came a cheerful voice from the foyer below. Liana smiled, though she did not draw her attention away from the flowers she stopped to tinker with, recognizing the voice of the woman who had been the supervisor of all goings-on within the estate since its inception.

"Is it still morning, Clea?" she asked as the woman climbed the stairs to join her. "I felt certain I'd slept the day away."

Clea laughed. "Almost, but not quite," she admitted. "Lord Chatelain gave us specific instructions not to disturb you. Now that you're awake, though, I'll have your rooms attended to right away."

At last, Liana turned to her. "I appreciate that, Clea. My husband was right—I needed the extra sleep. Yesterday's celebration was marvelous! You and the others did such a stellar job of getting everything done. It'll be the talk of Kynedal for months, I'm sure!"

"All thanks to your mother," Clea blushed. "We certainly couldn't have pulled it off without her. A going-away party for the young sir would have been audacious enough, but to combine it with the second birthday of the little one was extraordinary!"

"My mother is a miracle," Liana agreed with a laugh. "I don't suppose she's slept in at all?"

"Oh, no, ma'am! Mrs. Dhamon was already awake by the time I made it into the kitchen this morning. She spent time in the gardens and greenhouses as usual and selected some choice produce for us to use today. Should I put an order in for your breakfast, ma'am?"

"After I've looked in on the children," Liana said. "Perhaps the three of us can eat together."

"They've been up for a few hours already!" Clea said. "They're in the east garden with your mother."

"And my husband?" Liana asked lightly, the smile still firmly affixed upon her face.

"In his workshop, of course!" Clea laughed. "Probably coming up with a smashing goodbye present for the young sir. You know men..."

"I do, indeed," Liana said. "I'll join my mother outside. I'd like something light prepared for me and brought to the solarium in three-quarters of an hour. I have some last-minute details to iron out before our departure for Pandoufuli tomorrow morning."

"It will be so odd without our little man of the house about," Clea said with a sigh.

"It will be quite the adjustment, and it's important that Mahari's health and well-being are maintained during this time. The separation won't be easy for her."

"Yes, ma'am, of course!"

"Speaking of, I'm heading out. Will you also be sure to prepare an assortment of fruit, and have it brought out to my mother and the children? Don't forget the Moon Drops—my mother loves those."

Liana descended the staircase, making her way through the Den and out of the back doors leading to the gardens. She hugged herself, rubbing at her arms because of the slight chill of the air as she wondered why she did not bother to grab a wrap on her way out. She felt warmed, however, by the sight of her mother sitting with Mahari on one of the crescent-shaped benches in the garden. They were looking through one of Mahari's picture books, which lay open and flat atop the circular table as Jahd, on the bench across from them, looked on. Though both children were wearing light coats, the tips of Mahari's ears were tinged with pink, along with her cheeks. Liana could not see much of Jahd's ears, however.

"The barber will be here this afternoon," she said, greeting her son with a tousle. "I'd say we've allowed you to go woods-wild long enough. You need to get cleaned up for school."

"Yes, ma'am," Jahd said, shaking his curls back from where they had been jostled.

"Good morning, Mama," Liana said to Kaileih as she sat beside Jahd.

"Mo-ning, Mama," Mahari mimicked sweetly, as she beamed up at Kaileih.

"Good morning to you," Kaileih returned as she flipped a page. "Such an expansive wardrobe and you don't own a wrap?"

Liana laughed. "I've only come out for a moment," she said. "I have a few more things to square away before tomorrow, so I'll be working in the solarium."

"Ah, you and Evium will be in the solarium for the rest of the morning?" Kaileih asked lightly.

"I believe he is in his workshop," Liana said after a pause.

When Kaileih's gaze lifted to meet Liana's, the latter could only hold the look for a short time before averting her eyes.

"The dog ran," Mahari chirped to the book. She then looked up at Kaileih and tugged gently at a braid. "Turn, Grandmama..." Still staring at Liana, Kaileih absently turned the page, and Mahari focused on it for a few seconds before continuing. "...down the... r-ro... rod?"

Kaileih looked down at the page after smiling at the expression of incredulity on Liana's face.

"Road," she offered softly.

"Road!" Mahari repeated triumphantly. "Down the road!"

Liana put a hand to her mouth, stunned as both Clea and Alena approached the table. Clea was balancing a platter in her chubby hands as Alena hefted table settings.

"My goodness, ladies!" Kaileih said, eyeing the platter as Clea put it down. "Are those Moon Drops I see? You darlings! Would one of you be so kind and sit here with the children for a moment while I have a chat with my beautiful daughter?" She smiled at Mahari, who had already forgotten about her book and was reaching for a juicy slice of pluot.

"Your expression tells me you did not know," Kaileih said once she and Liana had moved away from the table to walk through the garden.

"No," Liana said dejectedly. "I've never seen her do anything like that before. I would have told you."

Kaileih nodded. "I've been watching her at playtime," she admitted. "Something about her style of banter had changed. You should have seen her a few months back, holding a meeting with her toys. She was teaching them things, and it made me wonder. So... I bought a set of books as one of her birthday presents and brought one of them out with us today."

"So, that was the first time?" Liana asked, feeling a combination of jealousy and relief.

"That she's done it in front of me, yes."

"Mama, Jahd was four when he began reading. Mahari is half that!"

"I know." Kaileih stopped walking and turned to her daughter. "You should start interviewing tutors for her," Kaileih said.

"A tutor?" Liana scoffed, lightly rubbing her forehead as she also stopped walking. "She's two years old!"

"And, in the swarm of the last few months she seems to have taught herself to read. Is it any wonder? Look at who you are. Look at who her father is. She's already advanced beyond her years, Liana. She's expressive and vocal... you didn't speak half as well at her age."

"Oh, Mama," Liana sighed.

"And, since things seem to go better than expected during visits to Dalenbeigh, perhaps Huison might also be consulted about this."

"Must he be?"

"Don't be daft, Liana. Mahari is his child. Why upset the apple cart?"

"He'll want to tutor her himself, Mama, you know that. He won't want to entrust her to the care of anyone else."

"He can tutor her when she goes to see him, but the decision is yours when it comes to her time at home. You and Evium must maintain a united front in this."

"United front," Liana said, shaking her head.

Kaileih studied her. "The two of you were recovering well enough. What's gone on?"

"I don't know," Liana conceded. "It's nothing I can put a finger on. We're so... polite to one another now. Things have been fine, it's just..."

"You'd rather that he rained a storm over your head every day?"

"Of course not, Mama..."

"He works hard, he's attentive, and the two of you are finally on common ground for the first time in a long while. Jahd has rebounded beautifully and has had no other seizures, and Mahari is happy, healthy, and highly intelligent. Why must you continue to invent problems?" Kaileih shook her head. "If you find that it's passion you lack, Jahd will be away at school and Mahari is getting to be of an age where she doesn't need to be attached to your hip at all times. She'll be especially busy once you've engaged a tutor. Divert some time and energy into your husband. He deserves that, as do you."

"You're right," Liana said, nodding. "As much as I don't want my son to go, it would be wise to invest that time in myself and Evium."

"Don't merely speak the words, Liana Rose," Kaileih cautioned. "You and your husband have rebounded from something that would tear most apart permanently. Don't squander it or take it for granted. I imagine it'd be a blow to your pretty ego to expect him to one day still be there for you, only to find that he's not."

Liana, horrified by the thought, stiffened.

"The feeling you're having right now," Kaileih said with a laugh, "keep it in mind. Use it to help keep you grounded. I'll help however I can."

"From Tilehn?" Liana scoffed.

"Are you on about that again?" Kaileih asked, smirking as she linked her arm with Liana's, and they resumed their walk.

"How long before we need to be downstairs and ready to go?"

"Hmm, about four hours."

203

"No," Liana groaned, her head resting upon Evium's bare chest. "It's too soon... much too soon."

"Hmm," Evium said again, his eyes closed as he held Liana's naked body against his.

"I'm going to be exhausted," Liana yawned.

"Serves you right," Evium said agreeably. "There I was in my workroom minding my own business when you strolled in wearing that red number."

"Burgundy," Liana giggled.

"Whatever!" Evium laughed. "What got into you?"

"You're complaining?"

"Oh, no! I'm just wondering so I can make sure it gets into you again!"

"Silly," Liana said, playfully slapping one of his pecs. "I just... had a talk with Mama. She made me realize how impractical we've both been over the last few months."

"Oh, that goddess!" Evium drawled. "She told you to do all that, did she? That bit in the workroom was her idea? I'll be picking those little pearls out of my backside for a month! What about the part in my shower chair an hour ago?"

"Vi!" Liana shrieked before burying her face in his armpit to stifle her giggles. As she calmed down, Evium squeezed her harder against him.

"I've been trying so hard," he said in his normal tone. "I haven't wanted to rush you... or put any pressure on you at all. What happened wasn't easy, Liana, I know that. I also know that it's different for you. I couldn't ever feel it the way you do."

"I felt the same of you," Liana confessed. "I feel so guilty, Vi."

"You've nothing to feel guilty about. It was out of our hands."

"She was our daughter, though—your daughter—and I lost her."

"Mahari is my daughter," Evium said gruffly, his grip tightening, "and I love her more every day." Liana took a deep breath and said nothing for several moments, causing Evium to stiffen. "What aren't you telling me?"

"Mahari is in the early stages of reading."

At last, Evium's eyes opened, and he stared up at the canopy billowing above them.

"She's... what?"

"She was reading a bit with Mama this morning and, to test it out myself later on in case she'd somehow memorized that book, I had her read something to me from another."

The ensuing silence stretched for so long that Liana could not help shifting into an upright position so that she could look down at her husband.

"She's two years old," Evium said at last, his eyes wide.

Liana nodded. "As I said when Mama told me. I don't think we should overlook this."

"How do we approach it, though?" Evium asked, pushing himself up into a sitting position and leaning against the headboard. He held an arm out to Liana and she joined him, snuggling close. "I suppose we could send another inquiry to the university in Claerendon. They'd know how best to handle this and suggest the best course of action."

"Do you think we could do it first thing in the morning?" Liana asked. "That way, we might have a response by the time we get back from seeing Jahd off at Pandoufuli."

"Liana," Evium began softly, "don't you think we should also consult Huison in this?"

"You, too!?"

"Ah," Evium said, chuckling, "so, your mother has also mentioned it?"

"I was prepared to ignore it!"

"As much as I'd love to do that, we must be fair, Liana! Why upset the apple cart?"

"You and my mother and your damned apples, Evium Chatelain, I am not having it!"

"What?" he said, laughing outright.

"Do you really think that he'll want someone else tutoring Mahari?"

"Do you really think we're giving him a choice? We're informing him because he's owed, and how he handles her schooling when she's in Scio is up to him. But, as her primary care is here, the ultimate decision is ours."

Finally, Liana smiled as she leaned over to kiss Evium.

"United front?" she said against his lips.

"Always," he answered.

"Good!" she said before pulling away and hopping up from the bed.

Evium, enjoying the unhindered glimpse of his wife's body, watched with great appreciation as she slipped into a robe and tied it closed.

"Do you think you could make this evening's raid a quick one?" he asked. "We have to be downstairs and ready for the road in three and a half hours."

"Shall I bring something back?" Liana asked, finger-combing her tangle of hair before bunching it into a knot at the nape.

"Only your stunning self in about twenty minutes, please."

Liana blew him a kiss as she left. The candles along the hallway, burning low and soon needing to be changed, provided ample lighting along the way. Despite the happiness she felt at being able to once again stoke the fires in her marriage, feelings of sadness involving her son soon conflicted her.

Liana still could not believe that Jahd was already eight years old. She could so vividly remember his birth, his first words, and his first steps. She knew she was being overprotective, but she felt fiercely determined to keep him with her—her precious little boy—for as long as she could, especially after losing his sister.

Time had flown by so quickly, though. Evium remained convinced that the best plans for Jahd included a stint at Pandoufuli. Liana's heart broke at the prospect, but she could not deny that it was the most ideal situation for their son. The alternative, should it ever be warranted, would be to send Jahd to Breaton, and the prospect of that often made Liana feel ill. She was, and not so secretly, thrilled that there was no reason to send her son there.

She paused, lightly toying with the sash on her robe. Liana was distraught on the morning of his birthday when he was overtaken by convulsions, and it reminded her of something she might have seen before but could not readily recall. Jahd had experienced no other such incidents, for which she was thankful. What would happen, though, if one occurred while he was at Pandoufuli?

Liana shook her head, taking a deep breath and willing away the uneasiness that was building inside of her. Jahd was fine. He was a perfectly healthy little boy, and in a few hours he would be on his way to an exciting chapter in his life with his parents there to support him. She wondered if she might wake her son and entice him into one last raid of the kitchens before his departure.

Smiling, Liana entered her son's suite, cutting through the playroom. Jahd was incredibly tidy for a boy, and not an item was out of place. Even his new toys—the ones he had received at his farewell gathering—were already neatly put away, some of them still in their original packaging. From the looks of it, he did not intend to take many of them with him to school.

She crossed through the moonlit room, heading toward the bedroom with the smile still on her face. When Liana reached Jahd's bedroom, however, she paused in the doorway and blinked. The bed was empty, though it was clear Jahd had been in it not long before.

Though no light shone in the bathroom, Liana checked it anyway and found it empty. Puzzled, she turned on her heels and examined the bedroom once more, as if her eyes were playing a trick on her.

Where could her son be?

After a short while, it occurred to her. There was a good amount of cake left over from the day. Liana was certain that Jahd was, at that very moment, enjoying his own foray. It would not be the first time. Perhaps mother and son could share a bit of cake and talk, just the two of them, before returning to bed.

Liana exited Jahd's suite, making a mental note to check on Mahari after she had tucked in her son. However, as she prepared to pass her daughter's room to approach the staircase, she saw a flickering light emanating from the crack beneath the door. She stopped and approached the door slowly.

What was going on? Perhaps Jahd was spending his final free moments with his baby sister since he was due to leave so early the next morning, and Mahari would stay behind with Alena. Liana put a hand to her mouth as tears burned behind her closed lids. He was such a remarkable and thoughtful child. After composing herself, Liana reached for the doorknob, freezing when she heard the soft voice of her son.

"*Sanguis*," she heard him say. "Blood of my blood. *Parva soror.* Awaken for me..."

Liana shivered. The voice sounded like Jahd's, but there was something in the tone that was wholly unfamiliar.

"Mahari Siera," he went on, "I have been unfairly restrained. I am stuck and stifled within a banal existence until I come into my own, while those of lesser worth lord over me in blissful oblivion.

"But they don't know what I do. They don't know what's coming. There will be someone... a prize to cement my place among the stars. I will never again be trapped as before, and the difference is you. I will rise and claim what's mine. Someday, my throne will be built upon the bones of non-believers. But, first... awaken for me..."

"Jahd!" Liana gasped as she burst into the room, closing the door behind her.

She gasped again at the sight of her son standing in the center of the room, a five-branched candelabrum in one hand and his baby sister balanced expertly on his opposite hip. Jahd calmly gazed from the blank-faced toddler to his mother, his expression unchanging as if nothing were amiss.

"Mother," he greeted, managing a polite bow despite his burden. "You're up late. Couldn't sleep?"

Liana marched over and snatched Mahari away from her brother, looking her over before fixing her son in an angry gaze.

"What are you doing in here?" she demanded. "What was that I heard you saying to your sister?"

"Saying, Mother?"

"About a throne being built on bones... and awakening..."

Jahd laughed, and the sound chilled Liana further. There was no mirth in it, and the smile never touched Jahd's eyes.

"Mother," he said with a shake of his neatly trimmed curly head, "it was a joke! I was only playing with Mahari and telling her stories."

"That is not any story I ever heard, especially one told to a baby. I won't have you filling her head with such things!"

"Mother," Jahd said after a pause, "may I have my sister back now?"

"For what, so you can tell her more of that garbage? You most certainly may NOT!"

"Mother," he said again, this time with an acidic tone, "she's only two. Do you really think she'll retain what was said? Calm yourself."

"Retain?" Liana repeated in a whisper, staring at her son in disbelief. "Who do you think you're talking to?"

"After all," Jahd continued, ignoring her question, "it's not like she's a thirteen-year-old girl dallying in things she would have done better to avoid. She is, as you pointed out, a baby."

Liana stared down at her son, ashen. She reached, almost blindly, for something upon which to support herself, and finally sank to her knees as she cuddled Mahari against her.

"You don't look well, Mother," Jahd commented. "Uncle Hui isn't here, or I'd ask him to come tend to you... again."

Liana closed her eyes, breathing deeply. The room was quiet, and she could feel her son's gaze burning into her. She finally opened her eyes again, gray locking onto gray as mother and son stared.

"I don't know what's gotten into you, but I want you out of my sight," Liana said firmly. "Go to your room. You will go there right this minute and go to bed. Is that clear?"

"But, Mother, I..." Jahd began in a sweeter tone.

"It's a shame that your last few hours at home have to be spent this way, but you give me no choice. Go away from me, Jahd Dhamon. Now!"

With a quick flick of his wrist, Jahd whipped out the flames of the candles within the candelabrum, shrouding the room in darkness, save for the strands of moonlight peeking from behind the closed curtains at the window. Liana blinked rapidly to make the adjustment and, as her vision cleared, the door to the bedroom opened and she saw her son framed in the doorway. He left without so much as acknowledging her command. She opened her mouth to call after him, but he was gone, closing the door behind him with an echoing click.

Chapter Twenty-Two

Evium wheeled backward up the ramp of the carriage, settling against the side of the cabin that lacked traditional seating. This carriage, one of three in varying sizes, was modified specifically for his use and comfort while allowing standard seating across from him for the enjoyment of others. As Evium strapped himself in, ensuring the mechanisms were secure, Fayal first lifted and then stowed the ramp inside a drawer-like compartment on the side for safekeeping before reaching underneath to pull a small staircase forward.

Liana exited the front door, the heels of her black velvet boots clicking along the pavement as she approached the carriage. Fayal bowed, extending a hand to help her up the stairs and into the cabin. She scooted left along the brocade-covered cushion, smoothing the satin lapel of her knee-length black wool coat and crossing her legs. Evium watched her, his head tilted slightly.

"You've been quiet all morning," he remarked. "In fact, you have said little since returning to bed last night." He waited for a response from her and, when one did not seem to be forthcoming, he sighed. "Liana, I know that this isn't what you wanted. Pandoufuli really is the best..."

"That isn't what this is about," Liana interrupted.

"Then tell me what it is about," Evium said.

Liana examined her fingernails before tucking a few stray curls behind one ear. At last, she shrugged. How could she rationally explain to her husband that their son alluded to an event, the details of which only five others had knowledge? He would think her mad, and rightfully so. She could not sleep at all after going back to lie beside Evium, all thoughts of kitchen sweets gone. As Evium dozed soundly beside her, it took everything inside of Liana to keep from going to Jahd's bedroom and shaking the truth out of him.

"I wouldn't even know where to begin," she admitted.

"Try," Evium said.

"I... came upon our son in Mahari's bedroom last night. He was telling her some horrible story, something that... was completely unsuitable for a child. I thought it might give her nightmares and told him off. He... was somewhat rude about it."

"Well, that's certainly unacceptable," Evium said, unable to lean forward because of the security of the straps but holding out a hand. Liana quickly grabbed it. "I'm sorry, sweetheart. I know that this is not how you wanted to see our son off, with tension between you. Maybe that's why he did it. He could be acting out because he's going away and doesn't know how else to process those feelings."

Liana pressed her lips together, not sure that she agreed with her husband, but lacking a logical rebuttal.

"We'll be on the road for a bit," Evium continued. "We can use this opportunity to reassure Jahd that sending him away isn't a representation of anything negative. He'll be home on breaks, and we can always go out to visit him if he really needs us, hmm?"

"Yes, of course," Liana said, managing a smile.

"Here we are—the man of the hour!" Fayal boomed from outside. Shortly thereafter, Jahd appeared at the opening of the carriage.

"There he is!" Evium said, releasing Liana's hand. "Hop aboard, son! Your future awaits!"

Jahd's eyes rolled toward his mother, who sat silently watching as he climbed the stairs to come inside.

"I hope that you'll forgive us for being overindulgent, my boy," Evium said later. "I was dispatched to Pandoufuli alone by train. My father couldn't get away from work and my mother couldn't bear to see me leave. But, I didn't want that for you... or for us."

Fayal had directed the horses to turn the carriage onto the lengthy road leading to the entrance of Pandoufuli. It had been a quiet journey, Liana saying little as Evium enthusiastically reminisced about his school days. Liana noted that Evium had carefully excised Huison from his recollections, but knew better than to comment. Jahd had interjected politely when warranted, but otherwise remained an attentive listener.

"Do the grounds look the same as when you attended?" Liana asked courteously, speaking for the first time in over an hour. Evium looked out of the carriage window to his left, while Jahd peered through the opposite side.

"Much larger," Evium said. "They've expanded a great deal. I also see newer buildings—dormitories, perhaps—as well as the extended library that those of us in the alumni contributed funding for."

As they drew nearer, Liana looked over the small clusters of students and their parents. Though the looks on the children's faces ranged from inquisitive to terrified, all the adults looked proud.

"I see quite a few young ladies here," Liana remarked. "Has the school become coeducational?"

"Girls were never really excluded, Liana," Evium said a bit sheepishly. "It's just that the curriculum rarely appeals to the fairer sex. But, it's very possible that Mahari could one day attend here, as well."

Jahd perked up at that, turning away from the window to look at his parents. "Mahari might be here with me?" he asked.

"Well, son, that would be quite a way off," Evium said, laughing. "By the time she came in through the Junior Academy, you'd be on your senior levels. The schedule becomes much busier by that point. You might only see her on weekends, if then."

"That's if she even comes at all," Jahd said, casting a sidelong glance at his mother. "She could very well end up at Breaton learning to be a spellweaver."

Evium arched a sandy brow at his son, who turned back to the window with a pleased expression as Liana stiffened. When the carriage at last came to a stop, the tension was palpable.

"Here we are!" Fayal said, having come around to open the carriage door before deploying the stairs, first helping Liana and Jahd alight the vehicle before tending to Evium.

"I don't want things to continue like this, Jahd Dhamon," Liana said in a low voice when they were alone. "I don't know what's happened or what has gotten into you, but... it ends here." She sighed. "It's hard enough letting you go, but to do so with friction between us is unimaginable." She placed her index finger beneath his chin, tilting his head upward as she looked into the eyes that so closely matched her own.

"I won't ask why you said what you did last night," she continued. "I will, however, stress that you are never to speak to me that way again. This is hard on all of us, but that will never be an excuse for insolence. Remember yourself."

"I do, Mother," Jahd said, locking eyes with her. "I do."

"Very well," Liana said, content to accept that as an apology as she released him.

"My goodness, am I glad to be out of that carriage so that I can stretch my legs!" Evium said when he joined them.

Liana blushed deeply as he came to a stop beside Jahd, but then could not help laughing at the joke. Evium reached for her hand, kissing it and pressing a few giggles of his own into her palm.

"Liana? Liana Dhamon, can it be you?"

Liana turned on her heels at the mention of her name and the smile froze upon her lips as the laughter seemed to stick in her throat. The other woman was nearly as tall as Liana, her curvaceous figure wrapped in a dark green wool coat with a ruffled hood and hem. Though the hood was up to help shield the wearer from the elements, lustrous dark waves framed an olive-hued face, and her dark green, heavy-lidded eyes sparkled with delight.

"Ani," Liana whispered, her own eyes wide. She then cleared her throat before shaking her head. "Aniela... I... I can't believe it..."

"Neither can I!" Aniela said, enveloping Liana in a hug. Liana suddenly felt very warm, and more than a tad nauseous. "When I saw you get out of that carriage, I thought my mind must be playing tricks on me! You've hardly changed since our school days!"

Liana cleared her throat again, turning to her husband and son. "Th-this is Aniela Guiden," she said. "We were at Breaton together. Aniela, this is my husband, Evium, and our son, Jahd."

"So wonderful to meet you both," Aniela said as she shook hands first with Evium, and then Jahd. Jahd's eyes narrowed the moment their hands touched, and he looked at Aniela from raven head to velvet toe. "I was Aniela Guiden then... it's Stefanidis now."

"Do you have a child starting this term?" Evium asked. "Or perhaps one returning for the new school year?"

"Starting this term," Aniela said. "My stepson, Jacinto."

Evium looked around. "Where is the young man?" he asked. "How wonderful! You and my wife were classmates and now our sons shall be."

"Isn't that remarkable?" Aniela asked, reaching over to give Liana's hand a squeeze. "I'm sure he's around here somewhere. He couldn't wait to leave our carriage so he could go off and explore. The driver barely had time to get it stopped before he bolted." She smiled again at Jahd. "Are you just as excited, young man?"

"It's already turning out to be an unforgettable experience," Jahd said, his gray eyes tracing Aniela's face with focused curiosity.

"I'll go find Jacinto," Aniela told him. "I'm certain he'll be excited to have already made a new friend." She beamed at Liana once more before departing.

"Isn't that a delightful surprise?" Evium said, clearly pleased as he smiled at his wife. "I'd say we're getting off to a grand start, wouldn't you?"

"Pardon me, please," came a thickly accented voice from behind Liana.

The trio turned to find that they were joined by an older man with thick, wavy hair that glittered under the morning sun. His eyebrows and neatly trimmed beard were of the same glinting silver shade, contrasting nicely with deeply olive skin and clear blue eyes.

He was holding the hand of a little girl, her long hair the same deep tint as Aniela's, and with eyes of a lighter green. She was wearing a coat identical to Aniela's, except in miniature, over a pale gold silk smock dress with lace accents and matching shoes.

"I believe you were just speaking with my wife," the man continued. "Would you tell me, please, where has she gone?"

"Mr. Stefanidis!" Evium greeted, holding out a hand. "It's a pleasure, sir! Aniela went 'round in search of your son—Jacinto, is it?"

"Yes, and please call me Sandro," he said, shaking Evium's hand and then turning to grasp Liana's.

"Liana Chatelain," Liana said. "This is my husband, Evium, and our son, Jahd."

"This is my daughter, Zoi," Sandro said, indicating the child. He then reached for Jahd's hand. "Hello, young man."

Jahd had already noticed the little girl. Almost immediately upon seeing her, he felt a chilled tingle creeping up the back of his neck. His entire body felt warm, as though he had been submerged in the bath, while both his stomach and chest simultaneously tightened and churned in opposite directions.

"Jahd, sweetheart, don't be rude," Liana said before having a closer look at him. "Jahd? Honey, what's wrong?"

He could hear the increasingly shrill voice of his mother echoing about, but could not respond. The surrounding air seemed to crackle and thicken as the tingle spread from the back of his neck throughout his body, bringing with it the sensation of his hair standing on end. Jahd's heart raced, and he began to sweat.

"What's happening here?" Evium asked.

"I don't know," Liana said, "he's suddenly gone cold. Feel his hands!"

Evium grasped one of Jahd's hands, and his eyes widened.

"Allow me, please," Sandro said, releasing Zoi's hand and kneeling in front of Jahd. "I am a physician."

At that moment, Aniela rounded the corner, accompanied by a tall young man with closely cropped dark brown hair and pale blue eyes. The smile on Aniela's face melted as she surveyed the scene before them, and she rushed over.

"What's gone on?" she asked as the young man, presumably Jacinto, walked over to take Zoi's hand, stepping back and away from the adults surrounding Jahd.

"Nothing very serious," Sandro offered, looking into Jahd's eyes. "Appears to be mild shock." He looked up at his wife. "I am without my bag, but it's easy to see that his pupils have dilated."

"Let me," Aniela said, as she and Sandro switched places and an anxious Liana hovered nearby with Evium. Aniela grasped both of

Jahd's hands, rubbing them. "His hands are freezing," she said to no one in particular. "Not much to it, since it's cold out."

"Should we move him inside?" Sandro asked.

"Not until he's come out of it," Aniela answered.

"Are you also a physician, Aniela?" Evium asked, to which she responded with a wide smile, even though her focus remained on Jahd.

"Of sorts," she said.

Evium looked to Liana, his brow furrowed in confusion.

"Healing is Aniela's gift," Liana said softly before swallowing the bitter taste building in her mouth. "Even in school, I'd seen nothing like it."

As soon as Aniela touched Jahd's face with both hands, he blinked and gasped. "Well," she said, still smiling, "hello!"

Chapter Twenty-Three

Liana glanced back toward the double doors of the infirmary, nibbling upon her bottom lip as Evium chuckled nearby.

"Looks like we have the start of a tradition," he joked. "I spent my first few hours in the Pandoufuli infirmary, and now so will Jahd!"

"Should we have left him?" Liana asked, still studying the doors.

"I know exactly how you feel," Aniela said, taking Liana's hand, "but he was fine. It was a little shock as San said, perhaps brought about from exhaustion after the journey. Time in the infirmary is merely a precaution. They'll hydrate him, have him rest for a bit, and then he'll join the others in enough time for orientation."

"Thank you both," Liana said to Aniela and Sandro, who was walking only a few paces behind them with Zoi.

"I am glad we were there to help," Sandro said with a smile, wrapping his free arm around Aniela's waist. "And as Ani said, he's fine. Jacinto is there with him, and it'll give the boys a chance to get to know one another."

Jahd lay propped up in one of the many beds inside the infirmary, though the one he occupied was closest to a bay of windows. An untouched cup of tea sat atop the bedside table, the liquid still steaming, as Jahd warily eyed his visitor. Jacinto, sitting in a chair beside the bed, blew lightly into his own cup before taking a sip. Pale blue eyes peered at Jahd over the rim.

"I don't need a babysitter," Jahd said. "You don't have to be here."

"I know," Jacinto replied when the cup was lowered.

"Then why are you?"

"Because it's getting me off the hook," Jacinto answered with a shrug. "Now, instead of focusing on me and the fact that I've left home to attend school, everyone can focus on you and your fainting spell."

"I did not faint," Jahd said, unamused.

"Whatever," Jacinto said as he shrugged slender shoulders. "You sure freaked your parents out, I know that much. Your dad practically had to drag your mother out of here."

Jahd flicked a gray gaze toward the closed infirmary doors and then at the matron who flitted through the space carrying various supplies. He reached over to retrieve his cup of tea.

"What's the story with your mother?" he asked idly. "Is she some sort of healer?"

"Oh, she's not my mother," Jacinto said amiably. "My actual mother died a few days after having me. Ani is the only mom I've known, though."

"The little girl is hers," Jahd said, feeling his skin tingle again slightly. He drew in a deep breath, held it for a few seconds, and then exhaled. It made him feel better immediately.

"Of course," Jacinto said, not noticing. Then he laughed. "What gave it away, the resemblance?"

Jahd's lips curled into a smile around the rim of his cup, and he did not answer. The boys sat in silence for several minutes, each taking turns drinking his tea. Finally, when Jacinto's cup was emptied, he arched a brow at Jahd.

"Were your parents disappointed you can't do magic?" he blurted.

"Excuse me?" Jahd asked.

"That's why we're at Pandoufuli, isn't it? I mean, I obviously can't do it, either." He shrugged again. "Both my dad and birth mother are from a non-magical lineage, though, so it was expected. Zoi is very different. Because of Ani, things have been really interesting."

"Oh?" Jahd said lightly, returning his cup to its place on the bedside table. He then smiled. "Have they?"

"I was glad to see our boys getting along so well together," Aniela said a short while later, standing outside with Liana as Evium and Sandro chatted nearby. "When we went back to the infirmary to say our last goodbyes, they were chatting like old friends."

There was a line of carriages waiting along the extensive driveway, some of which were still being unpacked, while others were being boarded by the still-sniffling relatives of departing students.

"It'll be so odd not having Jacinto at home," Aniela went on, "but he's already so independent that I imagine he'll do swimmingly without us. They grow up so fast!"

"I have the same fear regarding Jahd," Liana admitted with a sigh. "But Pandoufuli is the best place for him. I'm sure he'll do well here."

"I don't know if Zoi fully understands," Aniela said, glancing back toward her own carriage, a magnificent construct of dark green lacquer with gold trimmings. Zoi, peering at her mother from within the plush interior, waved solemnly.

"I have a daughter at home, too," Liana said as both she and Aniela waved back. "Not as old as your little angel, though. Zoi will understand. I'm uncertain that Mahari will."

"Such a beautiful name!" Aniela said with a laugh. "I'd bet she's such a darling. Does she look more like you or your husband?"

As Liana reddened, scrambling for a reply, Evium and Sandro joined them.

"We should go, lovely," Sandro said, kissing his wife upon the cheek. "So sorry to interrupt, but if we're not back on the road soon, we'll miss our late afternoon appointment."

"Well, it was certainly wonderful meeting you both," Evium said. "I hope we'll get to do this again, under less strenuous circumstances, of course."

Aniela reached for Liana's hands, squeezing them. "I hope so," Aniela said. "I've missed you, Li. I have thought of you so much over the years. I don't want to become strangers again."

"That's right!" Sandro said as Liana was about to speak. "I thought your name sounded familiar when we were introduced. You were school friends with my Ani! How wonderful is it that our daughter, Zoi, will attend Breaton in the spring? Following in the footsteps of you ladies, I'm sure!"

"Oh!" Liana said breathlessly as she reddened and cleared her throat. "How wonderful, indeed! I... I'm sure that little Zoi will be brilliant. She'll surpass us both..."

Liana was distant, tuning in and out during Evium's excited chatter on the journey back to Kynedal. He was so proud of Jahd.

Evium eagerly expected the accomplishments that Jahd would make and the opportunities he'd benefit from as a successful graduate of Pandoufuli. Though Evium hoped that Jahd might consider following in Evium's metaphorical footsteps and venture into inventing, he vowed to support his son in whatever undertaking he chose.

Though she shared the same overall sentiment, Liana could not stifle the conflicting feelings about encountering Aniela again. Seeing Aniela transported Liana back to that night so many years ago at Breaton. The dormitory matron, who was alerted by the candlelight streaming from beneath the girls' bedroom door during bedtime rounds, had discovered the quintet. It startled the matron to enter the room to find four of the girls huddled together in varying degrees of distress as the fifth, Vanja, sat apart from the others.

Spying the crudely drawn diagram upon the floor and the tome tossed haphazardly to the side, Matron came to an immediate conclusion that, per Breaton rules, unsanctioned magic was being performed. The headmistress was roused from slumber, and the girls were marched into her office for individual questioning.

The threat of expulsion was made, but it was a ruse. Had she burned the Breaton campus down to its foundation, Liana Dhamon could do no wrong in the eyes of those who idolized her father. Instead, she was offered a private dormitory, to get her away from the other girls, who were deemed a bad influence. It was ultimately Liana's decision to leave Breaton altogether. That leering, laughing thing had humiliated her, daring to renege on the agreement and deprive her of her birthright.

Despite everything, she had been such good friends with the other four girls—Aniela, Vanja, Rhia, and Elyse—and they all tried keeping in touch with her after her departure. Though she missed them to the point of almost daily tears in the months after their separation, she never answered the letters she received.

How could she respond? They had witnessed the most shameful moment in Liana's life. Liana felt as though she had no choice but to tuck away the memories of them and of the experience, doing her best to forget as she made the most of her life as someone who was simply born plain.

Liana's thoughts returned to Jahd, and she could not help wondering. Why did he speak to her in such a way while in Mahari's nursery the other night? What did he know, and how did he come to know it? He could not have just been lashing out—his words hit much too close to home and were cloaked in Liana's disgrace. Liana could not get a straight answer from him, but she knew who else she could ask.

"I hope that you'll keep in touch with Aniela," Evium said, breaking through Liana's reverie. "It was such a pleasant surprise to meet her and her family. Jahd and Jacinto are fast friends, and it would be brilliant if little Zoi could meet Mahari and get on well together, don't you think?"

Evium studied his wife, smiling gently. "Was a shock for you, wasn't it?" he continued. "When Sandro mentioned Zoi would attend Breaton, I noticed the change in you. Your recovery was commendable, but... I saw." He leaned forward as best he could in the protective straps. "Would you like to talk about it with me?"

"Vi," Liana said, licking her lips, "I... n-no. No. There's nothing to talk about."

"I mean it, Li," Evium insisted. "Whatever you need... you know I'll help you. Don't hide from me."

"I'm not hiding! I just..." Liana shrugged, shaking her head before turning to her right to gaze out of the window at the passing landscape. She recognized they were on the outskirts of Kynedal and would likely disembark within the hour. Liana turned back to her husband. "Evium, once we get home, I'll be taking the carriage out again on an errand."

He blinked, frowning. "What? Why go all the way home and then back out again? We can go wherever you need now..."

"No, no... we can't. It's only an errand, Vi, and I'd rather go alone."

"I thought you said that there was nothing to talk about," Evium said as he sat back.

"Am I not allowed a moment to myself?" Liana demanded.

"Of course! But, not if it means taking that moment to run from me when all I'm trying to do is to be here for you."

"I'm not running!"

"Riding in a carriage, then!" They stared at one another for several moments before Liana turned back to the window. "How long will you be gone?" Evium finally asked.

"Not long," she answered, still looking away. "I thought to drop you off and, while I check on Mahari and freshen up a bit, Fayal and Millard can see to changing the horses."

"Where are you going?"

"I need to get some air, Evium."

Silence continued to hang between them for what remained of the trip home. Once the carriage stopped in the driveway of the Den and Evium unlocked the mechanisms holding his wheelchair in place, he looked at his wife.

"I'll see to Mahari," he said. "She may not understand why you've just come home and are leaving again so soon. But, have someone come find me in the nursery so that I can see you off."

Fayal appeared at the carriage door, smiling as he assisted Evium from the carriage and into the house, where he was greeted by Clea and Alena.

"So glad to have you back, sir!" Clea enthused as Alena curtsied before going outside. "Is the young sir all settled in at his new school?"

"That he is," Evium said with a smile. "There was a slight hiccup before we left, but I know that he's sorted by now. He's even made a new friend already."

"Bless him," Clea said, dabbing at her eyes with the dishtowel hanging from her apron pocket. "He will be missed around here, but it does my heart good to know that he's already getting on so well."

"Where's Mahari?" Evium asked.

"Sleeping, sir. I've just put her down for an early afternoon nap. She spent much of the morning playing with Alena and the children, and she was quite worn out after. Alena finished tucking in her own brood not moments before your arrival."

"She's all right, then?"

"She didn't ask about her brother, sir, if that's what you mean," Clea said with a smile. "They kept the little one quite busy, and she didn't have a chance to think too much. Can I get you some lunch?"

Evium's stomach gurgled, and he chuckled. "What wretched concoction have you made today?" he joked.

"I've got a lovely pork roast with mushrooms and leeks," Clea offered. "I sliced a bit for sandwiches for the children, but I'll make something else to go along with it on the side for you, Lord Chatelain."

"If you insist," Evium said with mock sternness as his stomach rumbled its assent. He began steering himself toward the lift. "I'm going to have a shower and then come back down. Please let my wife know that she'll find me in the kitchen rather than the nursery."

"Of course, sir," Clea said, "and, I'll get to your lunch right away."

When Evium emerged from the shower less than an hour later, enlivened and refreshed, he changed into a simple dark blue tunic and soft gray pants. He could tell by the slight disarray in Liana's dressing room that she had been there and hoped that she was downstairs in the kitchen so that they could have lunch together before she left again. With Mahari sleeping, there was no longer any concern about unduly distressing the child. Upon arriving in the kitchen, however, he found only a single place setting at the table as Clea sliced into a rosemary-crusted pork loin.

"I'll be only a moment, sir," Clea said as she fanned a few slices of the meat onto a plate before spooning the leek and mushroom mixture over the top. "What will you have to drink?"

"Won't Liana be joining me?" Evium asked as he settled in at the table.

"No, sir." Clea placed crisp-edged polenta cakes on the plate, along with a cluster of blistered cherry tomatoes still on the vine. "Though she did promise she'd have something once she got back."

"Back?" Evium echoed as Clea walked over to place the plate in front of him before wiping her hands on the hem of her apron.

"Yes, sir! She's gone for her errand. She took Millard with her so that Fayal could have a moment with Alena while the children are napping."

Clea continued to talk, his thoughts closing in on him as her voice grew more distant. Why hadn't Liana come to him as he had asked? There was no need for concealment, was there? Evium sat unmoving as his lunch, which looked so delicious to him mere moments before, almost seemed to drain of color and appeal as his stomach twisted into varying configurations.

He barely heard Clea ask again what he wanted to drink. He did not know. He knew nothing anymore except that he was powerless.

Chapter Twenty-Four

Huison strolled through the gardens of Dalenbeigh, dismissive of the chill in the early evening air as he slid his hands into the pockets of his gold-threaded, maroon velvet sherwani. A light wind toyed with his dark curls as he walked. He smiled, knowing that this was the day that Jahd began his tenure at Pandoufuli.

He had so far received a single missive from one of his contacts at the school, describing an event that caused Jahd to be housed in the infirmary that morning. Huison was initially concerned, though nothing in the message described symptoms akin to that which afflicted Jahd on his eighth birthday. Obviously, Liana and Evium did not think it was serious enough to delay his enrollment or even stay in town for the evening, but Huison, in his return communiqué, asked to be kept informed regardless.

Everything was set in motion, and all Huison needed to do now was wait. Time would do his work for him. When it reached its apex, he would reap the abundant harvest of what had been sown.

In nine years, Liana would be near her mid-thirties. He had no doubts that she would still be incomparable. She would always be beautiful to him, and such a joy to his heart. Huison would continue to foster growth in the relationship with his daughter as well, and would be there for Mahari, as a comforting guide during her most dire need. He would be there for them both.

After all, they would need solace after Jahd's untimely death before his eighteenth birthday.

What a boon it was to discover the source of what tormented Rael Dhamon. The demon was trapped inside him, so willing to bargain with Huison for release. Huison was not naïve to the duplicity of such creatures, however, and had only agreed to help once assured of the benefit to him.

The binding ritual that necessitated the displacement of Jahd's original soul with that of the demon—a sacrifice that had to be made for, ironically enough, what Huison considered to be the greater good—ensured that the new inhabitant would be rendered unable to benefit from any of its existing abilities. There was no way that Huison was going to allow the thing to grow and manifest increased power. He was going to control it, stifle it until the moment he intended to place the blade in Liana's hand to set it free. By right of blood, she would inherit what she was due.

It would be fitting for her to turn to Huison as her redeemer.

This time, Huison laughed aloud. It was so easy to put the pieces together! How stupid was this creature to be so forthcoming? It actually thought that Huison didn't know and hadn't realized the connection: the way it latched onto Rael, the reverence with which it spoke of Kaileih Dhamon, and that it ended up trapped because it was lying in wait for a certain someone to visit Rael at Vespers Glen... someone who never came.

Had it not been for a secret, one shared with him on a warm summer night a few years ago amidst a tangle of cool silk sheets, Huison might have missed the opportunity of a lifetime.

"Huison?"

Huison stopped as a breath caught in his throat. Had she so saturated his thoughts that he could now hear Liana's soft voice swirling around him?

He turned around, exhaling explosively. It had not been his imagination at all. Liana was stunning, wrapped in a red wool asymmetrical coat with long ruched sleeves. Her dark curls were wildly loose, framing her face before spilling past her shoulders, and she lifted a black velvet-gloved hand to push a few of the curls away as she approached.

"Li," he whispered, drinking her in.

"Forgive me for dropping by unannounced, but I needed to see you."

"Of course! No forgiveness needed. I am delighted to see you! Come inside where it is warmer..."

"No," Liana said, shaking her head. "They offered to have me sit inside so they could come out and get you, but... I need to talk with you out here where there's no chance of us being overheard."

"O-Oh," Huison said. "As you wish, of course, but... is something wrong?" His eyes widened. "Has something happened to Mahari?"

"It's nothing like that, Huison, no." She glanced around the neatly manicured garden and smiled softly. "Your home is beautiful," she said, as if caught off-guard by this revelation.

"Thank you. I have longed for the day you would come to visit me here. I am pleased you find it to your liking."

"I've been wondering... why did you name this place Dalenbeigh? The décor of your home, and the design of the estate don't seem to fit."

Huison laughed, surprised by the question. "In a way, I suppose it does not. Dalenbeigh is the maiden surname of my mother. I wanted to build a place that is exceptionally beautiful, as she was. But, I also wanted to put her name on something belonging to me

230

that could not be as easily denied. While Dalenbeigh does not have the reputation of The Den, my mother cannot escape the fact that I am her son, no matter how hard she has tried."

"I can't imagine being estranged from my mother," Liana admitted.

"I envy that," Huison said. "I envy your relationship with your mother. I envy a lot of things."

Liana nodded, tucking a few curls behind one ear. "Huison, I can't stay too long. I came because I... needed to ask you something."

"Anything," he said.

"Huison, I hope that, despite the way things are between us now, you'll be completely honest with me." Huison, brow arched, only nodded. Liana took a deep breath. "Have you told anyone... anyone at all... about what happened at Breaton when I was a girl?"

Huison placed a hand against his midsection, as though able to caress his resulting relief. He was almost certain that anything Liana asked would have to do with Rael.

"Of course not, Liana," he said. "You shared your secret with me during an intimate moment while we were both laid bare and vulnerable. I know how difficult it was for you, how deeply painful an experience. I could never betray you in that way."

"Huison, this is important!" Liana stressed, her cheeks flushed.

"I am aware. I felt your pain then, and I feel it now. I cannot imagine why you think I would divulge your secret to anyone." The combined expressions of relief and disappointment in Liana's striking eyes puzzled Huison. He shook his head, shrugging helplessly. "You came all the way here to ask me this—why? What has made you think I could do such a thing?"

"I didn't think that you'd done it maliciously," Liana said, lowering her gaze as her voice trembled. "I thought perhaps you shared the story with Jahd to bring him closer to you. I know he has a fascination with magic and spellweaving, and..."

"Jahd?" Huison interrupted. "What has Jahd to do with this?"

"He and I had words last night. I found him in Mahari's bedroom telling her some scary story in the middle of the night, and I told him off about it. That was when he said that it wasn't as though he was a thirteen-year-old girl dabbling in something she shouldn't. Then he made some remark about you, and it just made me think..."

"What kind of story?" Huison wanted to know.

"Oh, it doesn't matter!" Liana sighed, pushing her hair out of her face as she sniffled. "If you didn't tell him, then it was apparently nothing, and everything I've been assuming has been about nothing! I alienated my son during his last hours with us, all because... I was afraid. I've been so afraid and so mixed up for most of my life!"

"Afraid of what?"

"Afraid of being a nobody! Afraid of being lost and forgotten and washed away in a torrent of reverence paid to my parents and my brother while I'm cast off..."

Huison uncoiled his lanky frame from where he stood, moving quickly to envelop Liana in an embrace.

"Do not do this to yourself!" he breathed in her ear. "You are not forgotten, and you are revered!"

"I lied to Evium! I lied to my husband because I couldn't tell him who I was coming to see and why." She looked up into Huison's amber eyes as her own filled with tears. "I have never told him what I shared with you. My mother doesn't even know!"

"That is why I hold your confidence so dear, because you blessed me with it when no one else was."

"You swear you've said nothing at all to Jahd?"

"Not to Jahd, not to anyone, on my life," Huison swore, transfixed by the sight of her and the feel of her in his arms. He reached up to brush at her tears with his thumb, his shuddering breaths forming clouds in a staccato mid-air.

"That's all I need to know, then," Liana said, though she made no move to release herself. "I stopped at my mother's shop in town. One of her people there gave me enough hybrids to justify the trip, and I've left some here with you that can be planted this month to secure the alibi with your people, if needed. I'll take the rest back with me."

"You do not have to go back," Huison said, indulging in the scent of coconut from her hair. "Stay with me, Li. Be with me."

At last, she broke the embrace. "That's impossible," she said, wiping her eyes.

"With us, there is no such thing."

"My home is in Kynedal."

"Your life is with me."

"Mahari..."

"Send for her," Huison said, "or we can go back together to get her..."

"Huison..."

"Everything you feel and what you have endured is because you are wasting away in a place where you are unappreciated!" he said. "No one there understands what it is like! Liana... if you could have but a taste of your greatest wish, you would be so much happier!"

"Oh, so now you're telling me that running off with you will somehow turn me into a spellweaver?" Liana asked with a laugh that sounded anything but merry.

"There are ways, Liana," Huison said determinedly, wishing more than anything that he could tell her everything, yet knowing that it was too soon.

"Oh?" Liana laughed again. "Will you teach me tricks? Shall I become a magician now? Will we go on the road?"

"No, no, no!" Huison grasped her hands, looking into her eyes. "I need you to trust me. Know that I have your best interests at heart! It will just take some time and you will realize all your hopes!"

Liana slowly tilted her head at him. He nearly wept at the sadness in her eyes.

"Huison, there is no hope for me," she said slowly. "I was so ready to lay blame on my son for making a harmless comment that stemmed from distress and meant nothing, all because I've felt inferior my entire life." She pulled back her hands and took a deep breath. "My mother is right. I need to let go."

"No, Liana! You need to be patient and you will have everything you want!"

Liana locked eyes with Huison, and he felt the warmth of her gaze flush through him. When she reached up to caress his cheek, he could have melted in her hands, and he closed his eyes to languish in her touch.

"Everything I want is at home," she said softly, causing Huison's eyes to snap open again as she lowered her hand and turned to leave. Huison opened his mouth to protest, but all that came out was a strangled gasp as he felt his stomach lurch and twist.

"Liana," he finally rasped. "It is just the two of us here. There is no danger of interruption from your mother... your husband... or anyone from your household. Tell me. Tell me truthfully. Did I mean nothing to you?"

Liana paused, turning to study him through her curtain of hair. Her look was a spell that he knew would bind him forever. He could feel himself growing warm as the tips of Liana's dark lashes briefly stroked the crests of her cheeks as she blinked before fixing her clear gray gaze upon Huison. The subtle curve of her smile was delicious, and Huison had to catch his breath again.

Chapter Twenty-Five

Jahd, still housed in the infirmary at Pandoufuli, groaned in his sleep. He was allowed to attend orientation and, after receiving his dormitory assignment, was ordered back to the medical wing to relax for the rest of the afternoon.

He did not argue. He had not felt the same since seeing Aniela again and encountering Zoi. Jahd felt an incessant pull from deep within, drawing him to the little girl. It was as if every cell in his body knew who and what she was even before they were introduced.

The feeling was so different from the experiences after his rebirth in the mine. Jahd felt bound to Liana and overwhelmed by Kaileih, but meeting Zoi was much like the primal magnetism of the first time he saw Mahari. He did not think there was anyone else like Mahari. He was wrong and had succumbed to a fitful sleep while thinking of what it all could mean.

"Father of Night, heed the call of your daughters..."

Jahd whimpered, beads of sweat dotting his brow as he turned over in bed. He desperately wanted to wake up, but could not. Fatigue had overtaken him and, as he lay trapped, he was transported back to that night.

"Father of Night, heed the call of your daughters..."

"They've started again," said Jahd, before he was called Jahd.

Back then he had another name, one not easily spoken by human tongues. Neither was that of his master, who had been given many monikers. One of them, "Father of Night," was the preference of those seeking favor or favors.

"I hear," rumbled the Master, closing his eyes as if reveling in the sound of the combined voices of the girls. "I can feel her pain." When he opened his eyes again, they appeared to pierce the darkness that surrounded them. "If it were anyone else, I would delight in it."

"Yet you have allowed none of us to go to her," Jahd said. "They've been at it for months and, each time they raise a plea, you bid us be still."

"Yes..."

"By granting her this, would you not be elevated?"

"In her eyes, yes," the Master said. "Not in the eyes of the one who matters."

Jahd turned back to the open portal through which they watched Liana and the others. "She is your way in, Master. When her wish is granted, she will have to tell her mother how it was done. Kaileih would be in your debt."

"There is a reason, though, why Kaileih stripped her daughter of her abilities when she was a child," the Master growled. "How can I go against her?"

Jahd paused, considering. "If I may offer a solution, Master?" Black talons flicked in Jahd's direction as if giving permission for him to speak. "Allow someone to answer her and give her what she asks—nothing akin to the power she held before, but enough to appease since she has no memory of her potential. She would, at some point, have to reveal herself to her parents."

"To that father of hers," the Master thundered. "That underhanded usurper!"

"To her mother as well, Master. What could Kaileih do but appeal to you directly to reverse the deliverance of the gift, since it was in your power? It's a window of opportunity, Master, one that could pave her road back to you..."

Jahd waited as his master paced back and forth before the open portal. Jahd took a moment to look back at each of the girls, focusing on Liana. This desperate, sniveling thing was the product of the greatest woman ever created?

Begging... simpering... what a disappointment she must be. But they were all so delicious-looking—sweet and vibrant—in varying hues and levels of beauty. They would grow into stunning women, the playthings of mortal men.

Even though this assignment would likely be given to someone of a higher rank, Jahd decided he could be content with only watching and with the joy of knowing that it was his idea that his master put into action. Someday, he hoped to be consigned to something tender and delectable for his very own.

"You go."

Jahd was startled from his musings and blinked. "Master?" he said.

"The idea was yours. You should be the one to bring it to fruition."

"I beg your pardon, Master, but," Jahd indicated his compact form, "those whelps are expecting something very different from..."

"It is of no consequence," the Master said. "You said yourself that this has been going on for months. At this point, she should find herself grateful that anyone answered at all." He pivoted away from the portal, the silver chains clinking as they held the dark cloak across his shoulders when he moved. "Go there. Give her a taste of what she craves. She'll become ours and, eventually, her mother will, too."

Jahd cried out in his sleep, tears streaming from his eyes as his body arched and stiffened. That wretched ingrate had sliced into his thigh with her silver, hook-handled dagger! What cruel madness was this? What heartless thing had Kaileih Dhamon conceived? This Liana harpy was no more gracious than the demons Jahd served with, and the immobilization spell cast upon him made it impossible to escape either the dagger or the churning of the wound that followed.

Why should she be given anything? She was wholly undeserving. Her mother showed wonderful sense when she took Liana's talents away, and who was he to go against someone of the caliber of Kaileih Dhamon?

But... he had given his master his word. How could Jahd back away from his own idea? He was entrusted with something of vital importance and, if he ever hoped to advance in rank, he had to deliver on the most basic level. Liana could have her gift, but he owed her a little something first.

Why wouldn't Liana listen to her friends!? Jahd was forced to lie prone while she contemplated murder. She was so impatient, hasty and irresponsible, that she was willing to eternally damn herself and the others during a fit of immature temper. The audacity of this scrap of a human!

"*I'll send it back!*" she had screamed, and Jahd closed his eyes as he waited for the last stroke. At least he would die in service, and he longed for an arduous punishment for all those involved in his demise.

The deathstroke had not come. When Jahd opened his eyes again, he was once again in his master's observatory, still bleeding profusely. The scene had continued to be surveyed through the portal, and he had been saved. Jahd struggled to get to his feet but found that he could not because of the agony of his leg.

"Master," he said, "I did what I could..."

"You dallied for too long!" the Master roared, his wintry gaze causing Jahd more pain than what he felt in his limb. "I should have known better than to leave it to you! You are like a child! This was not the time for your games, and now the moment is lost! Did you think I'd want her damned? If not for the importance of the endgame, I would have left you there to be skewered!"

Jahd whimpered in speechless mortification as his master turned away from him, stalking out of the observatory with a shout of frustration. A flicker of movement in his peripheral vision caught his eye, and he turned once again to the portal. Three of the girls were comforting Liana while the fourth looked on.

She was sobbing, that heartless bitch. She, who was so willing to sentence herself and her cohorts to a world of darkness, was now crying like an infant. Jahd narrowed his eyes. She did not yet know tears, but he promised himself that she would. He would find a way to get back at her and, as a bonus, the others as well.

Despite his pain, the imp chuckled.

Jahd's eyes snapped open. It took a moment for him to blink his surroundings into a state of recognition, and he recalled his presence in the infirmary during his return to the present.

Sitting up in bed, he reached down to massage the echoes of distress from his left thigh, as if it had been this body that was cut into rather than his former shell. His forehead was damp, as were his armpits, and as he turned toward the window while attempting to guess the time, he hoped they would soon release him so that he could go to his dormitory.

Rubbing at his throbbing temples, he swung both legs over the side of the bed as he sighed. Huison thought he was so clever. He was certain that he had everything figured out and had the upper hand. He knew nothing in comparison, and by the time he did, it would be too late.

It was hell, in many variations, when Jahd could not fulfill his master's task. Years of being shunned, denigrated, and humbled, but Jahd never blamed his master for it. How could he? It was her fault... Liana. He kept Liana in mind and heart for years as Jahd waited for the day he would avenge himself.

How fortuitous had it been to find her older brother, Rael, on the evening he stumbled between the planes? His father had been claimed, a prize the Master would never surrender except under extremely specific circumstances, and Rael was so clumsy in his attempts to retrieve him.

Rael was not yet strong enough to be of any use to his father, and it was nothing for Jahd to slip away and accompany Rael back to his own realm. As Rael had not summoned him, the only way for Jahd to make the journey was to discard his own body in favor of Rael's.

The acquisition of his new trophy distracted the Master enough not to notice that he was much closer now than he had ever been in his quest to reclaim his deepest love. He would at last get what he wanted, but what about Jahd? What about the years of castigation over an incident spurred by an entitled brat? Wasn't he also due some restitution?

He was, and Liana would be the source.

Jahd rubbed at his temples again, glancing over at his long-forgotten teacup. He was certain the tea had gone cold, but he was thirsty and needed something. As he reached for the cup, it budged slightly atop the saucer before rattling. Startled, he drew his hand back, amazed as the tremors ceased.

With his heart racing, Jahd once again trained his eye on the cup, this time without reaching for it. The cup shuddered, spilling a bit of its contents onto the saucer before becoming steady as it rose a few inches from the bedside table. He laughed in delight as tendrils of steam rose from the surface of the liquid and the cup floated over to him. He plucked it from midair, taking a deep and satisfying breath of the aromatic, and now hot, serving of tea.

What was the meaning of this? The parameters of the binding ritual ensured that Jahd was disallowed the use of his existing range of gifts. Huison had intentionally only given enough leeway for him to use his talents once after his rebirth at the mines. This was different. This source of power was unknown to him, and though he could feel the awakening of a pulsating whirr inside, he did not know its limitations.

"Zoi," Jahd whispered into the cup.

That strange little girl with the light green eyes had somehow stimulated something at his core, though he spent only minutes in her presence. Were these new gifts a result of an unexpected corruption in the binding, or was he coming into powers that the real Jahd—had he lived—might have developed organically?

He thought of those moments in the nursery with Mahari, when simply being in her company caused resonant feelings of warmth and wonderment. Mahari held a wealth of untapped potential that Jahd hoped to finally coax out of her the night before. He had, after all, been trying to do so for weeks. He wondered if he might have finally succeeded had they not been so rudely interrupted.

Jahd sighed. The increasing fatigue he was feeling after so little a display served as a clear warning. This power would need time to grow, and he would grow with it. It would have to be done in secret. Sure, he could let it be known that he was exhibiting the traits of a spellweaver, but then he would be sent to Breaton where they would test and measure him. While formal training might be nice, no one else could know, not until the right time. Pandoufuli would become his haven, and he would practice furtively.

The infirmary doors banged open at the other end of the room, and it surprised Jahd to see Jacinto approaching. Though he still wore the button-down shirt he was dressed in earlier, a few of the top buttons were loosened and the tie was discarded. Jacinto's soft blue gaze surveyed Jahd, and he smirked.

"They told me earlier that you could leave right before dinner," he said. "I'm sure you've had enough of this place by now. Are you ready, Jahd?"

Jahd took one more sip of the heated brew before smiling over the edge of the cup.

Chapter Twenty-Six

It was well after midnight when the carriage coasted onto the driveway of the Chatelain estate. Fayal greeted Liana, helping her to disembark as Millard began unloading the items from Kaileih's shop. As Liana entered the house, stripping off her gloves and smoothing her hair back, she detoured to the kitchen as she slipped the gloves into her coat pocket.

She was ravenous, seizing a cluster of grapes from the fruit bowl on the countertop. Liana sighed as she ate, plucking each juicy orb from its cluster even while eyeing the handful of date plums inside the bowl.

"Worked up quite an appetite, I see."

Liana coughed, whirling around in velvet-clad boots to face Evium. He looked exhausted; his blue eyes tinged with red as he surveyed his wife.

"I was just on my way upstairs," she said after clearing her throat and turning back to the bowl of fruit. She popped another grape into her mouth. "Thought I'd have a snack first."

"Where have you been?" Evium asked in that same soft tone.

Liana chewed carefully and swallowed, turning back to Evium with a smile. "I told you I was going out for some air."

"Air," Evium repeated, folding his hands in his lap. "You were out for ten hours getting some air?"

"Time got away from me."

"It seems I've heard that excuse before," Evium said with a nod. "The last time it was from our eight-year-old son. A child, Liana!" Evium's face reddened as he yelled. "Not from my wife—an adult who should know better and should also know not to take me for a fool!"

"I'm not trying to do that!" Liana said. "Vi, lower your voice!"

"Where have you been!?" Evium demanded.

"You'll wake Mahari..."

"Mahari cried herself to sleep because she thought you'd abandoned her to be with her brother! We both know that isn't who you were with. Where have you been, Liana?"

"I... I-I went to Scio," Liana said, tears building in her eyes as she wrung her hands together. "I... Millard... h-he, he's loading some things... I bought from Mama's shop... taking them to the greenhouse..."

"That's the only place you went... to Kaileih's shop and back... in ten hours."

They stared at one another. Evium's breaths were deep and even while Liana's were erratic as tears streamed down her face.

"No," she said before bursting into tears. "Vi, I..."

"Don't," he said flatly, glaring up at her. "The bit about the flower shop is a nice touch, but I know who else is in Scio. Do not lie to me again. My legs may not work, but there is nothing wrong with my brain. Now, tell me the truth and save the tears."

"I went to Dalenbeigh," Liana said, wiping the wetness from her cheeks.

"Why?" When Liana's answer was not forthcoming, he shouted the question again, causing her to jump.

"I... n-needed him to tell me if he ever spoke to Jahd about something I had confided in him."

"You confided in him," Evium repeated. "And what did my wife confide in my former best friend and her presumed former lover? Does it have anything to do with what Jahd said to get you so worked up last night and this morning?"

Liana wiped her nose with the back of her hand, sniffling. "Evium... I..." She shook her head. "It doesn't matter... it... it wasn't what I thought!"

"What about what I am thinking right now, Liana? What about what this looks like to me?"

"Evium... please..."

"I asked you... in the carriage," he said, his own eyes filling. "I asked if you wanted to talk about it. I saw you were hurt. I offered to be there for you. I wanted to be there for you..."

"I know, but..."

"Instead you turned me down, made up some excuses, and went straight to Huison fucking Loromin!?" he said. "Will we never be rid of him? You ran to him before when things were tense between us. Now, when there's NO reason for you to turn away from me, you open the door to him again."

"Please, I didn't mean..."

"You didn't mean to be caught! Was I not supposed to question you? Were you planning to come crawling back to bed after...?" He took a shuddering breath. "What happened while you were at Dalenbeigh? The two of you commiserated over yet another shared secret, and then what? What did you do for four hours?"

"Not that, Evium," Liana whispered. "I wouldn't do that."

"You mean you wouldn't do it again?" he asked. Evium ran a hand through his hair before steering backward a few paces in his chair. "I've tried so hard... so hard because I love you with every breath in me. I accepted Mahari, and she'll always be my daughter, but even I have my limits."

"What are you saying?"

"I won't stay this time, Liana," Evium said as his tears fell. "I won't sit by while this happens under my nose."

"I told you that nothing happened!"

"Were you planning to come upstairs and make love to me? Three months from now, am I to expect a pregnancy announcement from you?"

"I thought you forgave me for that," Liana wept.

"I thought you'd learned from your mistakes."

Evium steered backward again before turning to leave the kitchen. Liana fled after him until she was standing in front of him, blocking his way.

"I'll tell you!" she promised. "I'll tell you everything! Evium, please, it amounts to nothing!"

"If it were about nothing, you could have been honest with me from the time you came back to bed last night! We could have worked this out before even leaving for Pandoufuli. But, when I asked you again tonight, your first instinct was to LIE! I should not have to beg for your love or your confidence. It's exhausting, Liana, loving you!"

She gasped as a fresh stream of tears fell. "Exhausting?" she echoed. "But... I want to tell you everything."

"It's too late," Evium said, shaking his head. "There are consequences for your actions. That's something you've refused to learn as you go about doing as you like on a whim, and without a care for anyone else."

He wheeled around her and headed for the lift. Liana, practically frozen in place, continued to breathe shallowly as Evium moved farther away from her.

"But... you can't leave me here..." she breathed. When she finally turned to face him again, she saw he had stopped, and her heart leaped.

"What I can't do is just stay and watch," Evium said. "I don't want to keep up appearances anymore. I no longer want to feed what has become a lie, but I refuse to be separated from my children, so we'll have to work something out. Or is your intention to relocate to Dalenbeigh?"

"I don't want Huison!" Liana said brokenly. "I want you!"

"Well, you've had a hell of a way of showing it!" Evium yelled back as he faced her. "I keep falling for it, I... tell myself that everything's all right, that we're all right."

"Because we are!"

"Then why do you keep doing this!? Why hold yourself back from me? Why... why run to Huison as soon as you can sneak away? Now I find that you've gone and shared something with him... that not even your parents had the full story about, let alone me! You picked him—again!

"You don't know any better! You can't help yourself, can you? One of us has got to stop this madness before we're both consumed by it. Apparently, I'm the only one with the courage to do so."

Evium sighed, turning away again before wheeling the rest of the way to the lift, boarding without another backward glance.

Liana could not stop crying. How did everything go so wrong?

She had only meant to confront Huison about sharing her shame with Jahd, but it turned out that he had not. As she got ready to leave Dalenbeigh, he had looked at her with longing in those damnable amber eyes. She saw in them someone she could control, someone who found her superior. Liana held an authority over

Huison that she possessed in no other aspect of her life. It was exhilarating.

Liana sat cloaked in steam from the freestanding soaking tub. Her skin was red from a vigorous scrubbing, and her face was puffy from doing nothing but crying over the last hour. She had not heard Evium return. He must have slept elsewhere, perhaps in his workshop.

She understood he would need time. Evium had surely just spoken out of anger. He could not possibly be serious about leaving. After all, he had stayed with her after the discovery of Mahari's parentage. How could he leave now?

"Why?" she whispered, wringing out her bath sponge as if in the act of strangulation. "Why did you do this? You didn't have to go see Huison. You could have waited. You could have taken Evium along."

Liana shivered despite the hot water; her mother's most recent sentiments resonant in her mind.

"Don't squander it or take it for granted. I imagine it'd be a blow to your pretty ego to expect him to one day still be there for you, only to find that he's not."

"It won't happen," Liana vowed with a sniffle. "I won't let it. He just needs time."

When at last she emerged from her bathroom, shrouded in a cotton robe and with her wet hair pulled back into two thick braids, it disheartened her to find that Evium really had not returned to their bedroom. She went over to his side of the bed, taking up one of his pillows and holding it against her body. Liana caught his scent on the fabric and, though she knew him to be somewhere in the house, she missed him tremendously.

With a gentle hiccup, she returned the pillow to the bed. Had their son not been sent away to school, she might have crept into his room, enticing him awake to accompany her to the kitchen for a late-night bite.

Perhaps it was time for a new tradition.

Liana padded from her bedroom and down the hallway toward her daughter's nursery. While she walked, she wiped her eyes and affixed a smile to her face, so as not to rouse Mahari with a countenance that was too foreboding. She did not want to frighten the child into submitting to a trip to the kitchen.

When she got closer to her daughter's suite of rooms, however, the smile faded slightly. Liana heard laughing, the high-pitched and musical laugh of her youngest child. What in the world was that all about?

Suddenly, Liana's face lit up. Evium! That was where he went— to their daughter's room! Of course! He was so upset that Mahari cried during Liana's absence, so it was only natural that he would want to comfort her, and himself, by staying with her through the night. Liana would join them. Surely, Evium would not rebuke her presence in front of the baby, and it would give Liana the means to eventually win him over.

Liana smoothed the robe over her body and pinched lightly at her cheeks to give them a bit more color. She thought of rushing back to her rooms to apply something to her lips, but instead bit at the top and bottom lip to infuse color into them as well.

She opened the nursery doors with a flourish. Her daughter's exultant laughter drowned out Liana's gasping cry as Mahari twirled in the center of the room. Surrounding her was almost every stuffed animal, doll, and figurine she possessed, in a wide loop and dancing around her to a lively beat orchestrated by a set of drummer boy figurines lined up against a far wall.

"'ello, Mama!" Mahari said excitedly. "Dance! Dance! Come!"

Liana could barely breathe. What was this? What mockery was this? Why was this happening? She had lost one child, was forced to surrender another to Pandoufuli, and now... Her daughter, her precious baby girl... Was everyone going to leave her behind?

Mahari threw her head back, still laughing. The delight on her face as she danced was like a searing blade in Liana's heart. She was a baby. She was just a baby. She was only two years old and yet...

Mahari turned to her mother again, ceasing her breathless dance though the music continued. The menagerie broke the circle so that Mahari could walk over to her mother, arms outstretched.

"Come, Mama. Dance with us!"

The torrent of feelings had left Liana spent, and her body tingled as though her blood had carbonated. Standing in the heart of her daughter's nursery, with Mahari happily reaching out to her, Liana did the only thing she could truly, successfully manage after having replayed in her head all the events of the last couple of days, with each gut-wrenching occurrence guiding her toward the pinnacle of her emotions.

She fainted.

Chapter Twenty-Seven

Liana sat cross-legged atop the granite bench in the west garden, staring out at the cedar sapling rising over the memorial plaque at its base. Though Kynedal had experienced a rare dusting of snow that morning, Liana was quite warm in the light camel-colored cashmere poncho she wore, layered over a cream-colored turtleneck and matching pants.

Idly tapping the block heel of one suede knee-high boot against the cobblestones, she sipped from an etched glass of sweet red wine, mindful of the open bottle sitting below her hovering foot.

Liana sighed, slowly shaking her head as she remained fixated upon the sapling. She could hardly believe how things had changed and, as she had frequently, did her best to figure out exactly how and when things went wrong. Yes, she had made mistakes, but she was not a bad person. Others had done much worse. Yet, she was always the one in the wrong... always the one punished and forced to bear witness as others thrived.

When Evium packed up to move to D'alegne two months prior, Shaz and Fayal had chosen to go with him. Shaz had been no great loss, but Liana felt betrayed by the duplicity of Fayal.

Though Fayal and Alena did their best to live separately during that time, Alena finally came to Liana one night, a sodden, weepy mess as she explained how much she missed her husband, and the children missed their father. What was worse, she was expecting again! Liana could not be bothered to say goodbye as Fayal returned to the Chatelain estate to collect his brood. Mahari was inconsolable for days, having lost her most trusted nanny and all her playmates.

Mahari.

Before being officially cast off by Evium, it pained Liana to break the news that their two-year-old daughter was a spellweaver. Part of Liana hoped that, as heartbroken as she felt by this revelation, it might at least bring Evium closer to her. He instead accepted the news with an irritating calm before sending a modified inquiry to Claerendon for a more specialized tutor.

Oh, how the responses flooded in! Not only was this an opportunity of a lifetime to take part in the molding and growth of an obvious wunderkind, but also to serve the granddaughter of Amriel Dhamon! Who would not want this opportunity, even though it would be for a few short years until Mahari was old enough for enrollment in concentrated courses at the Junior Academy of Breaton?

Liana had no interest in interviewing candidates for the position. Even while supervising construction of his new home in D'alegne, Evium made periodic trips to Kynedal, sitting beside Kaileih as the consultations took place. Though Liana neither knew nor cared how it was done, it was arranged that Evium would conduct the preliminary roundtables with Kaileih, but Kaileih and Huison would preside over the final round of candidates.

Kaileih handled that, too. She was the one to send a message to Huison, advising him of his daughter's prowess. As expected, he demanded to be the one to instruct her, only giving up after Kaileih influenced him to exercise some sense not based solely on pride.

Huison had not yet been informed of the separation between Liana and Evium, and only accepted the temporary cessation of his visits with his daughter to ensure that her educational requirements took precedence.

Both Huison and Kaileih unanimously chose the winning candidate, apparently once a child prodigy. With dual specialties in both spellweaving and spellbreaking, besides a proficiency in various languages, Kaileih felt confident that all bases would be covered and Mahari would be in more than capable hands.

The first tutoring session was due to start soon. Liana had a full dossier on the young woman that would visit, but she had not bothered to read it. She instead spent the morning as she had the last several—in the comforting, warm embrace of a premier sweet red.

She heard footsteps approaching behind her, and Liana sighed again. They had not stopped pestering her all morning. How many times did she need to tell them she needed nothing, and that she was all right?

"Mama?"

Liana uncrossed her legs, getting to her feet. When she turned around, she was greeted by Mahari, who was beaming at her, being held by a somewhat stoic-looking Kaileih and trailed by Clea who, despite the short distance to the west garden from the main house, deemed it necessary to bundle up in a hat and puffy coat.

"I was wondering how long you planned to languish out here," Kaileih said, bouncing Mahari in her arms. "The new tutor will be here in three quarters of an hour, and I see you haven't even bothered reading the packet I left for you."

"There's no need," Liana said, taking another sip from her glass. "I trust your judgement." She then turned around again with her back to the others, resuming her place on the bench.

Kaileih's eyes narrowed as her jaw tightened, but the face she turned on her granddaughter was a cheerful one as she kissed

Mahari's forehead. "Why don't you go back inside with Clea? You can finish the puzzle you were working on."

Mahari nodded as Kaileih gently set her on her feet. The child first looked at her mother, and then at Clea before glancing up at her grandmother.

"Mama doesn't like me," she whispered before walking over to Clea.

Clea and Kaileih exchanged looks before Clea took Mahari's hand, and they walked together back to the house. The matter-of-factness of the statement coming from such a small child, combined with the fact that Mahari seemed a little too accustomed to the disdain coming from her own mother, caused tears to form in Kaileih's eyes.

"I could rip... every last curl from your head over the way you're treating that baby, Liana Rose," Kaileih said once she and Liana were alone. "None of this is her fault!"

"I never said it was, Mama," Liana said, lifting the glass to her lips.

With a cry of frustration, Kaileih's right arm shot out and the glass in Liana's hand shattered, spraying her with sharp fragments and spilling red wine all over her cashmere poncho. Startled, Liana got to her feet and shrieked when the bottle of red wine exploded beside her, covering her in even more shards and carmine splashes.

"What are you doing!?" Liana screamed when she faced her mother.

"What are YOU doing!?" Kaileih yelled back.

Panting, Liana touched her left cheek, knowing that she had been cut, but unsure of whether the wetness she felt was wine or blood. Her hands shook, and when she looked at them, she saw that the one holding the glass was pierced by several slivers. She burst into tears and, not caring that she was sitting in a small puddle of wine, lowered herself to the bench. Kaileih exhaled, shook her head, and sat beside her.

"You think I'm awful," Liana moaned, sniffling loudly.

"Yes," Kaileih said, "and what you're doing to that little girl is unconscionable. Jealous of a two-year-old, punishing the world for your mistakes…"

"It's a lot for me to deal with right now, Mama! My son is gone! My… my husband has left me… and now, my daughter is…"

"…an incredibly gifted child who will make you proud someday," Kaileih finished. "And, Jahd is not gone, he's away at school. Quit being so overly dramatic. As to Evium… I warned you."

"That doesn't help!" Liana wailed.

"I'm not trying to help. We've been through that already. I'm not here to coddle you. You insist upon doing things your own way. While there isn't much to be done about Jahd being at Pandoufuli, the other issues could have been avoided, or at the very least prepared for, had you only listened and acted accordingly.

"I cautioned you that Mahari would likely exhibit the characteristics of a spellweaver at some point in her life," Kaileih went on. "With a bloodline like hers, I would have been amazed if she hadn't. While I didn't expect it to happen so early, I'm not entirely surprised by that, either. It's innate."

"Innate," Liana said with a dry laugh. "You were wrong about me. I hoped you might be wrong about Mahari, too."

"I wasn't wrong about you, Liana," Kaileih admitted with a shrug. "I knew what you were, and I knew what you could do."

Liana gasped, turning to face her mother on the bench. "You mean you knew all along that I was a nobody?" Kaileih arched a brow without answering. "All the times we talked about it… and you gave me hope I could be like you and Daddy and Rael… and you knew I'd be nothing like you? Why?"

"Being a parent sometimes means making decisions your child will never understand, Liana," Kaileih said. "I did the best I could for you as your mother because I loved you so much and wanted you to live a good life." Kaileih got to her feet, pacing in front of the bench. "You were always so unhappy, even though I knew I'd done my best, so I sent you to the school. At the very least, I hoped they could teach you enough to satisfy you."

Liana stared at her mother in disbelief. "So, you sent me off to Breaton to what... turn me into nothing more than a magician?"

"Don't be so derisive of magicians, Liana Rose. I didn't raise you to be a snob." Kaileih took a seat again. "While it may be true that those considered magicians do not possess the native energy that comprises our abilities, some of them still do well with manipulating the elements as we know them. Some of the most talented magicians can even create enchantments that look exactly like the real thing."

"Parlor tricks. Illusions. Sleight of hand!" Liana spat. "You thought I'd be happy doing that, with all that you and Daddy can do? And Rael?" she laughed bitterly. "And, then there's me with an unlimited supply of hare to pull from a hat!"

"Being a spellweaver is more than about having power," Kaileih said, her dark brown gaze growing distant. "It's about being responsible to yourself and to others. It's about respecting your station and the natural order of things. Some aren't satisfied with that. For them, just having a taste is enough to place them on the road to madness, and there's no return from that."

"We're not talking about them, though, Mama! We're talking about me!"

Kaileih's smile was serene when she turned to her daughter, reaching out to caress her injured cheek. The shard of glass embedded beneath Liana's skin fell into Kaileih's palm, and the wound was instantly closed.

"Yes," Kaileih said softly. "Yes, we are."

"What about Mahari?" Liana whispered.

"You should not make your daughter suffer for your feelings of inferiority," Kaileih said gently. "Be that strong parent, Liana. Do the best you can by her, and by Jahd. Listen, this time! Listen, before it's too late." She studied her daughter. "You ought to get cleaned up. Mrs. Desmond will be here shortly."

"There's wine and glass everywhere," Liana said as she got up and looked around them.

"No worries," Kaileih said cheerfully. "I'll take care of that and then meet you inside." She stood up again, smirking. "I hope that you'll also stop by the nursery to give your daughter a big hug and kiss... after you've changed, of course."

Somewhat mortified by her behavior, Liana could only nod as she turned to walk back to the Den.

"What are you doing?"

Mahari looked up from where she sat at a small yet sturdy writing desk with a hutch that held a variety of colorful pencils, crayons, and even a small posy of flowers inside a compact vase. Though made of oak, it had been painted white and the recessed drawers, as well as the outer edge of both the desk and hutch, were coated in mauve. The initial 'M' was engraved on each brushed gold rosette knob adorning the drawers. Evium crafted both the desk and the matching chair, having sent them over the day before.

"Waiting," Mahari said softly, studying her hands.

"I see," Liana said with a nod, entering the room and having a look around. She could not suppress a wide smile.

Deciding that the library was too severe an environment in which a two-year-old should be tutored, Kaileih insisted that part of Mahari's nursery and playroom be converted into a study area.

There was ample space for her collection of dolls, toys, and other playthings, but they redesigned one section of the room into a dedicated, yet still colorful, haven for scholarship.

Liana had changed into a cream-colored crepe jumpsuit with satin lapels, her long hair pulled away from her face in a high ponytail. She had not yet bothered to put on shoes, and she walked almost silently over to where her daughter sat, lowering herself until she was seated on the floor beside Mahari's chair. Mahari reached over to touch the large gold hoop earring dangling from her mother's left ear and smiled.

"Pretty," she said.

"Thank you," Liana said, returning the smile. Liana looked at Mahari's face and could see the exact moment when doubt cast a shadow over her miniature features. "What is it?"

Mahari was finding it hard to look at her mother and instead focused on the gold hoop. But at last, her face crumpled as she asked, "Are you still my friend, Mama?"

Liana could not suppress a gasp at being asked such a question by her child, and feelings of guilt and self-loathing immediately overwhelmed her. She held her arms open and Mahari jumped into them, squeezing her mother with all the strength her small body contained. Liana dotted Mahari's face and neck with kisses as she held her, and they were still sitting there together a short while later when Clea entered the nursery.

"Forgive me," Clea said after gently clearing her throat. "Mrs. Desmond has arrived, Lady Chatelain."

"Oh, yes!" Liana said, gracefully getting to her feet with Mahari still in her arms. Mahari rested her head on her mother's shoulder, looking quite content.

"I've shown her to the sitting room and Linet is preparing a tray of refreshments. Would you like anything special brought to you there?"

"What has Mrs. Desmond requested?" Liana asked, kissing Mahari on the forehead before putting her down. Happily reassured, Mahari skipped to her collection of dolls, presumably to tell them the good news.

"Just some mint tea for now," Clea said.

"That'll do for me as well. When Linet's done, please have her come sit with Mahari until Mama gets back."

"Of course, ma'am."

As Clea departed, Liana turned back to smile at her daughter. "I'm going to have a talk with your new tutor, sweetheart," she said. "I'll be back with her soon."

"Yes, Mama," Mahari said before leaning to whisper into the ear of one of the dolls.

When Liana entered the sitting room a short while later, having momentarily detoured to her own suite to slip into a pair of soft gold moccasins, she stopped in the doorway and narrowed her eyes.

Mrs. Desmond, who was standing with her back to Liana as she gazed through the open window at the view of the east garden, was wearing a dark blue, sleeveless velvet romper over a metallic silver waffle weave turtleneck. Her thick, dark brown hair was pulled back into a braid, the end of which was nestled between her shoulder blades. Liana placed a hand to her stomach as tendrils of familiarity closed in around her. Linet's arrival, as she entered with the tray of refreshments, stifled Liana's resulting inhalation of surprise.

"Here we are!" Linet said cheerfully.

At that moment, Mrs. Desmond turned around and, as her eyes met Liana's, she smiled. Liana's gaze dropped, drawn to the small bulge at Mrs. Desmond's midsection, still visible despite the romper. She said nothing as Linet busied herself with the tea service for a moment before turning to Liana, cheeks flushed from exertion.

"Will you be needing anything else, my lady?"

"No," Liana said absentmindedly, her face slightly ashen as her eyes remained fixed on her guest. She then blinked and shook her head, finally focusing on Linet. "No, Linet, thank you."

"I'll head up to the nursery now, if that's all right."

"That's perfectly fine. I'll let Clea know if we need anything else." Linet nodded, curtsied, and then left the two ladies alone. One stared. The other smiled. "Please... have a seat."

"Thank you," Mrs. Desmond said, walking over to one of the cushioned slate gray chairs and sitting down. When she saw Liana gawking at her, she could not help laughing softly. "Um... I'm not really sure what to call you."

"Flabbergasted would be a good start," Liana said, walking over to sit on the large sofa across from the duo of chairs. "This is... quite a revelation. Apparently, I should have reviewed your dossier after all. When Mama told me we had hired you, she didn't mention that you were..."

"Expecting?" Kaileih said as she entered the room, a pleased expression on her face. "I didn't think it mattered. She's not due for some time. Mahari can have her break in the early winter months rather than in summer as is the norm. If we keep her in that habit, she'll have no trouble adjusting when it's time for her to attend school." She sat on the sofa beside Liana, reaching over to help herself to an almond cookie. "Hello again, Mrs. Desmond."

"Hello to you, Mrs. Dhamon. So good to see you again."

"No, of course," Liana said, almost to herself, "what was I thinking? You weren't there."

"I wasn't where?" Kaileih asked, turning to her daughter. "Liana, what are you talking about?"

Liana cleared her throat. "Mama, as you know, this is Mrs. Desmond," she said. "Rhia Desmond now, but when I knew her back at Breaton Academy, she was Rhia Angelo. She was one of my classmates and we shared a dormitory."

Kaileih turned to Rhia in surprise, the cookie forgotten. "Well, that's certainly unexpected! I knew you attended Breaton, but...why didn't you tell me during any of our conversations that you knew my daughter?"

"Forgive me, Mrs. Dhamon," Rhia said as her smile faded. "No deceit was intended. I would have acknowledged it had you inquired. I just didn't know if you might base your decision on any prior association with Liana. I hoped to be granted the position based on merit."

"Well, we based the collective decision upon your skill set," Kaileih said. "I won't say that you set out to deceive us, but you certainly lied by omission."

"I understand, Mrs. Dhamon," Rhia said, her eyes downcast. "I'm willing to step aside to allow someone else to..."

"Save the speech," Kaileih interrupted before turning to Liana. "Looks like you'll have some say in this after all. What do you think of this? What would you like to do?"

"Daddy met her once," Liana said after a few moments as she wrung her hands together. "Called her brilliant, which she was. Apparently, she's become even more so. The things she could do when we were in school... I'd be foolish to turn her away." Rhia looked up, a smile highlighting her smooth brown skin. "I have to do what's best for my daughter," Liana went on, looking at Rhia again. "That's all that matters to me right now. If you fail to follow suit, prior association will not be your saving grace."

"I understand implicitly," Rhia said contritely.

"Then, I'll let the two of you get reacquainted," Kaileih said, finishing her almond cookie. "I'll be in the nursery with Mahari when you're ready to join us, Mrs. Desmond."

"Thank you, Mrs. Dhamon," Rhia said appreciatively.

"Two down," Liana said wryly once Kaileih departed. "Two to go."

"Pardon?" Rhia said, adjusting her wire-rimmed glasses.

"Let's just say that you aren't the only former classmate I've reunited with recently." Liana could not help laughing. "It makes me wonder what else is coming." She studied her old friend. "I see you still love your dark blue," she mused. "Don't you find this the least bit awkward, Rhia?"

"No," Rhia answered with a shake of her head. "I wouldn't say awkward. Serendipitous, maybe?" She leaned forward in the chair. "We all missed you so much after you left Breaton."

"Even Vanja?" Liana asked dryly, reaching over to pour tea for the two of them.

"Her, maybe not so much," Rhia admitted, waiting until the tea was served before taking up her cup. "She asked to be reassigned to another dorm the day you left. She cut everyone off after that, stuck to her studies, and even graduated early just like you thought she would." Rhia smirked, chuckling into her cup. "Maybe the prospect of being offered for eternal damnation was a turnoff."

"Are you still in touch with anyone else?" Liana asked as she spooned a bit of sugar into her tea, stirring it before picking up the cup and taking a sip.

"Elyse and I used to get together a few times a year after graduation, but... once she became a royal it wasn't as easy to do."

Liana coughed, involuntarily spitting out some tea in surprise. "She became a what?" she asked, putting the cup back on the table and reaching for a napkin to wipe her mouth. Rhia grinned.

"She married well," Rhia said, still smiling as she took a sip. "Elyse Bourdillon has become Elyse, la Dauphine d'Allard."

"My word," Liana breathed.

"Indeed. As such, she can no longer travel as she once did—at least not without an entire retinue behind her. Because of that, we're down to one or two correspondences a year... if we're lucky."

"I'm sorry, Rhia," Liana said with great sincerity. "I remember how close the two of you were in school."

"She tried to have me appointed as *directrice* for the royal nursery," Rhia explained. "But, her husband insisted upon hiring someone with tenure directly from the university in Claerendon. Offered the man a year's wages upfront to abandon his post and become the *directeur*. Nothing but the best for their daughter."

Liana shook her head as Rhia chuckled. "So, we've all had girls so far?"

"Hmm?" Rhia asked, her brow furrowed.

"You mentioned serendipity before," Liana said, reaching for a cookie. "I ran into Aniela a couple months back."

Rhia gulped. "Did you? Where? How is she?"

"She's doing wonderfully. She's also married, with a gorgeous daughter and a handsome stepson who attends Pandoufuli with my son, Jahd."

"Pandoufuli?" Rhia asked.

Liana bit into her cookie with a wry grin. "I have a son, who can do no magic... and a daughter who's poised to carry on the Dhamon name in spectacular fashion."

"Liana," Rhia began carefully as she briefly stared into her tea, "are you okay? Forgive me for asking, but... you were so upset after... what happened... and then you left Breaton without another word said. Now Mahari..."

"Has come into her birthright and will do beautifully," Liana finished. "The road hasn't been easy, Rhia, and I'm sure there are bumps yet to come, but... I'm fine. I must be. It's always a mother's hope that her child will exceed her expectations, isn't it? I'd say she's off to an impressive start." They smiled at one another as Liana finished her cookie and nodded in Rhia's direction. "How about you? Your first?"

"Yes," Rhia answered, rubbing the small curve of her belly.

"Could you imagine if we all had girls?"

Rhia laughed. "Somehow, I don't think the world would be ready for that... a new generation sprung from The Original Five."

"Is that what we are?" Liana said, unable to help laughing.

"Ah, just making sure that I forewarn the aforementioned world."

"May they tremble in their boots," Liana said amiably as she got to her feet. "Shall we? You and Mahari can spend some time getting to know one another and then we will all have lunch together. Her session can begin afterward."

"That would be amazing," Rhia said, radiant with happiness.

When the two of them arrived upstairs in the nursery, they found Kaileih sitting on the floor, with Mahari standing in front of her. Mahari was using an antiquated stethoscope to listen to her grandmother's heart. After several seconds, Mahari pulled back, her little face scrunched and serious.

"I think you gonna live, Grandmama," she said gravely.

"Well, isn't that a relief!" Kaileih said, before glancing over at the others.

"'ello, Mama!" Mahari greeted, walking over to Liana and Rhia as Kaileih got to her feet.

"Hello, yourself!" Liana returned, smiling. "Mahari, sweetheart... I'd like to introduce you to someone." Mahari looked over at Rhia, who was grinning down at her. "This is Miss Rhia. She's going to be your teacher."

Rhia sank to her knees in front of Mahari so that they were closer to eye level.

"Hello, Mahari," she said warmly. "It's very nice to meet you."

Mahari peered down at Rhia's stomach before looking into her new tutor's dark brown eyes. Then she smiled.

PART THREE

Chapter Twenty-Eight

Jacinto stared at the card in his hand, light blue eyes filled with wonder. He and Jahd were sauntering down the white, marbled halls of Pandoufuli on their way back to their shared dormitory.

"Once again, you've saved my hide," Jacinto said. "I can't believe these final marks."

The term had officially ended a week prior, and they were among the few stragglers who had yet to pack up to head for home. Jacinto waved at a classmate who was going in the opposite direction, looking anything but thrilled to collect his final grades from the headmaster's office. Jahd, coolly aloof, continued to walk without giving the other boy a second glance.

"You ought to," Jahd responded, tucking his own grade card into his pocket without bothering to look at it. "I made you stay up late nearly every night for the last month studying for exams."

Jacinto laughed. "How many times were we almost caught by the curfew sentry?"

"How many nights are there in a month?" Jahd returned with a smirk.

"You're not even looking at yours?"

"No need."

"Of course not," Jacinto said. "Always top marks for Jahd Chatelain, even with a dual concentration in Supply Chain Management and Actuarial Science." He cast a sidelong glance at his friend. "Planning to take after your father?"

"I should be so lucky," Jahd said, chuckling.

"All I know is that with marks like that, you're a shoo-in for the ambassadorship next term."

Pandoufuli's reputation needed no defense. It was rare that a graduate of the academy did not become renowned within a specialized field. It had become a recent practice that the all-around top student among those of the Senior Level, selected based on grades, bearing, attractiveness, and overall likability, would become an ambassador of sorts and given a stipend to travel once monthly to targeted areas hoping to lure those of similar measure into Pandoufuli's ranks.

"We haven't even started senior levels yet," Jahd reminded Jacinto.

"So?"

"So... let's wait and see what happens." They passed another of the last-minute stragglers, an attractive girl with short red hair. This time it was Jahd who nodded in greeting, while Jacinto simply ignored her. "You ready to head home later?"

"Hmm, I guess."

"Guess?" They ascended the staircase side-by-side, as it was highly unlikely that anyone would need to come down. "You're always glad to see your family."

"I don't know what I'm getting into, though. The last letter I got from Dad and Ani didn't sound so good."

"How so?"

"It's Zoi," Jacinto sighed. "She's been having nightmares for a bit. Got everyone worried."

"Nightmares?"

"Yeah. From what my dad said in his last letter, she keeps having these dreams about someone being after her. Someone or something. She's never sure which... and can remember nothing about it when she wakes up. Ani and my dad are thinking of taking her to Vespers."

At the top of the stairs, Jahd halted. "Vespers Glen? Isn't that where they house the magical crazies?" he asked.

"Don't say that about my sister!" Jacinto flared, reddening.

"Apologies. I meant nothing by it." They resumed their walk. "But, why there?"

"Things are happening in her sleep. She's been hurting herself, waking up with marks on her. They can look after her at Vespers while they get to the root. If our parents take her there, it'll be during our winter hiatus... so that she can rest and be out before the next term starts at Breaton."

"Is she having any problems at school?"

"Pssh, no. She's aced all her classes and is at the top of her grade. She'll probably graduate early."

Jahd considered this. "Isn't she a healer like your stepmother?"

"Sort of," Jacinto said. "Her ability works differently... more on feelings and emotions than physical ailments. I don't understand it much, to be honest. All I know is that I never had a bad day when she was around. No bad dreams, wasn't ever sad about anything... there was just this warm feeling like something wrapped me up and made me safe..." He sighed. "Kind of ironic that she can keep everyone else from having nightmares and can't help herself. But now what she's apparently become great at is conflagration."

Jahd stopped in his tracks again. "She's what?"

"Now do you see why they need to get her to Vespers and under control?" Jacinto asked, shaking his head. "They've been keeping it under wraps at Breaton, but she's apparently set two fires already in her sleep. She'll be assigned a dorm to herself starting next term."

"Alone, huh?"

Jacinto nodded as they continued to walk. "Just feels weird to have a sister who could roast you alive for lunch and, at the same time, make you feel happy to have been invited to the picnic."

"Yeah, I guess so," Jahd said, almost to himself.

"Anyway, what about you? What are you doing this winter?"

"Dodging a million questions at home, I'm sure, even though my parents were here last month to sign off on the start of senior levels next term."

"Both of them at your place together?" Jacinto asked. "They still do that after all this time?"

"They try. They're both always there for the first week after the end of term. Then my dad heads back to D'alegne."

They reached their dormitory. Jacinto kicked off his shoes and yanked the knot from his tie as Jahd removed his uniform jacket and placed it on the coat rack. Jacinto's side of the room looked as though a tempest had hit it. Jahd's side was pristine.

"You've got so much to clean up," Jahd continued. "We're leaving in a couple of hours, and this won't be our room anymore when we get back in the new year."

"Eh, it'll get done," Jacinto said with a shrug as he draped himself across his bed, which was covered in various items of clothing. "Or you could do it for me."

"As if I'd touch your filthy plum smugglers," Jahd said with a laugh.

"Who said anything about touching them?" Jacinto asked lazily. "You could simply..." Jahd's eyes widened as he watched Jacinto wiggle his fingertips.

"What's that supposed to mean?"

"You really thought I didn't know?" Jacinto said as he sat up. He and Jahd stared at one another for a moment before Jacinto got up and walked over to the door, closing it. He then turned back to Jahd, folding his arms and fixing him in his light blue gaze. "It's been killing me all year not to say anything! I wasn't sure if you were hoping I'd notice and bring it up to you first because you were afraid to. Now, here we are within hours of leaving for home, and you still haven't said!"

"Said anything about what?" Jahd asked slowly.

"Don't play with me! I'm not stupid and I'm certainly not blind, though I wondered if I was really seeing..." Jacinto moved away from the door and closer to the center of the room. "What are you doing at Pandoufuli when you're a spellweaver?" Jahd continued to stare, not answering. "Come on, Jahd—talk to me! I thought we were best friends!

"For the longest time, I'd hear things from your side of the room in the middle of the night. I thought maybe you were just having a happy tug here and there and was trying not to be heard, but then I saw you! After all this time I finally saw!"

"What did you see!?" Jahd demanded.

"Why didn't you tell me?" Jacinto countered.

"Why didn't you say anything?" Jahd asked, eyes narrowed.

Jacinto ran a hand over his closely cropped hair. "I was waiting for you! Seems like we talk about everything else, why not this?"

"Because, as you well know, it could get me expelled!"

"So?" Jacinto said.

"So, what do you want?"

"What do I... Is that what you think? I want nothing! If I did, don't you think I'd have confronted you when I found out for sure? I mean... I guess... I want to know what it's like." Jacinto's eyes were rounded. "How does it feel? What all can you do? If I hadn't caught you, would you ever have said anything?"

"It's not a simple thing to discuss," Jahd said. "I don't want anyone else to know yet."

"Wouldn't you need to go to school for it, though?" Jacinto asked. "You're wasting yourself here."

Jahd sat upon his bed, shrugging. "I've thought of that," he said. "This is the best place for me. I can explore on my own with no one getting in the way." He eyed Jacinto. "Or, at least I thought I could."

Jacinto returned to his bed. "I remember hearing about some guy who's related to the founder of Pandoufuli," he said. "When his family realized he could do magic, they disowned him."

"I'm fairly familiar with that story," Jahd said with a straight face.

"Your dad seems like a great guy. He wouldn't do that to you. Is your mother the problem?"

"You have no idea."

"I won't tell anyone," Jacinto promised. "I wouldn't. I just..."

"...wanted me to tell you," Jahd finished. "What have you seen?"

"You can move things without touching them."

"Is that all?"

"Is there more?" Jacinto shot back.

"Yes," Jahd said at last. "But, there's only so much I can practice here in the room at night. I... can't do it anywhere else."

Jacinto nodded. "Is that what you've been doing, wait until you think I've fallen asleep and then start practicing?"

"I couldn't very well do it in broad daylight, could I?" Jahd scratched at his curls. "I do a bit here and there when home on breaks, but... most of the time I'm worried about getting caught."

"You can do it in our dorm from now on... starting when we get back next term." Jacinto's eyes lit up. "Show me something... what else can you do? What else have you been practicing?"

"Are you serious?" Jahd said with a laugh.

"What do you think?" Jacinto said. "I finally got you to ante up with the truth. The least you could do is show me something."

"You've already seen!"

"But, you said that wasn't all of it."

"No..." Jahd said after a brief pause.

Jacinto leaned forward on the bed. "So, show me!" he said eagerly.

Jahd looked over at Jacinto. A slow smile crept across his face.

"Are you sure? I don't want to scare you."

"Ha!" Jacinto said, almost giddy. "As if you could. Come on, show me what you've got!"

"Oh, all right," Jahd said. "If you insist. Close your eyes first, though."

Jacinto closed his eyes, unable to contain a grin as he waited, even bouncing on his bed a little. He was almost holding his breath, as he was so excited. He then heard his name being whispered softly. A crease formed in his brow, and Jacinto slowly opened his eyes again.

His resulting screams bounced from their shared dormitory and along the hallway, echoing throughout. As they were the only students remaining on that floor because of the end of the term, no one else heard.

The weather was warmer than usual, considering the time of year, and it seemed logical that those present at the Chatelain estate should take advantage of the beautiful morning. Millard partnered with Linet in creating several outdoor games and other festivities while Clea and Shaz labored inside the kitchens, making sure that there was enough food and refreshments for everyone by keeping a series of buffet tables fully stocked.

Skilled in neither party games nor food preparation, Liana was content to remain indoors in a prime position from which to watch everything and everyone. She was particularly amused by Shaz, as she did not know that he even had any culinary skills, and she surmised he had gained them after joining Evium in D'alegne.

Liana spied the sidelong glances Shaz occasionally made in Linet's direction, particularly when Linet tried something that Shaz had prepared, and Liana wondered whether she would soon need to interview a new housemaid. She watched Alena playing in the yard with eight of her own children and a handful of other offspring of present and past personnel of the Chatelain estate, including four-year-old Léah Desmond, Rhia's adorable daughter. No matter how hard Liana tried, though, her gray gaze always eventually returned to where Evium sat near the table.

It was not fair.

Liana peered through the glass double doors leading to the backyard, where she could surreptitiously peer at her former husband without his knowledge. Evium sat with his back to her, watching the activity in the vast backyard of the Den and laughing at the various antics around him. He looked the picture of health, color high in his cheeks as he tossed an errant ball back to one child playing outside.

Liana sighed, recalling that when she met Evium, as the charming twenty-one-year-old who came into her mother's shop in Tilehn to purchase an afterthought gift for his then-fiancée, he still had a boyish quality about him she found endearing.

By the time his marriage to Liana had ended, he was approaching thirty. Still, Liana did not think he could ever be more handsome with his refined features, distinguished manner, and irresistible grin.

At thirty-five, he had become thoroughly devastating. In the last several months, he had grown facial hair, and the neatly trimmed beard that was perhaps a shade darker than the thick, golden blond hair on his head, edged a delicately sculpted jawline and somehow made his eyes appear an even deeper shade of blue.

He lost a bit of weight in the months after their separation but had since rebounded in spectacular fashion. Evium now looked made of marble, his chest and arms massive and finely muscled, white teeth gleaming in the bright morning sun as he laughed again before charging over in his wheelchair to scoop up a giggling child and spin with her in fast circles. Liana felt warmed by the sight, even as daggers of bitter jealousy stabbed at her extremities.

"You'll set the man ablaze if you keep staring at him like that," Kaileih chided as she walked by carrying an empty porcelain vase, causing Liana to jump guiltily.

"I wasn't staring," she said, turning away from her viewing post to look at her mother.

Kaileih was another to whom Time had been exceedingly kind. Even the threads of silver appearing at her temples were flattering, and there was nothing more to show that she had aged at all. Her skin was still as smooth, her tongue was sharper than ever, and she was always effortlessly beautiful.

Conversely, Liana felt every bit of her thirty years, and then some. She had not accepted the finality of the demise of her marriage with anything resembling grace, and it was draining. Early on, Liana felt secure in the premise that she could get Evium back. Time away from her and away from the home he had so painstakingly built for the two of them would prove too much for him. How could he stay away?

Evium did stay away. Sure, he returned to Kynedal to visit Jahd during his breaks from school at Pandoufuli, and he also spent time with Mahari when she was not busy with her studies with Rhia or spending time at Dalenbeigh. Both children had expansive rooms on his own sprawling estate, ready for whenever they wanted to come and stay with him.

Evium even maintained an amiable relationship with Kaileih, not only visiting her at the Den occasionally but also helming various projects at any of four shops she now owned, the latest of which—at Evium's urging—was opened in D'alegne. That he worked so hard to preserve those other bonds, yet still insisted on breaking the one he had with Liana, was very painful to her.

Liana abandoned her post, walking over to where her mother stood, building a massive arrangement of creamy yellow calla lilies, bright orange roses, and dark red daisies within the porcelain vase, each flower taken from a large basket sitting beside it.

"You should be thankful that he's doing well," Kaileih said, focusing on flora. "Things could have ended differently."

"Or, they could have not ended at all," Liana said, picking up one of the large orange roses and bringing it to her nose.

"Regret is such a bitter condiment," Kaileih mused, tilting her head to study her creation before continuing her work. "I'd say you've had enough time to perfect your act of martyrdom. You've eluded much over the last several years, but big changes are on the way in a couple of months and decisions have to be made."

"What kinds of decisions?"

Kaileih turned to study her daughter, daisy in hand, as her brow arched. "Jahd will start his senior levels at Pandoufuli, and Mahari will begin her first term in the Junior Academy of Breaton," she said. "This will be the first time you have ever been alone in this house, bevy of servants not included, of course."

"And?"

"You're still young, Liana. You have cloistered yourself for the last five years waiting for something that, quite frankly, was a long shot from the start. Accept it and move on."

"You act as if you don't want us to get back together!" Liana accused.

"I want you both to be happy," Kaileih said, turning back to her flowers. "Of course, in an ideal world, you could be happy together as the family you were before. Time has passed, though. Things are evolving. It's no longer a possibility."

Liana scoffed, turning away to walk back toward the glass doors. Evium was now racing about the yard, two of Alena's children shrieking on his lap as he maneuvered into a series of sharp turns. Her eyes softened as she looked at him. After a few seconds, her brow slowly creased before her eyes widened and she turned back to her mother.

"Wait a minute," she said, returning to Kaileih's side. "Mama... what are you saying?"

"Same as I have been for a few years now."

"No, you've never said it quite like this," Liana stressed. "What do you mean that things are evolving?" Kaileih sighed and turned to look at her daughter. Liana stared into her mother's dark brown eyes, and then her jaw dropped. "Mama! He's... Is he...? Is there...."

"No," Kaileih said before taking the rose from Liana's hand. "But, I suspect that he soon will."

"When?" Liana wanted to know, her face reddening. "Who?"

"There is a young lady who manages my shop in D'alegne," Kaileih began.

"Mama, no!" Liana wailed. "Why... why do you think that... You have to get rid of her, then!"

"I will not," Kaileih said curtly and without raising her voice.

"How long has this been going on?"

"Nothing *is* going on, Liana Rose. But, as I've said, things are evolving." Kaileih shrugged. "It's been very gradual. They started out as cordial and business oriented... very polite to and respectful of one another during the times Evium's been out to the shop to work on enhancements.

"Lately, I've noticed a growing warmth between them... easy smiles, effortless banter... To be honest, I'm not sure that either of them has fully realized it yet, but when they do..."

Liana exhaled sharply, feeling her temples throb as she had been holding her breath the entire time. Her eyes burned, and she wrapped an arm about her midsection as she took a few more breaths. The redness slowly drained from her face as the crease in her brow deepened.

"I suppose she's younger than me?" Liana asked in a voice that seemed far away, detached from herself.

"A year or two older, I believe," Kaileih said, studying her daughter. "Whatever you're thinking about doing, stop. That's the sort of nonsense that was the catalyst for all this."

As Liana glared at her mother, a small, lanky figure who watched them calmly through a long tangle of dark curls as she nibbled upon a chocolate and honeycomb biscuit joined them. Kaileih's expression softened and, smiling, she winked.

"Well, hello there!" Kaileih greeted.

"'ello, Grandmama," Mahari returned softly.

Mahari had long since lost the musical lilt inherited from Alena in her early years, the one that might have caused her to be mistaken for a child of the northern region. Her preferred greeting, however, had not changed at all, becoming something of a hallmark to those around her.

Her large gray eyes moved to take in Liana's condition. "'ello, Mama."

"Hello, sweetheart," Liana said after clearing her throat. "I thought you were still outside with the others."

Mahari held up what remained of her treat, wordlessly showing that she had come inside for a snack. A perfect hybrid of both her parents, Mahari was skinny and long-limbed, with her father's olive complexion and her mother's striking gray eyes set in a heart-shaped face. When she spoke, which was not very often, her accent was crisp and gave her the unintended air of someone much older than her seven years. Mahari was a serious and studious child. Her smiles, though rare, could light up a room.

Kaileih, having finally finished with her arrangement, walked over to her granddaughter wielding the remaining red daisy, expertly weaving the stem through the tresses at Mahari's right temple and tucking the bud above her ear. Mahari, always spontaneously affectionate with her grandmother, leaned into Kaileih as she finished the biscuit.

"I hope you saved some of those for your brother," Kaileih admonished playfully as she smoothed Mahari's hair back, to which Mahari responded with one of those rare smiles and a giggle. "Do I have to send you back into the apiary, young lady?"

"You say that as though it's a punishment," Liana said, having recovered enough temporarily to join in on the conversation. She walked over, gently straightening the flower in her daughter's hair as she smiled down at her. "She spends about as much time there as she does with her studies."

"Did you remember the letter to your father, reminding him you and your brother will go out to Dalenbeigh in a couple of weeks?" Kaileih asked.

"Yes, Grandmama," Mahari answered, her tongue darting out to lick at a bit of honeycomb stuck to her bottom lip.

"Go on back outside for a bit," Liana said. "Jahd should be here soon, and you know he'll look for you."

She watched as her daughter left while Kaileih repositioned the vase and smiled at her handiwork.

"As if Huison needed reminding," Liana continued. "He's been beside himself, bursting with pride over Mahari's early admission to Breaton. He can't wait to celebrate her departure."

"It's quite an achievement," Kaileih said. "It was wise, though, to keep her here at home for the extra months, even though they would have gladly taken her a year ago."

"Off to school at five years old," Liana said with a shake of her head. "Who's ever heard of such a thing? As it is, I'm reluctant to let her go now as she's turning seven."

"Mahari will be fine. She's an extraordinary little girl with a great foundation."

"She's so solemn, Mama... so severe. She's not at all like I was at her age."

"There weren't very many children for her to interact with once Alena moved to D'alegne to be with her husband," Kaileih reminded her. "Once she settles in at school, she'll learn from others like her. It'll give her the opportunity to develop her social skills." Kaileih folded her arms. "And, you need to think about what I've said about your own life."

"Why haven't you ever remarried?" Liana asked suddenly. "You're telling me to go out and do something you haven't dared yourself."

"There's no one else for me," Kaileih said simply.

"Mama, you are still a breathtaking woman! I'll be lucky to look half as good at your age!"

"Oh, I don't disagree with that," Kaileih said, her dark eyes twinkling. "What your father and I have transcends convention. No one can replace him. No one will."

"No one can take Evium's place for me, either," Liana said.

"I think we've just finished chatting with the living proof of that not being the case."

Liana gasped. "Mama! You can't mean Huison!"

281

"Not as a direct example, no," Kaileih said. "But, it shows that you could be wrong and there might be someone else for you." She picked up the basket, now empty of the flowers it once held, playfully poking at the tip of Liana's nose before departing.

Jahd rinsed his mouth, spitting into the basin of the sink and watching his blood-tinged saliva swirl down the drain. Bracing himself on shaky limbs, he peered at his reflection in the mirror, noting with mild amusement that he looked as though someone had painted him in sepia because of the lack of color in his face.

His light laughter turned to gagging, though, causing him to cough before vomiting explosively into the sink again, expelling more blood as well as what remained of his breakfast. Groaning, he washed his mouth out again to rid it of the taste of bile and blood. Despite his coloring as it appeared in the mirror, having gone from sepia to grayscale, he felt much better.

He hiccupped, switching the hot water off until nothing but cold ran for several seconds. He then plunged his hands beneath the chilled flow, liberally splashing his face and running both hands through his curls as he took several deep breaths. Jahd reached for the empty glass water pitcher sitting atop the toiletry cart inside the bathroom and filled it to the brim with icy liquid. He turned the water off before going back to the adjoining bedroom and to Jacinto, who lay sprawled in the center of the floor, motionless.

A hastily dumped pitcher of water directly into Jacinto's face was more than enough to rouse him from his former state after having so hysterically lost consciousness.

"Hey, what the hell!?" Jacinto spluttered, scrambling to his feet.

Jacinto coughed, shooting water from his nose and mouth, and struggled to catch his breath as Jahd calmly sat upon his own bed and tossed the pitcher behind him.

"What the fuck was that you just did!?" Jacinto demanded after he had mostly collected himself.

"I provided you with a little hydration therapy," Jahd said.

"Not... that!" Jacinto said, coughing again. "Before!"

"What's the last thing you remember?" Jahd asked faintly, wrapping his arms around his midsection.

"We were talking. I asked you to show me something." Jacinto's eyes widened. "Then you told me to close my eyes, and... You whispered my name, but... Somehow... your voice went from being over by your bed to being beside me on mine, and..." He shuddered, swallowing hard. "Something was next to me when I opened my eyes. It wasn't you like I thought it would be... It was a... a... dark red and black blob of something." Jacinto blanched as his watery eyes bulged. "...wrapped up in this... swarm of smoke or vapor. What the hell was that all about!?"

"And... what else..." Jahd pressed, closing his eyes.

Jacinto was still breathing so heavily that he felt lightheaded. He tried sitting on the edge of his bed, missed, and instead dropped to the wet floor. "And... your body was still sitting on your bed," Jacinto whispered shakily, to which Jahd responded by smiling, his eyes still closed. "Your eye sockets were empty and black... I... Jahd..."

"Yes?"

"What did you do?"

"What did it look like?" Jahd countered.

"Like you left your body," Jacinto said, swallowing hard.

"Did it?"

"You left your body?" Jacinto asked, louder.

"It would seem so," he said, opening his eyes again.

"Why did you do that!?"

"You asked me to show you something, did you not?"

"Yeah, but... I mean... You couldn't just wave a hand and put the candles out or something, though, damn! Instead, you scare the shit out of me?"

Jahd chuckled. "I had to know."

"Know what!?"

"Whether I could for certain." He extended a shaking hand, turning it over to study the palm. "I've had these dreams of looking at myself from the outside." He looked up at Jacinto, his gray eyes seeming to crackle with life, though he still felt terrible. "Or, maybe they weren't simply dreams. I wasn't sure. I haven't been able to test it out until now. I was planning to when I got home."

"Why do you look so sick?" Jacinto whispered.

"That's the hardest thing I've done in five years," Jahd said. "Took more out of me than I expected."

"I don't think I've ever even heard of anyone who could do... whatever that was."

"I feel it's very safe to say that, as difficult as that was just now, it's highly possible that anyone with the ability to perform corporeal projection didn't live to tell the tale." Jahd's brows rose. "How many comatose slabs of flesh at Vespers stumbled onto this little nugget by accident, do you think?"

"You should see yourself," Jacinto said.

"I looked in the mirror," Jahd said with a dismissive wave of one hand. "It'll pass."

"You might have nearly killed yourself or become one of those slabs you just made fun of. You can barely sit upright, Jahd. You can't do that again!"

"Your concern is touching," Jahd said with a smirk.

"I'm serious!"

"I tried to touch you at first, before I said your name. My hand passed right through. Can you imagine what I could do outside of myself in a more solidified form?"

"No, not if doing that is going to end up hurting you. Promise not to do that again, Jahd!"

Jahd's smile widened. "I have to," he said, laying on his back and staring up at the ceiling. "How else will I get stronger?"

Liana stepped through the open back door, the light morning breeze toying with the fringed hem of her black sweater dress as the silver heels of her black velvet boots tapped across the cobblestones. Evium had finished giving rides for the time being and was back to watching the group of children playing nearby. Mahari was not among them, and Liana wondered if she had gone back to the apiary.

Heart racing, Liana moved to stand beside Evium as she also watched the group of children while lightly wringing her hands together. Evium glanced to his right, looking up at her. He made note of the busy fingers and the way she nibbled at the fullness of her bottom lip, and he frowned before turning away to watch the assemblage again.

"Mahari was just here," he said, trying to be helpful. "I believe you'll find her manning the hives."

"I thought she might be," Liana said. "It's been a chore keeping her out of it since Mama had it installed last spring."

"Ah, it does her no harm. I think it's a healthy hobby, and she'll miss them while she's away at school."

"I still find it so hard to believe that she's already old enough to go to school," Liana said with a sigh. "She's still a baby. She and Jahd both... they're my babies."

"They'll always be our babies, Liana," Evium said with a sincere smile. "That'll never change."

"Yet everything else has."

Turning the wheelchair to the right, Evium faced her fully, his blue gaze warm. "Within a couple of hours, we'll have both our children here at home," he said. "In roughly a couple of months, they'll both be away at school and, for the first time in our lives, we'll face how it feels to be without them."

"I always thought we'd face that time together," Liana said, staring down at her hands as she toyed with one of her rings.

"We'll face it as their parents, but not together." He reached for one of her hands and gave it a gentle squeeze. "And, that's okay. We'll both still be there when they need us."

"What about how I still need you?" Liana asked, her voice trembling. "I'll love no one else the way I do you, Evium."

"I should hope not," he said with shining eyes and a charming smile. "Hopefully, you'll love the next one better." He released her hand, sitting back and still smiling at her. "You'll always hold a place in my heart, Li. Through you, I have two remarkable children. I would never discount that or our time together as a whole—even with the way it ended.

"There are times I wish I could go back," Evium admitted, continuing, "to the night we met... with you in your mother's shop, and I'd swear I fell in love with you right then." His wistful look faded, and he shrugged as his smile grew sad. "Yet once I've taken myself through that wringer and come to my senses... here we are. Nothing's changed. This is what we've become. This is what we have left."

"If only we *could* go back," Liana said with a sniffle. "If I could erase the last several years..."

"Oh, then we wouldn't have Mahari," Evium said. "I wouldn't trade that for anything because I love her dearly. She's one of a kind. She's got something special to offer this world, and I can't wait to see what it is." He tilted his head. "I know we spoke of having a big family while we were married. That isn't totally out of the question for you, Li."

Liana scoffed. "As if I could think of such a thing now!" she said.

"Not right this minute, no," Evium agreed. "But, you have this enormous house. I built it to have children running up and down the hallways, Liana... and you're still young."

"I meant it for our children!" Liana practically hissed, wringing her hands together again. "Yours and mine!"

"That aspect can't be helped," he said. "We need to look ahead of us now. Don't shut yourself away, Li. Leave a door open a little."

"Is that what you're doing, Evium? Leaving the door open a little?"

Evium's smile faltered slightly, and he shrugged again. "All I can do," he began, "is hope to get from one day to the next... a little smarter and a little stronger than the day before. I owe that to myself and to our children. Everything else will happen as it's meant to."

Liana could not stop the burning sensation building up at the backs of her eyes as she placed a hand to her mouth, swallowing a sob. Evium opened his mouth, ready to continue, when someone else joined them. He turned to see that little Léah Desmond had wandered over and was smiling shyly at the two of them.

She was a lovely child with a mass of tight, dark brown curls in a fluffy cloud around her head and ears. Her gold-flecked, cognac-shaded eyes were widely set ovals that seemed to take everything in all at once. She was comfortably dressed in dark blue coveralls with a tab collar, and sturdy little black boots.

"Hallo, sir," she enunciated carefully in a piping voice, color high in her cheeks from recent play. "May I have another ride, please?"

Unable to suppress a grin, Evium glanced back at Liana. Not trusting herself to speak and, knowing there was not much left to say anyway, Liana simply nodded back. She watched as Evium held his arms out to Léah, who promptly clamored into his lap before they took off.

Liana watched as they became a blur, not only because of the distance but also because of the tears she could finally allow to fall.

Jahd and Jacinto stood together outside, their trunks nearby as they waited to be picked up and transported home. Both boys looked tired. Jacinto had spent much of the last two hours at Pandoufuli locating, attempting to organize, and packing his belongings, while Jahd had mostly recovered from his malady and was eagerly pondering the use and meaning of this latest gift.

"Hey, doesn't your sister have a birthday coming up?" Jacinto asked.

"In a couple of months," Jahd said. "I'm sure there'll be a huge celebration thrown for her. She's going off to Breaton soon after since she's qualified for early admission."

"Just like Zoi did," Jacinto nodded. "I remember what a big deal that was. There wasn't really a party for her, though."

"Don't let my mother ever hear you say that," Jahd snorted. "She lives for a good party. Anything to keep her name on people's tongues." He considered Jacinto. "You should come."

"What?"

"To Mahari's party. You could come, bring Zoi... and then you and I can come back here to school together afterward. You said your parents would try to have Zoi in and out of Vespers during break. She'd be out then, by that estimation."

Jacinto cast a sidelong glance at Jahd before edging closer to decrease the chances of being overheard, even though they were the only two standing outside. "Are you going to keep practicing that..."

"Are you going to keep asking me that?" Jahd interrupted.

"You have to be careful!" Jacinto insisted. "What if you're seen?"

"I'll do at home as I've done here and practice during the night when no one..." He raised both brows at Jacinto. "...is any wiser."

Jacinto laughed before both boys turned to peer down the long driveway at the sound of an approaching carriage. Jahd recognized both the coach and the coachman, his eyes briefly widening in surprise before he turned back to Jacinto.

"That's for me," he said. "We'll wait, though, until yours has arrived."

"No need," Jacinto said with a nod of his head, causing Jahd to turn around again. The familiar dark green vehicle with the gold trimmings made its turn onto the grounds of Pandoufuli and was now not too far behind. "You'll have your mother reach out about that party?"

Jahd nodded. "Let me know about Zoi, also," he said off-handedly as the coach drew nearer.

"Young Master Jahd!" Fayal boomed once the carriage came to a halt, and he jumped out of it. He bounded over, his eyes simultaneously bulging and brimming as he looked Jahd over. "You are certainly a sight! I remember the last time I saw you, sir... when I dropped you off for your first day here. Now here we are, and... you're how old now?"

"Thirteen," Jahd said, shaking Fayal's hand as he cast a sheepish grin over at Jacinto. "It's good to see you, Fayal. Been a long time. How are things in D'alegne?"

"Doing well, sir, very well! Been helping your father, as you know. My oldest started an apprenticeship with him during the summer, as well. But, since I just brought your father out to your place for a visit, I asked if I could be the one to come and fetch you this time instead of Millard."

"My father is there?" Jahd asked.

Fayal nodded. "For quite a bit, yes. With your sister leaving in a couple of months, he's wanting to make sure he gets enough time with you both beforehand." As Jacinto's coach coasted to a stop, Jahd exchanged a brief nod and a wave with his friend as Fayal looked over Jahd's belongings. "Is this all you've got?" Fayal asked. "I'd swear you had more things when I dropped you off."

"That was five years ago," Jahd said with a chuckle. "I've learned since then that I don't need as much, especially since they keep us in uniforms most of the time."

Fayal walked over to the carriage, opening the door and deploying the stairs. "Let's get you settled in and then I'll see to loading your things," he said. "I'm sure that your folks can't wait to have you back!"

Jahd smirked before walking over to the transport, waving again briefly at Jacinto, who was boarding his own carriage.

"We'll see," he said to Fayal before climbing inside.

Chapter Twenty-Nine

Jahd was deep in thought for the duration of the trip back to Kynedal, glad the carriage didn't have enclosed seating for the driver. He was certain that, if it had, Fayal would have been content to prattle on for the entire time, and Jahd wanted a quiet moment alone.

He cursed his own carelessness. How could it have escaped him that Jacinto had been stealthily watching him over the last several months? Though Jacinto had not fully confessed to exactly how much he had seen, Jacinto could not—now or ever—be made fully aware of Jahd's skill set.

But what a feat! Jahd was planning to make his initial attempt at corporeal projection once he was safely at home but being able to do so earlier than expected was thrilling. Jahd was willing to allow Jacinto to believe he had a bit of control in this situation to keep him close. Jahd also hoped he had frightened him enough with the display to keep his mouth shut.

The truth was that Jahd needed Jacinto. It was why Jahd had started helping him with his studies, to ensure that Jacinto would remain at Pandoufuli after having proved early on that he could not exactly be trusted to maintain the coursework on his own.

Liana was not certain to maintain a connection with Aniela, not after so willingly shutting her out in the years since her departure from Breaton. Jahd needed to maintain a provisional link to Zoi... until which time he could make a more permanent connection. Jacinto's presence would prove useful.

He had not seen Zoi since his very first day at Pandoufuli, but it was impossible for Jahd to forget her. Jahd had also learned from Mahari that another of their mother's schoolgirl friends had resurfaced—Mahari's tutor, Rhia. Jahd had not yet encountered her, as Rhia had usually departed for break by the time he arrived home. But, apparently, Rhia also had a little girl. Jahd would have to meet them both soon.

Three. At least three of the Original Five had daughters of their own. Mahari experienced the unusually early awakening of her abilities before she was three years old. Zoi, also a prodigy, had recently gained the additional ability to, albeit involuntarily, set things ablaze. What was Rhia's daughter like? What of the remaining two of the Five?

It was all so promising. What a lovely coterie Jahd would have when the time came. But how would the others be located? Kismet had returned Aniela and Rhia to him. Should he sit back and wait... or take a more active hand?

Jahd glanced out of the carriage window at the sprawling landscape, recognizing various landmarks on the outskirts of Kynedal. He pounded on the roof of the carriage with his fist, waiting as it slowly came to a stop. Within moments, Fayal appeared and opened the carriage door.

"What can I do for you, sir?" he asked.

"I won't be going all the way to the main house," Jahd said. "Drop me off just inside the gates."

Fayal removed his cap and scratched nervously at his short brown curls. "I don't think your parents would much like that, sir," he said. "They can't wait for you to get in, and there's bound to be others looking forward to seeing you as well."

"They'll hold," Jahd said. "I won't be very long. If they ask, tell them I insisted."

Fayal sighed, flipping the cap back onto his head as he nodded and then closed the carriage door. Jahd settled back in his seat with a smirk, shifting slightly as the carriage began moving again.

Shortly after coasting through the massive gates at the edge of the Chatelain estate, Fayal stopped the carriage once more to hop down and walk over to the door. After it was opened, Jahd stepped out and ran a hand through his mass of curls before grinning at Fayal.

"I'll be there before you even get the carriage unloaded and the horses back in the stable," he said.

"I still think your parents won't like this at all," Fayal warned.

Jahd flashed his most charming grin, winked, and turned to walk away from the carriage and toward the east side of the property. He slipped his hands into his pockets, inhaling deeply as the large greenhouse came into view to the right of the east gardens. Rather than continuing in that direction, however, Jahd stopped walking as the shadow of a nearby oak loomed over him.

His smile widened.

He turned to his left and looked up into the tree, his gray eyes sparkling with delight as he glimpsed Mahari, who was casually draped along one of the thick lower branches. She was almost entirely cloaked in shadow, peering down at him like some untamed fairy child.

"'ello, brother," she said.

"It'll be odd with you away," Jahd said nearly an hour later, when he and Mahari were finally on their way back to the main house.

They were walking side by side, hardly in a hurry as Mahari busily chewed upon a wad of fresh honeycomb, making soft smacking noises along the way. She carried another piece in one hand, palm-side up so as not to risk squeezing it.

"I don't know how much time we'll get to ourselves over the next couple of months," Jahd continued with a frown. "I imagine they're sending you to Dalenbeigh in a few weeks?"

"Yes," Mahari answered carefully around the wad. "You, too."

"I'm not going," Jahd said with a laugh. "I doubt anyone will mind."

Though the transition to solo visits with Huison had gone well over the years, the bond Mahari developed with him was one more out of convivial respect than love. She dutifully called him Father, but to her, Evium would always be Papa.

"He wants to go," Mahari said, the lump of honeycomb tucked securely into her left cheek. She stopped walking, turning to her older brother, her face resembling a lopsided chipmunk.

"Go where?" Jahd asked as he stopped, naturally inferring that she was speaking of Huison.

"Breaton," she answered, suckling the wad, "for my first day."

"He told you that?"

Mahari shook her head. "He told Mama."

"Father was planning to take you," Jahd commented with a chuckle, referring to Evium.

"Still is," Mahari shrugged.

"Oh, you've got to let me know how that goes," Jahd said with a laugh as the two of them resumed their walk.

As the duo took a shortcut through a large grove of assorted fruit trees, Jahd squinted as he spied a small, lone figure up ahead.

He froze, drawing in a deep breath. Mahari, who had continued to walk, finally stopped and turned to look back at her brother.

"What?" she asked, shaking her hair from her eyes as she studied him.

Jahd did not hear her. A sharp ringing filled his ears as the grove seemed to stretch before them, the color draining from the trees.

When it dissipated, he found Mahari anxiously tugging at his sleeve with her free hand as the figure, much closer and now glancing up at him, came into focus. She was a beautiful child, her hair a cloud of curls, clothed mostly in dark blue save for little black boots. Her eyes, beautifully shaped and strangely colored, locked upon him with curiosity.

"Well," he said at last, having found his voice as the ringing ceased, "You must be Léah."

"Who told?" she asked.

"No one needed to tell me," Jahd said, feigning shock at the suggestion. "Everyone knows you. You're famous."

Léah's disbelieving gaze shifted to Mahari, who answered the look with a shrug.

"My brother," Mahari said by way of introduction. "Jahd."

Jahd studied what looked to be the battered remnants of a kite clutched in one of Léah's hands.

"What's happened there?"

Léah frowned. "It got stuck."

"Where?" Mahari asked, to which Léah responded by pointing up at a nearby pear tree.

"How'd you get it down?" Jahd asked, confused. Léah smiled without answering, and Mahari chuckled.

The meaning of the smile, though Léah was again looking at the damaged kite, wasn't lost on Jahd as he contemplated the height of the tree. Wordlessly, Mahari extended the hand that contained the honeycomb to Léah, who accepted it with a nod before putting it into her mouth. Jahd looked from one girl to the other, amazement giving way to a slow, spreading smile.

Chapter Thirty

It was shortly before sunset as the festivities finally began winding down. Clea and Millard teamed up with Shaz, Linet, Fayal, and Alena to ensure that the grounds were cleared, the kitchens scrubbed, and the children accounted for.

Earlier, Mahari had taken Léah upstairs to her suite along with Alena's daughters, while the boys still lingered about outside. Jahd, finally free of the general commentary from the adults praising his manners, handsomeness, and growth spurt, wandered the halls of the Den before venturing into the library.

Browsing the tomes along the wall, he wondered which book he might take with him back to Pandoufuli. Though Liana would not dare keep anything inside the house that even hinted at spellweaving, there was a stellar collection of reading material covering a multitude of other interesting subjects. Despite the many things that had changed about Jahd since his rebirth, including the parameters of his soul, he had always loved to read.

He considered the dozens of titles before him, reaching out to run the tips of his fingers along the spines as he inhaled various scents: the woody aroma of paper, the faint metallic scent of ink, the adhesives in the bindings.

Jahd slid one book from the shelf, pausing to fan the pages inches from his nose as he closed his eyes and inhaled. Returning to the first page, he read the opening paragraph before deciding the book would do nicely.

He continued reading absently, holding the open book in his right hand as he walked, still trailing his left hand along the shelves. He then looked up, the smile fading from his face as he spied an antique, curved glass curio nestled against the wall. He lowered the book, closing it, and stared at the cabinet as he drew nearer to it.

The cabinet comprised three main compartments. The outer two were taller than the one in the middle and adorned with a bowed glass enclosure. Each of the towers housed four clear glass shelves with a variety of trinkets hidden behind the etched glass doors. The center section, however, had only three shelves with flat panes of clear glass. Jahd sucked in a breath as he saw the item on the top shelf of the middle section.

Nestled atop a black, silk-draped pillow was a silver, hook-handled stiletto dagger. He bared his teeth, a low growl rumbling in his throat as he recognized the piece as the one used by Liana during the summoning at Breaton.

"I'll send it back!"

Jahd shuddered as the book dropped from his hand and without thinking, he rubbed his thigh.

"I thought I might find you in here."

Startled, Jahd whirled around to find Kaileih standing in the open doorway. She took one look at her grandson's pallid complexion and hastened to him, placing a cool hand against his forehead. Jahd, wholly caught off-guard and discomfited by the sight of the dagger, wrapped his arms around Kaileih and hugged her tightly.

"What is it, sweetheart?" Kaileih asked as she held him. "Are you ill?"

He was not much shorter than her now, and she could rest her chin upon his curly top as she wound her arms around him, rubbing his back. Jahd took a series of deep breaths before clearing his throat, stepping out of the embrace to look up at her. In this new life, he could think of no greater gift than claiming Kaileih as kin.

"It's passed, Grandmother," he said, shaking his head. "I think I might have eaten one too many chocolate honeycomb biscuits."

Kaileih laughed, relieved. "You and your sister," she said, cupping his cheeks with her hands. "Are you sure you're all right?"

"Yes, ma'am, Grandmother." As Kaileih moved closer to the curio, he bent to retrieve the fallen book.

"Do you like this cabinet?" she asked. "I had it brought over a few months ago."

"Brought over from where?" Jahd asked, once again eyeing the shelf that contained the dagger.

"From my home," she said, wrapping an arm about his shoulders. "I took some things out of it, of course, so that your mother could fill it with items of her own. I left this, though... front and center."

"That belonged to you?" Jahd asked, unable to pull his eyes away from it.

"Yes," Kaileih said, as she smoothed back a few of his curls. "It's been in my family for years. It has always fascinated Liana for some reason. I even had to confiscate it from her a few times at your age.

"But... since she'll inherit it and many other things at some point, I decided she should have it outright." She tilted her head. "You know, I've always sensed that there were two of these, but I have passed only the one down. Perhaps one day its mate will be found." Kaileih planted a kiss upon Jahd's temple. "I'm taking Mahari out with me later this evening for some moonlight harvesting. Want to come with?"

"Another night, Grandmother," Jahd said, still eyeing the dagger. He then looked up at her and smiled. "I think I'm going to write to Jacinto tonight so that a messenger can take it in the morning."

"Oh?"

Jahd nodded. "I asked Mother about inviting him and his family to Mahari's party in a couple of months. I wanted to tell him to be waiting for it."

"It's good that you're forming bonds with others your age, Jahd," Kaileih commented, her eyes twinkling. "As wonderful as it is that you're so close with your sister, you'll need counterparts of your own—young, like-minded men and women of comparable years with whom you can plot to one day take over the world."

"I've been thinking about that," Jahd said, laughing. "It's precisely what I've had in mind."

"Of course! You are my clever grandson! I can only imagine the plans you've concocted!" Kaileih caressed his cheek again, turning away to head back to the door. "Let me know if you change your mind about harvesting!" she said as she departed.

Once he was alone, Jahd turned back to glance at the dagger inside the cabinet before exiting the library. As he headed toward the foyer, intending to cut through to the staircase and return to his room, his eyes widened at the sound of a wailing child.

He arrived to find Léah yowling as she darted about, dodging attempts to be squeezed into a small black pea coat by an exasperated, bespectacled young woman, already wrapped in an ankle-length blue sweater coat. Jahd, clearly able to recall the woman as she was years earlier, knew this to be Rhia.

"Léah, sweetie, come on now," she crooned. Spying Jahd, she reddened in embarrassment, ceasing her attempts to catch and capture her dissatisfied offspring. Léah, seizing the opportunity, bolted and ran over to Jahd.

"Tell her to make me stay!" she demanded shrilly, her tiny face scrunched with fury.

"Léah Adriana Desmond!" Rhia gasped, reddening even more.

Jahd lowered himself to Léah's eye level, giving her a conspiratorial wink.

"I can't go against what your mother says," Jahd said with mock humility. "You should listen to her."

"She wants to take me home!" she said with the stomp of a tiny, booted foot. "What for when your sister has two beds in her room!?"

Jahd's bottom lip quivered as he did his best to bite back a laugh. He looked past the child toward her mother, who did not seem to share the least bit of his amusement.

"We have beds in our own house, Léah," Rhia said, seizing the opportunity to wrangle her daughter into her coat, paying no mind to the protests as the child wriggled. "We've already stayed later than we should have."

Jahd stood upright, cradling his book as he watched. When Rhia was done, she sighed, smoothing away the wisps of hair that escaped her bun during the fray. She paused, arching a brow at Jahd.

"They did not officially introduce us," he said with a slight bow. "There was so much going on today." He extended a hand. "Jahd Chatelain, Mahari's older brother."

"I gathered," Rhia said, placing a hand in his. As their skin met, she jolted as if shocked, and then quickly withdrew her hand. In the silence that followed, Léah looked up between her mother and Jahd before rolling her eyes.

"This is my mama!" she offered, completing the introductions. Rhia blinked, staring down at her daughter before looking at Jahd again.

"Yes," Rhia said, recalling her manners. "Rhia Desmond. I've... heard a lot about you from your parents, of course, as well as from your sister."

"I'm glad to meet you finally, Mrs. Desmond," Jahd said. "Mahari speaks highly of you. I appreciate being able to put a face to such a favorably mentioned name."

"Your sister is a treasure, as I'm sure you know. She's extremely unique." Rhia peered at Jahd through her glasses. "Almost as unique as her brother."

"Sorry?"

"You have such interesting eyes," Rhia said.

"Not so much," Jahd said carefully, "since they're the same as my mother's and sister's."

"No," Rhia disagreed. "It's more than that. I can't put a finger on it, but... the eyes say a lot. Yours appear to be trying to say a bit too much."

"Oh, good! I haven't missed you!"

Jahd was still watching Rhia when she looked past him to smile at Kaileih. When at last he turned around, he saw his grandmother approach the younger woman, a closed wicker basket in her hand.

"Mahari and Jahd somehow didn't eat all the chocolate honeycomb biscuits," Kaileih said. "I've packed a few in here for Léah, and some slices of lemon-blueberry cake for you to take back and share with your husband."

"Oh, Mrs. Dhamon, you're a marvel!" Rhia said, accepting the basket. "Thank you so much!"

"Thank you!" Léah piped, grinning as she eyed the basket.

"It's my pleasure," Kaileih said to them both. "Let me walk you out. Your carriage is ready, and you should both get going before it's too terribly late."

Jahd watched the trio walk through the foyer, chatting softly as they made their way toward the front door. His gaze hardened as he

302

focused on Rhia, slowly shaking his head before he turned in the opposite direction, toward the staircase and up to his room.

Chapter Thirty-One

Evium steered his wheelchair across the marble floors of the Den, making hairpin turns around clusters of festive decorations and various members of house staff that hurried about on errands. Coasting into the kitchen, he surveyed the array of offerings with gleaming blue eyes: trays of brightly colored macarons, platters of succulent vegetables and tasty dips, and serving dishes sure to contain a variety of soups, stews, and casseroles.

He had been tormented by the combined aromas for hours, able to smell everything from the guest room in which he slept. It had finally become too much for him, and he hurriedly showered and dressed so that he could see — and taste — things firsthand.

Navigating closer to the table containing the desserts, Evium reached over to grab a bright green macaron with what appeared to be a soft cream in the middle. He bit into it, groaning as his eyes rolled upward, the gentle taste of mint spreading over his tongue and enhanced by the sweet vanilla from the cream.

He was eyeing the other colors, debating which to sample next, when Kaileih entered the kitchen. Her long, twisted braids were pulled away from her face into an updo and secured within a black head wrap. The hem of her long saffron-colored skirt brushed the tops of her sandaled feet and she looked comfortable in an oversized black tunic. Evium, caught with his hand in the symbolic cookie jar, nearly choked as he gasped while eating.

"I wondered how long it would take for you to make an appearance," Kaileih said, smirking. Evium guiltily coughed a spray of green crumbs. She walked over to where he sat, taking a pink one for herself. "Try one of the pale lilac ones next," she suggested after biting into it. "Elderberry. You'll love it."

"How long have you been awake?" he asked after composing himself, reaching over to pluck one of the recommended treats.

"Who's had time to sleep?" Kaileih responded. "It's been pandemonium for the last week or so with everything that's gone into Mahari's birthday and farewell party. Liana's determined to give her a proper send-off."

"I'm sorry I wasn't able to come sooner," Evium said, shamefaced. "There's been an influx of new contracts coming in. Shaz and I have been working double to get the added staff trained before delegating assignments."

"You have businesses to run," Kaileih said, as she disappeared into one of the nearby pantries. She emerged almost immediately, hefting a medium-sized basket filled with an assortment of raw vegetables, placing it atop the kitchen island. "With everything you have going on, I'm glad you could make it at all."

"Nothing would keep me away," Evium said as he finally took a bite of the macaron.

He could feel Kaileih's eyes on him as hints of elderberry and honey spread over his tongue. She giggled, sounding somewhat girlish, at the expression of appreciative bliss on his face.

"You're still seeing Mahari off to school in a few days?" Kaileih asked as she looked over the contents of the basket. The question was enough to lure Evium from his reverie as he swallowed.

"Nothing could keep me away from that either," he said.

"Huison is arriving a little later this morning. How will this play out, Evium?"

"I never intended to restrict him from seeing his daughter off to school," Evium insisted, "and I have remained objective about her visits to Dalenbeigh. She can even ride with him in his transport on the way to Breaton, and I plan to leave first so that the two of them can have that last moment alone. But I feel that I have as much of a right to be there."

"Of course, you do! I don't dispute that at all. I know Mahari appreciates it, and she'll look to you first for comfort... especially since her mother won't be going."

Noting the change in Kaileih's tone during that latter statement, Evium shrugged and finished the macaron.

"Her daughter is leaving to attend a premier academy based on merit rather than as a favor to famous parents," he remarked. "It's a lot for Liana to deal with, but she's made substantial progress since finding out that Mahari's a spellweaver."

"You've finally forgiven her, then?" Kaileih asked softly.

"I forgave her long ago," Evium said. "I had to... to heal and move on with my life."

Kaileih abandoned the basket, walking around the counter and over to Evium. Pulling a chair out from the table, she sat facing him and grabbed his hands.

"I've been waiting to hear you say that," she said. "It's not so much that I've been wanting you to forgive my daughter, but... you deserve so much, Evium. It brings me joy to know that you are healing, and that you're going to be all right."

"Thank you," he said. "I mean... thank you doesn't even cover it. You've always been incredibly supportive and a source of strength for me."

Kaileih shook her head. "Don't let your children be the only reason you stay in touch with me," she warned, her eyes moist. "Whatever you need or want... or even if you don't need or want anything..."

"Why do you think I keep suggesting locations for you to build shops in?" Evium asked suddenly, taking a shuddering breath as his deep blue eyes filled with tears. "If I have anything to say about it, you'll never stop expanding... if only so that I can have an excuse to spend time... at each site... and with you." He breathed in, held it, and then slowly exhaled before sniffling. "Kaileih, you've been the only mother I've known since I lost mine more than ten years ago."

"And I still will be," she promised, squeezing his hands, "for the duration."

Two hours later, the Chatelain estate was teeming with activity. A fleet of uniformed servants rushed between the main house and a newly constructed facility on the east side of the property, near the grove. The structure, built solely to serve as a means of entertaining large groups of people during periods of less-than-desirable weather, was fully outfitted in mauve, gold, and cream decorations. Dozens of beautifully appointed tables surrounded a large space at the center of the room that was earmarked for dancing.

Linet, in charge of organizing the place settings at each table, busily flitted about, unable to resist periodically glancing at the sparkling ring on her left hand. It had been such a surprise! Shaz had ridden out to the Den on his own the night before, after having spent nearly every moment of his spare time for weeks collaborating with a jeweler. The result of their collaboration was an exquisite ring, showcased by a small, rose gold lotus flower with a deep red ruby nestled within the petals. The ring trembled between his calloused fingers as he, breathless and flushed, asked Linet if she would consent to becoming his wife.

"Did you count the centerpieces?" Clea demanded, huffing and out of breath. Her plump cheeks were red from the chilly conditions outside. Linet, unbothered by almost being caught daydreaming, shook her head.

"No," she said as she moved around the table, placing silverware. "Didn't think I had to."

"Well, you should have!" Clea huffed. "Maybe if you had, you'd have noticed that we're missing a few."

Linet straightened as her jaw dropped. "What's a few?"

"Four," Clea confirmed. "I counted twice, and I've looked all over."

"Maybe they were routed to the greenhouse by mistake," Linet said. "Things have been getting shuttled back and forth all day. Twice now I've had to return something to the main house that's not meant to be up here. They could have been misplaced."

"I've looked everywhere," Clea said, shaking her head. "No one's seen them. Those centerpieces are huge, so they're not so easily lost."

"Well, did they bring them all? We're meant to have sixteen— did you count sixteen this morning?"

"I didn't have time to count!"

"And yet you thought I did?"

"Bah!" Clea said, throwing up her hands before turning away, grumbling over her shoulder. "Now, I'm going to have to tell Mrs. Dhamon that we've only got a dozen centerpieces. What a disaster!"

As Clea made her way back to the main house, a large carriage was traveling up the driveway. It was an older transport, unadorned and unassuming, though sturdily constructed. Once the carriage stopped, the driver, wearing a thick, long-sleeved sweater with rugged slacks and worn work boots, made an effortless drop to the ground below, startling Clea.

"Good gracious!" Clea gasped, clutching at her bosom.

"My apologies, ma'am!"

Clea looked up into the soft, tawny eyes of the woman standing before her. She was statuesque, with an oval-shaped face, high cheekbones, and a small gold hoop adorning the left nostril of a strong nose. She wore no makeup, her deep brown skin lustrous and smooth. When she smiled, two rows of perfectly straight white teeth enhanced an already striking beauty.

"I'm so sorry to have startled you," she said, her accent thick but easy to understand. "I was wondering if you might help me, please."

"Why, yes, of course," Clea said. "Are you lost, dear?"

"This is the Chatelain estate, is it not?"

"Yes."

The smile widened. "Then, I'm not lost at all!" the woman said. "Is Mrs. Kaileih Dhamon here?"

"Yes!" Clea said, also smiling. "She's the mother of the lady of the house. I'm Clea, the head housekeeper."

"It's wonderful to meet you, Clea," she said, shaking Clea's hand. "My name is Nikhila Granville. I'm the shop manager for Mrs. Dhamon, working out of the D'alegne location."

"My goodness!" Clea said, reaching up to grasp Nikhila's shoulders. "The centerpieces!"

Nikhila laughed. "Yes, ma'am! Claude assured me last evening that he'd carefully counted the arrangements beforehand and would do so again before loading up for the trip here. But, when I arrived at the shop this morning, I saw we left some behind." She indicated the carriage. "I brought them with me straightaway. I hope I'm not too late."

"Oh, you sweet darling, you're right on time!" Clea said with a clap of her hands.

Minutes later, Linet looked up from her work in time to see Clea proudly leading a procession back into the building. She held one centerpiece: a ring of alternating mauve and cream-colored roses grouped around a large and glittering golden crown. Behind her was Shaz, wielding two more of the centerpieces, and a third person who Linet did not know, bringing up the rear with the last. Linet was about to go over to ask how Clea found the missing arrangements when Liana walked in. Linet instead returned to her task.

"Shaz, take those to the main table," Clea said. "That's the only one meant to get two, so they can go there." She turned to beam up at Nikhila as Shaz went to do her bidding. "Please come with me, dear. We can place ours on the last two tables on the left."

"Things are coming along wonderfully so far, Clea," Liana said, stepping over. Her gray eyes took Nikhila in as she arched a dark brow. Nikhila returned the look with a welcoming smile.

"You must be Mrs. Chatelain," Nikhila said. "It's so nice to meet you finally!"

"Oh? And you are..."

"Nikhila Granville," she said. "I manage your mother's shop in D'alegne."

"You manage my..." Liana blinked and then she stiffened.

She looked Nikhila over; at the closely cropped auburn hair that was tapered on the sides and in back, but deeply waved at the top. She glimpsed the beauty mark above her right eyebrow, and the fullness of Nikhila's lips. Liana hated the suppleness of Nikhila's skin, the sparkle in her lively gaze, and her incredible smile. Liana noted the simplicity of Nikhila's garb but could still see the athletic physique beneath it and curves that Liana could never hope to have, even during the latter stages of pregnancy.

"There is a young lady who manages my shop in D'alegne," Kaileih had warned. Here she was, in the undeniably stunning flesh.

"What are you doing here?" Liana asked in an acidic tone.

"Ms. Granville came out after realizing that..."

Liana shot Clea an icy look, one that immediately silenced the older woman. "I did not ask you!" she snapped. "Take the flowers you're holding, and the ones from this person, too. You can finish setting them up and then help Linet with the rest of the table settings."

"Yes, ma'am," Clea said hurriedly, unable to meet Nikhila's eyes as the arrangement changed hands.

Clea struggled a bit, doing her best to balance them both as she made her way to the back of the room. Shaz, having finished with his, came over to help her. They exchanged a few whispered words, and Shaz was careful not to look back in Liana's and Nikhila's direction.

"How is it that those flowers weren't among the others?" Liana asked when she turned back to Nikhila.

"It was a mistake by Claude, Mrs. Chatelain," Nikhila said, no longer smiling after witnessing the mistreatment of Clea. It appalled her, but she knew it was not her place to comment. "I was told that he would take inventory before leaving, and he did not."

"Is that not your responsibility?"

"My responsibility was to help your mother create the pieces."

"Who's in charge of managing the orders that leave the shop?" Liana asked, raising her voice. She stepped closer. "I'd say you are, correct?"

Nikhila put her hands behind her back, curling them into fists. Her temper, usually easily maintained, was simmering. What exactly was this woman's problem, and why was she taking it out on Nikhila? Under other circumstances, Nikhila would be quick to regain control of the conversation. However, this was her employer's daughter.

"Mrs. Chatelain, Claude and I made certain that every centerpiece was accounted for after the shop closed last night," Nikhila said, standing straighter. "I charged him alone with returning to the shop before it opened this morning, loading the flowers onto the transport, and bringing them here.

"As his manager, I will discuss the issue with him later today. I might have done so immediately upon arrival, but he'd already departed for the return trip to D'alegne."

"Were these really left behind by mistake?" Liana asked, seeming to ignore all that was said. "Was it intentionally done?"

Nikhila frowned. "Ma'am?"

"Why would you come all the way here, hmm? It was hardly necessary. Anyone else could have made the trip."

"No one comes into the shop as early as I do, Mrs. Chatelain," Nikhila said, her velvety skin suffused with redness as she flushed. "I couldn't wait for Claude to return. The flowers wouldn't have made it here in time!"

"I'll be speaking with my mother about this," Liana advised.

"I don't understand!" Nikhila said, her eyes wide. "I realize that the oversight wasn't ideal, but that's why I came—to explain, apologize, and correct it!"

"An apology is neither welcome nor wanted. That sentiment also applies to you. Leave."

Liana turned her back to Nikhila, occupying herself with the straightening of table settings. Nikhila stared at Liana's back in confusion, tears of frustration and disbelief building in her eyes. She turned to leave, blinking rapidly and nearly colliding with Kaileih after only a half-dozen steps.

"Mrs. Dhamon!" she said, breathless and shaking. "Please excuse me, I..."

"It's okay, Nikhila," Kaileih said tenderly, touching the younger woman on the shoulder. "Are you all right?"

"Yes, ma'am. Mrs. Dhamon..."

"Nikhila, you don't have to explain anything." Kaileih smiled. "Go up to the main house. Get someone to show you to the bathroom so that you can wash your face and collect yourself." Nodding wordlessly, Nikhila rushed past Kaileih and through the door.

Liana guessed she had roughly an hour before needing to go upstairs to bathe and change into what she planned to wear to Mahari's party. The celebration had been in the planning stages for months, and it had come together more superbly than Liana dreamed... all except for the appalling appearance of that creature from D'alegne.

The audacity! How dare she show up with her ridiculous face and her flimsy excuses? There was no reason for her to force her presence into this joyous occasion... meddling in things that did not concern her... occupying herself with a husband that did not belong to her. Dismissing Nikhila from the property was only the beginning of what Liana hoped to accomplish.

"Are you proud of yourself?" came Kaileih's composed voice from behind her. Liana turned around, simpering.

"Oh, Mama, yes!" she said, perfectly willing to cast that Nikhila-thing out of her mind for the rest of the day. "Doesn't the room look fantastic? I also stopped by the kitchen to look over the food. Mama, you have truly outdone..."

"I don't mean that."

Liana laughed. "What else do you mean, then?"

"Oh, maybe I mean the way you spoke to Nikhila just now." Kaileih watched as the smile on her daughter's face twitched and then faded. They stared at one another, and then a worried crease formed in Liana's brow. Kaileih was unmoved. "Liana, what is wrong with you?"

"She had no business coming here," Liana said stubbornly as she turned back to the table, organizing the stemware with shaky hands. "Serving up some nonsense about why she had to be the one to bring those flowers."

"I heard what she said," Kaileih revealed. "You must have been too wrapped up in your delusion to notice that I'd come in and witnessed the entire exchange!"

"What delusion?" Liana asked, whirling around again.

"The one running rampant in your mind if you think for one moment that you have a chance to reconcile with Evium! That you can even find it acceptable to explain away the misguided and misdirected motivation to reproach Nikhila in that way..." Kaileih slowly shook her head. "What's the point? What are you still trying to prove? What did I tell you two months ago?"

"But Mama, she had no right," Liana said brokenly, wringing one of the linen table napkins that she was supposed to be organizing.

"You have no right, Liana! You squandered what rights you held!" Kaileih's eyes were fiery as she surveyed Liana from head to toe and back again. "You sad and simple creature," she continued, still speaking in a tone much lower than the one Liana used to address Nikhila. "Did that make you feel powerful, Liana, hmm? Browbeating someone for doing what any decent human being would if in her position, and for what?"

"Mama, you don't understand," Liana said as tears slid down her cheeks. "You never have."

"Unfortunately, I do," Kaileih said, "and, it's only proven what I've always suspected of you. You take entirely too much pleasure in having control over other people. You've done it with Huison for years. You tried and finally failed at doing it with Evium. You use control to amass what you feel you are owed as the ineffective member of a strong spellweaving family."

Liana placed a hand against her mouth, stifling her gasping sob as she wrapped the other arm about her midsection, her flood of tears unchecked.

"Grow the hell up, Liana," Kaileih said. "I honestly do not know how much more of this I can take."

Inside the bathroom closest to the kitchen, Nikhila had finished splashing her face with cold water. The conversation with Liana Dhamon still discomfited her, and Nikhila wondered where she went wrong or how she could have offended someone she had only just met. She knew she would have to do her best to dismiss it, though, so that she could regain clarity for the trip back to D'alegne and get some more work done at the shop.

Dabbing the excess water from her skin with a fluffy towel, Nikhila sniffled before folding the towel and draping it along the basin. Exiting the bathroom, she smiled at a passing group of uniformed servants before walking through the foyer and heading for the front door, which was opened to accommodate the constant flow of traffic between the main house and the site of the party.

"Ms. Granville?"

Nikhila had nearly crossed the threshold on her way out when her name was called. She turned to find Evium Chatelain, his luminous blue eyes bright as he smiled at her. He was not yet dressed for the party, looking quite comfortable in a soft blue cotton tunic and tan slacks.

"Mr. Chatelain!" she said, unable to suppress a grin. "Good morning!"

"Good morning to you!" he said as he approached. "What are you doing here?"

"Oh! I... well... there was a..." Nikhila cleared her throat and tried again. "Something happened with the delivery meant for the party. Claude left four of the pieces behind."

"So, you brought them?" Evium guessed. "How extremely thoughtful of you, Ms. Granville, thank you so much!"

Evium's genuine display of appreciation, the likes of which Nikhila had expected to elicit from his former wife, made the severity of her actual response much more hurtful in retrospect. Evium, reacting instinctively to the change in Nikhila's demeanor, looked more closely at her as his smile faded.

"What's wrong?"

Nikhila shook her head quickly. "Nothing," she whispered. She manufactured her smile when it returned. "I should get out of your way, Mr. Chatelain. I know you have a busy day ahead of you. So much to celebrate!"

"You're not in my way, Ms. Granville," Evium said. "What happened? Was something said about you bringing the flowers?"

"Said?"

Evium edged closer. "Is Kaileih upset with you over it? She has to know that it wasn't your fault."

"Yes, of course! I mean, no... No, Mr. Chatelain. Mrs. Dhamon was more than gracious. Of course, she understood."

"Then what's got you looking so rattled?"

Nikhila looked at Evium. She made note of the way he was watching her, with an interest in and care for her distress. He was quite easy to talk to and pleasant to be around. She enjoyed the times he had visited the shop. Nikhila had dealt with different types of men over the years, but none as physically enthralling or cerebrally stimulating as Evium Chatelain came close to duplicating the compassionate resolve that was his most attractive feature.

"I feel awful," Nikhila finally said. "It was a mistake that shouldn't have happened, and I feel foolish about it."

"You shouldn't," Evium said gently. "We all make mistakes, and though this one wasn't yours to resolve, you did it anyway... and in spectacular fashion." His smile returned. "It's a shame that you came all this way just to turn around and leave so soon. You should stay and join us."

"Oh... no!" Nikhila said, shaking her head rapidly. "I can't do that. Thank you, but I really cannot. It isn't proper." She indicated her attire. "I'm inappropriately dressed, and I really do need to get back."

"Okay, um... I get that. I won't keep you, then. But, thank you again, I... Have a safe trip."

"Of course, Mr. Chatelain," Nikhila said. "Have a wonderful party."

Nikhila turned to leave, her heart thudding in her chest as she wondered how far she would be away from the Chatelain estate and Kynedal before her palms stopped sweating.

"Ms. Granville?"

Nikhila stopped again before slowly turning back to face Evium. "Yes?" she asked.

Evium cleared his throat. "Ms. Granville," he said again, his face reddening as he brought his hands together, cracking the knuckles, "I'll be here a few more days yet to see my daughter off to school. W-When I get back to D'alegne, I... was hoping I could drop by the shop."

Nikhila's eyes widened as she, too, blushed. "Certainly, Mr. Chatelain," she managed, wondering if he could even hear her with as loudly as her heart seemed to beat. "I don't know that your mother-in-law will be in on whatever day you want to visit, but..."

"It isn't Kaileih that I hope to see," Evium interrupted softly. He bit his bottom lip as he lightly scratched an ear lobe. "I'd like to see you, Ms. Granville... and talk with you... I..."

He looked away. For the first time since meeting him, Nikhila saw he was struggling with something to say. Her soft gasp was involuntary. She had been tensed from the moment she discovered the four clusters of flowers still at the shop. She had practically raced to Kynedal, rehearsing in her mind every apology she planned to make upon her arrival. The thorough dressing down from Liana Chatelain had left her mortified, and Nikhila planned to flee the property so that she could finally breathe.

Now, looking at Evium, she could feel all that tension melting away. This moment was important to him. Nikhila was as certain of that as she was of her own name. She was equally certain that it was important to her, too.

"I'm sorry," he said at last, running a hand through his hair. "I didn't mean to..."

"Yes," Nikhila said.

Evium suddenly looked up, his eyes rounded. "Excuse me?" he blurted.

"I said yes, Mr. Chatelain. I would very much like it if you'd come by."

When Evium emitted an explosive sigh, she could see him visibly relax in his wheelchair.

"Evium," he said as he smiled. "Please... call me Evium."

"Nikhila," she said, smiling back.

"I'll be seeing you again very soon, Nikhila."

"I look forward to it, Evium," she replied before turning to leave.

Chapter Thirty-Two

The festivities were in high gear. The distinguished array of guests was dazzled by the lavish décor, astounded by the culinary exploits of Kaileih Dhamon and the supporting staff, and charmed by the quiet poise of the guest of honor, Mahari Chatelain, who would surely surpass her beautiful mother in style and grace.

Even though Evium had relinquished the title of Lord Mayor after deciding to move to D'alegne, the denizens of Kynedal had not forgotten the contributions made to their city's abundant economy. Dozens of gifts poured into the Chatelain estate to celebrate Mahari and her illustrious family.

It surprised no one that Mahari, as the granddaughter of Amriel Dhamon, had been granted early admission to Breaton Academy. The only surprise was that her older brother, Jahd, who had already claimed at least a half dozen hearts that afternoon, had somehow not exhibited any traits of a spellweaver.

Not that it mattered. Jahd had already made a name for himself as a scholar with top awards and accolades. The Yannic Pandoufuli Ambassadorship, a station implemented ten years prior, was rumored to be his for the taking once he returned to school and started his senior levels. From there, it was impossible to say how far he would go.

They would remember the names of Jahd and Mahari Chatelain for decades to come.

Jahd sat at one of the smaller tables in the back of the room, Jacinto by his side. Jahd had tolerated a place at the main table with his immediate family and a few choice guests for as long as he could. He slipped away the first chance he got, joined almost immediately by Jacinto, who also greatly desired an escape.

"You weren't kidding about your mother's parties," Jacinto said, still somewhat overwhelmed after two hours of revelry. "I've never seen so many people in one place."

"This building is new," Jahd said, sipping from a glass of carbonated pineapple juice. "We have a room inside the house that my mother would sometimes use for large gatherings, but even it wasn't big enough for what she wanted to do today, so..."

As if on cue, they watched Liana twirl past them on the ballroom floor, dancing gracefully with the man who had superseded Evium as Lord Mayor of Kynedal. He was a portly man with frizzy red hair and a sallow complexion. Jahd recognized him as the father of one of his and Jacinto's classmates.

"Is that going to be your new stepfather?" Jacinto remarked, to which Jahd responded by snorting bubbles into his drink.

As they laughed, little Léah Desmond meandered over to their table. Her hair was pulled back into two curly puffs. She wore a cap-sleeved shirt covered in gold sequins with a matching two-tiered skirt. Completing the delightful ensemble was the same pair of little black boots. Jahd imagined the boots were a source of contention between Léah and her mother.

"Hallo," she called, busily chewing on what Jahd suspected was a piece of fresh honeycomb.

Jahd graced her with a slight bow, though he did not get up from his seat. "Lady Léah," he responded, taking on an exaggerated accent. "So good of you to come. Such a pleasure seeing you again."

It reduced Léah to peals of giggles as her mother, Rhia, walked over to them. Rhia barely looked at Jahd when she took her daughter's hand.

"Come now, Léah," she said. "We should get back to our own table. Stop wandering off and bothering people."

"She's no bother at all, Mrs. Desmond," Jahd said, this time getting to his feet and directing a bow her way, though he had dropped the embellished affectation. "Are you enjoying the party so far?"

Rhia pulled the still-giggling Léah behind her and then looked at Jahd, brow arched.

"I like it just fine, thank you," she said a bit stiffly before turning on her heels and walking away, taking Léah with her.

"Damn," Jacinto said once she was gone. "What's her deal? She's going to be a problem when that kid grows up."

Jahd chuckled as he took his seat, picking up his drink. "No, she won't," he said.

The two watched as Liana flitted by again, having discarded the Lord Mayor in favor of a new dancing partner. Jacinto, who had gone back to studying the room, noticed Huison sitting alone at a corner table. Huison's golden-orange eyes were fixed upon Liana.

"You'd think your mother would dance at least once with Mahari's natural father," he commented. "In a way, this is his celebration, too."

"And sully her picture-perfect party?" Jahd said, hand to his throat as if scandalized. He shook his head as the hand was lowered. "Don't bet on it. Besides, the truth of Mahari's sire is a closely guarded secret. Hardly anyone outside of immediate family knows about it." He eyed Jacinto. "We should keep it that way."

They both looked from Huison over to Evium, who was engaged in animated conversation with Kaileih at the head table.

"Yeah, right," Jacinto said with a laugh. "Mahari's blonde hair and blue eyes make it impossible for her to be mistaken for anyone else's child."

"You ass," Jahd said, also laughing. "Mahari looks like me, and we both look like our mother. No mystery there." He settled back in his chair and then turned to Jacinto. "I'm sorry that your parents and sister could not come."

"Me, too," Jacinto said with a sigh. "I think a party like this is what they needed to help keep their minds off things."

"Zoi's not getting any better?"

"She is," Jacinto said, "in a way. The frequency of the nightmares has really tapered over the last couple of months. The fire incidents are at a minimum. She was given an almost clean bill of health at Vespers. She's just been really quiet and withdrawn."

"Will she be going back to Breaton next week?"

"Yeah, she wants to." Jacinto looked at Jahd. "She's looking forward to meeting your sister, too. I mean, Zoi will start her senior levels, but I still think she and Mahari would get on well together."

They both turned to watch as Mahari, a vision in miniature of rose gold and cream with her long hair pulled back into cascading ringlets, walked over to join Huison at his table. She carried two small dishes of Kaileih's champagne cake with strawberry mousse and champagne buttercream.

"Have you decided what you're going to do after we graduate in a few years?" Jacinto asked after a few moments. "My dad has been hinting about me joining him at the clinic, but... that's not for me. I have no interest in medicine at all."

"So, what do you want to do?"

"Not that. I don't know. Something that actually matters."

Jahd laughed. "You don't think you could find that by working as a doctor?"

Jacinto turned to look at him. "Are you telling me you'd be perfectly content with running a string of factories with your father?" He checked to make sure that no one else was close by, and then leaned closer. "Come on, Jahd. You're a spellweaver. You can't waste your life with the options you have available to you." He sat back again. "I might not be able to do what you can, but that doesn't mean I intend to settle."

"I don't intend to join my father's business," Jahd admitted after a period of silence. "I have something much bigger in mind. The coursework at Pandoufuli might seem inadequate, but it'll serve a purpose. I'll need power and influence as I get older. I'll need to keep building until the time is right."

"The time for what?"

"The time to claim what's rightfully mine. Until then, I need to balance both worlds—this one and that of a spellweaver. I have to keep hiding what I am for years yet."

"Have you told Mahari?" Jacinto asked.

"No."

"I thought you told her everything."

"Apparently not."

"So, we're both frustrated as hell, but for different reasons," Jacinto surmised. "We're both stuck."

"Stuck, yes," Jahd said. "But when my time comes... oh..." He closed his eyes briefly, his face a mask of tranquility. "When my time comes, it's going to be so... outstanding."

"I want to help."

"Hmm?" Jahd said absentmindedly.

"I said I want to help you, Jahd."

Jahd looked over at Jacinto, brows raised. The expression on the face of the other boy was solemn and resolute.

"I mean it," Jacinto said. "You had to know that... right? It can't be that much of a surprise. You had to know that I'd want to be there for you."

Jahd looked at him closely, his eyes narrowed. He then blinked, sighed, and shook his head.

"Jacinto..."

"I know what you're going to say," Jacinto interrupted, fiddling with a linen napkin. "I already know, and it isn't necessary. You're still my friend, Jahd. You're my best friend. The other bit doesn't matter and won't be an issue. I'm here and I want to help. I'm sure that whatever you have planned is a hell of a lot more interesting than having to deal with sick people at a clinic."

Jahd chuckled. "Well, yes," he said. "Yes, it is." He studied his friend. "You've already helped me much more than you realize."

Chapter Thirty-Three

Liana ventured out on the same early morning walk she took almost daily since sending Mahari off to Breaton Academy. She never set out with any specific destination in mind and did not always take the same path. For her, it was a cleansing walk and a time to reflect, though her reflections were rarely profound.

Instead, she often wondered what she was doing with her life and why it had not progressed the way she felt it ought to. Everyone else seemed to change, grow, and thrive.

Her mother had opened four more shops. Acknowledging some of the smaller florists who were struggling to compete with the wares of Kaileih Dhamon, she had brought them under her wing by joining forces with them. Kaileih knew she could not be in all places at once, and counted on other shop owners who were trustworthy and reputable to sell some of her specialized blooms in their shops.

However, to ensure that none of them could corner the market or surpass her own level of success, she only gave each store the rights to sell one of her premier hybrids, to be combined as each owner pleased among their own specialized creations. It proved to be a lucrative arrangement for all those involved.

Jahd maintained top marks while remaining committed to the monthly excursions that were required as an ambassador for Pandoufuli. Jahd was away for one weekend per month, traveling only to locales ideal for singing the praises of a Pandoufuli education. He was making quite a name for himself, and the school, by dining with mayors, local gentry, and even royalty—but only with families whose children possessed no magical talent.

Mahari was also first in her class at Breaton. Though she had yet to display a specialty beyond the movement magic she'd shown since childhood, she had an extraordinarily high aptitude for spellbreaking. Reassembling spells, however, still needed work. She could reconstruct any spell she dismantled which, while excellent in theory, concerned her instructors because Mahari had not yet grasped the danger of certain kinds of magic. Without that understanding, she risked stumbling into a power with catastrophic results.

As a result, they encouraged Mahari to spend extra time at Breaton after they had dismissed the other students for the winter. This was so that she could receive specialized instruction in a more private setting, something that thrilled Huison to no end. It was with Liana's permission that Huison journeyed to Breaton as a guest for those two weeks to be at his daughter's side and to serve as a spectator during those teachings.

Liana, meanwhile, was tired of being alone. She had enjoyed a periodic dalliance with the most recently appointed Lord Mayor of Kynedal, though she had eventually grown weary of picking the frizzled red hairs from her pillow on the mornings after. Even though Liana maintained a somewhat busy social calendar, Evium remained the standard against which every man was measured

Evium. He was flourishing in D'alegne. Already a success while Lord Mayor of Kynedal, he was ten times as productive since the move, with dozens of workshops and factories rising in his name along the coast. Shaz, after years of working under Evium, was now heading his own factory under the Chatelain umbrella. After training his successor, Fayal's oldest daughter, Dara, Shaz and Linet moved to Heingraf, no longer known solely as "Brothel City," thanks to the income flowing into its coffers from Evium's business acumen.

Evium's triumph in business was dwarfed only by the accomplishments of his personal life, after marrying Nikhila Granville... now, Nikhila Granville-Chatelain... and celebrating the birth of a daughter a year later.

Liana knew Nikhila would be trouble from the moment she laid eyes on her on the day of Mahari's dual celebration. Liana so wished that her mother had done as she asked and fired Nikhila. Had Kaileih done so then, there was little chance that Nikhila would have gotten her claws into Evium and given him both a daughter and a son in quick succession.

For that reason, Liana finally turned to Huison again, inviting him to spend the occasional weekend at the Den. She needed someone who loved her unconditionally. She deserved to be prized above anyone else. She required that someone belong solely to her.

Huison wanted to marry her. He had asked more than once over the years. In reply, Liana would smile demurely and ask for more time. As Liana stopped walking through the west garden, looking at the tall cedar tree, the one with the memorial plaque at its base, she could not help wondering. Precisely how much time would she need to convince Evium that Nikhila was not the woman for him?

Jahd walked across the courtyard, the strap of his leather satchel slung across his broad chest as he hefted its matching valise in one hand. He paid little attention to the stares he got along the way, long used to being gawked at.

A tall young man, Jahd had never experienced the physical awkwardness plaguing other sixteen-year-olds. He had settled into his six-foot-one frame with an effortless grace. Polite mannerisms and a disarming smile had served him well over time, even while breaking a few hearts along the way. He wore his dark curls long, as was the norm for young men his age, and the shoulder-length locks complemented a beautifully tapered jawline and made his gray eyes seem even brighter.

Jahd entered the large and homey cottage that had served as his home for the last three years. It was a lovely, single-story, ivy-covered building with a low, thatched roof, an arched entryway, and limestone walls. Though there was no fence to speak of, the cottage was surrounded by enough cherry laurel on three sides to offer more than enough privacy.

Though the cottage was awarded as a perk of being an ambassador for the school, Jahd had asked and received permission for Jacinto to join him. There was only one bedroom, but it was still much larger than the dormitory they had shared previously, so it worked out well. It was in the cottage that Jahd could freely practice his magic without the risk of being disturbed by a sentry.

Jahd spied Jacinto in the sizable bedroom, lying on his back in bed and with an open book balanced against his bent knees as he reclined upon a few pillows. Jacinto was taller than Jahd by a couple of inches. Though not as broadly muscled as Jahd, Jacinto was solidly built and moved with a balletic grace. An attractive young man, Jacinto had let his hair grow out in recent years. Though he kept it neatly trimmed on the sides, his dark brown hair was long at the top, smoothed back and enhancing the intensity of his light blue eyes.

"Don't you knock?" Jacinto drawled in greeting. "I could have been indecent in here."

"How would that differ from any other time?" Jahd said with a laugh.

"Lita came by here looking for you," Jacinto commented after chuckling, turning a page in his book as Jahd tossed the satchel upon his own bed. "I suspect she wants to ask you to the formal and tried to beat the other girls to it."

Jahd laughed, pulling the strap of his satchel overhead and depositing the bag beside the valise. "I'm not going to that," he said.

"Tell that to her and to any of the other half dozen lassies that keep coming by here. And when they don't find you, they try to chat me up as if I can give them an in." Jacinto rolled his eyes. "So gross."

"Ah, you simply haven't met the right girl yet, old chap," Jahd said as he opened the valise and unpacked.

"Oh, that old relic," Jacinto said with a laugh. "Same thing my dad told me when we talked last time I was home." He affected Sandro's thick accent. "Do not rule it out, my son. Life may yet surprise you."

"Not as much as you surprised him when he caught you in the observatory with Olly during visitation last month," Jahd commented, moving to his bureau to open a drawer and deposit the stack of neatly folded shirts he had just taken from the valise.

"Hey!" Jacinto protested in his normal voice. "He sneaked up on me! I didn't know he was coming!"

"Your father or Olly?" Jahd said with a smirk, finishing the last of the unpacking. He closed the emptied valise and secured the straps before sliding it beneath his bed and out of the way.

"Easy for you to say," Jacinto said, sitting up. "From where I sit, you've got it made. You get free rein 'round this place, and there's no telling what you've gotten up to on the road during the ambassadorship for the last few years. I get it in where I can."

"I don't want just anybody, though," Jahd said, sitting atop his bed and pulling off his boots. "I'm looking for something special."

"Yeah? How many 'something specials' did you come across this time?"

Jahd grinned, placing the boots neatly side by side on the floor near the foot of the bed. "One," he said. "Only one... a pretty little thing with long red curls and dark green eyes."

"Where'd you find this paragon of beauty?" Jacinto asked.

"In Allard," Jahd said offhandedly, unbuttoning the cuffs of his long sleeves. "I think she's a princess."

"Oh! Then you surely won't get a chance!" Jacinto said.

"You never know."

"Right... the day I call you a prince is the day you WILL see me shack up with a girl!" They both laughed. "What else did you get up to?"

"Not too much. But... I think I should go back through Guion one day soon."

Jacinto wrinkled his nose. "Guion? There's nothing out there but docks and fishmongers. They'll never send you there to pander on behalf of the school. The people of Guion couldn't afford the rates."

"It wouldn't be for the school. It'd be for me," Jahd said, undoing the first few buttons of his shirt.

"What? Why?"

"Not sure, really. But, when I went through there, I felt something. I need to go back and see what that's about."

"It's about another girl, I'll warrant," Jacinto said. "You know the chances of you heading back anywhere near there at this point are nil. There are only a couple of months left before we graduate. No more ambassadorship for you and no more trips."

"So, I'll go on my own," Jahd said, pulling his shirt overhead and shaking the curls out of his face. "Nothing to stop me once we've left here, and I can do as I like rather than being stuck on school business." He winked at Jacinto. "I might even spend a little more time in Allard."

Jacinto watched, shaking his head as Jahd changed into a clean shirt. "I suppose I could come with you... keep you out of trouble."

"You can certainly try!"

"Precisely how many girls do you need, Your Majesty, to get to where you're trying to be?" Jacinto asked.

Jahd looked at Jacinto and grinned. "Five. Only five."

Chapter Thirty-Four

Jahd had finally finished making the rounds through the large reception hall, pausing to chat briefly, shake hands, and thank those he deemed appropriate and some he didn't, before rejoining friends and family.

"After that speech you gave, they might end up changing the name of this place to the Chatelain Academy," Jacinto teased in good-natured greeting with a roll of his light blue eyes.

"If they do, I've got dibs on that cottage," Jahd said with a laugh.

"I am so extraordinarily proud of both of you," Sandro said. "To have completed your senior levels a year early is a remarkable feat. Especially you, Jahd, finishing at the top of your class while managing all your additional responsibilities!"

"I can't agree more," Evium said, beaming. "I did well when I attended here, but I didn't finish until I was nearly eighteen. Here you both are, just turning seventeen." Evium sat back in his chair, looking up at both boys. "What's this I hear about you two having plans to do some traveling now that you've graduated?"

"Well, sir," Jahd said, glancing briefly over to where Liana stood along with Kaileih, Mahari, and Aniela, amidst a group of other ladies. "I know the Pandoufuli Ambassadorship didn't exist when you attended, but the program is effective during the senior levels, from ages thirteen to eighteen. Having graduated early, I'm abandoning my post a year ahead of time."

"Well, don't think of it as abandonment, son," Evium said.

"I can't help it," Jahd insisted. "It's what they appointed me for, and I'd like to see it through."

"See what through?" Liana asked as she and the other ladies joined them. Sandro wrapped an arm around Aniela's waist as Mahari, who was excused from the two weeks of additional studies to attend Jahd's graduation, leaned against the arm of Evium's wheelchair.

"Jahd was explaining about continuing the ambassador's program," Evium said.

"Ah, your plans to circumnavigate the world," Kaileih said with a laugh, caressing the side of Jahd's face.

"Not quite, Grandmother," Jahd said. "It would only be for a few extra months, just enough to fulfill my obligation to the school by visiting the remaining sites I would have paid a visit to anyway had I not graduated early."

"And what's your role in this?" Aniela asked Jacinto.

"I don't have one," Jacinto admitted. "Honestly, it's an opportunity for me to travel and maybe figure out something to do after."

"There is always room for you at the clinic if you wanted something to do," Sandro offered.

"I know, Dad, but... I don't know that I want to be around a bunch of crazy sick people all the time." Immediately, Jacinto's eyes widened as he noticed the crestfallen expression on Aniela's face. "Oh... wait. I'm sorry. I didn't mean that."

"It's all right," Aniela said softly, her eyes glossy. She smiled at the others. "Please excuse me for a moment."

"Wait... Ani..." Jacinto called as she hastened through the reception area toward one of the side doors. He then turned to his father. "Dad, I swear..."

"No worries, son," Sandro said with a nod, reaching over to squeeze Jacinto's shoulder.

"I'll go see to her," Liana offered.

"No, no," Sandro said. "I'll go. We'll only be a moment."

Jacinto watched as his father left, shaking his head. "I shouldn't have said that," he said. "She thinks I'm talking about Zoi. I would never do that."

"Mahari," Kaileih said, turning to her granddaughter, "how about we go get some punch, hmm?"

Wordlessly, Mahari nodded, and she walked with Kaileih over to the refreshment table.

"We know you didn't mean it that way," Liana said in a comforting tone. "It's just difficult. Your parents have been dealing with a lot."

"All the more reason for me to have kept my mouth shut," Jacinto said, frowning.

"How has Zoi been doing?" Evium asked in a kind tone. "I thought she had gotten better. She graduated from Breaton, didn't she?"

Jacinto looked from him to Jahd and then at Liana as his face reddened. "Zoi is pregnant," he blurted, to which Liana responded with a gasp.

"What?" she said.

"We found out last month. Dad was willing to settle it... have her marry the guy who..." Jacinto shook his head. "But we don't know who he is, and she's not talking. She's... retreated into this shell and won't say anything about it when asked."

"Have there been any other episodes?" Evium asked. Then, as if remembering the use of the dismissive term to describe Rael's uncontrolled magic, he shook his head and thought better of it. "Is she still improving otherwise?"

"Yes, but this has thrown my parents for a loop. I mean, she's sixteen. We'll back her up if she goes through with the pregnancy, but we also need to make sure that she's completely clear of the rough patch she was going through." Jacinto shook his head again.

"I've told him she'll be fine," Jahd said solemnly. "This could even help in the grand scheme of things."

"Babies certainly can be a godsend," Evium agreed, and then he chuckled. "Though I'm not too sure that my wife would agree, considering that she's home on bed rest with our third."

"Do you understand why I need to get away for a bit?" Jacinto went on. "I need some time before I have to come back to help them deal with all of this."

"We do, sweetheart," Liana said warmly. "We understand, and we will all make sure that you both have whatever you need for your travels before you go."

"Make sure you're back before your birthday, young man," Evium said good-naturedly to Jahd, trying to ease the tension. "Turning eighteen is a pretty big deal, you know."

"Oh, I know," Jahd said with a smile. "I will come back before then."

Liana went over to Jacinto and enveloped him in a hug. Jacinto looked over Liana's shoulder at Jahd, and the two of them locked eyes.

"I still can't believe you're going to be gone another five months," Liana said later.

They were all standing outside among clusters of other graduating students and their families. The difference was that while the other students were boarding various types of transport with their families, Jacinto was saying his goodbyes to Sandro and Aniela as Jahd stood surrounded by Kaileih, Mahari, Evium, and Liana as he bade them farewell.

"It'll fly by, Mother," Jahd said with an affable grin. "It's nothing compared to the last five years of me being away."

"You'll send letters from the different places you visit?" Mahari asked.

Jahd turned to her. He would dearly miss his little sister who, at twelve, was not so little anymore. Mahari had sprouted into a tall and gangly sprite who, having gained her grandmother's great respect for nature, spent the bulk of her spare time outdoors climbing trees or cozied up in the apiary. She had grown so fond of bees that she convinced Huison to install an apiary at Dalenbeigh.

"For you?" Jahd said, playfully tugging at one of her long curls. "Anything."

"You should try to stop by D'alegne when you can, son," Evium said. "Nikhila's always happy to see you, and you ought to spend more time with your other siblings."

"I will, sir," Jahd said. "You're all coming out for my birthday, though, aren't you?"

"Wouldn't miss it," Evium said. "But that's months away. Try to come through sooner if you can."

"It wouldn't hurt you to visit your old tutor, either," Kaileih said pointedly. "It surprised me not to see Huison in attendance today." She shifted her gaze to include both Evium and Liana. "After all, he helped lay the foundation for the accomplishments lauded this morning."

Evium, Jahd, and Mahari all turned to look at Liana.

"I never said not to invite him!" she exclaimed, reddening.

"You could always come with Mahari and me," Kaileih said to Jahd. "I'm taking her out to Scio tomorrow."

"Jacinto and I are heading out at first light, Grandmother," Jahd said apologetically, "and we still have a lot left to do first."

"As you like," Kaileih said with a sigh, before turning to Mahari. "Time for us to get on the road. I'd like to get to Kynedal by nightfall."

Mahari nodded, making her way over to speak briefly with Jacinto and his parents before joining Millard, who was waiting patiently beside the nearby coach. She then waved enthusiastically to Fayal, who waved back from his place near Evium's transport. Millard then helped her to board before he turned back to wait patiently for the others.

"I won't say goodbye to you," Kaileih said, standing on tiptoe to kiss Jahd on the cheek. "I'll expect to see you again soon."

Jahd wrapped his grandmother in a hug, inhaling the floral scent of her skin and hair before stepping back to smile down at her.

"I'll see you soon, Grandmother," he promised.

"You've got the entire world in front of you, Jahd," she said. "Never forget it and never forget who you are."

"I won't," Jahd said. "I can promise you that."

Chapter Thirty-Five

Kaileih allowed the butler to take her cloak, smoothing the long sleeves of her dark red, shoulder-skimming sweater. Knowing they had arrived early, she moved through the living room and straight to the double doors leading to the backyard.

"I thought you'd be out here," she called moments later, after finding Huison strolling through the gardens of Dalenbeigh.

"Ah, good morning, Kaileih!" Huison said in surprise. "Forgive me. I would have met you, but I did not expect you for another half an hour." He shrugged, almost shyly. "I spend more time out here now. I cannot help but marvel at the improvements to the landscape since your last series of visits." His amber gaze roamed appreciatively over the space. "There is always something new to delight the senses no matter the time of year." He looked toward the back doors. "Where is Mahari?"

"She's checking on her bees," Kaileih said, traversing the small bridge under which dozens of colorful fish swam through a flowing body of water. "Millard could barely stop the carriage before she jumped out and ran for the apiary."

"Ah, of course." Huison smiled as Kaileih came to a stop beside him. "I am so pleased that she enjoys it. I should have had one installed years ago. The freshness of the honey is divine." He studied her. "I have asked the cook to prepare a grand lunch. I hope that you will stay."

"Thank you, I will." Kaileih chuckled. "I appreciate your hospitality, Huison, especially considering that none was extended to you." Kaileih looked over at him. "I'm sorry that they did not ask you to attend Jahd's graduation ceremony yesterday."

Huison waved a hand dismissively. "It is of no consequence," he said. "I had no expectation to be. It might have been awkward had I been there, and I would not have wanted to cast the slightest shadow upon the day."

"Evium has moved on," Kaileih said. "I don't think it would have been a problem."

"No reason to risk it. Besides, I'll be seeing Jahd soon enough."

Kaileih turned to look closely at him. "Are you all right, Huison? You seem weary."

"Does it show so much?"

"Yes. What's going on?"

"I have not been sleeping well," Huison admitted.

"Is something troubling you?"

Huison paused. How could he explain it? How could he tell Kaileih that he was within months of giving her daughter everything she wanted? How could he convey the magnitude of the nights filled with longing and the visions of the ways Liana was sure to display her appreciation for what he had done?

"No," he said at last. "I am simply overwhelmed by the changes in my life these last few months."

"Between you and Liana," Kaileih surmised.

"Yes."

"It has been a long time coming," Kaileih said with a sigh.

"Do you disapprove?"

Kaileih smiled and then turned to focus on the colorful clusters of fuyu-botan nearby.

"You have been relentless in your love for my daughter," she said. "Your persistence may pay off. Just try to keep your wits about you, Huison, and keep your eyes open. She still wants Evium."

"As you said, Evium has moved on," Huison said, frowning. "He has remarried and has other children."

"He has moved on. She... has not. Is it your intention to remain second best?"

"I am hardly that," he said, his scowl deepening. "I can give her something he cannot."

Kaileih studied him for a long moment and then reached up to pat Huison's cheek lightly.

"I'll see about working on something to help you sleep," she said finally. "No reason you should lack the ability to carry these grand dreams along with you in slumber."

Turning on her heels, Kaileih walked back toward the house, leaving Huison to stare after her with the crease still in his brow.

"I have something for you," Kaileih said later.

Huison sat at the head of the table during lunch. His cooks had prepared an opulent spread that began with a selection of decadent canapés that included Kaileih's favorite, mushroom and polenta, as well as the olive crostini that Mahari favored.

The trio had tucked into their roasted beet salads with goat's cheese when Kaileih, who was sitting to Huison's right, smiled over at him and made her announcement.

"Oh?" he said, arching a brow. Though a few hours had passed since their discussion in the garden, he was still feeling surly about it.

"Indeed," Kaileih said knowingly. "Well, I don't have it right here with me, but I've started the process on something that I'm sure you'll find quite helpful."

Huison sat back in his chair, the salad momentarily forgotten. "You have piqued my interest," he said.

"You have had the power to resolve your sleepless nights all along," Kaileih told him. "There is quite a bit of valerian in your herb garden."

"I would not know how to go about using it."

"I gathered, but this is where I've helped you out. There's a jar of valerian tincture sitting in your kitchen right now that I've prepared. Of course, it's not ready just yet and will need to continue to sit undisturbed for a few more weeks, but… when it is ready and after it has been strained, you'll only need half a spoonful taken about an hour before bed to get all the rest you need." Kaileih wrinkled her nose playfully at Huison. "I hope that you'll forgive me, though. I used a bottle of your best spirits in order to make the tincture."

"If it works half as well as you say, it will not matter in the slightest," Huison said.

"Oh, it will," Kaileih assured him, picking up her fork. "Don't be misled by the amount. One-half teaspoon is all you will need. Anything more than that…" She shrugged, spearing a small wedge of yellow beets with her fork.

Huison studied Kaileih in careful consideration.

"In the meantime, you can snip a bit of the fresh herb to steep in some hot water and sip on before bed," she continued. "It won't pack the same punch as the tincture but should make you relaxed enough."

"I can get you some honey, Father," Mahari offered from her place at Huison's left, "to help sweeten it."

"That would be a help," Kaileih said, "though, it would take a little more than honey to mask the taste of a valerian tincture."

"Oh?" Huison asked lightly. "Such as?"

Chapter Thirty-Six

L iana sat in the solarium, a large seating chart spread across the table in front of her. To her right was a glass bowl filled with scraps of paper. She extracted one, read the name written on it, and then placed it on the chart. She had gone through at least a dozen such scraps when Mahari walked in with a book tucked under one arm.

"Any sign?" Liana asked as she rearranged two names on the template.

"Not yet," Mahari said, reading over her mother's shoulder. "Mama, I don't think you want Mrs. Beauchamp and Lady Mathers at the same table."

"Oh, you're right!" Liana said, switching the latter to another table before she paused and turned to look at her daughter. "What do you know about it?"

"Nothing. Only what I overheard when Clea was talking with Filene."

"Well, I'll have to see about that," Liana said, shaking her head as Mahari made herself comfortable on the bench by the window and began reading her book. "Your brother is certainly cutting it close.

He was due back weeks ago. I'm not even sure if I should still plan this party for him tomorrow."

"His last letter explained how he and Jacinto got caught in a series of storms out east," Mahari said, not looking up from her book. "It was impossible for them to travel until recently."

"But it's so close!" Liana said again as she placed a couple more names. "I'm sure he does this to get me riled!"

"That's exactly why he does it, Mama," Mahari said with a straight face.

Liana looked over at her daughter. "Does he have a girlfriend?"

"How would I know?" Mahari asked, disgusted.

"He wrote to you the entire time he was gone. There was certainly opportunity for him to mention it." Liana went back to the seating chart and then paused again, looking up once more. "Boyfriend, then? He and that Jacinto are certainly joined at the hip, and no telling what else at this rate."

"How abnormally archaic, Mama."

"I just... there is so much that I don't know about my own son. It's as if we've become strangers since he went away to Pandoufuli."

"I don't know who Jahd is seeing, Mama," Mahari said, sighing. "You know, you could try asking him."

"You don't think that might be a little nosy of me?" Liana asked, placing a hand on her hip.

"Is that approach somehow any different from this entire line of conversation?"

Liana gasped. "I swear you sound more like your grandmother with every passing day..."

Mahari looked up from her book with a grin. "Thank you!"

Liana was about to retort when she heard horses approaching and a commotion outside.

"Is that..." Her eyes met Mahari's, and they both bolted out of their seats, rushing from the solarium to the front door.

"Finally!" Jahd said as he stepped out of the coach before shaking hands with Millard, who had been waiting nearby. "After nearly a week of riding, I didn't think I'd ever get here."

"It's about time!" Liana said as she exited the house with Mahari close behind. "We were expecting you weeks ago! I thought you'd end up missing your own party."

"Hello to you, too, Mother," Jahd said, giving her a hug.

"Who is that?" she said, looking behind him at the older man talking with Millard.

"I hired a coach to bring me back," Jahd explained, draping an arm around Mahari's shoulders. "Millard's going to let him bunk in over at the stables so he can rest before going back. It was a long trip."

"Where's Jacinto?" Mahari asked. "I thought he was coming with you."

"Change of plans," Jahd said, his eyes lighting up. "Zoi's had her baby, a little girl. We got word as we were leaving Guion, so he's gone straight home."

"Was something wrong?" Liana asked.

"No, Mother. But, I told him it was best that he check in on her."

"I suppose that Sandro and Aniela won't be coming to your party tomorrow, then," she said.

"I'd guess not, Mother."

"Well, your father and... the... others... won't be here until morning," Liana said. "Huison is here, though, and will dine with us tonight."

"One big happy," Jahd said with a grin, to which Mahari responded with a giggle.

"You need a bath," Liana said to Jahd, wrinkling her nose. "Once you've cleaned up, you can say hello to your grandmother.

She's been in the kitchen all morning planning menus for tonight and tomorrow."

Jahd bowed gallantly, still grinning, before kissing Mahari on the cheek and then going into the house. Liana then studied her daughter.

"You didn't ask," Mahari said.

"Ask what?"

"Whether he has a girlfriend."

Liana shook her head, watching as Millard led the other coach driver back toward the stables. She then turned back to her daughter.

"Mahari?"

"Yes, Mama?"

"Do you... like the other children your Papa has?"

"You mean my brother and sisters?" Mahari asked pointedly.

"I suppose," Liana said.

"I like them well, Mama," Mahari said. "I also like Nikhila very much. She makes Papa happy."

"Does she?" Liana asked as she headed back into the house, Mahari beside her.

"Yes. You need someone to make you happy, too, Mama."

"I am happy!" Liana said, crossing through the foyer to head back to the solarium. "I have an amazing life, and I have my children."

"Jahd has just come back after traveling the country for the last several months, Mama," Mahari said, retrieving her book and then looking at it. "I have the option of graduating in two years." She looked up at Liana and then took a breath. "It's an option I plan to take. After that, I'm going to Claerendon to continue my studies for a year, and then start a mentee program at the university so that I can go into teaching."

Liana pressed a hand to her chest in shock. "When did you decide all of this?" she asked.

"Honestly? Just now when I said it," Mahari said. "I've been thinking about it for weeks, though. Seeing my brother outside... looking so pleased about being away doing something that he obviously loves... made me realize I want that for myself."

"I can't think about this right now," Liana said, holding up a hand and shaking her head. "My son is turning eighteen tomorrow and will likely leave again to start his own life. I'm supposed to think about you doing the same?"

Mahari kneeled beside her mother's chair, looking up at her with large, earnest gray eyes.

"We still have two years, Mama," Mahari said. "But, it's something to think about. What are you going to do once we've gone?"

Mahari's question was still echoing in Liana's mind that night at dinner. It was just the four of them at the table, including Jahd and Huison. Kaileih had begged off, deciding instead to eat in the kitchen while she indulged in a bit of early prep for Jahd's birthday luncheon the following day.

The curly heads of Jahd and Mahari were buried in a book that Mahari had smuggled into the dining room as she showed off some notes from her tutoring sessions.

"What does any of that even mean?" Jahd asked as he frowned at his sister's neat handwriting.

"Ah, I guess you aren't so smart after all, brother!" Mahari said gleefully. "If you're lucky, I might show you a thing or two."

"You should be so very proud of her, Li," Huison said softly, the love of his daughter shining clearly in his amber gaze. "I am in awe of her myself! I do not think she will need the additional training for too much longer." He turned to Liana. "They are, however, thinking of placing her in accelerated courses for her final two years. You know she is on track to graduate early?"

"Yes, I know that," Liana said, settling back in her chair and fiddling with one of the silver bracelets on her arm. "But, did *you* know she wants to go off to Claerendon after graduation?" Huison's shocked expression was a clear sign he did not. "Yes... once she's finished at Breaton, she wants to complete her studies at the university and then become a mentee so that she can start teaching."

Huison exhaled slowly and appeared to deflate as he looked over again at Jahd and Mahari.

"No!" Mahari told her brother, slapping his hand away from the section of the book that he was pointing at. "That isn't it at all! You can't rearrange the spell like that, or it turns to gibberish."

"I think you're full of gibberish," Jahd countered.

"Silly... you know how words have a prefix, root, and suffix? You've got to keep that in mind when you break spells apart... because each word in the spell has its own components! You can't turn 'round and try to combine two prefixes with a root! Now, try that one again..."

"I think she will do well as an instructor," Huison remarked.

"Especially if hand-slapping is part of the curriculum," Liana agreed, the corners of her mouth twitching as she tried not to laugh. She then cleared her throat. "That's enough, you two," she called to her children. "If you're done with dinner, I'm sure that your grandmother has something delicious waiting in the kitchen for dessert."

Two pairs of sharp gray eyes twinkled at the mention of dessert. Jahd got up from the table, gently pulling Mahari's chair out before she also rose, closing her book and tucking it beneath her arm.

"I don't want you staying up too late," Liana cautioned. "Tomorrow's going to be quite a day."

"Outstanding and unforgettable, if I say so myself," Jahd said as he straightened an imaginary tie.

348

"The only thing outstanding or unforgettable would be if you learned what a prefix is," Mahari said, coming around the table to kiss her mother on the cheek. "I'm going up to my room after dessert. Good night, Mama." She looked over at Huison and smiled. "Good night, Father. See you both in the morning."

Jahd reached over to grab an asparagus spear from a platter on the table. "Yeah, coming out of the same bedroom," he said with a chuckle as he bit into the spear.

"Come on!" Mahari said in frustration, yanking Jahd by his free hand as they both left the dining room.

"She is more like Kaileih every day," Huison said after they had gone.

"I told her that very thing earlier," Liana said, laughing. "She had the audacity to thank me for it." She glanced over at Huison. "Though she posed an excellent question."

"What question was that?"

"She asked what I plan to do once both she and Jahd are gone... off living their own lives."

Their eyes met. "And you said?" Huison asked.

"I didn't," Liana said, her lips curled into a teasing smile. "I didn't tell her, but it is something I'd like to discuss with you."

"Oh," Huison said, and Liana could see hope spring into his eyes. "Li, I would very much like..."

"Liana, these children of yours are demolishing the banana meringue pudding that I made," Kaileih said as she walked into the dining room, hands on her hips in mock sternness. "I'd suggest that if either of you want the chance to have any, you'd best come wrestle it from their hands."

Liana smiled at Huison. "I guess we'd better," she said.

"But Li..."

"Shhh," she warned in a whisper, one eye on Kaileih. "We'll talk. Tonight. In the library. Around... eleven-thirty? Everyone should be asleep by then."

"In the library at eleven-thirty," Huison agreed. "I will be there."

Liana then got up, smiling, and followed Kaileih to the kitchen as Huison took a breath and sat back in the chair. He could not help laughing. Could this mean what he hoped? Mahari had asked what Liana planned to do with her life when she was alone, and Liana wanted to discuss it with him! She was going to be his! That had to be why she wanted to talk! Huison had not even bestowed the greatest gift upon her yet, and she was still finally going to consent to be his wife!

"Tonight... the library at eleven-thirty," he said again.

"You're looking awfully pleased with yourself." Huison looked over to find Jahd lounging in the doorway, a dish of dessert in one hand and a spoon in the other. "Get a flick in under the table, did you?"

Huison slowly got up, draping his napkin over his emptied plate before smoothing his embroidered silk thobe. He walked over to Jahd, smile still intact, and placed a hand on the younger man's shoulder.

"Tonight will be amazing," Huison said. "I am going to make your mother the happiest woman in the world, and I hope you will be there to witness it."

Jahd shook Huison's hand away before stabbing the spoon into the bowl of meringue and walking away.

Chapter Thirty-Seven

The house was quiet.

Huison was alone in the library, his amber eyes roaming over the collection of tomes among the many shelves lining most of the walls. Taking a sip of his drink, the finely etched glass cool against his lips, he reflected upon how comfortable he'd always been at the Den, particularly during the times that it was a second home to him.

Huison wondered what he might do about Dalenbeigh once he took up permanent residence in Kynedal. Dalenbeigh would have to be maintained, obviously, for Mahari's inheritance, but Huison did not really relish the thought of shuttering the property until that time. Perhaps, once the evening's unpleasantness had passed, she might consent to spending half the year with him in Scio. After he and Liana were married, and he was certain after their conversation at dinner that she was on the cusp of a decision, he would also insist that Liana change Mahari's surname. She should never have been branded a Chatelain to begin with.

Huison was mindful of the time. Liana was running late, but it would not be much longer now. Everything was ready and every fiber of Huison's being was taut with anticipation. This was it! Tonight,

Liana's lifelong dream would be realized and Huison's aspirations would come to fruition as well.

Walking over to the large desk, Huison took a seat and placed his glass atop the marble surface. It was time to put all the pieces into play. His eyes moved to an antique cabinet nestled against the far-left corner of the wall, and his heartbeat quickened. Huison took a moment to steady his breathing, reached for the book he had obtained earlier, and opened it to a random page.

As if on cue, the door to the library opened and Jahd walked in. On the inside, Huison was in an uproar, aching to demand that Jahd stop looking at him with that stupid smirk and die—just die right now!—so that Liana could receive her due, turn to Huison in love and gratitude, and Huison could finally get what he deserved.

Instead, Huison only looked up from the book in feigned surprise, reaching for his drink as he took a sip and said, "Well, I thought you to be asleep by now."

"Not yet," Jahd said as he entered, closing the door behind him. "I'm not very tired."

"No?" Huison asked lightly. "Excited for your birthday, are you?"

"You have no idea." Jahd walked over to the desk, leaning over to help himself to Huison's glass, taking it straight from his former tutor's hand. He lifted it to his nose, smelling it. "And more than that."

Huison watched as Jahd took a long drink, draining most of the contents of the glass in three swallows. "More than your birthday?" he asked.

"Oh, yes," Jahd said, after licking his lips.

Huison arched a brow. "Nice habit you have," he commented, "taking that which does not belong to you."

"Says the pot to the kettle," Jahd said, returning the nearly empty glass. Huison chuckled, getting up to walk over to the small serving cart of refreshments that Clea brought into the room earlier for his enjoyment.

"Did you come down hoping for an early taste of birthday cake?" Huison asked as Jahd studied the books along the wall.

Jahd turned to glance at him, only able to see the back of Huison's slender form as he busied himself at the cart. Jahd heard the bits of ice being added to the glass before a liquid was poured in. Huison then turned to him, stirring the contents with a long-handled silver spoon.

"No," Jahd said, taking a book from the shelf and leafing through it. "But, I knew you'd be here. You practically invited me, so I thought I'd humor you and we'd have one last chat."

"Our last chat, is it?" Huison removed the spoon from the glass, placing it atop the cart before returning to the desk with the fresh drink and sitting again.

"You never saw fit to advise what it was you brought me here to do," Jahd said. "Instead, you've allowed the last nine, almost ten years to go by while you've done nothing." He smirked. "You realize that, once the clock strikes midnight, I am no longer beholden to you."

"Is that a requirement, that you are beholden to me? Can it not be simply that you owe me for saving you?"

"If that's what you think, you are grossly misguided about how my kind operates."

"No," Huison countered. "I am very well aware of how your kind operates."

Jahd laughed, reaching over to once again pluck the glass from Huison's grip. Huison sat back in the chair as Jahd helped himself.

"This is quite delicious," Jahd commented after lowering the half-empty glass. "What is it?"

"A little something to help celebrate the evening," Huison commented softly. "The recipe belongs to your grandmother, but I may have added a flourish or two."

"What a renegade you are, Uncle Hui. Don't mind if I do." When the glass was nearly empty, Huison got up again and began pacing the room.

"About your kind and how you operate," he began, "Liana came to me... years ago... to ask if I had ever shared with anyone the details of an event that took place when she was thirteen and enrolled at Breaton Academy. It was an incident so heart-wrenching and painful for her she had not fully shared it with anyone.

"Her parents, and perhaps Evium, may have been told one version or another, but... she shared the full extent of what took place with me. Yet Liana mentioned you alluded to it on the evening before your initial departure for Pandoufuli. She did not understand how you could have known anything about it."

Huison stopped, turning to look back at Jahd. Jahd was staring at him over the rim of the glass.

"I had already gleaned that there was something more to you and to the reasoning behind your adhesion to Rael. After speaking with Liana, however, I had no doubts." Huison pointed a finger at Jahd. "Liana and the others summoned you. You were the one she planned to kill for reneging on the agreement."

Jahd shrugged, lowering the glass with a sigh. "Of course, it was me. I told you that day at the mine... I like to play with fresh things. I was only toying with her and her friends. I would have given her what she asked for had she only waited. She's the one who, by trying to kill me, broke the agreement. That's why she ended up with nothing."

"I initially thought that perhaps you were trying to make up for that night... for the renunciation of the power that you owed Liana," Huison continued, his eyes locked on the glass. "I assumed that was the reason you latched onto her brother, because you hoped to satisfy the pact. Had she just come to visit Rael once, she would have found you and she would have been made whole. However, so much time has passed since your release while you have sat by and done nothing."

"I didn't sit by," Jahd smiled, ice clinking merrily as he swirled the glass. "I haven't been idle at all."

"With her you have been! Have you never intended to fulfill your end of the bargain?"

"Why should I!?" Jahd suddenly yelled. "She tried to kill me! That bitch! That greedy, self-serving bitch planned to massacre me in cold blood rather than accept the fact that she's nothing!"

"She is everything!" Huison countered in a thunderous voice.

"Oh, her talent lies between her thighs and nowhere else!" Jahd sneered. "Look at you, still dancing to her tune after all this time with nothing to show for it and no guarantees! And, once the clock strikes midnight, you both end up with nothing!"

"You are wrong," Huison said, slowly shaking his head. "I have a guarantee—you."

Jahd laughed as he brought the glass to his lips again, sucking in one of the ice cubes. "Right... sure you do," he said. He crunched into the ice and then paused, noting the expression on Huison's face. Jahd's head tilted slightly, his eyes narrowed, and he shifted the ice in his mouth. He then frowned, allowing the ice to fall from his mouth and back into the glass. His eyes slowly lowered to study the glass in his hand before he looked up at Huison again, swallowing hard. "What have you done?" he asked in a whisper.

"What I intended all along," Huison said calmly, as he watched Jahd's grip loosen until the glass fell from his hand and splintered against the flooring. "You, my friend, should have known better than to grow complacent."

"W-What is this?" Jahd asked with a groan, his footing as unsteady as a newborn colt as he moved around the desk to brace himself against the bookcase. "What was in that glass?"

Despite having recently consumed two substantial drinks, Jahd's mouth seemed dry. His tongue was leathery and felt engorged. He felt rippling spasms in his abdomen as Huison swayed and shuddered in his vision.

"I told you," Huison said. "The recipe came from Kaileih... I merely added a couple of teaspoons of valerian tincture for an added kick."

Jahd groaned again, blinking rapidly as Huison doubled, tripled, and then quadrupled in his sight.

"Despite what you are at the core, you are still subject to the restrictions of your human shell," Huison explained. "You are right, Jahd. I have let the last nine years go by, but thoughts of what I want from you and what you will do for Liana have never been far from my mind."

Jahd winced as he felt another cramp. If he could only get free of this body, even for a moment, it could buy him the time he needed to recover himself. But, how could he? He could not focus. He felt dizzy and extraordinarily fatigued. Each limb felt as though it weighed a ton.

"I'll do nothing for her," Jahd managed thickly before swallowing. "I never intended to."

"Then why are you here? Revenge?"

"At first," Jahd said, a line of sweat dampening the curls at his brow. "I wanted her to pay... for what she did to me. I planned to make her regret it." He managed a smile. "I've learned... and I've grown... thanks to you... and all because you forced me to remain in this body. You were so right when you told me on that first day that this body was the best one for me, but you did not know all the reasons why.

"I am tied to Liana by blood... the blood she took and drank from me that night... blood passed down through Jahd's veins helping me to become stronger than I ever thought possible..."

"I already knew that!" Huison said.

"But what you didn't count on... was the blood Liana already had in her, inherited from her father after the oath he took while on a quest for knowledge and the ability to transcend the realms..."

Huison flinched. "What?" he said, gasping. "What are you saying?"

"I said you did not know," Jahd grinned, though his eyelids were heavy. "How did you think that Amriel Dhamon gained that skill? Why do you think his son thought himself able to replicate it? In the end, though, none of it meant anything, and your love of Liana is nothing when compared with that of my master's love for her mother.

"Kaileih was to be his long ago. He adored her, and planned to claim her... but, she encountered Amriel Dhamon during a visit to this realm and Amriel fell madly in love with her. He was determined to see her again, and he sought my master out... invoking a pledge... a binding of the blood to gain the ability to move between the realms... Only my master didn't know then that Amriel was doing it hoping to find Kaileih, and it shattered him once he realized that his own power had been used to undermine him."

Huison's mouth was dry from hanging open for so long. "Kaileih," he croaked, "was visiting this world? She is not from..."

"No," Jahd answered with a throaty chuckle. "Kaileih knows the taint of absolute authority. She stripped her own daughter of everything that would have made her an extremely powerful spellweaver. She did it because she knew their bloodline was infected with voracious ambition, and that a desire inside of Liana could be twisted just enough to have Liana be the means by which Kaileih could be forced to confront a reality she has no intention of ever returning to."

"But Kaileih had to know that Rael would try to follow what his father had done!" Huison protested. "Rael was the catalyst, not Liana!"

"Rael was intelligent, but he lacked his father's genius," Jahd said. "I hardly think that Kaileih ever realistically expected her son to come close to duplicating his father's efforts."

"You had taken possession of Rael," Huison reminded him. "If Amriel Dhamon passed along the bloodline of a supreme malevolence, why did you not use Rael as your weapon of vengeance?"

"He had the mental fortitude of a carrot by the time I got to him!" Jahd said with a dry laugh. "He was useless to me!"

Huison opened his mouth to say something more, but then the door behind him opened and they were no longer alone.

Chapter Thirty-Eight

Liana hadn't yet changed out of the dress she'd worn to dinner, the chiffon overlay swirling around her legs as she rushed in. "I'm sorry to be late, Huison," she said. "There were a few last-minute things I needed to—"

Her words trailed off as she looked past Huison and over to Jahd, who was barely standing as he slumped against the rows of bookshelves. She shook her head in disbelief as she surveyed Jahd's sweat-slick face, the feverish flush of his skin, and Huison's look of devastation.

"What the hell is going on?" she asked, rushing into the room and over to her son. "Sweetheart, what's happened? Are you all right?"

"Mama," Jahd said in a pitiful voice, his eyes filling with tears, "oh, Mama, I'm so glad you're here..."

Huison moved quickly to the door to close it before turning back to Liana and Jahd. "Li, please listen to me... listen to me this moment and come away from him now!"

"What the hell do you mean I should come away from him?" Liana demanded, returning to Huison and glaring up at him, eyes blazing. "What is this? Why is there glass all over the floor? What have you done to my son, Huison?"

Huison clasped his hands together, interlacing the fingers as he moved closer. "To your son? Nothing."

"Oh, so I'm imagining things, is that it?" Liana said in a nasty tone. "Why does he look so ill?"

"Mama," Jahd said, panting, "please... help me. Uncle Hui is killing me."

Liana's blood did not run cold. It burned as she looked from the quivering body of her son to Huison, who was looking back at her without appearing to be even remotely chagrined by the accusation levied against him.

"What is this?" Liana repeated in a raspy whisper. The way she felt toward Huison at that moment was the opposite of what she had been considering when she initially entered the room.

"Liana, I promise," Huison said, "if you would allow me to explain... it will all make sense... you will see and understand that this is for the best..."

"What is for the best!?" she yelled.

Behind them, Jahd groaned. No longer able to support his own weight, he fell to his knees.

"Baby!" Liana cried, about to return to his side when Huison grabbed her around the waist.

Liana opened her mouth to scream when the sound was stifled by one of Huison's hands as he used his other arm to sustain the grip around Liana, preventing her from moving away from him.

"Shhh! Quiet, Liana!" he pleaded as she twisted and struggled.

It did not matter which way she moved, Huison maintained his wiry embrace even as she used her legs to kick at him and she ground the spiked heels of her strappy sandals against his ankles and the tops of his feet.

"Listen, listen—I need you to listen to me, please, Liana!" Her scream against his hand was muffled, and his hold on her tightened even more. "There is not much time," he went on, speaking quickly. "I realize how this appears. Even though I have had years to think on this, I could never decide how this should play out. I admit that my methods at this juncture were more than a tad haphazard as a result.

"I could only settle upon the means of subduing Jahd once he came into the library, and improvisation would prove necessary from that point. I know what he has alleged, but that is not the case! I have provided him with a beverage, Liana, infused with something that will not prove fatal. I only needed to make him unwell, mollifying him while you carry out what you must."

Liana, feeling sick from a combination of fear and rage while growing weary from thrashing about, wailed a single-word question into Huison's palm.

"I will tell you, Li," Huison said. "I will tell you why. The fact is, Liana, that I have hidden something from you... something kept in trust for the last nine years..." Liana cried out in frustration, the tears from her eyes streaming down and over the hand clamped against her mouth. She did not know what he was talking about. "I have given you a gift... a gift that needed to be cultivated.

"Think of your formidable mother, Li. Think of Kaileih and her gift of growing things. She plants a seed, and it is provided shelter and nourishment... After a while, that seed grows. It assumes the preliminary shape of what it is eventually meant to be. What I have sown has needed nine years to blossom. That is what Jahd is. It is what he has become—now ripe for harvest."

Liana continued to sob as she remained pressed against Huison. To her, he sounded like a raving lunatic. He spoke of Jahd as though he were some creature or inhuman entity. She could not understand why Huison seemed so detached from the boy he had cared for and loved for almost eighteen years.

Why would Jahd need to be subdued? What was it that Huison expected Liana to carry out? Had Huison finally cracked under the strain of repeated rejections over the last dozen years? He could not possibly think that this would be the means by which Liana would be his, and Liana could not believe she had been considering asking if they could try to make a relationship work. She was convinced that Evium would want to kill him after this. Liana had no plans to interfere.

"It is time, Liana," Huison was saying before moving his lips mere inches from her left ear. She shuddered, repulsed. "He is incorrect tonight in saying that I am killing him," Huison said softly. "I know this because... Jahd is already dead."

Huison felt Liana's body stiffen as he held her. She was no longer struggling, and her cries were reduced to the occasional sniffle. Her breaths were sporadic, and he knew she was trying to puzzle out what he was saying to her. He had to press on.

"You know what it was I tried to do for your brother," Huison said. "My intentions were genuine, but I discovered early on that Rael posed a more unique challenge than I realized.

"A demon possessed him. It came back with him after he tried to go after your father. The demon drove Rael mad, and extracting it caused his death." Huison sighed. "I did not mean for that to happen, Liana," he said, still speaking into her ear. "I wanted to return Rael to you, but the discovery of the demon presented another opportunity altogether."

It was at this moment that Huison felt sure that he had Liana under his control. She had remained still. She was no longer crying. There was little doubt that she would want to know the rest of the story, and what brought them to the events of the night.

Huison slowly loosened his grip. If her lack of motion was a ruse to encourage him to let his guard down, he would simply have to snatch her up again. As much as he abhorred the use of physical force, using magic to control her was entirely out of the question.

Liana stepped out of his arms, glancing briefly at Jahd before slowly turning to face Huison. Her face was red and splotchy because of her misery, but she looked no less beautiful to him. After she came into her power, he would dry her tears and be more tender when taking her into his arms again.

"Go on," she whispered. He could see that she was trembling.

"There are rules on every plane," Huison said. "Of course, there are stories of demons plaguing their victims, but a demon cannot remain for long in a realm that is foreign to it except through possession.

"Even when one is summoned, such as what you could do with your friends back at Breaton, the parameters of the visit are such that the situation is only temporary. Had you been able to bind it into a body, it would have been yours to command for the duration of that pact, usually until the body exhausted itself, forcing the demon to vacate. The typical human form is not meant to house that kind of creature for too long."

"Rael had that thing inside of him for six years!"

"Rael was different!" Huison said. "I did not find out exactly how different until tonight, however."

"What does that mean?" Liana demanded.

"What that means is not the point and we do not have time to discuss it! What I am saying to you is... the typical human form is not meant to contain a demon for too long."

"You told me that already!"

"Liana!" Huison pleaded, silencing her. "Because you drank the blood of a demon on that night... it made you an exception. You... or any of your descendants... are uniquely prepared for a successful, lasting demonic binding. A child sharing your blood could be that seed, growing over time until harvest."

He watched as Liana's eyes widened. He could see the moment that realization dawned, and her eyes filled once again with tears.

"No," she whispered. "You mean... Jahd? My baby?"

"On the early morning of his eighth birthday, I took Jahd away," Huison said. "He was so perfect, Li... the perfect vessel. We... went out to the mine, and I performed the binding."

"But why?" Liana wailed. "Why would you do such a thing?"

"For you! I did it for you, Liana. But... now I cannot harm him. That is the condition of my covenant with him. Just as you would have broken the pact by killing the demon then, I would break it if I did so now."

"Then what? You let it walk around in the body of my son!?"

"I told you how special your bloodline is," Huison said. "How, because of that, the effect of the binding is different. The age of the host is also a factor. Had Rael not been afflicted by a psychotic break, he might have been able to carry the demon inside of him for the duration of his life, benefitting from an amplification of the power Rael already possessed, if you will excuse the pun.

"Jahd was eight years old. His body was still developing. He had not yet come into his own. He would flourish, as would the demon inside of him, and they would mature together and turn into something brilliant. Following the natural course of things, his traits would be honed until he reached adulthood."

"At eighteen years old," Liana whispered, to which Huison responded with a smile.

"If we halted the process right before that very moment, you are left with a power that is at the peak of potency. Jahd is seventeen years old, turning eighteen at midnight. Liana, he is at his peak."

"You just said that you can't kill him!" Liana said. "Just as I almost killed that thing at school, you'll be damned if you do!"

"No, Liana, I cannot kill him," Huison confirmed. "You can."

Liana gasped. "What? Why would I do that!?"

"Because, the power inside of him would be yours to claim by right of blood."

Liana froze. "What did you say?"

Huison slowly reached into the left pocket of his thobe. From it, he extracted the silver hook-handled dagger taken from the cabinet earlier.

"Take his life," Huison said. "Claim your destiny."

"My son!?" Liana screamed through her tears. "You expect me to kill my own son for power!? Have I seemed so desperate to you, Huison!?"

"He is not your son, Liana!" Huison pleaded, his own eyes shining because of the distress of the woman he loved. "Not anymore. Your son died on his eighth birthday. He died so that you could have the life you have wanted since you were a young girl—the life you deserve. I wanted to give that to you because I love you!"

"Huison," Liana said, hiccupping through her tears, "where is he? Tell me the truth. My boy... my precious, sweet baby boy... where is he?"

Huison wrapped his arms around Liana's waist, gently this time, reveling in the feel of her in his arms again. Even in her distress, she had never been more breathtaking.

"He is gone," Huison said, pulling her closer to him. "I took him away and replaced him with everything you wanted."

"No!" Liana said, breaking from the embrace and reaching down to snatch the dagger from Huison's hand. She shook it at him. "Not like this! I didn't ask for this!"

"No, you did not," Huison conceded. "I did it for you. Do not think of it as killing Jahd because that is not your son."

"You mean to tell me that there's nothing... nothing left of my baby in there? Rael lived with that entity for six years. Surely, there's hope for Jahd—my Jahd."

"No," Huison said with a shake of his head. "Rael was merely possessed. Jahd has been supplanted."

"Noooo!" Liana wailed.

"Remember that night, Liana," Huison begged. "Remember how badly you wanted to be a spellweaver. You and your friends together at Breaton... something finally answered your call after months. You drank the blood. Since that moment, he has been a part of you."

"I was infected!" Liana spat in disgust.

"You were enhanced," Huison corrected. "The blood has been inside of you for all these years; dormant, needing to be awakened. He was returned to his plane before he could grant you the gift that night, so this is the only way to receive it now.

"You must close the circle. Jahd was the perfect host, as he inherited your superior bloodline and could carry your gift unscathed for all these years. But, for this to work, Jahd had to be wholly consumed."

"Consumed," Liana repeated in a whisper. "What have I been raising for the last nine years?"

Huison shrugged. "Your legacy. It must end—tonight. Now, before it is too late. Liana, everything you could ever want is all within your reach." He took a step closer, his voice taking on a soothing tone. "All you need do is one thing... and everything you crave is yours."

Huison's eyes suddenly widened as he looked past Liana. She turned to look behind her. Jahd had somehow gotten to his feet and was stumbling toward her. Visibly startled, Liana screamed, and her arm snapped forward.

Jahd cried out, his eyes bulging as the stiletto blade slid easily into his flesh. He fell to the floor atop a scattering of broken glass, his hands pressed against his lower right side.

Liana gulped. Motherly instinct made her inch toward Jahd before she stopped, remembering what he had become. She began crying again.

"Do it! Do it, Liana!" Huison was panting behind her, practically chanting the words. "Finish it... take him... claim what is yours. Begin your new life!"

"You shut up!" Liana screamed, turning on Huison and pointing the tip of the bloodied weapon at him. "You're out of your mind! All of this is madness! That you can stand there trying to force me to do this..."

"Liana, we are running out of time!" Huison yelled, his wiry frame a confused knot of trepidation and eagerness.

"I don't care!" Liana said. "I won't do it! This is ridiculous! It's just..."

Liana sucked in a sharp breath. Her panicked, gray gaze flew to Huison, her brows twitching together in uncertainty. She then looked down at the tremors in her hands and at the bloodied dagger in her grip. Liana's vision grew cloudy as a slow buzzing crept from the back of her neck and over her ears.

"What is happening to me!?" she cried as the heat in her body was magnified and she broke out in a full sweat.

"Li," Huison whispered with rounded eyes as he reached for her.

"Don't touch me!" she screamed as a bolt of pain raced through her spine, bowing her body backward.

Liana cried out again as she sank to her knees, the dagger clattering to the floor as the fingers of each hand stretched to impossible lengths before snapping back into tightly contorted fists. As her spine bowed again, she threw her head back and howled, a distressing cry of agony and terror. With a violent shudder and a rapid series of audible cracking sounds along her vertebrae, she finally crumpled onto the floor and lay still, her eyes closed.

Huison's exhalation was explosive. He did not know what to do or what to think. What had happened to Liana? What could have possibly caused what looked to be a vicious attack on her person?

"No," he said breathlessly. "No, this cannot be..."

He could not have lost her. He could not lose her. She was everything to him. He had done everything for her. The night was hers. The light was hers. Liana must endure.

Huison went to her, turning her limp form onto its back and pushing her sweat-soaked hair out of her face.

"Li," he said, his voice quivering, "Li, my beauty... my love... Please, please wake up! I cannot do this without you! Liana!"

As if in response to Huison's desperate cry, Liana's eyes snapped open. Huison looked into them and then recoiled, hurriedly scooting backward away from her, hardly feeling the bits of glass that embedded themselves into his palms. Liana's eyes drained of color, becoming almost entirely white as even her pupils appeared to have vanished.

Liana sat up, feeling wobbly only for a moment. Getting to her feet, with no assistance from a traumatized Huison, she briefly closed her eyes as she took in a deep, cleansing breath. She stretched languorously and then looked around the room. Her surroundings had never been in such great focus. She could see every minor detail, including the intricate designs in the art on the walls, down to the individual strokes made by the artist's brush in the paintings.

She felt cloaked in endless, reverberating warmth, and the hum in her ears was like the whisper of a lover. Liana hugged herself, running her hands over the skin of both her arms and shoulders, delighting in the gooseflesh that resulted. Feeling audacious, she flicked a gaze toward the branch of candles along the far wall, laughing in delight when the previously low flames burst with renewed energy and a curtain of fire rolled up the wall, igniting a nearby canvas. She then turned to glance at one of the windows. The panes of glass shuddered, warped, and then imploded as crystalline shards and splinters of wood blew into the room.

Huison's resulting gasp recalled Liana to his presence, and she turned to him with a chilling smile. "Tell me what you know of this," she said in an unnaturally calm voice.

"It is the blood," Huison panted, sweat dripping from his brow as he struggled to get to his feet. "It is his blood. The wound you inflicted with the dagger has begun the process. It is as I told you. The power in you is awakening."

Liana held Jahd, who was still writhing in pain with a hand pressed against the wound at his midsection, within her snowy gaze. Her nostrils twitched. Jahd's gray eyes seemed unusually large in Liana's augmented sight, and her eyes narrowed as she glimpsed the traces of blood leaching from between his fingers. He had a sour aroma about him. It was one she had never noticed before. It thrilled her to the point of arousal. He smelled of fear.

"That little cut has done this for me?" she asked Huison, though she was still staring at Jahd.

"Yes," Huison said, edging closer. "There is so much more. End this. End him, and the rest is yours."

"There's more?" Liana asked in delight, paying no mind as the scorched painting on the wall dropped to the floor and landed beside a plush rug, the edge of which was smoldering.

"So much more," Huison crooned, bending to hastily retrieve the dagger. He pressed the handle into her palm. "You have only to finish what we started. You will have everything that should have been yours from the start. But, we are almost out of time, Liana!"

"What is time to me now?" Liana asked with a shrug as she looked at the dagger with indifference. "Surely someone of my restored capacity isn't governed by something as pedestrian as time."

Her laughter was musical, even as the large area rug behind them was engulfed and a few tendrils of fire began licking at the bottom of the lavish curtains adorning the window on the other side of the room.

"We have only minutes, Liana!" Huison said, nervous amber eyes darting about the room as things crumbled around them.

"We have centuries!" she countered, holding her arms above her head as she stretched again. "We have as long as I want, and I have so much to do! Wait until everyone sees!" Her white eyes sparkled. "Everyone who looked down on me or felt sorry for me for being plain... won't they be surprised?" Her eyes narrowed. "Wait until I show them." She lowered her arms, tapping the bloodied tip of the dagger against her lips.

"You!" Liana said, suddenly glaring at Huison. "You say that thing on the floor isn't my son... that you took Jahd when he was eight and brought that back in his place. I've had him here... for nine years..."

"Yes," Huison said, confused.

"Nine years... you knew what he could do for me. Why'd you wait so long to tell me!?"

"I... I... what?" Huison stammered, taken aback and clearly startled.

Liana took a step toward Huison, the flaming curtains falling from their position at the wall and landing across an armchair.

"You made me wait all that time to get what was mine," she accused, before shouting the words at him. "Do you realize how different my life would be had you told me sooner!?"

Huison was shocked into appalled silence. "Liana, I have explained this to you," he said at last. "I have explained why it was important to wait..."

"This should have been mine long ago!" she screamed. Huison could only stare at her in dawning horror as he recalled Kaileih's words from so long ago.

"Huison, I adore my daughter. I also know her well enough to be acutely aware of what would happen if she ever tasted a mite of what spellweaving is. Things happen for a reason."

Tears filled Huison's eyes as he slowly nodded in silent acknowledgement of Kaileih's forewarning. Liana scoffed, thinking the nod agreed with her assessment of Huison's failure.

"I'll still get what I want," she vowed. "I intend to finish up here, and then it's time to take a little trip to D'alegne."

"D'alegne?" Huison asked, ashen. "What is in..."

"My husband," Liana said sweetly, tittering. "I'm going to get Evium back." She closed her eyes, her face taking on a serene look. "He'll have no choice but to love me again. How could he resist me now?" Huison shuddered when the pupil-less eyes opened and focused on him again. "Of course, I'll have to kill his wife and children, but that certainly poses no problem. I might even persuade him to help. Wouldn't that be fun?"

Huison could not staunch the flow of the tears that ran unchecked down his face as he slowly shook his head.

"She was right," he whispered. "She knew."

"Hmm?" Liana said, distracted by plans of reclamation and resurgence.

"Liana," he said shakily, his breaths ragged, "despite all... that you say and plan... nothing you want will come to fruition if you do not hurry and..."

"Oh, to the hells with you!" she screamed as her right arm extended in a sweeping arc.

Bewilderment spread across Huison's face, both brows lifting as his eyes widened. He stared at Liana with incredulity as she appeared to shift slightly out of focus.

Huison felt a dizzying rush. The edges of his line of vision seemed hazy. His mind could make no sense of what was happening, so it drifted off in search of more pleasant thoughts. He recalled the first time he and Liana met.

It was on the evening celebrating the completion of the Den. Huison, having missed the wedding of his former best friend, arrived at the gala intending to offer polite congratulations, have a few drinks, and perhaps leave with someone warm for the evening. Instead, he met Liana, and from that moment every inch of him belonged to her. He was hers from the moment she laid beautiful gray eyes on him, even though it would be years before she knew. When they met was the night Huison's life truly began.

Every moment they spent together, from the innocuous to the intimate, was embedded within Huison's soul. He could not imagine life without her. But, as dear as she was to him, Liana had become increasingly infatuated with Evium. The definitive loss of Liana, realized after so many years, presented an irony that was not lost on Huison even as his vision darkened. As his life had begun with Liana on the Chatelain estate, so would it end.

Huison opened his mouth to speak. He wanted to utter parting words of devotion to the woman to whom he had dedicated so much. All he could manage was a bubbling gurgle as one stream of blood trickled from his mouth, followed by another and another. His head tilted back slightly as a seam opened across his throat, curving along the smooth olive skin.

Blood slowly seeped from the slit created by Liana's vengeful stroke of the dagger, and she continued to glower at him even as he coughed and choked and gasp for air. Stepping away from him as he reached for her, Huison fell to his knees as the dream of Liana's beauty distorted, became obscured, and finally faded when he collapsed to the floor.

Liana sank to her haunches, tilting her head at Huison's wheezing form. She closed her eyes again, swaying slightly to the sounds of his struggles to breathe, opening them again once he was eternally silenced and the hand that was reaching for her had grown limp. She grinned and then stood fully erect, turning to the place where Jahd was cowering.

"Now for you," she began before pausing, her eyes wide.

Jahd was no longer there. Gritting her teeth, Liana spun on her heels, intending to search the smoky room, but was startled to find him standing behind her. His eyes, white like her own, were blazing with anger.

"Think again," he said as he grabbed her by the throat.

Liana's scream was squeezed out of her as she pounded ineffectually at the grip around her neck with her left hand while shakily raising the dagger in her right.

"Try it!" Jahd taunted, sneering. "Go ahead! You stupid little bitch!" He shook her. "You impetuous, weak thing! Blubbering idiot! Undeserving cretin!"

Liana rasped as the dagger fell from her hand. The milky whiteness of her eyes ebbed until they were once again gray, edged in red and filled with tears. Jahd threw her backward, where she banged against the wall before landing on the floor, her body twisting as she struggled to breathe and found her lungs filling with smoke rather than air.

"Jahd," she moaned.

"No," he said simply. "I mean, of course that's the name I've been answering to and will continue to be known as, but... as Huison told you, your son died a very long time ago." He reached down to pick up the dagger, intrigued by the etchings on its hooked handle. "Jahd was such an immaculate little thing, so vibrant. I could have played with him all day."

"You... monster..." Liana croaked before coughing again.

"Hmm, yes," Jahd said agreeably before tossing the dagger to the side. "I am and always have been, though once I was your faithful servant... your captive servant, actually, even if only for a very short while." He studied Liana as she inched about the floor and toward the desk.

"You always were absurdly obstinate," he continued. "Had you only listened to Huison... poor, poor deluded Huison... you not only would have at last been given the power you wanted as per the original terms, but my reign would have ended..." He smiled. "...rather than just beginning. I suppose I should thank you for that. In a way, you helped me out a little."

Jahd grinned before inhaling deeply, not at all troubled by the falling levels of oxygen in the room. Liana, meanwhile, had used the desk as leverage to pull herself up from the floor to stand on quivering legs.

"There's... no way you can... get away with this," she said, panting.

"Oh, sure there is!" he said in that same conversational tone. "Besides, you killed Huison." He pointed at the carmine stains at his midsection, still wet though the wound had closed. "You also attacked me while I was trying to save him. Poor Uncle Hui.

"You were mad with jealousy after learning that my father is expecting yet another child with his wife, the beauty who deposed you. You tried seducing Uncle Hui and he, at long last tired of being used, rebuffed your advances." Jahd giggled, his eyes twinkling.

"There's a fire in this room!" Liana said. "Someone will know! Someone will come!"

The smile faded from Jahd's lips, though his eyes were still alight. "No, they won't," he said acidly.

Liana bristled, bracing herself against the desk. "You can't hurt me," she warned. "If you do, you'll pay and pay dearly. My mother will see to it. She... knows powerful people. She'll hunt you down."

Jahd's expression became wistful. "Ah, your mother. She's a beautiful woman, your mother," Jahd said, slowly pacing the room. "This world could be hers—this one or any she wanted. She had but to ask... yet never would."

"What do you mean?" Liana asked through clenched teeth.

"My master has a longing so deep that it makes Huison's obsession with you seem like a hastily forgotten stable romp. He could never claim Kaileih as his. He's tried to manipulate things, yes, but he would never force her outright. So, he waited and hoped. Instead, she chose your father... who was underhanded in his dealings with my master and used what he learned to win the love of a woman that did not belong to him.

"It seemed so bleak for a while. My master was desperate for a way into her life and, one night, there you were. You were begging to be a spellweaver, not knowing that your extraordinary mother somehow already knew what you'd turn out to be had you been able to keep the power you were born with. He sent me to you, that night so long ago... when you and your friends were playing at summoning a demon to do your bidding.

"My master hoped that sending me to give you your greatest wish would finally be his way in." He glared at her. "But you tried to renege on the deal. You were ready to kill me when all I was doing was having a little fun. I was toying with you that night and you were so impatient, so impulsive... had you only waited, I would have given you everything you asked for... You would have been more powerful than the other four girls combined."

"The power... I was born with?" Liana repeated in awe.

Jahd snorted. "See? Even now with everything else I've said, that's all that permeated that one-track mind of yours."

"If what you're saying is true, you'll have a lot to answer for!" Liana shot back. "If your master loves my mother so, he won't like what you're doing."

"I thought of that," Jahd admitted. "You're wrong again, Liana. What has happened here, what will happen to you, will still ultimately benefit him and bring him closer to what he wants—which has always been to have your mother by his side. You are an acceptable casualty."

Liana pressed herself against the desk as Jahd approached her. "You won't kill me," she said, her voice trembling.

"No, I won't," Jahd said. "It's almost at the top of my wish list, though. I could spend years infusing every inch of your body with blistering pain if there was time. I will do something else. I will give you what you've always wanted... what I've owed you for over twenty years."

Liana's scream was silenced as Jahd grabbed her by the throat again. "One last thing," he murmured. "Thank you. You are the catalyst for what has happened and what is yet to come. Your impulsive nature, your refusal to accept your fate, is the reason that you and your friends came calling. It is because of you that the events of that evening will come full circle. My master will eventually have his bride on the planes... and I shall have mine here. It will take time... but, she will be well worth the wait."

Jahd stared into Liana's eyes. Liana thought she had cried out again, but could hear nothing but an increased roaring sound as Jahd's face, so close to hers, appeared to grow large, warp, and change into something grotesque as the whiteness of his eyes slowly leeched back into hers. Liana was inundated by pulses of heat being directed at her, making her skin feel as though she was being roasted alive.

With each pounding wave that coursed through her, Liana became less aware of her surroundings. She so desperately wanted to look away from Jahd, but found herself unable to break the stare. In the recesses of her mind, she thought she could hear Mahari distantly screaming and there was nothing she could do about it.

With the last of her strength, Liana beat at Jahd, clawing at his face to no avail. As her arms grew heavy, slack, and fell limply to her sides, Jahd released her. She fell against the desk, sliding down to her knees, the quickening beats of her heart punctuating the bellowing in her head as her body began sizzling with vitality.

Liana blinked; her vision sharpened again as the vibration in her ears ceased. She got up on legs that were now energized and strong, looking just in time to see Jahd fleeing the burning room. The smoke no longer bothered her. She felt no pain. In fact, she had never felt so energized.

Her nose wrinkled as an acrid aroma began filling the room. She turned to see that flames had crept up Huison's pant legs, charring the flesh up to his knees as the fire continued to climb along his body. With a hand to her nose in disgust, Liana was almost at the door when she was startled by the heavy sections of marble crown molding falling from the edges of the engulfed ceiling and crashing around her.

Liana jumped away from the door, a heavy chunk of marble barely missing her. She clenched her jaw in annoyance. This was nonsense! It was only fire, and wasn't she above that now that Jahd finally returned her birthright? Walking through a blazing room was nothing when compared with what she would do when she got out.

She shook her hair back, whipping out an arm as she directed her power to quench the nearby flames. When they only rose higher, she frowned. No! That was not right! Liana remembered her early days in the garden, and the way she watched as her mother channeled her gift into the earth.

Quickly crouching down, Liana placed her palms against the floor and closed her eyes, focusing with everything in her on dousing the inferno. As she concentrated, she also vowed that, once this was all over and she had been avenged, she would go to Breaton. They would have to acknowledge her. They would have to train her. She would be invincible. Liana Dhamon would be even more famous than her father!

Liana smiled as the power coursed through her. She was doing it! She could feel it! As proud as Liana was of her mother then, she was certain that her mother would be proud of her now. Everything would be as it should.

Liana's eyes snapped open as she gasped, a crease forming in her brow. Something was wrong.

When Liana's Den violently exploded in a constellation of flaming splinters, the resulting vibration was felt throughout the city of Kynedal.

Chapter Thirty-Nine

Despite the lateness of the hour, Kaileih was still awake. She was comfortably situated in the study of the guest home that served as her residence each time she visited the Chatelain estate. Sipping from a steaming mug of chamomile tea, she reviewed the final list of appetizers, entrees, and desserts she planned to either supervise or cook firsthand for Jahd's birthday celebration.

The tea, into which she had mixed a few drops of valerian tincture, was delicious. The concentration she used was nowhere near as potent as the one she had given Huison, but it served its purpose on those nights she wanted to be sure of getting a restful sleep. It was already past midnight, but Kaileih hoped to get at least five good hours of solid rest before going back to the main house to begin preparations.

The detonation snapped Kaileih to her feet.

She slammed the cup of tea onto the desk, hot contents splashing about, and jumped to her feet. She ran into the hallway as tremors rolled beneath her feet.

She hadn't made it two more steps before the windows to her right shattered. Glass sprayed across her skin, cutting deep. She was then brutally jolted off her feet as the entire guest house seemed to rock on its foundation, slamming the left side of her body against the opposite wall before she crumpled to the floor.

Jahd was in a hurry. He needed to get as far away from the Den as quickly as possible. There was no telling what the moronic Liana would do—novice that she was. Jahd had given her power, the power she had always wanted, but he had not given her the innate ability to use it properly. She had not grown up with those abilities. She was untrained. It would be all too easy for her to blunder into something catastrophic, and he did not want to be there when it happened.

Jahd ran from the smoldering library, thankful the billowing smoke had not yet alerted anyone. The staff had already gone to their own quarters in servants' row. Kaileih was safe in one of the guest houses. The only one that Jahd was deeply concerned with was Mahari, who was still inside the house. He raced to her room, startling her awake as he pulled her from the bed and threw her over one shoulder.

Turning to one of the large bay windows, he huffed at it, causing it to explode outward, scattering the array of stuffed animals and dolls that once graced the sill. Shifting a hysterically weeping Mahari from his shoulder and into his arms, he peered over the edge of the gaping hole created by the destroyed window. He jumped through it, landing below with effortless agility before breaking into a run.

Mahari was shrieking. He knew she was frightened and that he would have to concoct a story to tell her later. Damn that Liana Chatelain! Her willful stupidity was the reason Jahd's plans would have to change and likely accelerate. He would figure that out later, but for now...

Then he heard it—an ear-splitting eruption that caused him to wince. Jahd felt the air at his back grow hot as his surroundings stilled. The ground vanished beneath him and he gasped as the force of the detonation propelled him and Mahari forward through the air and into darkness.

The Chatelain estate was shrouded in silence. A vast, smoldering crater was all that remained of the Den. Wreckage from the explosion was scattered all over the property, and the barrage caused extensive damage to every other structure. Half of the houses in the servants' quarters were destroyed outright, and the others were in flames. The dairy, butchery, stables, and greenhouses were leveled. The concentrated heat of the blast boiled away half the contents of the lake and dead fish smoked along what used to be the water's edge.

One of the guest houses was razed. The other was barely standing. It was easy to enter the one that remained, as the front door was blown completely away. In fact, the entire front half of the house was strewn about the yard.

A tall, lanky figure moved easily over the debris. He traveled over what used to be the porch, stepping up and into the house. All the candles in the home were extinguished, but seeing in the dark had never been a problem for him. Venturing to the left, he finally came upon what, at first glance, looked to be a collection of rubble sitting atop a pile of rags. Bending to push away the fragments, he unearthed the battered body of Kaileih Dhamon.

Though it seemed at first that she was wearing a red outfit, it became clear rather quickly that she was drenched with blood. The lacerations marring her beautiful skin were innumerable. Her left shoulder seemed crooked, and the arm was twisted and pinned beneath her body. There was swelling on the left side of her face and head, and blood dripped from her mouth.

He was careful, more careful than he had been with anything in his entire life, as he slid his arms beneath Kaileih and lifted her from the floor, cradling her to him as he got to his feet. He looked down into her face as her uninjured cheek rested against his chest, and he exhaled shakily.

Long strides carried them away from the guest house and, as he crossed what used to be the threshold, the remains of the building folded in on itself as one might crumple a bit of paper, before crashing to the ground as he—and Kaileih—disappeared into the night.

Chapter Forty

Mahari groaned, turning over as she pushed a tangle of dirty curls from her face. Her fingers grazed her temple—wet. Her head throbbed. Her entire body ached, and a shiver traveled through her as she tried to sit up.

She coughed, blinking as she looked around her, feeling a warm fluid streaming slowly down the side of her face. Mahari didn't need to see it to know that she was bleeding. She struggled to remember what had happened.

She'd been asleep. Then Jahd was there, dragging her from bed. She thought it was a cruel joke... until he hurled them through the window.

She could barely see as they ran, and she could not get him to let her go. He did not even bother explaining what the issue was. She only knew that one minute they were running away from the house, and then she was careening through the air.

She coughed again, and the sound echoed around her. Wherever she was now, the air smelled slightly damp and mildewed. Mahari still could not quite see well enough to determine her whereabouts. The entire space seemed cloaked in a strange reddish-black haze.

She looked left and gasped.

She wasn't alone.

It had to be Jahd.

As her eyes strained to adjust to the darkness, she carefully crept over on her hands and knees, grimacing in pain as she felt what was likely the edge of a sharp rock slicing into her knee. Drawing closer, it relieved her to see that it *was* Jahd, wedged against what seemed to be a jagged wall.

"Brother," she whispered, placing a hand on his shoulder and shaking him gently.

She turned him over onto his back, but the haze made it hard to see his face or whether he was hurt.

When he did not respond, she sat back on her haunches and looked around again, finally recognizing their surroundings. They were inside the mine. Jahd must have brought her here after leaving the house. She'd demand answers the moment he woke up.

Mahari grunted, getting to her feet as she slowly turned to study the space, peering into the expanse as best she could. She knew of the mine but had never found it interesting enough to visit very often. Mahari knew them to be closed during this time of year because of the stifling heat of some of the lower levels. She also knew that her papa was considering having them closed altogether, as he was developing much safer methods of harvesting the metals contained therein.

But the mine should not have been completely emptied of the equipment. After briefly glancing back toward where her older brother lay, Mahari considered venturing about, hoping she could find a light source. It would make sense for there to be one or several. She would have expected to find some inside the entrance for the workers to carry within, but she could see none in the area she presently occupied. Jahd had brought them well past the entrance and deep inside the mine. Mahari would have to backtrack, find a lantern, and return with it, maybe even using it to look Jahd over to make sure he had not been hurt.

Mahari slowly made her way toward what she assumed was the direction of the entrance, skirting the wall so that she could keep her bearings. She allowed her feet to drag along the mine's floor—heel to toe, heel to toe—so as not to risk cutting her soles on something she couldn't see. Her face itched, but she did not dare touch it again and risk getting dirt into the wound.

Barely a minute had elapsed during Mahari's slow stroll, when she could hear pebbles skittering behind her. She gasped, stopped, and turned, but could see nothing.

"'ello?" she called softly. "Brother? Did you wake up?"

Mahari did her best to ignore the way her heartbeat pounded between her ears. This was so silly. She was twelve years old, hardly a baby. For a moment, she wished she could be like Zoi... poor, ill, institutionalized Zoi, who seemed to be slowly going mad despite having given birth to her first child.

Zoi could light fires, albeit involuntary ones, but still. Mahari would love that ability, if only for long enough to light her way so that she would not have to be stealing about inside some dank and dusty cave. Movement magic was not a great help to her here.

Mahari screamed as something brushed her ear and shot overhead. She tossed herself flat upon the floor, covering her head with her arms as the echoing squeak of the thing gradually grew distant before stopping.

Bats!? There were bats in this place? Forget it! She would go back to Jahd and either wake him up or stay beside him until he awoke on his own. There was no way she would continue alone to find a lantern.

Something icy clamped around her ankle. She screamed again. It tightened, creeping up her leg as she was dragged backward. There were high-pitched squeaking noises above her and what sounded to be the dry, leathery rustling of dozens of wings flapping. Mahari reached down to snatch away what had fixed itself to her leg, recoiling as a glacial chill penetrated her hands and caused the bones to ache.

"Brother!" she called. "Help! Help me! Something's got me! Jaaaahd!"

Further along the wide corridor lay Jahd Dhamon Chatelain. He was flat on his back, unresponsive to Mahari's frenzied cries. He only lay there staring up into nothing, the sockets of his eyes— hollow. Black.

Epilogue

The girl scurried along the mud-slicked road, squinting against rain that blew nearly sideways. Cradling a rusted bucket of fish to her chest, which had taken her half the day to catch, she hopped across the large puddle at the center of the path, skittering and slipping, though she kept her balance.

She was drenched, with rainwater plastering her dark-blonde hair to her head and dripping from the end of the thick braid swaying between her shoulders. Turning down a single leaf-strewn lane, she ran along the pathway until she reached a modest, two-story cottage and hopped up the single step leading to the porch.

"I'm home!" she called upon entering the four-room dwelling, placing the bucket on the rug before kicking her muddy work boots off at the door. "Aunt Hedda?"

"Oh, my goodness!" Hedda exclaimed when Solvi came in, wiping her hands on her apron. "You're drenched! You should have come home hours ago."

"I couldn't," Solvi said, picking up the bucket and holding it out to her aunt, her eyes sparkling. "See? They weren't biting because of the downpour. It took much longer than normal, but I got them."

"You sweet girl," Hedda said, taking the bucket by the handle. "I could have easily stretched what you caught yesterday. No sense in you catching a cold."

"It's fine, really!" Solvi turned to close the door and straighten the placement of her boots. She then reached into the left pocket of the gray smock she wore over a simple blue dress, pulling out a small packet of letters. "I stopped at the exchange, too, for the mail."

"Bless you, sweetheart," Hedda said, taking the packet in her free hand. "Now, you go get out of those wet things before you catch your death and I'll see to cleaning these fish. I don't think your father will make it tonight. Storms have been terrible these last few weeks."

"Do you need me to help with anything?" Solvi asked.

"You've done more than enough, I'd say! If this weather keeps up, we'll have to talk about other options for food. I don't want you going out into that squall again or anywhere near those docks."

"Yes, ma'am," Solvi said before jogging upstairs.

Hedda looked first at the letters in her hand before considering the bucket of fish, shaking her head. She glanced over at a painting on the wall of a striking young woman with golden-blonde hair and blue eyes. Tears came to Hedda's eyes as she smiled.

"You'd be so proud of her, little sister," she said to the painting. "She's grown into such a responsible little lass... much like you. Sixteen years old and such a treasure. I wish you could be here to see it, Vanja. I wish you could see what her life has become."

Upstairs in her room, Solvi had changed into a clean and dry smock, with her wet hair loose over her shoulders. She carefully removed a letter from the right pocket of the wet smock before draping both the smock and dress over a nearby chair to dry.

Her blue eyes danced over the elaborate handwriting upon the envelope. She sat at the foot of her bed as she opened it, extracting the letter as her heart beat wildly.

My dearest Solvi—

When traveling through Guion months ago, I felt in my soul that there was something special there—someone special—and I promised myself that I'd return to find her. I'm so glad that I did, because that someone is you.

I've waited so long for you. You are the embodiment of a dream. I had one night to indulge in the pleasure of you. I feel assured that it was only the beginning of what's to come.

J.

The story will continue in Book Two of the Heirs of the Five series...

PRONUNCIATION GUIDE

Allard **Ah-LARD**	Amriel **Ahm-ree-EL**
Aniela **AHN-yel-ah**	Bourdillon **Bor-dee-YOHN**
Breaton **BRAY-eh-ton**	Chatelain **Shah-teh-LANE**
Claerendon **CLAIR-in-dun**	Clea **KLEE-ah**
D'alegne **Dah-LANE**	Dalenbeigh **DAHL-in-bee**
Dhamon **DAH-mun**	Elyse **Eh-LEECE**
Evium **Ee-VY-um**	Fayal **Feye-AHL**
Filene **Fy-LEEN**	Guion **GUY-on**
Huison **HWEE-sahn**	Jahd **Jod**
Kaileih **Ky-LEE-ah**	Kynedal **KIH-neh-dahl**
Léah **LAY-ah**	Liana **Lee-AH-nah**
Linet **Lin-EHT**	Mahari **Muh-HAHR-ee**
Nikhila **NEE-kee-lah**	Millard **Mil-ARD**
Rael **Rayl**	Pandoufuli **Pan-DOO-foo-lee**
Scio **SY-oh**	Shaz **Shahz**
Rhia **REE-ah**	Solvi **SAHL-vee**
Tilehn **Tih-LEN**	Vanja **VAHN-ya**

Acknowledgements

Vitae is the first book in the **Heirs of the Five** series. It has taken a lot for me to finally have the courage to formally introduce these characters—and others you have yet to meet—to the world. The reasons for the delay are too long to share here. But, know that most of these nuggets of fancy have occupied a special place in my heart for over twenty years, and I feel blessed to be sharing them with you.

For years, I dreamed of what it would like to become a published author. While visualizing that moment, I never stopped to consider the other wonderful things that might come along with that accomplishment.

My debut novel, **Duality**, was named a 2019 IAN Book of the Year Awards Finalist in the Paranormal/Supernatural category. I am now an award-winning author. The experience has been incredible, and the response has been humbling.

It has always blessed me to have the support of an amazing group of people. This includes family, old friends, and the new friends I have made that are part of the Writing Community of Twitter. Making a list of everyone who has championed my quest would likely need a novel of its own, but there are some that I would like to thank individually, and in no particular order:

Suanne Fried-Goodman	Donna Cooper
David Mitchum	JC Paulk
John Kent Edwards, Jr.	Nickey Davis

Incredibly special thanks to my mother, who has been among my biggest cheerleaders. She spreads the word on my behalf and is diligent when checking on my progress. A huge thank you to my sister, one of the strongest women I know. She may be younger, but

I often feel she is wiser. Gigantic hugs to my other family and my friends. I absolutely love you all.

Stay tuned—there are so many more great things in store!

About the Author

Ametra S. Rayford spends a concerning amount of time arguing with the characters from *The Fractured Soul Saga* and *Heirs of the Five*. While she is fully aware that she is the cause of their behavior, she has yet to make any meaningful changes.

Visit her blog at ametrarayford.com.

Also by Ametra S. Rayford

The Fractured Soul Saga

Duality
Hey, Roomie!

Heirs of the Five

Vitae
Far From the Tree

ARRAYED FORMATS
PUBLISHING

www.ingramcontent.com/pod-product-compliance
Lightning Source LLC
Chambersburg PA
CBHW030933020726
47498CB00001B/229